Loyalty's Reward

Book Two of the
Victoria Chronicles

 To Hanne

 Happy reading

J.R. Whittle

J. Robert Whittle

By J. Robert Whittle

The Lizzie Series

Lizzie: Lethal Innocence

Lizzie Lethal Innocence - *Audio Book
narrated by J. Robert Whittle*
(CD/Tape/MP3 formats)

Lizzie's Secret Angels
Streets of Hope

* * *

Victoria Chronicles

Bound by Loyalty

Loyalty's Reward

* * *

by J. Robert Whittle and
Joyce Sandilands

Moonbeam Series

Leprechaun Magic

Leprechaun Magic - *Audio Book
narrated by Joyce Sandilands*
(CD and Tape formats)

Loyalty's Reward

Book Two of the
Victoria Chronicles

J. Robert Whittle

Publisher's note: This book is a work of fiction set in the City of Victoria, Municipality of Saanich, and other areas of British Columbia, as well as Washington State. To enhance the story, real places and people's names have sometimes been used, although the characters are fictional and are in no way intended to represent any person living or dead.

Whitlands Publishing Ltd.
4444 Tremblay Drive, Victoria, BC
Canada V8N 4W5 250-477-0192
www.whitlands.com
info@whitlands.com

Original cover artwork by Barbara Porter
Cover design by Jim Bisakowski, Desktop Publishing
Back cover photo by Terry Seney

National Library of Canada Cataloguing in Publication Data

Whittle, J. Robert (John Robert), 1933-
  Loyalty's reward / J. Robert Whittle.

(Victoria chronicles ; bk. 2)
ISBN 0-9685061-8-6 (bound). -- ISBN 0-9685061-6-X (pbk.)

I. Title. II. Series.
PS8595.H4985L69 2003   C813'.54   C2003-911171-7

Printed in Canada by Friesens, Altona, MB

In Memoriam
of my mother-in-law
Dorothy Carlson
1919 - 2002
Mother, grandmother, trusted friend.
A woman of rare loyalty
who saw beauty in everything and everyone.
Memories we will treasure forever.

Acknowledgements

The words 'thank you' just don't seem enough to show my gratitude for the response I have had from you, my readers, for the first book in this series. Due to your support, *Bound by Loyalty* will very soon be a Canadian Bestseller (joining the first book in the Lizzie Series, *Lizzie: Lethal Innocence*, which became a bestseller in 2002) and, if I am to believe your comments, waiting even a few months for the conclusion was an extreme hardship! Over the past 18 months, Joyce and I have continually found ourselves in the enviable position of having to explain when Book Two was going to be published. We hope you find it was worth the wait.

Many of you already know that the two books in the Victoria Chronicles were actually written as one for which I spent over a year to research. As always happens when undertaking such a project, your attention is drawn to other fascinating facts that further draw you into your subject. Thus, my book on Victoria soon grew into much more of a project than intended and this old history buff enjoyed it thoroughly.

Having lived in Victoria for only 32 years, unlike my wife, Joyce Sandilands, who is a 3rd generation Victorian, learning the history of Victoria was a journey achieved the hard way—by studying microfilm at the archives and reading many, many books. Thank goodness for archives and libraries!

My grateful thanks go again to our mostly local team: Barbara Porter, for utilizing her marvellous talent to provide a stunning new cover image of the British Columbia Parliament Buildings in Victoria C1910; Jim Bisakowski of Desktop Publishing, for working his graphic-design magic utilizing Barbara's image for the new cover design; Deborah Wright of Precision Proofreading, for her assistance with the final proofing; and Carey Pallister, City of Victoria archivist, for her assistance throughout the project, her proofreading of the historical data in both books and also for her invaluable suggestions.

The newest member of our team is Tara Poilievre, our first staff member and office assistant, who joined us late in 2002. Hired initially to organize our mailing list, we thankfully discovered her talents are much farther reaching and she has become an integral part of our team.

Due to Tara's efforts, we hope to keep you abreast of what is happening at Whitlands in a more expedient fashion—especially if we have your email and we're not bounced as spam! We would be most appreciative if you contacted us with any new contact information you wish us to have on file. Our list is nearing 6,000 names and, naturally, emails will have priority due to their cost efficiency and ease of sending. If you wish to be contacted and, have never heard from us we apologize. Please feel free to contact us anytime by email, snail mail or phone using the Whitlands contact information at the front of each book. If at all possible, please ensure that you consult a recent book in case our contact details change.

I would again like to thank all the local archives, individuals and family historians for their assistance and suggestions and, in particular, Sherri Robinson of the Esquimalt Archives, whose enthusiasm often spurred me on to greater efforts. Thanks also go to: Shar Houlihan; the Gala Van Party Shop; Terri Hunter; the independent bookstores of Victoria and Vancouver Island; you, our friends; and our family, for their loving support and understanding.

In July 2002, our family and friends suffered a monumental loss when Joyce's dear mother, Dorothy, our oft companion, first and greatest fan, passed away after a short illness. One of the biggest thrills of her later years, was visiting and travelling with her family and, in April 2002, Joyce and I were fortunate to have her accompany us to the UK. She loved to share in her family's achievements and was eagerly awaiting this book, but it was not to be. We miss her terribly and know she still shares our success.

Despite our rigorous schedule, we gain so much enjoyment from the friendships we make and, recently celebrating my 70th birthday, I only wish I were 30 years younger. The literary journey, on which Joyce and I embarked five long years ago, continues to amaze even ourselves and, in 2003, we will at last be taking our 6 books off Vancouver Island to two mainland BC shows.

Joyce and I are exceedingly grateful for the support we receive from the many thousands of readers who come from the far reaches of Canada, virtually every corner of the United States, and over 36 other countries. Many of you write to us and come back year after year to see if I have written a new book.

We have been told that we are probably the most innovative self-publishers in North America, if not the world; however, time is passing far too quickly and Joyce complains our readers are too demanding! We love it! Therefore, we will be taking the advice we hear so often, of seeking a publisher to lighten our load and make our books easier to find. We wish that was as easy as it sounds and we would be eternally grateful for any assistance!

On behalf of both Joyce and myself, thank you for your encouragement, your friendship and your love. We often say, 'people who read our books are *very* special people.' We love you all.

J. Robert "Bob" Whittle
August 2003
robert@jrobertwhittle.com

www.jrobertwhittle.com
www.whitlands.com
www.lizziebooks.com
www.mistermoonbeam.com
www.leprechaunmagic.com

Main Characters (in order of appearance)

Dan Brown – former whaler; partner in Brown and Wilson
Nancy Wilson – waitress; partner in Brown and Wilson
Sam Smith and Flash – hermit and his dog
Jebediah Judd – retired Pinkerton detective
Meg MacDonald – Nancy and Dan's adopted aunt
Jack Dumpford (Dumpy) – Nancy and Dan's dock manager
Terry O'Reilly – Seattle gangster
Waldo Skillings – owner of Victoria Baggage Company
Jack Duggan – builder with Parfitt Bros.
Harry Tabour – Balmoral Hotel Dining Room manager
Katherine (Kate) Flounder – waitress at Balmoral Hotel
Mary – cook at Balmoral Hotel
Fred Barrett – manager of Coast Guard station
D.W. Griffiths – Hollywood producer
Mary Pickford – Canadian actress
Ezekiel Plunket – hermit friend of Jebediah
Egger Brothers – notorious Seattle area riff raff
Jim Goodwin – tugboat operator
Ben and Asha Wall – American cousins of Bill Wall
Bill Wall – Negro living on Salt Spring Island
Willis Balcom – owner of Sechart whaling station
E.J. Martin – one of Balmoral Hotel owners
Mr. Simpson – general manager of Balmoral Hotel
Ken Macpherson – superintendent of Point Hope Shipyard
Emerson Turpel – owner of Point Hope Shipyard
Gus and Beth Jorgensen – Seattle businessman and wife
Capt. Percy Neville – British army officer
John Muir – Muir Lumber Mill, Sooke
Mr. Plimley – Plimley's Auto Repair
Francis Rattenbury – Victoria architect

(cont'd)

Tom Irvine – local farmer
Billy – Nancy's native friend
Nellie Duggan – wife of Jack Duggan
Eva and Thomas Todd – Gordon Head neighbours
Jean and Edith Dunnett – children of Malcolm and Jenny
Malcolm and Jenny Dunnett – Gordon Head neighbours
Algenon and Lolitia Jean Pease – Gordon Head landowners
Susan White – Victoria singer and friend of Nancy
Nellie Cornish – Seattle music teacher and pianist
James Moore – owner of James Moore Theatre, Seattle
Charles Blanc – Seattle restauranteur and chef
Hiram Gill – Mayor of Seattle
Albert and Hattie Rhodes – Seattle friends of Jorgensens
Johnny Schnarr – rum runner
Dorothy Poulton – Eva Todd's driver
Sgt. Roy Olmstead – Seattle Police Officer
Harry Maynard – owner of Crystal Springs Brewery
Emil and Eliece Layritz – owners of Layritz Nursery
Bill and Christopher Jorgensen – Gus and Beth's sons
Millie Maynard – pianist, wife of Harry Maynard
Commander Jackson – Chief Medical Officer in Esquimalt
Major General Green – Commander at Camp Lewis, Wash.
Billy Robinson – tap dancer
Bill Baker – entertainer
Will Rogers – entertainer
Fanny Brice – singer/actress
Harry Lauder – Scottish singer
Charlie Chaplin – comedian

Loyalty's

Reward

Chapter 1

With only a ripple on the Straits of Juan de Fuca and a gentle June breeze blowing from the south, Dan looked over at Nancy one more time before easing back on the throttle of the little blue boat. Sitting in the stern with her red hair streaming out behind her, Nancy looked out across the Strait. She smiled as they slowed to watch a fisherman land his catch and she couldn't help but reflect on the day's activities.

Only hours earlier they had said farewell to dear friends, Ned and Tim Joyce, now on their way to Newfoundland aboard their whaling ship *Belfast*. The Joyces had been Dan's employers for more than 10 years—the years Dan had been away from the orphanage where they had originally met.

She didn't remember arriving in Victoria harbour that October day in 1900 when she was only 4-years-old, nor could she remember what would be the last few minutes she spent with her father. Later, this proved to be a blessing as she found herself suddenly amongst strangers, not fully comprehending that her father had gone to seek work in the coal mines north of Victoria. For this poor motherless child to be told by her father that he was leaving her after all they had endured together was more than either of them could bear. Their sad parting almost broke the hearts of those attending on the Victoria dock that day.

But Nancy remembered none of this waking the next morning in the orphanage surrounded by children. Amidst the confusion, Dan, a lad eight years her senior, had taken her hand and done what he could to help her, becoming the brother she had never had. However, four years later, another sad event was to greatly affect her life when Dan turned 16 and left the orphanage to seek his fortune.

They did not see each other again until a fateful meeting in the restaurant at the Occidental Hotel eight long years later. Dan was a Highliner making his fortune as a whaler. He had an excellent reputation and was well-known on the Pacific Coast particularly for his sharp shooting. When Nancy, then a waitress, recognized him that day, Dan decided he must pick up where he had left off, looking after Nancy. As a result, they had become a family adopting each other as brother and sister. Now, with the Joyce brothers gone and the whales dying out, they found themselves embarking on a much different adventure, but then times *were* different.

"LOOKS LIKE WE'RE IN FOR A SQUALL TODAY," he shouted over the wind and noise of the powerful little speedboat. The boat was a gift from Gus Jorgensen, a Seattle millionaire who had suggested Dan utilize his talents in a business appropriate for the times … rum running.

Dan pointed to a black cloud developing over the Olympic Mountains behind Port Angeles. Having been a man of the sea since a young lad, he was very aware of the changing patterns of weather on the Pacific Coast. Knowing they were sailing to Seattle later in the day he was growing a little concerned with the weather but Gus had assured him that the boat was able to withstand quite rough weather.

Making good time, they passed Clover Point and several picturesque little bays taking a wide berth off Oak Bay avoiding an over-enthusiastic amateur yachtsman trying to catch the wind in his sails. Turning northward around the tip of Vancouver Island they roared past Discovery Island steering clear of the treacherous rocks along the ragged coastline, rocks which had already ruined many a sailor's dream.

Keeping well away from Ten Mile Point with its dangerous rip tides, they moved up through Haro Strait toward Gordon Head and the cove at Cunningham Manor. They were almost to the entrance when the bow of a small boat popped out from under some overhanging trees, then disappeared just as quickly.

"Was that Sam?" asked Nancy. "He must have borrowed that rowboat again, no one else seems to be using it."

A little dog barked excitedly from behind the rocks, giving his master's position away.

"What yer doing, Sam?" called the young whaler, knowing Meg fed the hermit in exchange for his keeping an eye on the property.

"Watchin!" the hermit growled back as he climbed onto the shore then, whistling for Flash, they both disappeared into the bushes.

Nancy took over the controls and eased the little boat up to the new dock which stood at the base of a steep rock cliff. Dan jumped out to secure the lines and all went quiet as the girl cut the engines.

"DID YOU FILL UP WITH GAS, LAD?" came a deep voice from the direction of the cliff stairs where Jebediah was sitting.

2

"Sure did. Didn't expect to find you home so quickly though," called Dan.

"Meg was feeling sorta low after seeing Tim and Ned off, so we decided to come home," said the old man, coming down to meet them.

Jebediah Judd was the newest member of their unique family—a former Pinkerton detective who had become a special friend and now lived with Nancy, Dan and Meg. Their home was Cunningham Manor, newly built by Dan and Nancy with the financial help of an old gold miner named English Jack.

"I think she's going to feel rather lonely for a while. That office was her life for so many years," Jeb continued.

"She'll be all right, Meg's a tough lady. I think it's probably more the shock of saying goodbye to them that's affecting her," explained Dan. "They've been her only family since her brothers were drowned."

"But now we're her family," added Nancy, "and at least *we* won't be out at sea chasing whales all the time!"

"No, but we might find the prohibitionists chasing us!" chuckled Dan.

"Once she gets the office cleared out and turned over to you young'uns, she'll find plenty to keep herself busy," laughed Jeb. "I reckon she's already enjoying her new role as our mother!"

This brought a smile from the others although Jeb was still thinking about Dan's statement. Not wanting to say anything that would concern Nancy, he kept silent although he knew that prohibition was going to cause a great deal of interest in the illegal trade of liquor. He vowed to himself that he would not let them travel to Seattle on their own for although they would be in a legal position as far as Canada was concerned, in the US it would be a different story once Washington went dry—now in the foreseeable future.

"All right, we've got work to do so best get onto it," Jeb reminded them. "We need to take out the back seats. Gus said there would be plenty of room in the hold."

Nancy watched as they removed the seats revealing a well-hidden trap door.

"I'll go up to the workshop and send the boxes down," said Jeb, heading for the stairs.

The young couple went into the cave and not many minutes had passed before the first two boxes sailed down the chute arriving in front of them. Ten minutes later, they had a stack of boxes by the boat and were having difficulty staying ahead of him.

3

Up in the workshop, Jeb sent the last box of liquor down the chute and stood looking at the mechanism that Jack Duggan had built only months before. Grinning devilishly, the American climbed onto the chute. Laying down flat and gathering his clothes about him, he grasped hold of the raised sides and gave himself a push. Initially surprised at the speed, he pressed his feet against the sides to slow his descent. In no time he saw daylight and found himself at the bottom. Dan and Nancy were nowhere to be seen. Feeling a bit dizzy, he stood up gingerly before walking outside and suddenly appearing at Nancy's side.

"How in heaven's name did you get down here so fast?" she gasped.

"I came down the chute," he laughed. "It was great!"

"Good gracious, Jeb, you're a bit of a devil aren't you!"

Telling Dan what he had done, they all had a laugh as they loaded the boxes into the boat. Outside of having some lunch, they were ready for their new adventure which would begin in a few hours.

"Lunch time," sang Meg's whistle from the top of the cliff and they headed up the stairs.

When they finished lunch Dan went to the closet and began pulling things out. "I think we're in for a rough ride tonight," he announced, pulling out several waterproof coats left over from his whaling days. "Try this one on, Nan, it's the smallest one we have."

Her slim body was lost in the huge coat and she giggled as Jeb helped her out of it, trying it on himself.

"That'll be a good fit when you get your Hudson Bay coat on under it," Dan chuckled.

"You'll need to get her one," Jebediah growled.

"Yes, you're right. I've got time so I'll go into town and get her a smaller size ... should be back by 4 o'clock," he announced, heading toward the back door. "Anything else we need?" Receiving no answer, he closed the door.

As he drove toward Victoria, Dan kept an eye on the black clouds which were coming closer each hour. It was beginning to blow and he noticed the trees were now bending in the wind. Growing somewhat concerned, he drove as quickly as he dared on the rough, hilly road.

About 45 minutes later Dan walked through the door at McQuades, the ship's chandlers. After selecting a waterproof coat for Nancy, he drove the short distance over to their dockside office to check with Jack Dumpford, for any messages.

Arriving home, he parked the truck and went over to the cliff's edge noting the wind was now whipping up great whitecap-topped waves out in Haro Strait. He shook his head worriedly and went into the house. Giving Nancy her new jacket, he helped her on with it.

"It doesn't look very good out there," he whispered into her ear, not wanting to worry Meg.

By five o'clock they had eaten and were getting dressed to leave. Inwardly, he hoped the worst of the storm had passed but leaving early would give them time to wait out any bad weather in the lee of the islands.

They carried their extra clothing down to the boat, stowing away what they weren't going to need until later. Jeb huddled in the back corner with a blanket wrapped around him. Dan took the helm and Nancy sat next to him. Stinging salt spray attacked their faces as Dan sent the craft out into the channel and opened the throttle. Surging forward, they bounced across the waves of the changing tide causing the redhead to grip tightly to Dan's arm. Rain began to fall, lightly at first, but as they approached the invisible border between the two countries, the dark clouds emptied and the wind rose again forcing them to contend with even angrier seas.

Grim-faced, Dan pressed the little boat onward toward Port Townsend while Jeb and Nancy watched for obstructions and deadheads. Passing into the protected waters of Admiralty Channel, Dan followed the eastern shoreline of the narrow waterway leading to Puget Sound. Here they found visibility was even more limited but as they entered the shelter of the islands, the sky began to lighten and the rain eased off. The wind dropped and a welcome sun allowed them to remove their constricting raingear. Old Jebediah, who had been quietly suffering with sea sickness in the stern, began to get some colour back into his cheeks.

"I'm all right," he lied, when Nancy looked at him sympathetically.

She noticed black clouds were still beating up the coast of Vancouver Island, probably raining on Cunningham Manor, but they were able to enjoy the last leg of their journey in warm sunshine. West Point welcomed them to Seattle as they flashed down the coast toward the Jorgensen's commercial dock.

It was almost eight o'clock when they tied up at the jetty. Smiling sheepishly, Jeb allowed Dan to take his arm to help him over the side where he flopped gratefully onto a nearby seat.

"I'm no sailor!" he whispered hoarsely.

Terry O'Reilly's car pulled up at the gate. Pushing the door open before his driver could assist him the gangster sprinted down the walkway to meet them. He greeted Dan and Nancy, whom he'd met previously, then broke into laughter seeing the state of his old detective friend.

"What's the matter with you, old man? Haven't gotten your sea legs yet?" he teased, receiving a stormy look from the former Pinkerton detective.

Minutes later, a cloth-covered truck screeched to a stop and four burley men climbed out and ran toward them. Receiving the go-ahead from their boss, they set to work and quickly began to unload the shipment of liquor. Twenty minutes later they were finished and driving away just as hurriedly.

"Easy money," the Irish-American chuckled, handing the redhead a sealed envelope. Giving Jeb a sympathetic slap on the back, Terry said goodbye, then hurried back to his car and they drove away.

On the way home Nancy took the helm and they were please to find the weather greatly improved and Jebediah was able to enjoy the return trip. He pointed out several places on the islands where he said friends had gone to live in their retirement or for other reasons, not easily explained. To this he added an evil chuckle.

Two freighters steaming toward Seattle were the only vessels they met on the way up through the narrows. It was already dark as Nancy looked for the cove, smiling when she saw the glow of the lanterns Meg had said she would place on the cliff steps—her effort to safely guide them in. The welcome aroma of steaming hot food greeted the weary trio as Meg laid out their meal, insisting on being told all the details of the trip.

"You feeling better now, Uncle Jeb?" Nancy inquired.

"Seasick, lad?" the Scottish woman chuckled while going to get the rum bottle from the cupboard. She poured a healthy portion into the American's teacup.

"Oh doctor!" moaned Dan, jiggling his mug on the table. "I feel awful sick, too."

"Go find your own doctor!" Meg laughed, putting the cork back in the bottle and returning it to the cupboard.

It wasn't long after dinner that tiredness settled over the group sending them off to their rooms. Lying awake in her bed, Nancy looked around her in the gathering darkness. This was the first bedroom that she could call her own and it was a wonderful feeling. She had watched the building of this house almost disbelieving that it belonged to her and Dan. They had named it after old Jack Cunningham, the gold miner who had secretly named Nancy as his beneficiary. *Poor old Jack*, she thought. *He had thought of me as a daughter and I didn't even know it.*

Looking over at the open window, she watched the moon rise through the wispy curtains that moved slightly in the light breeze. *English Jack must have watched this moon rise every night up on those goldfields—I wonder if he realized how much his gold was worth*, she mused silently, remembering the day the police chief had delivered Jack's belongings to her at the Joyce Bros. office.

As the bright orange sphere moved behind the clouds, she finally drifted off into a dream-filled sleep. Moaning a little as her mind took her back to the orphanage and its pain, she felt Dan's hand in hers and his soothing words of comfort. Then the picture changed and there was Louise, the cook who had found her the means to escape that wicked place.

A long parade of characters walked through her dreams that night— English Jack, Harry Tabour, Jebediah, the Jorgensens, and Waldo. But always Dan was there, holding her hand and keeping her safe and, Meg with her warm smile, watching over them all.

A seagull's scream shattered her sleep as it stood at the window squawking abuse. Pans rattled in the kitchen, advertising Meg was already up and about and she realized it was morning. At breakfast, Dan asked about the envelope Terry had given her in Seattle.

"Good gracious, I clean forgot all about it!" she exclaimed, scurrying off to retrieve it from her coat pocket. She tore it open and extracted the contents. A personal note from Gus fluttered onto the table followed by five one-hundred dollar US bills. At the top of the note he had written, *Please give this to Harry Maynard - same schedule for delivery on the 19th of June.* The next liquor order was listed below.

"I can deliver that to Crystal Springs Brewery for you," Jebediah offered. "Harry knows me now."

"But he wants it on Friday and I'm back to work on Monday," Nancy moaned, looking at the calendar and remembering the end of her two-week holiday had arrived. "I want to go with you."

"Talk to Harry Tabour. You get most everything else you want from that poor man," Dan teased. "I'll want you away from the Balmoral by three."

"Maybe you should only take Jeb with you," Meg interceded.

"She goes," Dan growled with finality, "and him, too!" As he pushed back his chair, he winked at the redhead.

Leaving Meg and Jeb discussing a day out in the city together, Dan and Nancy said their goodbyes and went out to the truck. They drove along in silence for awhile but when they reached Feltham Street, Nancy began to chatter incessantly.

"It's nice to see our neighbours more often now that spring has come," she mused. "Everyone is so friendly out here, Danny. We should try make an effort to get to know more of them. I met Eva Todd the other day and she said the Vantreights had a large farm at the top of the hill on Tyndall. She said they'd invite us to the next picnic they had." They were almost to Hillside when she pointed at some homes down Edgeware Street. "Look at those pretty gardens, Danny. I wonder who lives in them?"

"I know some of them," he replied. "Fred White and his dad live next door to each other. Fred's a house mover for Johnson's and his wife, Susan, is a well-known singer. You've probably heard of her."

"Yes, I know Susan and her children ... James and Winnifred, a really nice family. Do you know any of the others?"

"Nope, can't help you, love," returned Dan grinning at her as they arrived at the junction with Hillside. Crossing over, he took the right fork toward town and pulled off the road knowing Nancy loved the view from here. "We don't think about this much but from here we can see all over the city."

"The mountains are so clear today and look at the snow on them, Dan. They are so beautiful."

"Victoria is sure growing. When Jack built on Spring Ridge over there, he said there were hardly any houses around except near the springs."

Moving back onto the road, they went slowly down the steep grade and onto Bay Street. A block closer to town they noticed a heavily-loaded Victoria Baggage Co. dray standing in the road. Jack, the driver, and his helper, appeared to be checking over one of the horses. Easing the Model T to a stop, Dan got out.

"Hello Jack, having some trouble?"

"Seems to have gone lame, lad," replied the older man, recognizing the whaler. "Looks like we're going to need a replacement. Could you call in and tell Waldo on your way?"

"Sure we can," Dan replied, glancing at Nancy who had a deep look of concentration on her face as she watched the men's antics.

"Jack, why don't you send your helper back to the stable with the horse," she suggested. "If he went straight down Bay then onto Store, we'll tell Mr. Skillings he's coming and they can send the replacement to meet him. If they swap horses partway into town it should only take half the time."

"Good thinking, Miss Nancy," agreed Jack, waving them off.

Arriving at Wharf Street, Dan pulled off the road before turning down to the dock. Nancy jumped out and ran across the busy street to find Waldo who was standing outside the Victoria Transfer stables, another of his businesses, puffing on his pipe. He watched the lovely young woman run toward him, her flowing red hair blowing in all directions. *She's in a mighty hurry*, he thought.

"Morning, Waldo," she called. "We saw Jack down by Bay Street. His horse is lame and he's sending it back. He wants you to send a replacement."

He quickly cracked out some orders to one of his men. "Well done, lass, that was good thinking." As they stood talking, a stablehand came outside leading one of the big draught horses. Waldo quickly moved after him. "Get onto his back, man! Time is money."

On her way back across Wharf Street, she dodged past a streetcar, some horses and an automobile full of young men. They had the top down and whistled at her. Smiling self-consciously she got to the other side and halted, looking down toward the office. The signwriter's men were removing the old Joyce Bros. sign from their roof. She swallowed hard thinking how much she already missed Ned and Tim. Then, thinking happily about their own sign, soon to be erected, she hurried down the hill.

Inside, she found Dumpy talking to a stranger.

"Nancy, this man wants to show a friend what a whale looks like," he explained.

"A live one?" she asked, "but why?"

"Just for the thrill of seeing such a magnificent animal," the stranger replied haughtily.

"Tomorrow at ten," she replied, breaking into a smile. "The cost will be twenty-five dollars, sir."

With a stoic expression the man removed a bulging money clip from his jacket pocket. Peeling off several bills he handed them to Dumpy then tipped his hat and strode past her out of the office.

Dumpy looked at her quizzically but she ignored him and went to find Dan. He was at the end of the dock looking intently toward Shoal Point, shading his eyes from the glare.

"I just made a booking to see some whales," she said casually.

"That's an easy one," he muttered, without averting his gaze. "Look, they're drilling the reef. That should make it a bit safer."

After lunch Jebediah and Meg turned up at the dock, followed by one of the Crystal Spring's brewery trucks carrying a large new fuel tank.

"Harry says you'll be needing this to store extra fuel for the boat," explained the driver.

"At Cunningham Manor?" Nancy asked, turning to Dan who nodded. "It's awfully big, how will we get it down the cliff?" she asked, watching the men unload it.

"No problem, Nan, we'll just put it on floats and tow it around."

"You're right, lad," came Waldo's gruff voice from behind them. "Harry Maynard just phoned and told me Jack Duggan is on his way down here with lumber and two carpenters. When they've finished, we'll drop it in the water with my crane."

Being a man of few words, Waldo winked at the redhead and stalked off waving to Jack Duggan who was just arriving in one of the Parfitt Brother's trucks. Jebediah and Meg also took their leave saying they were going to have tea at the Poodle Dog Restaurant before leaving for home.

"Hi Jack," called Nancy. "Dan, I'm going over to the Balmoral to talk to Harry Tabour," she announced. He waved and she knew he had heard.

Smiles greeted her as she entered the back door of the hotel kitchen. Dottie, with a loaded tray of food, and one of the dishwashers moved about through the hot, steamy room. She went over to her employer's office in the corner and finding the door closed, tapped lightly and entered.

The restaurant manager raised his head from his papers, his eyebrows shooting up in surprise. "Nancy! I need you," he moaned.

"Now what's wrong?" she asked, slipping into a chair. "Why aren't you out on the floor?"

"I can't face all those young soldiers," he wailed. "I'm a German."

Springing onto her feet, she leaned over the desk shaking her finger angrily under his nose. "Get on your feet and get yourself cleaned up, mister. We'll go and face them together as soon as I get changed."

Quaking at Nancy's declaration, Harry stood rooted to the spot as he watched her walk away leaving the door wide open behind her.

"Are you on the warpath again, young lady?" Mary, the cook, inquired, wiping the sweat from her brow with the corner of her not-so-clean apron.

Katherine Flounder, Nancy's holiday replacement, came into the kitchen with a tray full of dirty dishes. Worry spread across her face when she saw Nancy and her stormy expression.

"What have I done?" she asked, frowning.

"It's not you, love, it's him," Nancy reassured her, jerking a thumb over her shoulder.

Dottie and Mary exchanged knowing glances as Nancy went into the staff room. She changed into her uniform and was tying her hair back with a ribbon, when she returned. Not seeing Harry, she marched back into his office to find him nervously straightening his tie.

"Right, let's go," she snapped, heading toward the restaurant door. Harry meekly followed.

Sergeant Walker smiled when he saw the familiar, determined set of Nancy's jaw. Something was up and he decided he was in no hurry to leave. *This could be worth sticking around for. I'll wager she's going to talk to that group of noisy soldiers.* Behind her Harry was feeling distinctly uncomfortable and showed it.

"What's all the noise about boys?" she asked, stopping at the soldiers' table. "I'd like you to meet Mr. Tabour, our manager."

"Send him for another round of beer!" one of the soldiers said cockily, slurring his words slightly.

"Young man!" Nancy snapped. "Do you realize what uniform you're wearing? Show some respect when you represent your King and country."

The redhead's words hit like a hammer. His face turned ashen and he quickly climbed to his feet, coming smartly to attention.

"Ma'am," he began, an obvious catch in his voice. "Please accept my apology on behalf of myself and my friends."

"Well done, soldier," a voice spoke quietly from the corner, causing an instantaneous reaction as all the soldiers scrambled to their feet and stood stiffly to attention. "You can go now," the voice said crisply.

Nancy watched the young soldiers as they quickly pulled some money out of their pockets, dropped it on the table and left without a backward glance. She turned to the stranger who, gauging from his uniform, was a soldier of high rank. A *man of class*, she thought, as he came to his feet and extended his hand toward Harry.

"I'm Lieutenant Colonel Currie, Commanding Officer of those young scallywags," he explained. "Please join me."

Harry hesitated but Nancy urged him forward with a gentle jab in the back. Perching nervously on the edge of his chair, the manager watched his Number One waitress and friend hurry off in the direction of the kitchen, fully aware of her intentions. In less than two minutes she returned carrying a tray with a fresh pot of tea, cups, and two steaming hot muffins.

"It's on the house, sir," she murmured to Colonel Currie, beginning to move away from the table.

"You're a very bright young lady," he complimented her, motioning her to come back. "I would like to commend you for the way you handled that situation. This girl is a credit to your hotel, Mr. Tabour."

Blushing at the colonel's comments, Nancy excused herself and hurried away quite confident that Harry would feel better now. In the kitchen, word had already been passed around about the incident.

"She's a marvel with people, Kate. You're still new here, but you'll get used to it," Mary whispered. "She knows how to handle our Harry, too!"

In the staff room, Nancy changed back into her street clothes and, returning to the kitchen, the empty tip jars caught her eye. "No tips this week, Kate?" she asked, frowning.

Mary's eyebrows raised and she glanced at Katherine.

"Oh yes, lots," she answered, "but the girls decided to keep them for themselves."

"Oh, did they?" Nancy replied with a knowing glance toward Mary who turned back quickly to her cooking, rattling pans busily. "Well, you tell them all, from me and Harry, that we want two dollars from each of them for the kitchen staff." Sensing the girl's objections as she stammered for words, Nancy added, "Ask them how many tips they'd get if Mary didn't produce good food? She's entitled to a fair share, don't you think she's earned it, too?"

Katherine was seeing a different side of the head waitress now and Nan's quiet argument got her point across quickly. She had never known anyone like Nancy. They locked eyes for a moment then Nancy smiled and, with an impish wink at the American girl, she was gone.

Brilliant sunshine caused her to shield her eyes as she stepped outside and crossed Douglas Street. Traffic was heavy at this time of day and the main street was crowded with pedestrians out to enjoy the weather. She made her way along Broughton Street past the open doors of Law and McNeill, and the stables of Victoria Transfer. Noticing something shiny in a nearby window, she stopped at the fish and game shop. Continuing on, she ran the next block down to Government Street. She noticed Mrs. Rogers outside the grocery store a few doors down, watering her planter.

"Lovely day, Mrs. Rogers!" she called to the chocolate maker's wife.

"Hello Nancy," the woman called back, returning her wave.

At Wharf Street, she waited for two horsedrawn drays to pass, both emblazoned with the words R.P. Rithet, Wholesale Merchant. Arriving at the office, she saw Dan engrossed in conversation with Dumpy and Fred Barrett, the customs officer. Fred was an old friend of Dan's and they seemed to be talking about the impending war and the men who were joining the militia.

"Not me," declared the whaler. "We've a business to get started."

Inwardly Nancy breathed a sigh of relief but she wondered why everyone was getting obsessed by a war so far away in Europe, one that hadn't even begun yet. She noticed though that there seemed to be a marked enthusiasm in the young soldiers she saw—a strange morbid sense of adventure that she couldn't quite understand. Nancy realized that loyalties could run deep, like her feelings for Dan, but they were Victorians and their life was here.

Chapter 2

There was no escaping the mood of the city. As she and Dan made their way home, a small platoon of soldiers marched through the streets while citizens cheered on every corner. Children ran alongside waving to fathers and brothers. Brooding quietly at the madness she saw all around her, Nancy curled up in the corner of the little truck, racking her brain to find a reason why any nation would send its young men away to a foreign country to get possibly wounded ... or worse.

"Isn't it peaceful looking?" Dan's voice cut into Nancy's thoughts as they went past a field of sleepily grazing red and white cows. She never answered and Dan became aware of her unusual quietness as the Model T bounced along the road through the multi-coloured Saanich farmland. Glancing over at her as he turned into their drive, he smiled when he heard her whisper, "Home!"

Leaping from the vehicle she dashed over to Meg and Jebediah who were standing on the cliff looking out at the San Juan Islands. It was a marvellous view today with Mount Baker standing proud and tall with its snow-capped peak shining in the sun and a cloudless blue sky. She hugged the Scottish lady fiercely and Dan momentarily wondered about her strange behaviour then put it from his mind.

However, for the rest of the afternoon it continued to pop up in his thoughts. He knew the dark threat of war was looking more and more imminent and although they had not discussed it very much he still harboured the hope that it would never take place. His first duty was to Nancy and the family they'd created. *I'll not sign up*, he thought stubbornly, *not if I can prevent it.*

After supper they were all out sitting on the porch when he broached the subject. "The threat of war is certainly causing some reaction amongst people in town," he said cautiously, watching their faces. "All everyone talks about is that we'll have to help in the fight, our loyalties must lie with Canada."

Meg, in true Scottish fashion agreed exuberantly. "If I were young, I'd be going home to Scotland if she were attacked," she said steadfastly, causing a ripple of laughter.

Nancy moved her chair closer to Dan affectionately laying a hand on his arm. "I know what you're doing, Mr. Brown," she whispered. "You don't have to worry about me. I know that if war starts, some day you'll have to go. It's your duty, but I don't have to like it."

This opened up some more conversation giving Jeb the opportunity to tell some lighter stories. As the shadows lengthened Flash, Sam Smith's little terrier, came confidently out of the forest and wagging his tail wildly, trotted up the steps to Meg.

"He's even learned who gives out the food in this place!" laughed Jebediah. "You out there, Sam?" he called, peering into the darkness.

Old Sam timidly stepped out of the shadows, limping with the aid of a gnarled tree branch. "You had visitors today," he growled.

"Sam, you're hurt, are you hungry?" Meg asked, leaving her chair and heading into the house without waiting for an answer.

"Who was it, Sam?" Dan asked.

"Don't know, but I scared 'em off good," he rasped, wobbling on his bad foot but keeping his distance at the bottom of the steps.

Meg returned and handed Jeb the parcel of food.

"Good man," Jebediah continued, going toward the hermit. "You need any help with that injury?"

"No!" Sam replied, recoiling slightly as Jeb came toward him. Grabbing the parcel, he backed away. "Sea water make good," he said, then he patted his leg for Flash to come and shuffled off into the trees letting the darkness close in around him.

Dan gazed pensively out the kitchen window the next morning at the fog shrouded water and his mind went back to other foggy days— aboard the *Belfast*. Remembering the exhilaration he used to feel out on the ocean his thoughts wandered back to the long years he had spent at sea whaling with his great friends, the Joyce brothers.

"You know, there were days when we couldn't see a thing the fog was so thick out there," he mused. "But it didn't matter much to us, even through the stillness Tim could smell those whales. He had some nose that man!"

"You boys sure teased him about it, too," added Meg.

"Everyone did, but the crazy thing was, he was always right!"

Nancy came into the room and heard the end of the conversation. "We're going whaling today, Aunt Meg," she said happily. "I'm going to put Dan's nose to the test and see if he can find some whales to show our clients from The States."

"You mean people will pay you just to see a whale? You'd think they could find a better way to spend their money!" clucked Meg.

Eating quickly, the young people were soon heading down the stairs to the dock. With the redhead at the helm, they chugged slowly out toward the racing tide before she opened the throttle.

"Easy now!" Dan reminded her as the engine roared into life. He came closer and spoke directly into her ear. "This fog likes to sit right down on the water ... makes deadheads even more difficult to see."

Nancy loved it when Dan came so close she could feel his breath on her neck. She also loved the thrill of the open water and even though she had reduced the speed this morning, the boat still bounced over the tiny waves. Excitement enveloped her when the powerful blue boat answered her wishes.

Dan watched as a look of complete contentment washed across her face and her red hair blew wildly in the wind. *She's a picture when she's out here*, he thought, as they turned westward to Victoria and came out of the fog bank. He grabbed for the side when Nancy increased the power, making a face at him.

Watching for other boats and remembering the Rules of Courtesy Dan had taught her, she skilfully moved past Ogden Point noting the progress on the growing breakwater development. There was a liner tied up at Rithet's Wharf but they couldn't see a name on it although it was flying a U.S. flag. Moving farther into the harbour past Shoal Point and the dredgers, they eased around the last corner past the soap works at Laurel Point and headed for their dock.

Dumpy was reading the newspaper in the new office of *Brown and Wilson Speedy Deliveries By Sea*, although it hadn't really changed much since it belonged to the Joyces. He heard them arrive and, smiling to himself, glanced at the tray he'd prepared with freshly made coffee and his mother's tarts and spice cookies.

"Oh, I like this kind of a welcome, Dumpy!" Nancy complimented their only employee. Her eyes eagerly searched the goodies on the tray as her hand moved to the plate. She knew Mrs. Dumpford's butter tarts were a well-known favourite.

"She made them especially for you," Dumpy chuckled. "Better get one before Danny sees them; he and Tim always fought over them!"

A rap sounded on the open door and the dour unsmiling client they had met the previous day stepped inside, apologizing for being early. He was followed by a diminutive, yet fragile-looking, attractive young woman with curly blonde hair. She appeared to be in her early twenties and shyly stayed behind the man as they entered.

"Come in," Nancy greeted them. "Pour some coffee, Jack, and offer them a chair," she ordered, using Dumpy's proper name.

Reluctantly the two visitors sat down at the table, declining the offered cup of coffee. Nancy noticed the young woman was studying her intently.

"You should try these butter tarts. Jack's mother made them," she said, not too enthusiastically. "Your taste buds will never have had such a treat."

Smiling expectantly, the blonde reached out her hand, but before her fingers closed on a tart her companion raised a stubby finger in warning. The girl's hand stopped short of the plate and the smile slipped from her face. Nancy's hand flashed out, smacking the offending finger, startling the blonde into wide-eyed amazement as her companion leapt from his chair, wheeling to face the redhead.

"Don't even think about it, matey," Dan growled from the door.

"You have a tart if you want one, love," Nancy encouraged with a wink. Ignoring the girl's sulking companion, she held the plate out to her.

It all happened in the blink of an eye for recovering her composure, a smile of amusement crept over the blonde's face as her hand reached out confidently.

"Sit down D.W. and behave yourself!" she purred.

"Coffee now?" Nancy asked, watching the girl shake her head.

"Do you know who I am?" she asked, giggling as several crumbs fell into her lap. "I'm Mary Pickford and he's D.W. Griffiths."

"So …," the redhead murmured, having no idea she was talking to the queen of moving pictures or that she had just slapped a world-renowned director.

"You're so refreshing, my dear," Mary laughed, standing up and moving toward the door. "I hope you're coming with us."

"I wouldn't miss it," Nancy declared, grinning at Dan.

Arm in arm the two young women walked down the dock chatting amiably. Behind them Dan beckoned the still-pouting D.W. to hurry. Slipping in behind the wheel while Dan started the engine, Nancy manoeuvred the blue boat out into the harbour. Mary squeaked with delight when she saw the waving workmen at the building site near the water.

"Everyone is so friendly here!" she declared, waving back at the men.

A freighter, coming slowly into the harbour, blew his whistle and Nancy pulled wide, bouncing in his wake.

"WEST TO BEECHY POINT, NANCY. LET HER RUN," Dan's order cracked through the wind. "THEN EASY UP THE STRAIT."

Slowly, Nancy opened the throttle of the powerful engines, forcing the bow of the blue boat to lift out of the water, pitching and tossing as it sliced through the waves.

Dan tapped Nancy on the shoulder, pointing to Mary Pickford's companion. Hanging over the side, D.W. was making a valiant effort at depositing his last meal into the water. Cutting their speed, Nancy went to his aid but he sat down with his head in his hands groaning loudly.

"WHALES!" Dan shouted, pointing his arm as they moved into the Strait. He slowed the boat to a crawl.

Mary leapt to her feet screaming with excitement as several of the huge black and white mammals came sliding through the water, not more than 30 feet away.

"Follow them!" cried the actress, ignoring D.W. who was groaning that he was dying.

Dan shook his head in amusement and turned the speedboat around to face Victoria. Chugging along gently through the choppy water, he instructed Mary to watch over the stern. Another scream told him the whales were coming back again, this time there were six or seven of the majestic creatures leaping into the air in a great show of power just off their portside.

Arriving at the dock Mary jumped out of the boat and raced off to find Dumpy. In her excitement, she completely forgot D.W. who wobbled precariously between Dan and Nancy.

Two cups of coffee heavily laced with dark rum and he seemed to be on the road to recovery. Mary sat giggling behind her hand as she watched this man of power struggling to focus his eyes. Nancy sympathetically handed him a cold cloth and slowly D.W. Griffiths came out of his stupor.

"Are you all right?" asked Nancy.

"Yes, I believe so," he groaned, helped to his feet by Dan. "I'm afraid boats don't agree with me at all."

Holding tightly to tiny Mary Pickford's shoulder, D.W. staggered toward the door. He grabbed the doorway and reached into his pocket with fumbling fingers for his billfold.

"Here, let me do it, D.W.," Mary laughed, taking the billfold from his sagging hand and deftly removing a $50 bill. Then she stuffed it back into his pocket. "Take this," she said, handing it to Dan. "That's been the most exciting hour of my life, and the funniest!"

"But he's already paid $25 for the trip, Mary," interrupted Nancy.

"Well, it wasn't enough," she said, pushing the money away. She glanced at her companion then put her hand over her mouth and smiled again. Refusing any help, she led the staggering director up the boardwalk where they disappeared into the crowd on Wharf Street.

"Lunch is it?" Dan asked watching Dumpy open his lunch box.

"Oh no you don't, lad," Dumpy grunted. "You've eaten all my butter tarts and you're not getting one mouthful of my lunch!" Taking out his sandwich, he slammed down the lid.

"Run up to Charley Miller's, will you, love, and get some sandwiches," he said, handing her their newly acquired $50 bill.

Taking the short cut through Bastion Street, past the great clock that kept the trams on time, she made her way up to Broad Street to Miller and Griffin's lunch counter. Giving her order to one of the staff, she walked down the row of counter stools full of people and found a vacant one.

"Where's Danny, Nan?" Charley Miller, an ex-whaler himself, called out when he saw her.

"Down on the dock waiting for his lunch!"

"But the *Belfast's* gone south," Charley said, frowning.

"We've started a new delivery business," she explained, as she accepted her parcel of sandwiches, paid for them, then hurried off.

Walking quickly back to the office, she wove her way through pedestrians wandering lazily in the summer sunshine. Dan and Dumpy had been busy in her absence. They had just finished attaching the large fuel tank to the side of the boat, ready for the task of getting it to open water and around to Gordon Head.

Sitting on the edge of the dock she unwrapped the beef sandwiches and handed one to Dan. Dumpy announced that some lady had inquired about transporting a family to Salt Spring on Tuesday, but had made no firm commitment of her intentions.

"Who told her to come here?" Nancy asked. "We don't even have a sign up yet."

"Waldo told her," Dumpy called over his shoulder as he ran up the jetty to answer the ringing phone. Two minutes later he stuck his head around the corner of the building. "Nine o'clock on Tuesday, all right, Dan?" Seeing the whaler wave, he disappeared inside again.

The satisfied grin on his face as he returned, told Nancy they had another job. "That was the lady I told you about. She's a relative of the Lineker's from Ganges. Now, let's see how that tank is going to manage."

An hour later the 30 ft. speedboat awkwardly manoeuvred its way out of the harbour under Dan's control, avoiding a Hudson's Bay freighter as it moved up the channel. Out in open water, Nan watched carefully as he made adjustments to the heavy towline, allowing for drag and the effect of the tide on the raft carrying the fuel tank.

"Take her away, Nan," he instructed, "but keep well away ·from the rocks."

Engine growling, the speedboat took the weight of the tow, moving forward into the light chop, its stern dipping low in the water. Dan grinned when he noticed her compensating with the steering, allowing for the drag of the heavy cargo. Passing Gonzales Point, the changing tides gave her a few anxious moments but again she made the necessary adjustments.

When they turned past Ten Mile Point the water flattened out, as if welcoming them home. On the clifftop Jeb was watching, aware that Sam had also spotted them from the tree line but when he looked again, the hermit was gone.

Chapter 3

"I'm going to find someone to help me get started this fall, Nan, I'm told that's a good time to plant young saplings," Dan exclaimed as they drove into the city early Monday morning. "I think 5-acres would be a good size and much of it has already been roughly cleared with only stumps to remove. I'll hire some of the local farmers who already have the horses and equipment."

This was a subject Dan hadn't mentioned for some time. Nancy was well aware of his plans for laying out an orchard on their land; it had been a dream of his since purchasing the property.

Nancy knew the war could change everything and really didn't want to get into the discussion again. They were almost at the hotel and she leaned over and kissed Dan silently on the cheek. He looked at her and smiled back, patting her arm. He knew what she was thinking. He had gotten very good at reading her mind of late. Stopping the truck in front of the Balmoral, she jumped out, suddenly feeling quite happy to be back at work. She turned and waved but he had already pulled away.

"Welcome back, Nancy. Tea's ready, love," announced Mary as she came through the swinging door.

Kate came around the corner and hearing Mary's loud comment, dropped her handful of cutlery onto the counter and went to hug her friend.

"Gosh, I'm glad you're back," she exclaimed. "It's been hard without you but we managed somehow!"

Nancy's eyes flashed over to the manager's office, noticing the open door and the empty room. Immediately taking charge, she told Katherine to finish what she was doing and get ready to open the doors.

Mary smiled, *Now that's more like it,* she thought, as she flipped the bacon over.

"What's on the lunch menu, Mary?" asked Nan.

The cook shrugged her shoulders, knowing Nancy's eyes were staring at her back.

"Ok, let's make it lamb, new potatoes, mint sauce, fresh peas … and whitefish for dinner." Nancy's instant decision was neither questioned nor disputed as she moved toward the manager's office.

Goodacre Meat Company, at the corner of Government and Johnson, answered the redhead's first phone call promising to deliver the lamb chops within the hour. Next was Chungranes, the fish shop run by a Greek family just down Broughton. They were a small shop and were always delighted to get the Balmoral's sizeable orders.

Katherine looked surprised as she came to the office doorway and stood listening, totally unaware that cook was watching and chuckling to herself. Redfern's clock began to chime in the distance and Nancy jumped up and came to the doorway. Seeing Katherine, she stopped.

"Doors need opening, young lady!"

The startled girl's hand flew to her mouth and she hurried off.

It was a busy day and the two waitresses found it difficult to keep up as businessmen and soldiers filled the tables, all chatting noisily. Two more waitresses came on at 8 o'clock, easing their burden as hotel guests and tourists began filling some of the now empty tables. Harry Tabour walked in at nine looking unusually fresh and dapper. He was swinging a cane with a jaunty air, smiling greetings to all he passed.

Eyes blazing fire, Nancy followed him into his office. "And what time do you call this, Mr. Tabour?"

"It's my new time schedule, sweetie," Harry smiled. "I'm the manager so I start at nine."

"No, sir," the redhead purred, getting a grip of her temper as she marvelled silently at Harry's newfound confidence. "If you're not here at 6:30 a.m. in future, the doors stay closed!"

Listening from the kitchen, Mary winced at Nancy's threat, knowing full well she'd carry it out. A moment of panic flashed across Harry's face, never dreaming the redhead would oppose him so dramatically. Doubt crept into his mind and the assertive angle of his chin sagged a little. Nancy was not only his head waitress but his friend and the one whose opinion he most respected.

"Gee Nan, when that British officer told me officials give orders and staff carry them out, I thought it would work well for me."

"Listen, you chump," she replied, leaning over the desk. "In case you hadn't noticed, this is not the army. We're a business and you're our leader, so lead and we'll respect you."

"Yes, yes, you're right love." Harry squared his shoulders and looked down at the desk. "I shall be here at 6:30 in the future."

Nancy returned to her routine and a few minutes later she made up a tray of coffee and a muffin delivering it to Harry.

"Friends again?" she asked coyly.

"The trouble with you, my girl," he sighed, "is you're always right, damnit!"

Over dinner the next evening Meg told them about the excitement of the day ... watching Waldo's truck arrive to fill the fuel tank down on the dock. Then, Nancy asked Dan about his trip to Salt Spring.

"It was a lady and two young children. They wanted to go to Ganges. The youngsters were well-behaved and their friends were waiting when we arrived. It was uneventful, although I did make several new contacts while I was at the wharf."

"What sort of contacts, Danny?" asked Jeb.

"Well, I met this coloured man named Bill Wall. He was a nice fellow who invited me to visit his family at Vesuvius Bay on the northwest side of the island. He's an older man, the youngest son of one of the original settlers, he told me, and a lifetime resident. He's done all sorts of things, fishing, farming ... when he mentioned he had an apple orchard he had my complete attention!"

"You're still thinking on that orchard are you, Dan?" asked Meg. "Did you ask him for any advice?"

"No, not yet, but I don't think he would mind at all. He was a right friendly sort."

On Wednesday the red and white sign painted by Mr. Hagenbuch was erected over the doorway of the new office making their delivery business official. It didn't take long to catch a great deal of attention and they were soon swamped with enquiries. By the time Friday arrived, excitement over their next trip to Seattle had gripped Nancy and she could hardly wait to get home begging Dan to drive faster.

As they sat down to an early dinner, Jebediah announced that the boat was fuelled up, loaded and ready to go. Nancy smiled at Meg's motherly attention, packing sandwiches and offering advice as she moved about the large kitchen. She was totally unaware how worried Meg was about this trip even though Jeb had assured her that she was being silly.

Half an hour later, Dan eased the little boat out of the cove. As the others waved and shouted to Meg standing up on the cliff. Dan beckoned Nancy to join him at the helm, sitting back on the seat so there was room for her in front of him. Putting his arms around her she snuggled up to him. Together they guided the craft through the currents until they entered the open waters of the Straits of Georgia. Pointing the boat toward Port Townsend, Dan stepped aside and went back to sit with Jeb.

Growling engines seemed eager to please as Nancy carefully opened the throttle and the boat surged forward. Way up ahead she noticed a stream of black smoke coming from a small freighter ploughing its way to Seattle through the light chop. It was a beautiful evening with light clouds and when they passed down the side of Whidbey Island with its cliffs and shadowy beaches, Jebediah leaned toward Dan.

"Have Nancy pull over close to Kingston. I've a friend lives in a bay just north of there," he announced into the lad's ear. "We'll pay him a short visit."

After they had passed through Admiralty Inlet, Dan moved forward to talk to Nancy. He pointed across the Puget Sound to Edmonds. "Our first stop will be at Kingston on the opposite shore just past Apple Point."

She nodded, although she wondered why they would make such a stop, knowing they hadn't spoken of this earlier. She thought they were in a hurry but decided not to say anything. Easing the motorboat down the sound she moved in closer to the land. Apple Cove beckoned with its tranquil and inviting patches of sandy beach. Easing back on the throttle she turned to Dan for further instructions.

"Keep going," Jeb called, watching the coastline intently. "There, there," he pointed eagerly, "see those overhanging trees? That's his secret entrance."

Nancy pointed the boat at the trees and Dan scrambled out on the bow guiding her in. As he parted the branches a wonderful hidden cove with a small building that looked more like a dilapidated shack than anything else, came into view. The area was overgrown with scrub and tall grass but close to shore a small fishing boat bobbed gently at anchor.

Jeb pointed toward the shore and a darkly tanned man with a massive growth of white beard came into view. He was sitting on a log near the water facing them. He blended in so perfectly with his surroundings one would have had difficulty realizing he was there. As they came closer, Nancy realized he was cradling an old long-barrelled rifle in his arms.

"ZEKE, YOU OLD MOONSHINER," Jebediah yelled.

The reaction from the man on the beach was alarming at first as he jumped up from the log with rifle ready. But seconds later, he let out a whoop, flung his hat onto the sand, propped his rifle against a log, and began to run across the beach to meet his old friend who had now leapt into the shallow water.

"I think they know each other," Dan chuckled as they watched the two old men shake hands and hug each other. Taking over from Nancy he eased the boat toward the shore until they felt the keel just touch the sand. Dropping anchor he, too, slid over the side and into the water. "Come on Nan, I'll carry you."

Looking doubtful but not relishing the alternative, she climbed up onto the side of the boat. Gathering her skirts about her she dropped into Dan's waiting arms, allowing herself to be carried to the beach.

"I want you two to meet Ezekiel Plunket," said Jebediah laughing heartily as he broke the dark-skinned man's grip on him and turned to the young people. "He's an old, old adversary of mine!"

"Chased me clean across two states, he did," Ezekiel added, grinning broadly, "then he locked me up for a year!"

"You mean you were on opposite sides of the law?" asked Nancy.

"Hell, yes," Jebediah chuckled, thinking back to the days when Ezekiel was a bank robber not much younger than he was, and had terrorized the west by holding up trains and stealing from the rich people on board. Jeb always thought it was fortunate that Ezekiel had worked alone because he had a soft heart and no one ever got hurt. As a young man he had spent more years in jail than out and it was when he moved into the Seattle area that Jebediah was brought in. "This old bird cost me many a night's sleep."

"And who are these two young'uns," Ezekiel asked abruptly.

"Kinfolk."

"You ain't got any!" declared the former train robber, who had spent many long hours talking to Jebediah as their paths crossed during his younger years. Long ago forgiving Jebediah for jailing him, they had become fast friends and had often talked of their families.

He knew Jeb had no family left and had never married. Upon his last release from prison, Jebediah had decided to try keep his friend from returning to his old ways, the only life he had ever known. He found this little cove and quietly purchased the property knowing it would be the perfect place for Zeke to protect him from society ... and vice versa.

"Well, I have kinfolk now! Meet Dan and Nancy," the old detective murmured, a serious tone creeping into his voice, "and if they ever need help?"

"Stop!" growled Ezekiel, throwing up his arms. "Damn it, J.J., you didn't need to ask."

"Had to introduce them though, didn't I," Jeb argued. "Now tell them your code."

"All right ... look up there." Ezekiel pointed to an odd-looking old chimney up on the hill. "I hang a light in there after dark. Line it up with the lights of Edmonds and you'll find my cove on the blackest night. Five quick flashes on a light, after you come through the trees, tells me you're a friend."

It was clear the old man meant it. Sitting down on a log, Ezekiel told them some of his story, laughing as he told of his many brushes with the law and finally meeting J.J. He was born in Kentucky, part of a moonshine-making hillbilly clan who just naturally drifted away to find adventure. Cowboy, seaman, train robber ... he'd tried it all, even spent a few years locked in jail until Jebediah caught up to him. Friendship with the Pinkerton man had been easy. It was Jeb who had met him upon his release, offering a helping hand and his trust, moving Ezekiel into this cove where he'd been living for almost ten years.

"We've to be in Seattle by eight," Dan reminded them about half an hour later. "I reckon it's about 18 miles or less."

"An hour in that fancy boat," Ezekiel estimated, cocking an eyebrow with an unspoken question at the whaler.

"Half if we push it!" came Dan's instant reply.

"Beautiful hair," the old mountain man murmured, turning his attention to Nancy who had stayed close to Dan. "Married?" he asked bluntly.

"No," she replied, "he's my brother."

"Sure don't look alike!" Zeke growled, looking from one to the other but they merely smiled.

Back in the boat some minutes later, Nancy was at the helm with the whaler standing by her shoulder.

Ezekiel watched, standing motionless on the beach as thoughts ran wildly through his head. From past experience he knew Jebediah was a thinking man, cunningly planning his moves. *This is a safe harbour close to Seattle, but why?* he puzzled, scratching his beard as the blue boat disappeared behind the trees.

"Push it hard," Dan ordered, checking his watch. "I'll time us to the Jorgensen's."

Smiling impishly, Nancy eased open the throttle and the boat surged forward with a roar. Flashing past other boats they screamed down Puget Sound. Dan's eyes searched the water ahead for deadheads. A freighter anchored in the harbour caused him to lay a hand on her shoulder.

"Slow down now," he cautioned into her ear.

Nodding, Nancy eased back on the power, surprising Jebediah who pitched forward in his seat. As they pulled into a jetty at the end of the Jorgensen dock they saw the familiar figure of Terry O'Reilly casually sitting on the hood of his car, waiting. A wave of his hand sent five men running to meet them. Dan and Jeb tied the boat up as the girl shut down the power.

"How long did it take from Ezekiel's cove?" she asked.

"43 minutes," Dan grinned.

Terry, stopwatch in hand, watched his men quickly load the cargo into their truck then, without a word, they drove off. At that moment, a flash of light from a building at the far end of the dock attracted Jebediah's wary attention and he raced up the steps toward O'Reilly, gesturing frantically. Terry waved, hurrying to his car as his driver started the engine. Burning rubber, the vehicle flew down the dock and out onto the driveway.

"We're leaving!" the detective called, quickly untying one of the lines as Dan loosened the other and they jumped aboard.

They were away just as Terry's car disappeared onto the main road. Moving in close to two anchored freighters, Dan kept close to them until he was sure they weren't being followed. He opened the throttle, handed the helm over to Nancy and moved to stand right by Jeb's elbow.

"What was that all about, Jeb?" he inquired.

"We were being watched and at this time of day it's too easy to hide in the shadows. I don't want any surprises and although we're not carrying a cargo those pirates don't know that," Jeb growled. "Do you have the field glasses?"

"Yes, they're right here," he said, handing them to him, "what pirates, Jeb?"

"Tell Nancy to slow down. I want her to keep us in the shadow of that northbound freighter." Waiting until Dan had done so, he continued, "You don't have any firearms do you, lad?"

"No," Dan replied, suddenly realizing the situation was a bit more serious than he realized, "just that miniature cannon that Ned gave me and a box of firing caps, but no powder or balls."

"Hmm, we'll be fixing that soon enough," he said, almost too softly for Dan to hear. "The pirates are three brothers known as The Egger

27

Gang," Jeb continued, answering Dan's previous question." They've run roughshod on this area for some years now. They must think they're modern day pirates because when you least expect it, they show up. They're also a bit gun-crazy. So far the law hasn't been able to catch up with them and no one has been badly hurt, but with prohibition starting I would expect they'll be extra vigilant—and there will be others just itching to get their hands on our cargo, too!" Looking over at Nancy he called, "STOP STRAIGHT OPPOSITE KINGSTON, NAN."

A couple minutes later, after Richmond Beach and Point Wells had slid past their stern, she slowed and turned to get more directions. "PULL IN THERE," he said, pointing to a nearby dock. "That's the jetty at Woodway. I know these people and they'll have just what we need," he said mysteriously.

Nancy turned the speedboat toward the almost deserted jetty and they tied up behind the building. Jeb took one more look around with the glasses and handed them back to Dan.

"Wait here and keep an eye out for trouble," he commanded, climbing out onto the jetty. He quickly disappeared into the shadow of the building.

Watching the water, Dan scanned up and down the coastlines. He thought he noticed something moving and upon closer scrutiny realized it was a wisp of black smoke coming from a boat that appeared to be slowly moving back and forth close to the shore. *Is it looking for something ... if so, what*? Raising the glasses, he turned in the opposite direction and found the chimney above Zeke's cove.

"What is it?" asked Nancy.

"I think someone is searching for Ezekiel's cove," said Dan. "That must be what Jeb was concerned about. I wonder why they are interested in him?"

They heard a board creak and Jeb came out from behind the building. He handed Dan two cans, which turned out to contain black powder, and a Winchester rifle. He climbed over the side and they realized he was also carrying a metal bucket from which he took a small pack of wadding, laying it on the seat.

The detective grinned at the young couple. "These stay on board the boat from now on. Load that silly musket of yours, lad."

"Cannon," Dan corrected him, as Nancy moved to help. "But we have no balls."

28

"We'll try some pebbles, they should be sufficient to put flight to whoever it is," replied Jebediah chuckling softly. He handed the bucket to Nancy. "You'll find lots on the beach. Better be quick. We'll leave just before dark."

By the time she returned less than fifteen minutes later, the shadows were lengthening and they had to move quickly. Dan loaded the cannon as she pulled away from the dock. Moving slowly across the choppy swell, seemingly unnoticed, they closed in on the suspicious craft.

Muttering to himself, Jebediah watched intently through the field glasses. "It's them, just as I thought!" he snapped, laying down the glasses and picking up the Winchester. "Get ready, Danny m'boy. Move in quickly now, Nancy. Get to within a hundred feet, then run alongside them."

Smoke billowed from the other boat's engine as its alarmed occupants poured on the power to get away from them. No one heard the shot, but Dan saw the flash of light from the direction of the other boat's stern. Then he heard the ominous ping as the bullet hit their windscreen.

"GET DOWN, THEY'RE FIRING AT US," he screamed.

Nancy crouched down as low as she could behind the wheel. Increasing the power she sent the speedboat forward then cut the power when they were in position.

"NOW!" Jebediah yelled, and Dan pulled the trigger.

With a surprising roar, flames erupted from the cannon's mouth. Leaping backward it flung the whaler onto the floor, but the result was stunning. When the hot pebbles became airborne, sparks lit up their path and a loud whistling sound gave warning to all around. In the dim light, the mystery boat could be seen veering suddenly then rising into the air. A loud crash ensued then some grating noises were heard as it bounced onto the rocks. Almost instantly a tirade of cursing and screams was heard.

"Let's go home!" Dan called, rubbing his backside.

The rest of the trip was uneventful although the men kept a careful watch as they travelled north. By the time they reached Cunningham Manor, a clear sky illuminated by a bright, rising moon gave them enough light to dock.

"You're late!" Meg chided, glancing at the clock before Nancy hugged her. "Get yourselves washed up, I'm dishing up before it gets anymore overcooked!

As they ate, Dan related their adventure, noticeably startling the older woman when he mentioned the use of the cannon.

"Don't you put my Nancy in danger," she warned.

"She's my Nancy, too," Dan replied softly.

"Stop your worrying, woman," Jeb interjected. "It was only the Eggers. They may be the worst scum on this coast, but now they know we're prepared for a fight, they won't want to mess with us again any too soon!"

After the old folks had gone to bed, Nancy and Dan went outside on the porch for awhile.

"Do you think Uncle Jeb's right about them bothering us again?" she asked.

"You're not worrying your pretty head about those Eggers, are you?"

"I guess I am a bit," she admitted.

"Well, I want you to know that Jeb is right. By the sound of our little altercation tonight, they won't have a usable boat thanks to our little cannon! And they're not going to want to fool with us again anytime soon," he assured her.

It was almost midnight when the last light in the house went out and Sam, who had waited patiently in the rowboat behind the rocks, now dipped a paddle into the water sending the craft gliding silently into the cove. Inquisitiveness was driving him and he urgently needed to see the blue boat with the powerful-sounding engine up close. He'd never seen anything like it and yearned to touch its sleek sides.

Tying up in the shadow of the boathouse, his moccasined feet padded across the moonlit jetty as he stealthily moved toward the boat and made his inspection. Flash padded silently along beside him. Pleased with himself, he ran his dirty hand along the smoothly painted sides. But a shudder ran through the old hermit when his nose picked up the distinct smell of gunpowder. Guns made him nervous and he quickly backed away. Snapping his fingers for the terrier, they returned to the boat and departed in a hurry.

Chapter 4

Jebediah leaned against the boathouse and puffed on his pipe as he watched Dan climb into the boat early the next morning.

"I need to find a place to mount that cannon properly or I'm going to break my neck one day!" exclaimed the whaler.

"It delivered quite a wallop, didn't it?" agreed Jebediah, chuckling. "Sam's been here during the night." He pointed with the toe of his boot to some fresh dog dung.

It needs more stability, but how? Dan thought, taking no notice of Jeb. Suddenly, a whistle sounded from above. He jumped out of the boat and began to run up the steps when he looked up and saw Nancy at the top.

"DUMPY JUST SENT A MESSAGE," she shouted excitedly, waiting as Dan came closer. "He's already booked two jobs for Victoria this week. Meg says breakfast is ready, too."

Forty-five minutes later, the young people were heading toward Victoria in the boat. Jebediah and Meg waved from the clifftop, his other arm draped nonchalantly around her shoulder.

"You were right, Meg. Nancy sure can handle that boat."

As they neared the Victoria dock, Dan suggested Nancy go over to Turpel's shipyard so they could fill up with fuel. "May as well save our own for emergencies."

However, seeing Dumpy frantically waving at them, Nancy circled around and pulled in beside him.

"WE'VE GOT AN URGENT DELIVERY," he yelled, holding up a small package. "WILLIS BALCOM NEEDS THIS AS SOON AS YOU CAN GET IT THERE."

"That's a long run, we'll have to leave right away if we're to be back before dinner," said Dan, cutting the motor. "Looks like we'll have good weather but it will be an awfully quick trip."

"We're not leaving before we get our heavy coats and something to eat," Nancy called as she headed toward the office.

"Top up our tank will ya, Dumpy. I better do as I'm told!"

Fifteen minutes later they were back with raingear, warm coats, a thermos of coffee and whatever Nan could find for food. Stepping

31

aboard, she dropped her load on the back seat and instantly took the helm, opening the throttle as Dumpy and Dan released the lines. In minutes they were out of the harbour.

Taking a wide berth to avoid an incoming freighter they waved to the captain of the *Dominion*, one of the Goodwin Towing Company's tugs. Jumping its wake sent spray flying over them as they turned westward toward the Pacific.

"We're lucky to have good weather today and I'm sure glad it's Saturday so you can go with me!" Dan said into her ear after stowing away the supplies. "Let me know when you want me to take over." She turned and grinned and he knew she was enjoying herself.

The run to the whaling station at Sechart up the West Coast was a lot easier than Dan had initially thought. About four hours later they entered the calm waters of Buckley Sound. He gave Nancy back the wheel and pointed out some buildings on the north shore. Noticing several other boats, they kept clear of them and soon had the station in sight.

This was her first glimpse of a whaling station, something she'd only heard Dan and the Joyces talk about over recent years. Gripping her nose against the stink that permeated the air, she looked over the side in revulsion as Dan avoided several floating carcasses. In the clear waters of the pristine inlet, she noticed they had become a feeding ground for numerous fish. Nearing the plant, the water grew quite murky and even more gruesome.

Willis Balcom, standing on the wharf watching them, smiled to himself when he saw Nancy's shocked expression. She was the first woman he could ever remember having been on the station and he doubted she would ever want to return. Steeling herself to the sights, Nancy stepped onto the landing jetty and handed him the parcel.

"You must be Nancy," he said, smiling pleasantly. "Danny's talked a lot about you."

"She's the captain, Willis, and we did it in just under four hours," Dan called from the stern.

"Well done, captain, it's a grand day to come visiting," he replied, disappearing into the building with the parcel. Returning a minute later, he continued. "You were bucking the tide this time of day but your trip back could be even faster. That's one powerful engine you have, I watched you enter the inlet with the glasses." He looked over at Nancy. "Come on in, young lady, we'll give you a tour of the plant."

A helpless expression came onto her face and she turned quickly to face Dan. He shrugged his shoulders.

"Thank you, but I don't think so," she said, making a face. "Besides, we're in an awful hurry."

Willis understood perfectly and, smiling broadly, lent her a hand to climb back into the boat. "Nice to have met you Nancy, come back and see me sometime." He winked at Dan.

Dumpy was surprised when he saw the blue speedboat come sweeping up the harbour at 20 minutes past four.

"You had a good run. How did you like the whaling station, Nancy?" he chuckled, watching her grimace as they tied up the boat. "I've got some nice hot stew on the stove. Mom's stew is so thick I just watered it down a bit and thought you'd like some," he explained as they walked toward the office. "Your next job can be done on the way home."

They looked quizzically at him.

"Two really nice people—they need a ride to Salt Spring. They ... oh, here they are now," he said glancing through the open door. "I told them to watch for the blue boat. They must have seen you come up the harbour."

Nancy stopped dishing up the stew and turned to watch the newcomers as they came down the boardwalk. She tried not to show her surprise when she realized the middle-aged couple were black-skinned. She had seen only one Negro person before but was aware that several families made their home on Salt Spring Island.

"They need help, Dan," she whispered, seeing them struggling with their baggage. He leapt from his chair. "Don't forget to come back for your stew."

"Just leave your baggage there, folks. Get the handcart will you Dumpy," called Dan as he went out to greet their new clients.

Dumpy found the cart, loaded their baggage and set off for the boat. Dan took their payment of one dollar each and asked if they minded waiting for a few minutes while they finished eating. Receiving a silent nod he ushered them into the office and invited them to sit down, asking if they would like a cup of coffee.

"No, thank you," said the man, in little more than a whisper.

"This is my sister and partner, Nancy Wilson," Dan continued. "She'll be going with us."

Nancy smiled as she had her mouth full but the couple still didn't say a word, looking at her quite suspiciously. The uncomfortable silence caused them to eat more quickly and soon they were all out on the dock getting settled into their seats. As soon as they stepped aboard, Dan realized that they were not familiar with small boats and appeared quite nervous.

Checking with Dumpy about the next day's schedule, it was only a few minutes before Dan cast off the lines and leapt aboard. He noticed the wide-eyed look of alarm on the woman's face when Nancy slipped into the captain's seat.

"STOP! WAIT DANNY!" Dumpy yelled, running down the jetty after them. "Jim Goodwin's heading this way in his tug ... seems to want something."

Cutting the motor, Nancy waited as the harbour tug chugged up alongside them. Jim Goodwin was the owner-operator of *Ping Pong*, an older gas-engined tug. He and his brothers Cal and Charlie ran the harbour towing service pulling log booms to the mills and schooners out of the harbour past Brotchie Ledge.

"Where are you heading, lad?" Jim called.

"Salt Spring ... why?"

"There's a log boom loose somewhere off Maple Bay," he called. "We just got the message. I'm heading out now, but you'll be there a long time before me, so be careful." He turned to pick up several red flags attached to sharpened steel poles and handed them across to the whaler. "Flag it if you see it," he called, giving them a salute before easing back on the throttle.

"Sorry for the delay, folks," Dan apologized to his passengers. "We'll soon have you over to Salt Spring."

"That girl won't be steering, will she?" asked the wide-eyed woman, breaking her silence.

"Yes, ma'am, that girl is most capable as you will see," said Dan. "Where on Salt Spring Island are you folks heading?"

"Bill Wall's farm, north of Vesuvius," came the man's deep mellow voice sending a thrill through the redhead's body. *I'll wager that man can sing*, she thought as she poured on the power and the speedboat swept out of the harbour.

The woman was now looking even more nervous and she began to moan, rocking her body back and forth as she stared down at her feet. It seemed that as the roar of the engine increased so did the sound of her moaning and Nancy felt terribly sorry for her. Rounding Gonzales Point, Nancy looked over at Dan and began to sing. Before long two more voices keeping perfect time joined her, singing softly at first and then growing louder. Dan and Nancy looked at each other and raised their eyebrows. She turned around and smiled at their passenger.

"SING GIRL!" the coloured man ordered.

"Take over, Danny," grinned Nancy, slipping from her seat.

She moved to the back of the boat and knelt down in front of the startled couple. Reaching for the woman's hand Nan began to sing again, this time more loudly. Several nearby boaters turned their heads to gawk.

As they travelled along the coast, they took turns selecting songs and if they didn't know the words they just hummed along. Nancy thought some of the songs were probably Negro songs from the South. She was thoroughly enjoying herself and thankfully the woman was more relaxed now.

After they passed Sidney harbour, Dan swung around the end of Swartz Bay and across Saanich Inlet toward Salt Spring keeping to the middle of the channel.

"THAT LARGE BAY OVER THERE IS CALLED COWICHAN BAY," he shouted pointing to Vancouver Island on the port side. A minute later he called, "I need you, Nan," as he cut back on the power. "We'd better watch for that log boom."

He immediately scrambled out across the bow and, hanging onto the bowline, balanced himself in a standing position as he searched the dark waters. Nancy carefully manoeuvred the boat watching Dan as they bobbed gently in the now choppy sea.

"STOP!" he yelled suddenly, pointing up ahead.

There, off to their starboard side, just below the tops of the waves lay a monstrous dark shape. It was the log boom all right and it was moving very slowly with the tide. Nancy cut the engine and allowed the boat to come up alongside.

Dan gaffed one of the logs and turned to his male passenger. "Hold this," he ordered, handing the man the end of the gaff. Then picking up the flag poles, he leapt out onto the boom. The woman gasped. Racing across the logs he set the flags firmly in place. It looked like he was walking on water. The poor woman covered her eyes as Dan jumped from log to log then returned to the boat. Leaping over the side, he nodded to Nancy and she pushed down on the throttle.

As they continued on toward Vesuvius Bay, Dan went back to talk to their passengers. With patient prodding, he finally ascertained that the man was Ben Wall and the woman his wife, Asha. Bill Wall, whose farm they were going to, was his father's cousin.

"You're good people," Ben commented, "and that little girl sings like an angel."

"She sure do," his wife agreed.

Now more relaxed, Ben began to tell them the story of how he and his wife were the children of slaves freed from a southern plantation only years before. They were coming to join their relatives on this small Canadian island wanting to spend their last years in peace and security with friendly folk. When Ben mentioned he'd worked on an apple orchard all his life, Dan smiled.

"I've thought about having an orchard," he admitted.

"FISHERMAN!" Nancy interrupted, cutting back on the power.

She stayed as far away from the little motorless boat as was possible in the narrow channel. Its lone occupant was so engrossed in landing the large fish on the end of his line he hadn't even noticed them. Scooping it laboriously out of the water with his net, he finally saw them just as their boats passed not two feet away from each other.

"That's one big fish," Asha gasped, looking curiously at the black man.

"I knew it was you, Dan," Bill Wall called. "Only one boat goes that fast in these parts!" He looked over at their passengers but showed no sign of recognition as Nancy and Dan exchanged glances.

"Are you heading in now?" asked Dan, considering he should be making some introductions, yet knowing it would be quite awkward on the boat, he decided to wait.

"Yes, done for today."

"We'll tow you in. Come on aboard, Bill."

Awkwardly scrambling over the side, Bill came face to face with his relatives, although none of them seemed even aware of the possibility. It only took a few minutes to reach the Vesuvius Bay dock and after Dan had tied up they all climbed out.

"I have a surprise for you, Bill. These folks are your relatives. Say hello to Ben and Asha Wall."

For a moment silent astonishment hit the three coloured people, then whooping with joy, Bill hugged the shy young woman and shook hands joyously with his cousin.

"That's worth more than money, love," Nancy whispered, her arm creeping around Dan's waist as they said their goodbyes and climbed back into the boat.

Just as they were about to leave, Ben turned and came back to the boat. "You talked about an orchard, Dan. If you need any help, just let me know."

Waving his thanks, Dan turned on the engine. Deeply touched by their new friendship, Nancy stood watching the happy family reunion as the speedboat slid away from the dock. As they sped down the channel, the sun was setting behind Mt. Tzouhalem and she began to sing. The sweet sounds of her voice rang across the water, bouncing off Salt Spring's rocky cliffs. Dan spotted Jim Goodwin and his tug at the log boom, a breeze now whipping at the red flags showed that the huge grey mass was on the move.

"Looks like Jim could use some help," Dan announced, moving toward the tug.

Gratitude showed on the tugmaster's face as the redhead squeezed the speedboat in by his side. Dan grabbed the ladder and pulled himself aboard.

"Hold the *Ping Pong* in tight to the logs, Nancy," Jim growled, leaving the controls.

Heaving on the heavy towline, the men worked furiously while the blue speedboat, buffeted by a now fast-running tide, heaved under Nancy's expert control. Minutes later, soaked to the skin, the two men jumped back onto the deck of the tug.

"GO!" Jim shouted urgently, grabbing his controls as Dan jumped across the widening space between the two boats.

Turning up the power, Nancy moved the speedboat safely away. Looking back, Dan could see the mighty little tug dip her stern in the water and, with engine roaring, the logboom began to move away from the rocks.

"He'll be fine now," Dan muttered, stripping off his wet shirt and grinning as he looped it over the back seat. Shivering, he found his jacket and put it on. "Take us home, love."

Later, as they sat down to a tasty salmon dinner, the young couple related the events of the day.

"I haven't seen many black people," whispered the Scot, raising her eyebrows.

"Well you're going to meet one now," Nancy laughed. "Dan's going to get Ben over to help him lay out the orchard next year."

"Apple farmers?" Jebediah muttered in disgust. "What an adventure!"

Later, out on the porch, they watched as dusk settled over the tranquil scene. Mount Baker loomed above the islands although a haze hung over its foothills.

"When we were in town today, we were surprised to see several large groups of men standing around on the street corners," said Meg. "Seemed they were out of work and talking of enlisting so they could put food on their tables."

"Yes, and prohibition is a big topic as well," added Jebediah.

There are no easy answers, the redhead thought tiredly, yawning as she said goodnight and headed indoors. *We have our own little piece of heaven right here at Gordon Head,* she thought, going slowly up the stairs to her room.

On the last day of June, Nancy found the Balmoral in an uproar as early morning businessmen voiced their loud opinions to the news of the day. Uncharacteristically, they shouted between tables and waved newspapers high in the air expressing their indignation and disappointment.

Harry Tabour, having just read the startling headlines in the Colonist, tipped his chair back, covered his head with his hands and groaned. It had finally happened—a student in Serbia had assassinated the heir to the Austrian throne and his wife. Harry listened to the noise filtering through the kitchen to his office and shuddered. His mind was already planning his future. *If I can get to the United States unnoticed, a German citizen would be much safer down there.*

Setting to his task, he worked frantically on the menus for the weeks ahead and was writing out orders to the traders when Nancy walked in.

"Are you going to sit here …?" she began, her words tapering off when she saw the pile of menus. "What's wrong?" she whispered.

"I'm getting organized so I can take a holiday," he lied unconvincingly.

"Permanently?" she asked solemnly, watching him nod without looking up. She noticed his trembling hand that fumbled for a cigar.

Finally he looked up at Nancy with a mournful expression.

"Don't worry," she murmured. "We'll take you to Seattle with us on Friday, if that's what you want?"

Harry's only answer was a relieved nod.

Chapter 5

The new delivery business was already a huge success and Jack Dumpford was proving himself to be an excellent dock manager. When he informed them near the end of the month that the blasting of the reef at Shoal Point was going to take place in a few days, Dan decided to make it into a family outing even though Nancy had to work. So, on the morning of July 1st, he and Nancy persuaded Meg and Jebediah to join them in the boat and, after dropping Nancy off for work, they sailed over to Lime Bay in Esquimalt where they would have a safe, but front-row view.

At 11:45 a.m., the dynamite loaded reef exploded with a terrific bang, sending a tremendous waterspout high into the air. The large crowd cheered and the underwater shipping hazard was finally gone forever. The boom of the explosion was heard all over the city, causing a moment's panic in the minds of many uninformed citizens. Shoppers came running out of stores fearing the worst and dock workers leapt for safety as a giant wave swept up the inlet.

At the Balmoral, Nancy shook her head as men jumped from their tables, rushing outside in alarm. Waldo Skillings and Charlie Goodwin were also well aware of what was happening. They didn't even flinch as they talked business over lunch, grinning at the redhead when the restaurant cleared of inquisitive patrons.

In his office Harry Tabour also leapt from his chair. His nerves, already raw, were now shattered by the explosion, nervous that a crowd of patriotic British had begun a rampage through the city. Sweating profusely, he was relieved to hear Mary's explanation for the blast and he settled back onto his chair.

The next day as they were finishing work, Nancy told Kate she needed to talk to her and they walked over to the Brown and Wilson office together. She told her of Harry's dilemma, laying out her plan to keep the restaurant running just as though he were still there.

"You'll be in charge, Friday, Saturday and Sunday," Nancy told her. "I'll do it Monday, Tuesday and Wednesday, and we will both be there on Thursdays."

A chuckle of amusement escaped Katherine's lips, wondering how long they could keep up the deception before the owners found out, and what kind of retribution they could expect for their part in the conspiracy. Her decision to go along with Nancy's plan was not a difficult one. Her friend's honesty and compassion had surprised her many times already. She'd witnessed the girl's amazing strength and resolve and found her envious of Nancy's attributes. She always seemed willing to give her unwavering help to her friends.

Dan and Dumpy sat listening to the girl's plan not sure if they could pull it off for long but interested enough to support them. Dumpy's interest in Kate was becoming more obvious and when he offered to chaperone her home, Kate blushed a little and accepted.

"Now there's two people with such a lot in common," Dan murmured as they watched Kate and Dumpy walk up the hill to Wharf Street. "I hope they become good friends."

"Softy!" Nancy smiled, slipping her arm through his. "Take me home, I'm starving."

On the way Nancy mentioned the Joyce brothers, wondering where they were on their trip back to the East Coast.

"The Panama Canal is open," said Dan. "It was in the newspaper last week. Ned and Tim were probably the first through!"

"Mmm, smell those blossoms!" Nancy murmured, sniffing the air as they made their way along Cedar Hill Road. "Some day our place will smell like that."

"Hungry love?" Meg asked, as Nancy came through the door.

"I could eat a horse!"

"Did the shipment come?" Dan asked, watching Jebediah nod.

After the meal they went to sit out on the porch and Nancy disclosed her plan to help Harry Tabour leave the city.

"I don't blame him for getting out," said Jebediah. "I've seen angry mobs before and it can be very frightening."

A sudden cool breeze blowing in over the cliff made Meg shiver and she reached for her shawl.

"Time to go in," Dan announced. "There's rain in the air."

The next day, rain was still beating heavily on the windows as Meg dished up breakfast and they prepared for their trip to Seattle.

"Looks like we'll need the oilskins today," said Dan.

"Do we have an extra one for Tabour?" asked Jeb.

"Yes, we do, I brought one home yesterday. It's in the boat. I'm going into town but I should be back by half-past three with Tabour," he said, heading for the door.

Harry Tabour was waiting at the dock. Seeing the truck pull in, he grabbed two of his several cases of baggage and began to drag them over to it.

"No need to do yourself an injury, Harry. We're not leaving for awhile. I have some things to do. I thought you were going to wait at the hotel," said Dan, looking at him curiously. The man was obviously nervous or very eager to leave.

"I couldn't sit around there, Dan," he said self-consciously.

"I understand, why don't you get your cases loaded and Dumpy will have some coffee in the office. I'll be back in about half an hour."

Harry took his time stacking the baggage in the back seat of the little truck but instead of going into the office he climbed into the passenger seat. In the office, Dumpy told Dan that Harry had arrived by taxicab about an hour before and had been pacing up and down the wharf ever since.

"I tried to get him to sit down by offering him a coffee but he said he had already drank several cups!"

"Thanks Dumpy, we have to appreciate his anxiety. I'll have him out of here shortly. Now, anything I need to know about?"

On the drive out to Gordon Head, Dan found Harry quite subdued compared to previous meetings and the dark clouds and intermittent rain seemed to reflect the poor man's dismal mood.

Arriving at the house, Jebediah had already seen to loading the cargo so Dan only had to send the baggage down the chute. There was still room in the hold but Jeb had rigged up a tarp over the back to help protect their passenger. Then, Dan blew his whistle to signal Nancy they were ready.

The rain was falling heavily by the time they slipped out of the cove. With Nancy at the helm, the speedboat's engine seemed to growl in protest as they moved off through foam-tipped waves whipped up by a stiff northerly breeze.

"Take it easy, sweetheart, we've lots of time," the whaler advised getting very close and speaking directly into her ear. Gently resting his hand on her shoulder, his eyes searched the water ahead.

The dark storm clouds seemed to hang just overhead as the blue speedboat swayed and bounced through the turbulent sea. Rain lashed their faces as the warning lights marking the channel between Keystone and Port Townsend Harbors blinked out their message of danger. Then the rain began to ease and a ray of sunlight broke through the heavy clouds.

"Stupid weather!" Dan mused, sweeping off his rain hat and shaking it overboard. He looked back at Harry huddled in the corner next to Jeb. *I don't think he's moved since we left.*

Halfway to Edmonds, the sea grew calm and the clouds seem to roll back behind the mountains. Brilliant sunshine bathed the Washington coast.

"LET'S CALL ON ZEKE," shouted Jeb from the rear and Nancy turned the boat toward Kingston.

She slowed when Ezekiel's chimney came into view nosing through the greenery covering the cove. Harry watched in silent fascination as Jeb pointed out the wild Kentuckian sitting on a log watching them. Rising, Zeke spat out a stream of tobacco juice then lay his rifle down and walked slowly to the water's edge.

"Howdy, Ezekiel!" Jebediah called, scrambling overboard as the boat bumped the shore. "We brought you a visitor."

"Howdy, Nancy," Ezekiel grinned, wading into the water and beckoning to the girl. Taking her into his arms, he moved back to the shore. "Golly it's nice when you find time to visit an old man like me!" he said grinning, as he put her down onto the sand.

"Not her, you chump ... him!" Jebediah laughed, as he pointed at Harry who had removed his shoes and socks and had gingerly jumped over the side of the boat and into the shallow water.

Scowling fiercely, the old hermit watched the stranger wince as he came toward him across the stones. He spit a stream of vile-smelling tobacco juice at Harry's bare feet, making the restaurant manager leap backwards.

"Don't want him!" Zeke's voice rumbled.

"I really don't want to stay here," Harry whined, turning to look desperately at Nancy. "Aren't you taking me to Seattle?"

Ezekiel turned to Dan and Nancy, winking at the young couple and completely ignoring Jebediah and Harry.

"It's all right, Harry. We're not leaving you here," Nancy quietly reassured him.

They made their way up to the beach and sat down on the logs.

"We weren't sure how long the storm was going to last so we left early. Now we've got some time to kill," explained Jebediah.

"I've got some tea on at the house," offered Zeke, turning to walk away, but then he stopped. "'Course Nancy might not like it much—sorta looks likes dirty dish water. My water comes from a stream out back and has a pretty strong taste. You might need to get accustomed to it."

"Let's have a look, Zeke. I'm sure the others would love some of your tea," she teased, looking over at her companions. "I'll help you." She disappeared into the ramshackle cabin after him.

Harry, deciding not to take a chance on being left with this wild man, gathered his shoes and socks and made his way back to the boat. Dan and Jeb exchanged smiles when they saw him scramble aboard. Nancy returned carrying several dirty-looking cracked cups, placing them on a flat log. Zeke was not far behind, gingerly carrying an old tin coffee pot stained black with soot.

"These were all the cups we could find so we'll have to share," she announced. "Where's Harry?"

Dan pointed to the boat. "I guess he didn't want to share!"

"He was making sure we weren't going to leave him with this wild man!" Jebediah chuckled.

Zeke poured them each a half cup of the horrid-looking brew and they sat back and let the sun warm their faces. He asked if they'd seen the Eggers because he hadn't seen them at all recently.

Laughing loudly, Jebediah told him about their previous week's encounter. "You're not going to see those boys until they find a new boat or do some major repairs!"

This set Zeke off telling stories of the days when Jebediah chased him around Washington State. Jebediah got up and began to stomp around the shore, kicking at pebbles and occasionally stopping to scream a tirade of abuse at the old man.

"Ain't he somethin!" Ezekiel chuckled, glancing over his shoulder. "I love winding up the old coot, he'd go on like this for hours."

"Uncle Jeb," the redhead snapped. "Come over here and listen for a minute."

Frowning, he turned and came to sit down curious what she was on about.

"Zeke, when we come here and find you sitting on that log holding your gun, it makes me terribly nervous," she began. "It gives me an awful uneasy feeling that you might not recognize us one day. So, I have a suggestion." She put her hand in her pocket and brought out two of their whistles. "This is what we use at home to signal each other. It works really well."

"That looks mighty like a duck caller," Zeke said with astonishment.

"It is, and this is a regular whistle." Then she explained how they used the whistles at Cunningham Manor.

A smile crept across the Kentuckian's face when he heard her blow a sharp note on the whistle followed by a very realistic duck call.

"That's good, I like that," exclaimed the hermit. "That would be sure to tell me it's you comin in."

"And," Nancy emphasized, squeezing the old man's hand, "if there's danger coming in with us, we'll only use the whistle, with two long blasts."

Ezekiel chuckled. "My Betsy loaded with buckshot will be waiting to give somebody a nasty welcome!"

"Well … you be careful, you old coot," cautioned Jeb, as they prepared to leave. "Don't you go stirring up trouble."

When the speedboat arrived at the Jorgensen dock, Harry was still looking miserable. Terry O'Reilly gave Harry a questioning look then ignored him as he put his men to work unloading the shipment. Jebediah, always wary, vigilantly kept a lookout. He relaxed a bit more only when the truck disappeared past the end of the dock.

"I need a favour, Terry," said Nancy, taking the Irish American's arm and giving him an entrancing smile. "My friend Harry needs spiriting away … South."

Terry's eyes narrowed as he stared unblinking at the stranger, then he slipped his arm over Nancy's shoulder. "For you, girl, consider it done." He instructed his driver to load Harry's baggage in his own car. Nancy went over and talked briefly to her former boss giving him a hug.

"Good luck, Harry," she said sadly, knowing they would probably never see each other again.

"Thanks for all your help, Nancy. Thank Dan and Jebediah, too. Have a good life. I'll never forget you," he said quickly, stumbling over the words. Then kissing her cheek, he hurriedly climbed into the backseat of the big black car.

Nancy waved until the car went out of sight. Thoughts of the hotel without him kept going through her mind and she hoped he would be all right. She joined the others going to sit down beside Jeb as Dan started the engine.

"You know what, Nan," said Jebediah, putting his arm around her as she gazed silently off in the distance. Someone once told me that 'friends are for now, but memories are forever.' Your lives have been enriched by knowing each other and I suspect his even more than yours." Then, as he often did when sharing his words of wisdom, Jebediah sat back and closed his eyes, and Nancy moved a bit closer.

It was after ten when Meg, from her vantage point on the porch, heard the speedboat coming. She smiled as she recognized the roar of the engines and went over to the steps to check her lantern. Then making her way back into the kitchen, she pulled the kettle back onto the middle of the stove and put another stick of wood in the fire box under their meal.

With barely enough light to make out the shadow-filled cove and its jetty, Nancy brought them in.

"We sure could use more lights down here," Jebediah mumbled, tripping over a rope.

"And a proper beacon up there," said Dan, looking up the stairs. "Well, one day it will happen when electricity gets out this way."

Over their meal they discussed many aspects of their regular Friday trip to Seattle, the impending winter months, and the darkness they'd have to contend with. Dan felt his pocket for the envelope Terry had given him and flipped it across the table to Nancy. Extracting the money, she read the hand-written note.

"Did you read this, Danny? They want double the order from now on!"

"That's better than three quarters of a ton," he murmured. "I'll take the boat into Turpel's on Monday and see how she sits with that weight although I'm sure Gus has already approved it."

"Better get a bracket for the gun, too," Jebediah yawned.

"I'm going to bed," Nancy announced pushing her chair back, as she stifled a yawn. "Have you seen old Sam lately?" she asked as she hugged Meg. "How is his foot?"

"I fed him today," she replied. "He came over straight after the storm, but he was dry as a bone and walking without his stick."

"He's a woodsman," offered Jeb. "He knows how to keep dry. I wouldn't be surprised if the old geezer doesn't share a cave with a cougar somewhere on Mount Douglas."

"A cougar!" retorted Meg, shivering.

"Oh, cougars have plenty to eat with all the deer and small animals about, you don't have enough meat on you to interest them!" teased Jeb.

In the Brown and Wilson office the following morning, Fred Barrett was talking to Dumpy about some relatives in Sooke who were interested in using their delivery service. He was attempting to strike a bargain when laughing voices were heard outside. Going to the door, he saw Meg and Jebediah coming down the boardwalk arm-in-arm.

"Who is that man with Meg?" he asked with a puzzled expression.

"It's probably Jebediah, how the heck do I know? I'm not as nosy as you are!" Dumpy snapped.

Fred's head swung sharply back to the dock manager but before he could say anything the old folks walked in.

"Now what are you two up to?" Meg asked, smiling when she saw her old friend. "You've met Jebediah, haven't you, Fred? What are you gawking at?"

Realizing she was right, he tried to cover his surprise. "Yes, we've met. Dumpy and I were trying to make a deal for Danny's delivery service but it's like talking to that wall."

"What do you mean?" Dumpy objected. "All you've said yet is that you've got relatives in Sooke."

"That's a long trip by road," Meg muttered, hanging up her coat, mischievously adding, "even if there were one!"

"But not so long by sea in Dan's speedboat," admitted Fred.

"So what's the deal?" asked Dumpy, still scowling.

"Once a week you take their orders to Sooke and bring back whatever they're sending to town. It's just that easy," explained Fred.

The sound of a high-powered engine alerted them that Dan and Nancy had arrived. In a few minutes quick footsteps sounded on the boards and the redhead burst into the room.

"He's going to throw me in the water, Aunt Meg," she giggled, taking refuge under the old lady's protective arm, as Danny appeared at the door. "Truce!" she called, throwing a towel at him.

He quickly wiped his face and continued toward her.

"Stop it you two," Meg demanded. "What has she done, lad?"

"The she-devil threw half a bucket of water over me," he chuckled, trying not to laugh.

Fred and Dumpy howled. Many, many times they'd been the brunt of Dan's tricks and this was poetic justice.

"Serves you right," Fred chuckled. "Remember when you pushed me off the Hudson Bay jetty?"

"And many a time you've dropped ice down my shirt with nowhere to go but over the side!" Dumpy added, as Dan threw up his hands in surrender.

"All right ... truce!" he laughed. "I can see you're all agin me, so I'm off up to Turpel's."

Nancy, hearing Fred and Dumpy's problem, quickly made a deal that suited Fred, gaining the concession to sell oil by the barrel in Sooke Harbour. Dan would tow a barge in for the purpose. Fred left for work and Jebediah, who had been quietly reading a newspaper, looked up with a deep frown on his face.

"I got this two-day old Seattle newspaper from an American sailor this morning and at last I know what's happening across the line," he announced. "More than half the counties in Washington State are dry already!"

"Prohibition," Nancy whispered.

"Not state-wide yet, just local," Jebediah grinned, "but it's coming."

Later that morning the sound of bugles were heard from the direction of the Parliament Buildings. Soon after, the pounding of hundreds of heavily booted feet as solders marched through the streets. The city was firmly in the grip of war mania.

An icy-cold feeling of dread stole through Nancy's body as she watched these young Canadian warriors proudly march by the Balmoral realizing deep in her heart that Dan would soon have to go. With eyes turned upward she sent a silent prayer screaming into the heavens. *Dear God,* she begged, *please don't take my Danny away from me.* Then shaking herself from the mournful feeling of self pity, she bit her lip, stiffened her back with resolve and went back to work.

At the Point Hope Shipyard, Superintendent Macpherson was loading weights onto the speedboat in an effort to settle the whaler's mind. Two tons were gently set in the craft before Dan decided to try the boat out on the harbour. Twisting and turning he tried to gauge the speedboat's reaction.

"You were right Mr. Macpherson, she handles just fine," he admitted when he returned to the dock.

Glancing up as the crane began removing the weights, Dan saw Emerson Turpel walking down the jetty toward them. He was frowning as he stopped to look out the harbour as the steam tug *Delta* chugged its way in. It had been following Dan but was very slow and puffing unusually black smoke.

"Now what's wrong with the old lady?" the shipbuilder growled.

"Blocked flue," Macpherson diagnosed, with hardly a glance.

When the crane had finished, Dan handed the superintendent some money and backed the speedboat away from the dock. His eyes roamed over the old wooden-hulled steam tug that had been around since before he could remember. He knew well the history of this little tugboat, built at the Point Hope Shipyard in 1889 by Emerson Turpel's father. It had once been the fastest tug on the West Coast, but past her heyday now she had been demoted to pulling log booms for the Emerson lumber yard.

Seeing a familiar old captain in the wheelhouse, Dan gave them a salute. "What a grand old lady of the sea," he said softly. Carrying on, he went to visit Turpel's blacksmith explaining what he wanted done with the cannon. The man laughed in disbelief when he saw it scratching his head when he heard Dan's explanation and how the Joyces had given it to him.

"That thing's blasted lethal, but I can see the Joyce boys having it!" snorted the blacksmith. "It's so old she needs a new barrel fitted. It'll be a lot safer and will spray shot over a wider area."

Confident with the man's suggestions, Dan left the boat saying he would be back at 4 o'clock. With a jaunty air, he made his way back up to Johnson Street and found Prior's Hardware. It turned out they were happy to supply him with whatever he needed … pre-measured black powder, wadding, starter shot and a quantity of ball bearings. They said they'd send a boy with a handcart to deliver it to the boat. Feeling more secure now that the craft would have its armament in place, he went back to the office. Jeb was there with Dumpy and he told them what he had arranged.

"Where's Aunt Meg and Nancy?" he asked, looking around.

"Shopping, where else!" exclaimed Jebediah, raising his eyebrows and pointing to the food supplies stacked by the door. "We'll be lucky if there's room for it all in the car!"

Down Wharf Street, Nancy was steering Meg toward Moore and Pauline's automobile show room. The older woman stopped and looked in the window.

"Why are we coming here?" she asked.

"It's time I made some preparations for the future," said the girl, holding the door open without looking at her.

48

They had barely entered when a salesman came toward them. "Hello Miss Wilson, what can I help you with today?"

"I require some advice, please. How long would it take for me to learn to drive a Model T truck?"

Meg suddenly realized what Nancy was doing. It gave her a heavy heart thinking of the possibilities; realizing they may not be able to ignore the issue much longer. Nancy had always been a determined girl no matter what situation she faced, but this problem would be much more difficult to surmount.

Chapter 6

July passed quickly as more and more soldiers filled the city's military camps, coming from all over the Island to receive training in anticipation of war in Europe. Kate was proving to be a marvellous partner in running the Balmoral Restaurant and, strangely, no one seemed to be missing Harry Tabour. There was talk in the restaurant that the government was about to fall and also the rumour that Premier McBride was negotiating to buy submarines from Seattle.

It was Tuesday, August 4th, when the newspapers blazoned across their headlines that war had been declared in Europe sending the city into a frenzy of excited activity. Volunteers rushed to enlist and the local militia were immediately called to active duty.

On their next trip south, Gus Jorgensen surprised them by meeting them on the dock. As he handed Nancy her envelope, she could tell by his manner that something was terribly wrong.

"Will Danny be enlisting now, Nancy?" he asked in a hushed tone.. Receiving a solemn nod, he continued, "Beth and I just got word this week that both our boys have been listed as missing in action in Europe."

"Oh Gus, how dreadful!" She hugged the shipowner as tears of concern welled in her eyes. She thought of what he and Beth must be going through and she knew it would be horrific. She remembered seeing the pictures of the boys on a table in the Jorgensen's upstairs apartment. They had made the surprising choice to join the Belgian Army over a year ago and she'd thought how handsome they looked in their Air Force uniforms. *It could so easily be me one day*, she thought, then pushed the thought from her mind as Gus went to talk to Jebediah.

"I heard that your Premier McBride purchased three of our submarines," he stated, watching his friend's reaction.

"Oh, so the newspaper was right then," Jeb replied.

"What will happen to our business if Dan goes away?" Gus asked.

"Nothing," Jeb grunted. "Me and Nancy will still carry on."

Dan, coming up beside them, had heard Gus' question and was surprised at Jeb's instant reaction. The determined note in his voice brought a measure of relief to the whaler. Now that war had been

50

declared, he found himself torn between loyalty to Nan and family and his natural feelings for his country.

"What's going to happen when winter sets in?" asked Terry coming to join them as his men drove away. "It'll be black as old hell out on the water ... and bloody cold!"

"Stop worrying," Nancy interrupted. "By that time I'll know these waters like the back of my hand."

"There are a lot of lights," Dan interrupted. "She knows them all up and down the sound now."

"It's not blasted lighthouses I'm thinking of," Terry muttered fiercely. "It's obstructions of the human kind!"

"Spell it out, lad," Gus snapped at the man who was his protector. "What have you heard?"

"Oh, just a whiff that the Eggers are out to get 'em."

"Then stop them!" the shipowner ordered.

"No, don't," Dan returned. "That boat has a big surprise waiting for someone."

"I know," Terry said quietly. "You've got a high-powered shotgun."

"A shotgun?" the whaler laughed. "No, we don't. It's a blasted cannon! Come and take a look."

"Holy jumping jeepers," Gus chuckled when Dan pulled the oilcloth off the little cannon. "Do those two know how to use it?" he asked, pointing to Jeb and Nancy.

Nan looked at Jebediah who put his arm over her shoulder and they both grinned.

"I would suggest to the Eggers they might want to keep out of your sights!" laughed Gus. "Now let's all get out of here."

Hugging Gus again, Nancy manoeuvred the boat out into the harbour. Jebediah, who hadn't suffered at all from seasickness on this trip, was watching the lights of Kingston as they went by. Dan went to sit down beside him.

"I'm glad you didn't tell 'em about our secret weapon," said Jeb.

"What secret weapon?" asked Dan.

"Ezekiel Plunket," Jebediah laughed. "That old coot is a one-man army when he's annoyed. I don't think he'd take kindly to someone trying to hurt Nancy."

Dan returned to his seat beside Nan and very little conversation passed between the three after that—they were too busy watching the dark shadows for trouble. Only the slosh of the waves and the thunder of the engine accompanied their thoughts. The dim shapes of San Juan and Lopez Islands came into view, lit only by the weak rays of the setting sun.

Nancy was the first to see the almost invisible shape of a boat as it slid out from between the islands, mysteriously devoid of lights.

"KILL THE LIGHTS!" Dan commanded sharply.

Running in almost total darkness gave the redhead an eerie feeling as she used the Oak Bay harbour light as a guide.

"Turn toward Oak Bay, then shut off the engine," Dan ordered into her ear, then he bent down and loaded the cannon.

As the speedboat settled quietly in the water, Jeb stood up as the phantom boat came closer. Finally, over the noise of the stranger's spluttering engine, they could hear singing.

"What is it?" asked Nancy.

"Drunks singing!" growled Jeb.

"Canadian drunks!" Dan corrected him. "Listen to them!"

Several out-of-tune singers were belting out the British Navy's fighting song, *Rule Britannia* as Nancy manoeuvred the blue speedboat alongside the unfamiliar craft. No one on the boat even seemed aware that they were nearby but they couldn't make out how many there were in the dark. Dan reached over and hooked a line onto its bow. Nan eased forward until the line twanged tight, then she pushed on the power and the tow began. The lights at Cunningham Manor guided the redhead into the cove but the singing had long ago stopped. There was now total silence from the boat and going to investigate with a light they soon realized there were five men, now sleeping soundly.

"Leave them to sleep it off," Jebediah suggested with a chuckle. "Unless they wake up cold, they'll probably sleep till we come down in the morning."

"If they do wake up, they'll be mighty confused at the surroundings," laughed Nancy, adding, "serve them right, too!"

Next morning Meg had the breakfast plates loaded by 7:30 and they sat down to eat.

"No sign of our visitors yet?" asked Dan, wiping the crumbs from his face as he walked over to the door and opened it. "Well, I make no wonder!" he exclaimed, causing the others to push their chairs back and go to join him.

There, at the top of the cliff stairs sitting still as a statue, was old Sam cradling his ancient rifle in his arms.

"Well bless my soul!" Meg gasped, returning quickly to the kitchen. She dished up a plate with leftover breakfast and headed purposefully outside.

Sam heard her coming and turned his head, stoically nodding a silent greeting. Climbing to his feet, he accepted the plate.

"Sam watch men in boat," he muttered, then shuffled off into the trees.

Meg could hear a voice yelling from below and she beckoned to the house for the others to come and see. Standing at the edge of the cliff they all looked down at the dock. Five dishevelled men were pacing the jetty in obvious frustration.

"Hey, you on the cliff!" one of them called. "Where are we? What country are we in? Who is that fellow with the gun?"

"They're streetcar drivers from the city!" Nancy whispered. "I recognize that one's voice and two of the others, I think."

Mischief gleamed in the American's eyes. Chuckling aloud, he answered their question … loudly, in his version of Mexican-Spanish.

"You old devil!" Nan giggled, watching a reaction of desperation run through the group as she tried to stay out of sight fearing she might be recognized.

Jebediah waved an invitation for the men to climb the stairs as the women went into the house to make some more breakfast. Baffled and looking quite dejected, the men were shown silently into the kitchen and seated at the table. A couple of them showed more interest in the house than the others and Jeb noticed them looking around. Suddenly, one of them saw the Colonist lying on a chair.

"Halleluiah boys, we're in Canada!" he gasped, picking up the paper and realizing they had been taken.

"Of course you are," Meg giggled. "You're in Gordon Head and this is Cunningham Manor."

A ripple of laughter passed through the group and soon they were all asking questions.

"If we hadn't picked you up you might have been out in the middle of the Pacific by now!" Jeb laughed, thoroughly enjoying the fun they were having at the expense of these foolhardy Victorians. Finally, they settled down to a welcome breakfast explaining that they had gone fishing in the Strait, calling at Friday Harbor for a beer.

"You certainly had more than one!" Dan interjected. "And you had no running lights so we might not have even seen you if Nancy hadn't been so observant."

Red-faced the men looked sheepishly at the girl, recognizing her but not sure why. Obviously repentant, they revealed they were all streetcar drivers in Victoria.

"The wife is going to kill me!" one of them muttered as another agreed and the rest laughed nervously.

After breakfast, they returned to the dock to see if the visitors' boat would start. Several of them tinkered with the engine, to no avail.

"Looks like we're going to have to tow you into Victoria," Dan announced.

Ushering the five back to their boat, Nancy climbed onto the captain's seat amid sarcastic comments from the men. "If you men don't behave, you'll be glad to get back to your wives!" she threatened, grinning wickedly at them.

Dan attached the tow rope while she started the engine and they moved slowly out of the cove. However, once they reached the Strait, she held nothing back. Watching them out of the corner of her eye, she noticed they were hanging on for dear life as their little boat bounced about in the speedboat's wake.

"You really are making them pay their penance, aren't you?" laughed Dan, beside her.

She merely grinned.

When they reached the outskirts of the harbour, laughter and whistles sounded from the freighter docks as Nancy slowed and nearby workmen got a good look as the little procession entered Victoria. The tram drivers handled it well, a couple of them standing up cautiously in the boat and bowing to the jesters. Dumpy stood back silently and watched them dock. Nancy noticed the smile on his face as the men walked toward him.

"I suggest you hurry home, boys," he chuckled. "Your wives have had everybody out looking for you!"

"Oh, Lord help us!" one of them murmured.

"So much for fishing trips," another commented dryly.

But they thanked their rescuers for their help and hospitality. Vowing to repay their enormous debt, they took their leave.

"What about the boat?" one of them asked calling after the others.

They all stopped in their tracks looking totally perplexed as they looked back to the wharf.

"Go!" Dan called. "We'll look after it. I think you've got enough to deal with at the moment! Come back and see us tomorrow."

The men called their thanks and hurried off toward town. Dan turned to look across the harbour and noticed the CP Steamship Princess *Margaret* loading a large contingent of uniformed solders.

Dumpy saw him and read his mind. "Don't even think of it, Danny," he murmured. "There are thousands volunteering every day." Pausing for a moment, he looked across the harbour. "Did you know that several US submarines were delivered to the Esquimalt Naval Dock early this morning?"

"We heard the rumour in Seattle," Dan muttered. "So it's true."

Throughout the month of August the newspapers reported anything newsworthy about the violent catastrophe that had erupted in Europe. Dan's heart went out to the families of Canadians grieving for the loss of their once-vibrant souls. He thought of the Jorgensens and sincerely hoped they had received good news about their sons by now, although he thought that unlikely or they would have called.

The following Friday they made their regular trip to Seattle and saw Gus for the first time in several weeks. They thought he might be delivering good news until they saw his expression and knew it was bad even before he spoke.

"They're gone," he announced softly, his voice breaking. "They've been missing in action for four weeks now. The military won't tell us anything and poor Beth is frantic."

Nancy rushed to her friend's side, wrapping her arms tightly around him. No words could fit the sad occasion. This man and his wife had become such an integral part of their lives ever since he had befriended them that day on a Victoria streetcar coming from Gorge Park. It suddenly seemed so long ago.

Terry's men unloaded the boat and he indicated it was time to go, leading his boss back to the car. All the way home, Nancy sat quietly in the stern holding onto Jebediah's arm, her thoughts a mixture of grief for her friends and terror for her own future. As they passed Pender Harbour she fell into a fitful sleep and didn't wake until Dan shut down the engine at home.

Meg watched Dan help her up the stairs, fearing something had happened. He helped her off with her coat then swept her into his arms, carrying her up to her room. He kissed her cheek and laid her on the bed, covering her with the comforter.

"Leave her," he whispered to Meg, who had followed them upstairs with the lamp. "She's all tuckered out. It's not going to matter what she wears to bed tonight."

Downstairs, Meg was stunned as Jebediah began to tell her of their meeting with Gus. She knew the pain of losing a loved one as her own tragic memories flooded into her mind.

"Life has to go on," Jebediah muttered, never having had much of a family of his own.

The next morning's sunshine was greeted with only a wisp of a breeze, helped to lift the sorrowful mood that hung over Cunningham Manor. Nancy, steeling herself against painful thoughts, ate breakfast and joined Dan at the boat. On the cliff, Meg and Jebediah, their hands firmly clasped, watched them go.

"You know, Meg, I've never had such strong feelings for anyone in my life before," the American admitted in a whisper. They turned to walk back to the house. "But I seem to care a whole lot for the three of you."

"It's because we're a family, Jeb," Meg replied in little more than a whisper, looking up at him. "Them two youngsters mean as much to you as they do to me."

He squeezed her hand lapsing into silence as they walked up the steps to the house.

Nancy cased the boat around the breakwater construction, slowing to follow a steamship into Victoria's picturesque harbour. *Another ship to carry our boys away,* she thought. She soon realized it was the *Princess Sophia,* the CPR boat that serviced the northern coast, although it, too, would soon be pressed into war service.

Gently bumping the dock, they tied up the boat. She stood and looked around the harbour—abuzz with activity and uniformed military everywhere. Walking slowly up to the office arm-in-arm, it was almost as if Dan was reading her thoughts and dared not break into them.

Captain Percy Neville paced the floor as he waited for them. Having already talked to Dumpy, the dock manager sat silently at his desk pretending to read the paper as their footsteps approached.

"Hello Nancy ... Dan," Percy greeted them when they opened the door.

Dan noticed right away that his friend was not his usual exuberant self. Nancy's heart skipped a beat, seeing the uniformed man who had already tried to persuade Dan to join the army not too many months before. Feeling suddenly weak, she went and sat down trying not to show her distress.

"Hello, Captain," returned Dan, solemnly shaking his hand. "I assume you're waiting for me. What can I do for you?"

"Dan, I won't mince words, we desperately need your expertise and I'm here on behalf of the army to convince you to join us."

Dan indicated a chair and the men sat down. Dumpy brought over the coffee pot and poured them each a cup. Dumpy couldn't help but feel how lucky he was to have lost three toes in a boating accident several years before. It gave him a medical reason not to join up. He looked cautiously over at Nancy who suddenly looked pale and frightened like a wounded animal.

"Your country needs you, Dan," said Percy, looking the whaler in the eye.

"And so do I," Nancy snapped, almost in a whisper as thoughts of the Jorgensen boys went through her mind.

But Percy's argument was compelling. "Nancy, Dan will be in very little danger. His job will be instructing artillery gunners before they go overseas. The war is going to be over within a year anyway, they say."

Reluctantly, Nancy nodded. "You mean he won't be going to Europe?"

"Not to my knowledge," he replied, hoping he was right.

"I know that every able-bodied man must go when called by his country … I just don't want it to be Dan," she said with a sigh, looking from one to the other.

Not risking a change of heart, the captain took some papers from his inside pocket and handed them to Dan with a pen.

"I'll need you to report to the Willows Camp at seven on Monday morning, Dan."

"So soon!" Nancy gasped.

When Captain Percy Neville left, Nancy stood at the door and Dan put his arms around her as they watched him walk smartly toward town, his mission accomplished.

Then her brain whirled into action. "The truck, Dan!" she said in an urgent tone, turning to face him. "I'll need to drive it and we've also committed to making those deliveries to Sooke on Monday."

"Hold it, hold it!" he replied, scratching his chin. "Is everything ready for Sooke, Dumpy?"

"It's all here," his friend replied. "It just needs loading."

Half an hour later, leaving Dumpy sweating on the dock, they started the boat's engine and, towing the barge behind them, they headed for Sooke.

"This could get a bit scary in winter, Nan," Dan murmured.

"Too late to worry about that," she replied. "I can always use Dumpy."

Choppy water caused very little trouble for the redhead who had become such a confident sailor she could handle the boat better than most men. Rounding Beechy Head they found a turbulent sea and she was mighty glad to see the sheltered entrance to Sooke harbour and the calm water leading up to the dock.

They enlisted the help of two fishermen who were repairing their nets nearby. One of the fishermen called a local boy over and asked him to fetch John Muir and he went running off up the road. The fisherman came over to the boat and explained that they knew where the barge was to be set up. By the time the kindly-looking bearded man arrived, introducing himself as John Muir from Woodside Farm, quite a group of locals had gathered and the unloading was almost finished.

"Well done, laddies," Muir greeted them in a strong voice with a Scottish accent. Handing Dan the pre-arranged fee and a page of written orders for the next week's delivery, he thanked them profusely.

At the same time several of the men left in a horse-drawn wagon while others struck up a conversation about what was going on over in Victoria. They were friendly hard-working people, farmers, loggers and fishermen, all eager for word from the city. A couple of them couldn't contain their curiosity and went over to the blue speedboat to get a better look.

"We'll have cattle to go to Victoria next week, lad," said Muir. He chuckled jovially when he saw the look of surprise on their faces.

The men in the wagon returned bringing with them bales of what looked like high-quality hay, loading it onto the barge for the return trip.

"Dan, have you met Tom Barrett?" asked Muir.

"Fred's uncle, yes, sometime ago. Nice to see you again, Tom," exclaimed Dan shaking his hand.

"Now that we know the deal is going to work, they'll want to build a special barge over at the Muir Lumber Mill," he said winking at Dan. Then laughing heartily, he continued, "Folks will want to transport their animals in luxury, I fear!"

Arrangements were made with Tom Barrett that he would look after their oil barge when it arrived, pointing to a place at the government wharf where he wanted it locating.

Waving goodbye, the blue boat eased the barge out of the harbour. It was still early afternoon when they arrived back at their own dock greeted by the strains of the Navy Band playing somewhere near the Parliament Buildings.

Dumpy was waiting for them on the dock.

"Who's the hay for?" he called, grabbing one of the lines.

"It's for Waldo," Dan replied, unhooking his towline. "I'm going to fuel up the boat."

Nancy leapt onto the boards and the whaler quickly spun the speedboat away. They finished tying up the barge and she hurried into the office.

"What's the rush?" Dumpy inquired, watching her set about making some sandwiches and tea.

Spinning around on the startled dock manager, Nancy wagged a finger in his face. "I only have one day to learn to drive that infernal truck!"

"Can't be done, love," he muttered sympathetically.

"We'll see about that!" she said, with determination and he knew she meant it. Hearing the speedboat return she quickly finished what she was doing. "Fill a liquor bottle with coffee will you please, Dumpy," she ordered. Putting her sandwiches in a brown bag she added a cup, the bottle of tea and hurried out of the door. "See you on Monday."

Dumpy followed her outside. Scratching his head, he stood in the doorway and watched the boat pull away. "Good luck!" he said quietly.

Chapter 7

Racing along the coast, the boat bounced and rolled in the waves. They ate their makeshift lunch and shared a mug of tea, laughing as it splashed all over them as the boat dropped between the waves off Ross Bay. She silently reflected on all they had been through together and apart over the past 14 years—the tears and sorrow and above all, the fun and laughter. She knew she'd have to hold it all together while Dan was away. *I can do it*, she told herself determinedly, feeling his comforting hands grip her shoulders.

Docking quickly, they surprised Meg and Jebediah when they arrived laughing into the kitchen.

"You're home early," murmured the Scot.

"I'm going to learn to drive the truck!" Nancy announced, going immediately back outside before they could question her.

The shocked couple looked at each other and followed them outside watching them climb into the truck with Nancy behind the steering wheel.

"Something has happened," said Meg, in an ominous tone.

"Well, they seem happy enough. I reckon they'll tell us when they're ready. They're not going to get far with Nancy driving. Why don't we go for a little walk," he suggested, with a chuckle.

"Yes, let's do that," she replied, getting her sweater then closing the door.

Taking his arm, they walked down the drive and, staying clear of the driving lesson, walked slowly out to the road. They stood for a few minutes and watched. Hearing laughter coming from the vehicle, they knew they were still having fun. They decided to get out of their way and continued up Ash Road.

"I just remembered something, Jeb," Meg said excitedly. "When we were shopping last Saturday, Nancy and I paid a visit to the automobile dealership where they bought the truck. She asked the salesman how long it would take to learn to drive."

"What did he say?"

"He said it would take about a week to become confident."

"It certainly sounds like they're preparing for Dan's leaving," Jeb mused. "Nan will find it very hard when he does."

"She knows, and she's trying to hide it so we don't worry about her. I can tell."

For the next hour and a half Nancy drove that truck back and forth along the drive. Confidence seemed to consume her and even though the actions of changing from gear to gear, braking and reversing, became so monotonous, Dan said her progress was truly amazing.

The older couple returned and walked cautiously by them pretending to be afraid.

"Looks like she's getting the hang of it," Jeb commented, watching her drive out to the gate without grinding the gears.

"I'll make a cup of tea, if you'll all come in for a rest," Meg called, when the truck pulled up nearby. Receiving a wave, she proceeded into the kitchen leaving Jeb on the veranda to watch.

Over tea, they finally learned what was happening when Nancy told them about Percy Neville's visit. Fighting back her emotions the Scot clenched her hands under the table but was unable to speak.

In an emotional tone, Jebediah spoke for both of them. "We wouldn't expect you to do anything less, son. We'll look after things here."

Supper that night was somewhat subdued although Jeb tried his best to keep the mood light. Meg chased the young people outside to enjoy the moonlight volunteering Jeb to help with the dishes.

Walking arm-in-arm, they walked along the cliff and down through the tall timber that enveloped their 25-acre property. The evening light was growing sparse but hardly a word was spoken between them. They felt such joy and contentment in each other's company, it was difficult to comprehend that it was coming to an abrupt end in less than 36 hours.

It was getting quite dark as they walked back toward the house. Hearing a noise in the water below, they walked over to the edge of the cliff and listened. Nancy rested her head on Dan's shoulder and he put his arm around her.

"Oh listen, Danny, it's the seals playing on the rocks. It sounds like they have some new pups! I wish it wasn't so dark so we could see them," she cried, and then her mood abruptly changed. "It's odd how tragedy springs up to tear people apart," she whispered.

"Blasted war," Dan growled, drawing her closer.

"Percy said he thought you wouldn't be leaving Canada. I certainly hope he is right."

She lifted her head and he kissed her tenderly on the nose and then the forehead. "Let's go in before you get cold," he said.

On Monday morning at 5:45 a.m., Nancy tried to keep her mood light but she was finding it extremely difficult. She wasn't sure what she was most apprehensive about, leaving Dan or her first experience driving the truck into the city.

Meg swallowed hard as she said her goodbyes to Dan and, Jeb shook the younger man's hand, murmuring his best wishes. Then, silently, they folded their arms around each other.

An hour and a quarter later, Nancy drove through the gates to the makeshift army camp set up at the Willows Fairgrounds. It had been an unnerving drive but Dan was patient and until now she had barely had time to think about her next task.

As she entered the camp, Dan directed her to stop and she turned off the engine. Choking back tears, she looked around and saw a line of men in civilian clothes waiting outside a tent. She grabbed Dan's hand with both of hers and kissed it, then silently wrapped her arms around his neck and held him.

"I'll be all right, Nan, I promise you. I'll call you as soon as I know anything," he said, trying to sound confident.

She closed her eyes to keep her tears back, desperately wanting to say the right words but they wouldn't come. His lips softly caressed her cheek and she didn't want to ever let him go, but he was pulling away. She felt suddenly weak and her arms fell to the empty seat. Quickly opening her eyes she looked up just as he closed the door and their eyes met again for an instant. He turned away and strode the short distance toward the tent where the line of men were standing, now watching them. Tears streaming down her face, she saw Percy step out of the tent and shake his hand. She was grateful he didn't turn around. As they went into the tent together, she started the engine and carefully turned the truck around.

Driving into the city, streetcars and trucks rattling past caused her a good deal of apprehension and she sighed with relief when she arrived at last at the Brown and Wilson dock. Shouting a quick hello to Dumpy, she set off at a run for the Balmoral.

He came out to see her and noticed the truck. "By George, she did learn it in a day!" he mumbled.

A streetcar stopped at Government and Broughton spilling a load of shop workers out onto the street in front of her. As she dodged the crowd, she waved to Dick, the newspaper vendor. He seemed to have extra hands this morning as he yelled out the headlines at the same time handing out papers and pocketing the coins.

The warm kitchen and Mary's smiling face helped to ease Nancy's tattered nerves. "Your teapot's ready, love," she called as the redhead entered the back door and hurried into the staff room to get changed.

Going to the swinging door, she took a quick look around the restaurant then came back and poured out a steaming cup of tea. She took it into Harry's office and sat down in his chair, sighing heavily. Her eyes caught sight of the day's menus all neatly printed and stacked on the desk. Katherine was proving to be a treasure. *Her efficiency is astounding,* Nancy thought as she opened the top drawer of the desk. She saw the unopened pay envelopes marked with Harry's name and closed it quietly when Mary appeared at the door.

"My goodness, love," cook whispered, taking a sip of her own tea, "you've trained Katherine well. She's a joy. She introduced me to her new man friend. A real gentleman … treats her like a lady."

"Man friend?"

"Yes, a Mr. Dumpford." Mary's eyes turned soft. "He's a dock manager on Wharf Street, maybe you know him." Startled at Nancy's involuntary giggle, Mary looked at her inquisitively.

Unsure of how much Katherine would want her to tell the well-meaning, but gossip-loving cook, Nancy changed the subject abruptly and told her Dan had joined the army. Before the surprised cook could question her, a clock chimed and she hurried off to open the doors.

After work she went down to the dock to talk to Dumpy, deliberately neglecting to mention Mary's revelation. She had other problems on her mind as she discussed the oil barge that needed delivering to Sooke.

"You'll have to deliver it," she told him.

Dumpy's eyes sparkled. He'd been hoping that Nancy would give him more responsibility now that he felt comfortable with the dock manager's job. He was feeling quite grateful that Dan and Nancy had given him the inspiration to make more of his life than being a deckhand.

"All right, but who's going to look after the office?" he asked.

"Uncle Jeb."

Nancy had answered his question almost without thinking and although it hadn't been discussed in any detail, Jeb always wanted to help so she was sure it wouldn't be a problem. The problem was how Victorians would take to his gruff ways. *Well, we shall just wait and see,* she thought, slipping into her coat and heading for the door. Setting her controls in the truck, just as Dan had taught her, she walked round to the front and cranked the Model T's engine. Nancy sighed with relief as it popped, chugging into life. Passersby stopped and stared in disbelief when they saw the redhead at the wheel of the lurching truck.

Pursing her lips in harsh determination, she manoeuvred the truck out into the traffic on Wharf Street, causing shouts of alarm from draymen when she skimmed past their horses. It wasn't until she turned onto Cedar Hill Road that relief flooded through her knowing she would now have nearly all the road to herself. Half an hour later, she turned into the drive and began to relax.

"I've made it!" she squealed pulling up to the side of the house.

Jebediah was sitting on the porch. "Well, how was the driving, love?"

"Hellish!" came back the muffled answer.

Dinner was ready and Meg was hovering over the table making sure she had everything just right for Nancy's first busy day. So, when Jeb and the girl came laughing through the door, Meg was finally able to relax a bit. Dropping her bag, Nancy rushed into the Scottish woman's outstretched arms.

"You had me worried, lassie," Meg whispered, wiping her eye with the corner of her apron. "How ever did you manage today?"

"Easy," Nancy lied flippantly. "I'm a much better driver than Dan!"

Laughter once again filled Cunningham Manor as the girl related her tales of terrified pedestrians leaping for safety and their strange looks upon seeing a lady driver.

"I don't think the draymen could figure out what was happening so the air turned rather blue when they thought I was disturbing their horses. Of course, I probably was!" she snickered. After dinner she broached the subject of Jeb helping to run the office.

"Don't you worry, my dear," Meg assured her. "We'll work it out together."

Interrupted by the phone's loud ringing, Nancy jumped up to answer it. It wasn't very often the phone rang, so it was usually important. An instant lump came into her throat when she heard Dan's voice. Meg and Jeb looked at each other and stopped talking. Nancy stared at the wall, biting back her tears as she listened. She whispered something into the phone and hung it slowly back on its cradle.

The house was absolutely still as Nancy leaned against the wall and began to sob. Jebediah looked at Meg and raising his hand for her to stay seated, he went out into the hall. Wrapping his arms around her for a moment, he led her back to her chair. Wiping her tears with the cloth napkin Meg handed her, she tried to talk.

"He-he's not coming back u-until the end of October," she explained in a halting voice. "Almost three months!"

Meg went over and silently hugged her knowing there was nothing she could possibly say to make the situation better. She stroked the girl's forehead and wiped her tears as if she were a child. "Now, lassie, the best think for you right now is to keep busy. Let's get the dishes cleaned up. You've had a full day but you'll no doubt sleep like a baby tonight."

Nancy didn't sleep well at all that night, or for several nights after. But finally, knowing that everything was going well so far at the Balmoral and, that the delivery business was continuing to flourish, thanks to Jeb, Meg and Dumpy, she began to relax. At last, on Thursday night, sleep caught up with her.

Friday's trip to Seattle could have ended in disaster when they almost ran over a deadhead out in the Strait. Nancy's young eyes and quick thinking narrowly averted the impending catastrophe almost dumping Jebediah into the water as she swung the boat around. Terry met them on the dock muttering his surprise when told Dan had joined up. There was no sign of Gus and no mention of his boys.

"What a week!" Nancy groaned, when they arrived home. "I'm sure glad we've got that one over."

"It will all be downhill from here on, my girl," said Jeb with a wink. "Just you wait and see."

And each week did seem to get easier as she steeled herself to the task, becoming an accomplished driver and enjoying the attention she attracted being the first woman driver on Victoria's streets.

CPR ships regularly came into the harbour empty and departed full of cheering young soldiers, displaying a strange sense of euphoria as they left for the war. Nancy quaked at the stories reported in the Colonist of the barbaric slaughter going on in Europe and tried not to think about the Jorgensens and the possibility of Dan having to go there one day.

She noticed a shift in the mood of many of the old businessmen who were patrons of the restaurant. Their conversations began to take on a cautionary note, no longer so sure when the war would be over.

Three months later, little had changed. Juggling her jobs had grown a bit easier but the long days and warm weather was now in the past. By the time she and Jeb arrived home late on a Friday evening she was exhausted. So far there had been no more trouble from the Egger boys but they were very careful not to let down their guard. They stopped in to see Zeke from time to time and he seemed very grateful for the company, even if it were only for a short visit before darkness closed in on them.

One Thursday morning late in October, there was a moment of anxiety for Kate and Nancy when Mr. Martin, one of the owners of the hotel, appeared in the kitchen. Nancy hurried into the office after Katherine whispered the alarm, churning over in her mind the excuses she had recited over and over in her brain since Harry had left town. A sinking feeling hit her as she walked through the door and saw the open drawer and Harry's pay envelopes in Mr. Martin's hand. Sighing with resignation, she knew the charade was up.

"My office in ten minutes, please Nancy," the man said kindly, taking the envelopes and closing the drawer. He stood up and left without another word.

After he had gone, Nancy and Katherine huddled together in urgent conversation. Nancy insisted that she would take the blame, and with a toss of her head she was gone, hurrying through the labyrinth of corridors to the top floor and the owner's sumptuous, but little-used office.

Tapping lightly on the partly open door, a man's voice invited her in. The person sitting behind the desk was the general manager of the hotel. Mr. Simpson had been with the company for a long time and she had spoken with him briefly several times before. He was a kindly, heavy-set man of middle years whose greying, mutton chop whiskers surrounded his face. He slipped off his spectacles and laid them down on the shiny maple desk.

E.J. Martin and a woman she did not recognize sat stoically in black leather upholstered chairs. The woman stared blankly at her across the thick luxurious carpet as she entered, as if waiting for her to speak. *She's probably one of the owners, too*, thought Nancy, trying not to look nervous. This was the first time she had been in this room and her attention was drawn to the well-stocked liquor cabinet whose door

66

stood partially open. She noticed the almost-empty glasses on the desk. A large bookcase and two lone family portraits completed the decor.

Nancy took a step closer and turned toward the desk.

"Now, Miss Wilson," boomed the man behind the desk. "I think you owe us an explanation."

"Mr. Tabour has gone," she said simply, "and any problem is my fault because I've been running the restaurant."

"Gone where?" the woman asked in surprise.

"Doesn't matter," Mr. Simpson's stern voice interrupted, already suspecting the reason. "So you're to blame, you say."

"Yes, sir," she nodded, looking him squarely in the eye. "I'll pack my things and be gone in an instant." She started to turn toward the door.

"Stay where you are!" E.J. Martin's softer voice, relaxed her a bit. He stood up and came toward her, pointing to the chair he'd just vacated.

"Sit down," he said quietly.

It was an order which drew a stern look from the woman but Nancy moved slowly across the room and sat down looking at the wall behind the man.

"Now," Mr. Martin continued, "how long have you been running the restaurant?"

"Three months, sir."

"Three months," he repeated slowly. "Well, my girl, we think you'd best carry on. It's making a remarkable profit. We were going to give Tabour a bonus!"

"Oh my ... n-no sir," Nancy whispered, taken aback by the man's statement. "Katherine Flounder is the best person for the job."

All eyes focused on the redhead, unable to believe she'd just refused their prestigious offer.

"Please, don't think I'm ungrateful," she added quickly, "but my brother is in the army and I have his business to run. Katherine has more time and she's a wonderful organizer and very honest."

"Your honesty is not a factor," growled Mr. Simpson, picking up Harry's unopened pay envelopes and dropping them with a clunk onto the desk. "Would you carry on a while if we gave you these to use in whatever manner you thought proper?" he asked, pushing the envelopes toward her.

This is more than I could have ever expected, she thought, then watching their faces she gave them a surprising answer. "I'll do it, but only if you'll make it a dual responsibility between me and Katherine."

There was complete silence for a few seconds then the woman cleared her throat.

"If my colleagues will agree, I believe we could do that for you, Miss Wilson," she said, looking around at the others and watching as they nodded solemnly. "Take your money, dear. You may go back to work now."

There was a bounce in Nancy's step as she hurried down the hall eager to tell Kate of their new official positions. Clutching the envelopes tightly in her hand, she entered the kitchen and made for the manager's office. Katherine was just entering with an empty tray and Nancy beckoned her in. Seeing her friend's smile, she breathed a sigh of relief and followed her.

"They didn't fire you?" she asked, quietly closing the door.

"No Kate, they didn't fire me," Nancy laughed, turning to put her arm around her friend's shoulder. "They made you and me into joint managers!"

Kate flopped onto the nearest chair. "You mean ...?" she gasped.

"Yes, yes," Nancy replied excitedly. Then a serious note crept into her voice as she went around behind the desk and sat down. "We've some hard thinking to do about what to do with these." She brought her hand out from behind her back and lay the envelopes on the desk.

"Why, those are Harry's pay envelopes. Aren't you going to give them back?"

"Mr. Martin found them in the drawer but he gave them back to us. Their instructions are for us to use them as we see fit!"

"Oh my, I see what you mean ... I think. What do you have in mind? I'm sure you already have an idea!"

"You're right, I do, but we don't have a lot of time right now with customers waiting. Why don't you go ahead and tend to them and I'll work out a plan. If you need me come and get me, you know where I am!" Nancy smiled, already writing some figures onto a piece of paper.

"All right, I suppose we had better keep the customers happy," said Kate, grinning as she opened the door.

It took about half an hour before Nancy had the answer and was just going out to help Kate when her co-manager arrived to enlist her help. Clocks in the city were chiming 6:30 by the time the girls left work that evening.

"Come on, let's go tell Dumpy our news," giggled Nancy.

Kate looked at her strangely but Nancy had already started out. Her friend had never included her quite like this before but she eagerly hurried after her. *I wonder if she knows about me and Jack. Surely she would have said something.* Catching up to her they dodged traffic, giddily leaping over tram tracks, as they hurried down Fort Street.

Dumpy looked up frowning when they burst through the door. "You're late," he muttered, looking surprised when he saw Katherine.

"I know, I'm sorry, Dumpy," Nancy replied. "We had some business to attend to."

"They made us joint managers today, Jack," Kate blurted out.

Total elation overtook Dumpy's normally subdued demeanour as he leapt from his chair to hug his girlfriend. "Well done, love, how did that happen?" He suddenly stopped and turned blushing to his boss.

"Well, do you two have something to tell me?" Nancy asked coyly, putting her hands on her hips and trying to look serious.

Suddenly feeling very ill at ease, Dumpy tried to explain, stammering so hard Kate took over, gently laying her hand on his arm.

"Jack and I are walking out together, but you already knew that, I suspect. Nothing escapes you, Nan," she admitted as her cheeks displayed a blossoming pink tinge.

"I'm so pleased for you, truly," said Nancy, putting her arm around Kate. She looked over at Dumpy and smiled brightly. "And Danny will be, too, he comes home on leave tomorrow!"

"You didn't say anything, Nancy. I guess we've all been busy with our lives of late. That is so wonderful!" said Kate. "Now, let's tell Jack our plans for the Balmoral."

"Yeah, Nan swore me to secrecy about Danny, love. So what are these plans all about?" asked Dumpy.

They all sat down around the table and Kate and Dumpy listened as Nancy described her meeting with the owners and the windfall of cash they now possessed. The simple logic of the two women was quite noticeable, obviously determined to be fair to everyone, including their employer. He shook his head in surprise when Nan detailed a plan to hold most of the cash in surplus in case one of the staff was sick and needed help with their bills. Then she stood up and put her coat on.

"Can I give you a ride home, Kate?"

Kate looked over at Dumpy.

"I'll walk her, Nan. We're not in a hurry, are we Kate?"

"Not in the least. Granny is now able to start the dinner for me, but I get it ready the night before. Grandfather is coming along, too, feeling a bit better of late, thank goodness."

"That's wonderful, Kate. They are so fortunate you were able to come home to look after them," said Nancy, as they all walked out toward the truck.

"They're really sweet people. It was terribly hard for a while, though now with Jack around he's been helping with some of the outside work and doing some repairs for us."

Nancy looked at Dumpy and smiled. *Well, this is a different side of Jack!* she thought, as she climbed into the cab. Dumpy turned the crank once and it started immediately. With his arm linked in Kate's, they watched her drive away and quickly disappear into the traffic.

"She'll be a great woman one day," said Dumpy.

"Yes, she will," Kate agreed, looking up at him, "and is!"

Driving up Johnson Street, the redhead's thoughts were centered on home and Dan's arrival when suddenly a pedestrian ran out in front of her, causing her to violently swerve to avoid him. As she continued on her way, she noticed that the truck was not driving properly and pulled over to the side of the road in front of Jim Wo's laundry. A group of uniformed soldiers stopped to watch as she got out of the truck and circled the vehicle.

"Fiddlesticks!" she muttered, seeing the flat tire.

Waving to the soldiers, they sauntered over laughing and talking amongst themselves. It didn't take much to coax them into pushing the Model T back to Plimley's auto repair shop, a block back toward the city.

Mr. Plimley and one of his mechanics were just leaving as the curious looking group arrived. The old man was well-known to the redhead and generously offered to stay and fix her tyre.

"Go have a tea over at the London Cafe," Mr. Plimley suggested. "We'll have it ready when you get back."

Throwing her leather gloves and woolly hat onto the driving seat, Nancy let her red hair cascade over her shoulders then turned back to the soldiers. Surprising them, she flashed her brightest smile inviting them to join her.

"Wow!" one of the soldiers whispered, "she's a beauty, too!"

"Aye lad," Mr. Plimley muttered, knowingly, "and she has a big brother, as well!"

Irene, the waitress at the London Cafe, had once worked with Nancy at the Occidental, although they hadn't seen each other in a long while. When she saw the four soldiers enter with Nancy in the lead, she recognized her friend and stood open-mouthed as the men followed her to a table. When she arrived to take their order, she was greeted with noisy laughter.

"Hello Irene, I'm treating these fellows," Nancy said brightly, bringing some order to the group. "Two of them would like Coca-Cola and the rest of us will have ginger soda, please."

When the drinks arrived, there were comments about the new Coca-Cola bottle which Nancy hadn't seen before, then the soldiers told her they were all in their last week of training. Excitement touched their voices as they broke into laughter, explaining they were being shipped out next week. With little or no thought of disaster, they readily talked about their plans of going to war. Drinks finished, they walked out into the darkness and accompanied the girl back to Plimley's. After paying Mr. Plimley and saying goodnight, she thanked the boys again and wished them good luck. They saluted her as she drove away.

It seemed a much longer drive in the dark, having to be extra careful and watching for ruts in the dim glow of headlights. She was never so glad to see their open gate when she turned into the driveway. It was very dark amongst the trees but the glow of the house lights were inviting and she parked and turned off the lights.

As she started toward the steps, a movement at the corner of the house attracted her attention. Thinking it was Sam, she was going to say something when the tall, straight figure stepped into the light thrown by the kitchen window. Instantly noticing the hat, she screamed. Dan was already moving toward her but before he could take three strides she was in his arms.

Meg and Jeb, already knowing Danny was home, heard the commotion and looked out the window.

Trembling, the Scot took Jebediah's arm and whispered, "It's not fair, Jeb, they belong together."

"The time isn't right yet, Meg ... one day." Then hearing the door, he turned and, a big grin lit up his face. "I see you found him!" he chirped. "You're late, love. Have some trouble?"

"Yes, as a matter-of-fact, I had a flat tire!"

"No!" Dan chuckled. "How'd you deal with it?"

"I found some good-looking soldiers to help me!" Nancy grinned.

"Jezebel!" he laughed, pulling her onto his knee. "I think I had better get these two to watch over you more closely in my absence."

A series of giggling and tickling followed, until Meg put her foot down and announced dinner was on the table. "He's not going anywhere after dinner," she said, "so behave yourselves and let's eat."

Over dinner, Dan told them what it was like living in an army camp. "I'm now a Sergeant Instructor in the Canadian Royal Artillery," he explained proudly. "I'm training gunners, thanks to Captain Neville's influence. It's an interesting job and I'd like it … if it weren't for the damned war." He suddenly changed the subject. "Is the boat in Victoria?"

"Yes, Dumpy's managing well with the deliveries," Nancy replied. "The Sooke job is off to a fine start."

It was getting late and Meg quietly reminded Nancy she had to work in the morning.

"Walk with me, Nan," Dan suggested, going to get her coat. "We won't be long, Aunt Meg," he called as they went out the door.

Leaving the house they slowly walked over to the clifftop. Arm-in-arm they stood listening to the crash of the waves. The wind whipped through Nancy's hair blowing it in all directions and she gathered it together and stuffed it into the collar of her coat.

"Sing to me, love," he pleaded.

"Not here," she laughed. "It's cold." Tugging him over to the cliff stairs they slowly descended. Halfway down they realized they were mostly out of the wind and they sat down on the step, huddling together.

At the house, Jebediah had gone out to the back door to pick up some wood for the fire and hearing the familiar sound of Nancy's singing, he hurried back inside. Gathering their coats and hats, he bustled Meg out onto the porch. Standing close for warmth, they stood and listened until the wind brought the haunting sounds up to them.

"It's nice to have her happy again," Meg murmured, as she felt Jeb's fingers press into her shoulder. *Lord, please keep him safe.*

The next day brought another dark, wet morning. Dan started the truck for Nancy and waved goodbye as he watched the lights of the vehicle disappear down the long drive. Two large deer wandered nervously along Cedar Hill Road as the Model T bounced through water-filled ruts, but there were no surprises as the roads were almost devoid of traffic.

The fountain, at the junction of Gorge Road and Douglas, usually stood stark and lonely in the half-light, but today there was a dray pulled up alongside and a horse was taking a leisurely drink as she putted by. She thought it a rather comical picture as his driver sat patiently waiting, hat pulled well down over his face, as the rain pelted down.

She was almost at the dock when the first streetcar of the day rumbling by up on Douglas Street. A light in the office sent her scampering across the boardwalk to tell Dumpy that Dan was home and would be coming for the boat later.

"I've a run to Metchosin this morning with Fred Barrett and his aunt," Dumpy announced looking up from the newspaper. "I sure hope it stops raining soon. It's supposed to be a much easier trip by boat but they may not think so in this weather. Fred said it would take all day to get there by wagon. Have you seen today's list of war casualties? It's getting longer each day," he said sadly. As soon as the words were out of his mouth he realized his mistake by the painful expression on Nancy's face.

"Blast you, Jack Dumpford," she said fiercely, reaching for the door handle. "I don't want to know! It's bad enough that Dan is in the army without being reminded of the risks, by you of all people."

The door banged shut and her feet could be heard running up the boardwalk. *Fool,* he chided himself, going out to ready the boat.

An hour later, with daylight pushing away the darkness of the harbour, the rain stopped and Fred Barrett led his aging aunt out the door of the Coast Guard office and started down the boardwalk. Dumpy greeted them and they helped the old lady into the boat. Fred wrapped a blanket around her legs and Dumpy started the engine.

Easing the speedboat away from its mooring, they moved quickly out of the harbour. Dumpy took them at an easy speed past Esquimalt and on to the beach at Metchosin. Here the two men helped the old lady out of the boat, carrying her across the rocky shoreline by fashioning a seat with their hands.

"We'll be all right now, Dumpy," said Fred, shaking hands with his friend, after seeing his aunt sitting safely on a log. "A cousin is coming to meet us. He lives out here and should be here any minute now.

The old lady looked cold and frail but, speaking for the first time since they had left the dock, she smiled at Dumpy. "That was a very exciting ride, young man!" she said slowly. "Thank you for giving an old lady such a thrill, Mr. Dumpy!"

Chapter 8

The rain had let up a bit as Nancy walked head down along the wet streets to the Balmoral, mumbling to herself. She was annoyed with herself for losing her temper over Dumpy's innocent comment. Young Dick was also telling everyone about the war casualties as Nancy passed his position on the corner of Douglas and made the hazardous crossing over the myriad of slippery tram tracks. *You just can't get away from it,* she groaned inwardly. By the time she reached the other side of Douglas, her thoughts were running wild and she almost bumped into Katherine on the corner as they both ran for the back door of the hotel.

Later in the morning, during their normal Friday discussion of menus and ordering problems, Kate could feel the tension in Nancy's usually happy demeanour. The girls had grown so close they were almost like sisters now. Mr. Martin dropped in and told them the owners were delighted with their efficiency and concern for their staff. After only a few minutes, he was gone again.

"What's wrong?" Kate asked gently, taking her friend out of her trance.

"Oh, just thinking about Danny and the war, Kate. It's so hard to get it off my mind."

"I know it must be terribly hard for you, Nan. Maybe he won't have to go away. Stop worrying about something that might not happen. We can't do much about it anyway, love. You have to go on living, you know. Enjoy your time with him, right now beef is our problem. It's getting mighty scarce."

The abrupt change of subject jolted the redhead out of her self-pity just as Katherine had expected.

"Beef, but why?" she murmured thoughtfully. She looked up at her friend then answered her own question. "The army's buying it to feed the soldiers, aren't they?" She remembered a conversation she had heard yesterday between several prominent traders who had talked about the exorbitant costs associated with shipping beef from Alberta. As she listened, it became obvious that prime meat was much cheaper in Seattle.

A plan began formulating in her mind, one that put a sparkle into her eyes when she explained it in detail to Katherine as they sat in their office at 2 o'clock. It was quickly agreed between them that Nancy should find a way to purchase their beef in Seattle, saving them the shipping costs would make an enormous difference to their cost.

"The price to the hotel," Nancy exclaimed, "must never exceed the price we paid on July 1st here in Victoria. Brown and Wilson will be paid from the profits so I will need to get a good price for it."

Katherine nodded. "Perhaps we should look into getting our vegetables down there as well," she laughed, "except your boat's not big enough to carry all that we need. We'll just have to continue to purchase them at local merchant's prices."

"Hold it," Nan said softly. "Haven't I told you about Farmer Irvine in Esquimalt, and my Indian friend, Billy?"

"No, you haven't."

"Then let's just wait until I get a chance to go see them. It may be too late for this year's crop but I'll ask anyway. I've got to run. It's Friday and Dan's going with us to Seattle!"

On her way back to the dock, her mind was full of ideas and she was so glad that Dan was home so she could talk to him. She ran down Broughton and arrived at the office out of breath.

"Has Dan been for the boat?" she gasped, finding Dumpy.

"He's here now," the manager grinned. "Gone to Turpel's to fill up with fuel and says you're to wait here for him."

She went inside to get what she needed to take home and smiled as she heard the roar of the familiar engine. Her heart skipped a beat as heavy feet rattled on the boards outside. Beaming, he stepped into the room and she rushed over to hug him. They were soon on their way down the harbour passing a liner that was just docking at the CN station. A nasty chop out in the Strait kept them busy until they rounded Ten Mile Point. She felt Dan's hands tighten on her shoulders sending a thrill up her spine. As she took the boat into the boathouse she noticed Jebediah sitting on the rocks, puffing contentedly on his pipe as he waited for them.

"Where's Danny?" asked Meg, when Nan walked into the kitchen.

"He and Uncle Jeb are loading," she called as she rushed upstairs to change.

As they ate dinner, Nancy told them of her idea to buy two sides of beef in Seattle to supply the hotel and why.

Jebediah scratched his head. "Interesting idea. It's a bit odd but I would think it can be done. I'll make a call and see if I can set it up. We may need to go a bit early, Dan.

"Don't you think you've enough worries, lass?" Meg chided her.

"Got to keep my mind off him," Nancy laughed, picking up her empty plate and ruffling Dan's hair as she went to the sink.

Jeb got up and went to the phone. Ten minutes later he put the phone down and came back into the kitchen. "There, it's all arranged, the meat will be delivered to the Jorgensen dock at 7:30 tonight."

Now it was an urgent matter to be on time and they hurried down to the dock. Rough seas again buffeted the blue speedboat as they left the protection of the cove and, by the time they arrived in Seattle, darkness was covering their movements.

Jebediah's watchful eyes scoured the waterfront for any sign of trouble before leaving the boat and going out to look for the meat truck. It wasn't long before the sound of a heavy truck alerted the couple and Jeb reappeared for a moment before stepping back into the shadows.

A spotlight knifed through the gloom sweeping along the jetty and the couple ducked low in the boat. Suddenly the light snapped out and two dim headlights moved toward them as the truck came closer.

"Mr. Judd?" a frightened voice came through the darkness.

"Danged fool!" the American snapped, stepping out of the shadows.

Two more vehicles raced down the dock and skidded to a halt, as Terry O'Reilly's men spilled out of them and surrounded the truck.

"It's all right, Terry, it's a delivery for us," Jeb called.

O'Reilly flashed orders to his men who quickly moved down to the boat and transferred the liquor boxes in record time. Speeding away, they left their boss shaking his head and talking to himself as he walked over to Nancy.

"What the hell's going on?" he asked, handing her the envelope.

"Uncle Jeb ordered two sides of beef for me," she explained quickly. "They're the delivery men."

"Ok, bring them over, Jeb," Terry called into the darkness.

The other truck engine started again and moved slowly forward, its headlights shining along the dock. Two very nervous young delivery men got out and hurried around to the back unloading two large bundles. When they got closer, it became more obvious that these were frozen carcasses encased in cloth. They all went down to the boat where, with Jeb directing them, the two men wrapped the meat in the large oilcloth before loading them into the hold.

"Can we go now, boss?" the driver pleaded warily.

"How much do we owe you?" asked Dan.

"You don't owe them nothing," Jebediah snapped, already having examined their bill while they were waiting. "They've doctored the bill and over-charged us by 2¢ a pound."

There was a moment of ominous silence before O'Reilly cleared his throat. "You go, I'll deal with these two birds," he said, with an unmistakable threat in his voice.

The driver let out a low curse turning his back on them as the second man slinked warily around to the other side of the truck.

"I don't want them hurt, Terry," Nancy interjected, feeling Dan's hand on her arm.

"GET OUTA HERE, before you wish you hadn't seen me!" Terry screamed at the men. The suddenness of the order definitely surprised them and they scrambled into the cab and roared away.

"Holy Toledo, there goes two grateful boys!" Jebediah laughed. "That's not what they were expecting. I don't think they'll stop until they get to the state line!"

"The beef's free," said Terry with a little chuckle. "Two sides every week and I'll get it for you, and it will be boxed next time. Now you get going, too."

Sitting on his heels the young gangster lit up a cigar and watched Nancy take the speedboat out into the shadow of a freighter. He remained there until the drone of their engine faded into the night.

Dan was impressed by the way Nan handled both herself and the boat. He was also happy to have witnessed Jeb's actions because he realized now that these two could handle just about anything in his absence. They had chosen their friends well and he knew they could be trusted to watch out for Nancy. As the cold wind and spray whipped about them, he remained protectively behind Nancy.

"Let's cut in close and check Ezekiel's light," he called into her ear as the light at Kingston came into view.

Moonlight and a break in the clouds assisted as she slowed the boat and turned for the shore. Jebediah instantly got onto his feet and came to stand next to Dan, their eyes searching the hill.

"Remember what Zeke said. Line up Kingston and Edmonds and we should see his light." Dan reminded her.

Wheeling the boat around Nancy cut her speed, lined up the lights and ran straight for the shore. But before they reached the entrance to the cove, Dan put his hand on her arm and told her to stop.

"He's not home or something's wrong," called Dan. "There, on shore!" Lit only fleetingly by a cloud-covered moon, they could barely see the outline of a dark boat, larger than Zeke's, and suspected it was the Egger boys.

Jebediah picked up his field glasses and waited for the clouds to pass again. "There's dirty work afoot tonight," he growled to Dan, seeing enough to be concerned. "Them Egger's are up to no good!"

"Come around again, more slowly, Nancy," Dan ordered, going to set up the cannon.

"What are you going to do?" Jeb asked.

"Bring them pigs out of there," he chuckled, setting the gun at the ready. "Run past them keeping about a hundred feet away."

Nancy gritted her teeth and sent the boat on the directed course, jumping a little as the explosion rendered the air and flames spurted from the barrel of the cannon.

They heard metal shot tearing through wood and a crash as the boat reeled against the rocks. Darkness hid the full extent of the damage but Dan said later he suspected they had hit the wheelhouse.

On the shore, the three Egger boys heard the blast and, yelling at each other, came crashing through the undergrowth to investigate. Ezekiel, meanwhile, rolled out from behind the log where he had hidden from the intruders. His flickering campfire cast eerie shadows across the cove in front of his cabin. Raising his trusty old shotgun, he fired once at the fleeing men then, cocking his shaggy head on one side, the old Kentuckian listened intently. He chuckled aloud when the sound of a sharp whistle penetrated the air followed by a duck call. Then he spotted the shadow of the familiar boat coming slowly through the trees. He threw some more branches on the fire sending sparks and flames shooting high into the darkness flinging its light across the water.

Meanwhile, moonlight momentarily exposed the Egger's mangled boat as they burst through the trees. Cursing violently, Milo was the first to reach the boat and tried unsuccessfully to push it into the water. Joined by his two brothers, together they succeeded and scrambled aboard. Milo next tried unsuccessfully to start the motor. As the others tossed debris overboard, they cursed loudly, but the motor remained silent and they struggled to keep the boat afloat.

Zeke, with his gun over his shoulder, walked down to the shore to meet his friends while Nancy brought the boat in and cut the engine. Zeke suspected that the Eggers had sustained some damage from his

78

friends because he couldn't hear the sound of their motor. Then, the sound of angry voices reached their ears and they distinctly heard the lapping sound of oars. He chuckled again as the others came ashore to join him. A few minutes later they were all sitting around the blazing fire.

"What the hell alerted ya?" Zeke asked.

"There was no light in your tower, Zeke," replied Nancy, looking up at Dan and pulling his arm closer.

Zeke was silent as he turned over the chew in his mouth then sent a stream of tobacco juice hissing into the fire.

"They won't be back," Dan predicted. "That's twice they've tasted Ned's cannon."

"Don't be too sure, lad," growled the old detective. "Those three add a new meaning to stupid. That was quick action you took back there, Danny." Then dropping his voice, he added, "I believe the army has already changed your thinking."

"Don't care who dun it," declared old Ezekiel, again spitting into the fire. "I reckon you got here just in time, son. I got me some hot coffee here I'll share with you," he laughed, grabbing a forked stick and pulling a tin kettle out of the fire. "Or a taste of my whisky might suit you, too. I brew it in me own still, set in the rocks out back. That's what they were lookin fer, but they'll never find it in the dark and they'd have trouble in the light!"

Smacking his lips, Jebediah suggested they should try the whisky and Zeke went off to the cabin to get it. When he returned, Jeb was the first to taste the fiery liquid, letting it slowly trickle down his throat, warming his insides. "Kentucky firewater," he whispered hoarsely, taking another mouthful. Dan took a little sip, to be mannerly, but choked on it and refused any more.

Meanwhile, the Egger boat had reached the tide line and without their engine it was gradually sweeping them toward Kingston.

"Who the hell was that anyway?" Ariel, the elder brother, snapped, kicking Milo out of the way so he could take a turn at the engine.

"Has to be a new Coast Guard boat with that big gun," whined Ted, the youngest.

"Wonder why they were out here?" Ariel growled, as he wrapped the rope around the starter and pulled. Finally, the little engine putt-putted into life and the other two boys pulled in their oars, cursing gratefully.

"Thanks for the help," Ezekiel muttered, shaking hands with the men as they prepared to leave.

Nancy went over to hug him and he returned it more willingly than ever before. As they pulled away into the darkness, they looked back and saw the dark outline of the old hermit standing motionless in front of his fire. The speedboat slid slowly out of the cove and into the dark waters of Puget Sound. Now, even more wary that danger could be lurking in the shadows, Nancy's eyes picked up the light at Scatchet Head. Her hand automatically opened the throttle, hurtling the boat toward Port Townsend and Vancouver Island.

Startled, Meg sat up in the chair where she'd fallen asleep, pulled the blanket around her shoulders and listened intently. Over the sound of the wind came the distant growl of the speedboat's distinctive engine. *They're home*, she thought with relief, putting away her knitting. Bustling over to the door she quickly put on her heavy coat and tied her hat under her chin. She picked up the kerosene lamp from the window sill and went outside to light her beacon lights. It was a difficult task with the wind blowing from all directions but she finally got them all lit and hurried back into the house.

"It's a nasty night out there," she grumbled as the door opened about 20 minutes later and the three came inside, having trouble shutting the door.

"It wasn't too bad, Aunt Meg, we're late because we stopped to say hello to Ezekiel," Nan explained. Her eyes flashed across the table sending a silent warning to the men.

Jebediah smiled, winking back at her.

Soon after they had eaten, the lights in the house flickered out one by one. From the shelter of the trees, Sam and Flash kept their vigil—a task which had become an obsession—watching over these people who fed him and called him friend. He waited for a while, standing like a stone statue before venturing across the clifftop, a blanket pulled tightly around his shoulders. Like a ghostly apparition he kept his nocturnal watch, disappearing silently into the forest at dawn when the first sign of life appeared in the house.

Chapter 9

The blustery October morning didn't bother Nancy as she scanned the white-capped waves on their way to Victoria. She welcomed the nearness of Dan knowing the luxury of his presence was not going to last much longer. Percy had told him they would probably have a week's leave but he shouldn't count on it. Dan didn't mention this to Nancy for fear he would spoil their time together.

Rounding Clover Point they both saw the sailboat at the same time—its mast broken in half and the tangled sail causing panic as the two occupants desperately tried to cut it free before the badly listing boat went onto the rocks.

Nancy's hand instantly opened the throttle, sending the powerful craft surging over the surf. Waves were now crashing over the sailboat's deck and she wallowed uncontrollably. Then thankfully, the mast broke free and the boat came upright again water washing across its deck. Nancy's quick action brought the two boats together safely and Dan's experienced hands caught the line thrown by one of the men.

"Easy on the throttle, Nan," he shouted, tying the line to their stern. "They must be getting full of water by now."

Nancy eased the line tight, and then moved forward ever so slowly, pulling the unfortunate craft and its occupants after them. Bailing furiously, the two sailors hardly noticed passing Shoal Point, only reducing their efforts when they realized they were in calmer seas.

Dumpy was watching as the two boats came alongside the jetty. Catching Dan's line in mid-air, he secured it to the stout ring while Dan ran back to check on the partially submerged boat.

"That could have been disastrous," said Nancy, relief crossing her face as she ushered the exhausted and wet sailors into the office.

Removing some of their outer gear, they stood around the warm stove and Nancy made them steaming mugs of rum-laced coffee which were gratefully accepted.

"I'm Chief Davis of the fire department," the taller man volunteered sheepishly, holding his hands over the stove. "My first mate here is Hugh Lynn, one of my firemen. We can't thank you enough for your help. It was getting mighty cold in that water."

"I thought I knew your face," murmured Nancy.

"Of course you do," Davis replied with a rueful smile. "You're Nancy from the Balmoral."

"That's right," she nodded, and then with realization flooding her mind, she continued, "you're a good friend of Mr. Skillings."

Voices outside interrupted them as Dumpy and Dan arrived.

"We've loaded the truck, Nan," Dan announced, reaching for his steaming mug. He turned to the sailors. "You're welcome to leave your boat at the dock for a day or two while you organize your repairs."

Nancy introduced Dan to the firemen who again expressed their appreciation for the timely help they'd been given.

"Probably averted a nasty situation for us," the fire chief mused, going to gather his clothes.

However, Hugh Lynn remained sitting, his eyes on Dan and a frown on his face. "I've just realized who you are. You're the Joyce brothers' famous gunner. You were the one who shot the freighter before it went down that night in a storm off Metchosin," he said, his tone indicating the utmost respect as he got up and went to shake Dan's hand.

Dumpy looked at his friend knowing he would not admit to anything. "You're right, and now he's teaching the army how to be gunners."

Davis came back to the fire and vigorously shook Dan's hand. That's a fine boat you have, son," he commented, "and your wife is a darn good driver."

Dumpy grinned impishly as he looked over at Dan, wondering what explanation he was going to give for this.

"The boat's more Nancy's than mine," Dan said softly, locking eyes with her, "and she's my sister."

Seeing the surprised looks on the firemen's faces, Dumpy moved toward the door. "We're glad to be of service, fellows," he said, dismissing them, "now you'll have to excuse us, we've got work to do."

Around the city, noon-hour chimes mixed with the rattling sounds of streetcars as Dan and Nancy got into the Model T and headed for the hotel. The back of the little truck was now weighed down with beef carcasses. Off in the distance, the familiar strains of a military band floated across the harbour.

Dick waved to the couple as they passed by his newsstand, flinging a paper into the cab as Dan flipped him a dime.

"All the news is about depression and death," Nancy grouched disapprovingly. "It's all so frightening. I hate it."

Dan glanced at the headline which blared, MINER'S STRIKE CONTINUES in large bold print, and below was a war story with a list of Victoria men killed in action.

Blowing her horn to hurry on some pedestrians talking in the middle of the road, they bumped across the tracks at the Douglas intersection and turned into the alley behind the hotel. Bouncing through the water-filled potholes from an overnight rainfall, they made their way to the kitchen door. Nancy hurried ahead to open the door and found Katherine in the kitchen.

"We've got a real grouch sitting over in the back corner this morning. He's very well dressed, take a peek and see if you know him will you, Nan?" she said, before disappearing back into the dining room.

"Mary, will you show Dan where to put the beef we've brought," she called as she went and looked into the dining room.

"Beef? Good gracious, what are you up to now, Nan? Hello Dan, nice to see you. Where on earth did you find the meat?" the cook cried in surprise. "Come, I'll show you how to get them into the cooler."

Nancy surveyed the roomful of diners, noting Waldo Skillings was eating with Charley Goodwin, one of the tugboat company brothers, and a familiar-looking freighter captain. Beyond them in the corner, staring fiercely at the table and drumming his fingers impatiently on the table, was the architect Francis Rattenbury, obviously agitated about something. She wasn't surprised Kate didn't know him as she hadn't been in Victoria long and he certainly wasn't a regular customer of theirs.

Nancy slipped her coat off and when Dan returned he was just in time to see her exit the staff room wearing her uniform.

"You're not going to work now, are you, Nan?" he asked sounding disappointed.

"No, of course not! I'll be back in a jiffy," she assured him.

Mary looked up to see her boss pick up a tray and turn toward the swinging door, shaking her head, she went back to the stove.

"Careful, he's really nasty," Katherine whispered, as the two girls passed each other in the dining room.

Greetings welcomed the popular redhead as she threaded her way through the tables but conversation dropped to a murmur when they saw her determined look and the direction she was taking. She stopped at Rattenbury's table.

Scowling, he sat back in his chair and pompously looked her over, his moustache bristling.

"Well, what do you want?" he snapped.

"Your order, sir?" she replied, smiling sweetly.

"Damn you ...," he snarled, not completing his statement before Nancy noisily set her tray down on the table. A look of surprise flashed across his darkly handsome face.

Placing her hands on the table, she leaned toward him, her eyes flashing like hot coals. "Manners, sir," she hissed, "are a necessity in this establishment. Please find yours ... or leave!"

Conversation had stopped in the room as all eyes watched and ears strained to hear the confrontation. It was obvious to any that knew his reputation that the esteemed architect had met his match and been startled by the waitress' action, although he was trying to hide it.

Francis Rattenbury had no illusions; this girl did not mince words. He carried no weight in this room. Looking around, he realized from the frowning faces and the manner in which Waldo Skillings had turned in his chair that these men would be ready to assist the young waitress, caring not a damn about him. Lowering his eyes, Victoria's premier architect muttered an uncharacteristic apology. He'd been deeply hurt when the army turned down his application, just an hour before ... due to his age.

"May I take your order, sir?" Nancy's voice cut into his thoughts.

"Just the coffee," he mumbled, reaching into his pocket and sliding some coins onto the table. Coming to his feet, he nodded slightly to the girl and strode quickly toward the door looking neither left nor right.

The hum of conversation once again filled the dining room. Cook, watching from the kitchen doorway with Kate, breathed a sigh of relief.

"That's the lot," called Dan, returning from the cooler. "Where's Nancy, why did she put on her uniform?"

"She's just sorting out a little problem for me," Kate laughed. "She'll be back in a moment."

"You'll go too far one of these days, young lady," Waldo growled his friendly warning, as the redhead cleared the adjoining table.

"Hard, but fair, Mr. Skillings," she quipped. "Learnt it from you!"

As Nancy drove out into the traffic, they calculated their profit on the beef and chuckled over the easy way it had been earned.

"Now where are we going?" Dan inquired as she drove down Wharf Street to Store and made no move to turn toward home.

"We're going to take the Point Ellice Bridge. I want to visit Irvine's farm and say hello to Tom and Billy."

"Hmm, if I know you, you have more reason than a simple hello," teased Dan.

Black smoke spewed from the Albion Iron Works chimney as grime-laden dust and fumes filled the air. Whipped up by the wind, the smoke billowed about the area and Nancy pressed harder on the accelerator. They found themselves behind a loaded tram making its way slowly over the Point Ellice crossing. Once on the other side, they turned onto Craigflower Road. This was a lovely area with few homes and many wooded areas and farms on the way to the countryside and the Indian land beyond.

"I think you're deliberately aiming at every water-filled hole you can find," Dan grumbled, bouncing about on his seat.

"I wonder who fixes them, cause they sure need to be filled more often?" she replied, slowing at last to turn into Tom Irvine's own muddy, potholed lane.

At the end of the long drive, it gave way to a yard neatly gravelled and bordered by open-fronted sheds full of farm implements and drays. Across the yard, the large barn doors stood open framing the old farmer and his Indian helper, Billy, Nancy's childhood friend.

Watching the truck pull up in front of them, old Tom smiled, always happy to have a visit from Nancy. "Want a job?" he called.

"Doing what?" she asked, her eyes twinkling.

"Bagging carrots," Billy laughed. "It's really tiring work."

Looking around the barn, Nancy noted the sacks of potatoes and huge mounds of turnip, carrots and onions. "Sales not good this year, Tom?"

"Late crop," the farmer grumbled, "and the Chinese traders haven't been round yet."

"Money a bit tight, perhaps?" she asked, watching the old man nod. "Want to supply me at the restaurant again?"

Billy's face lit up as he looked over at the old man.

Tom frowned. "No charity, lass," he muttered sternly. Tom had been born in Victoria and was already a second-generation Canadian of a pioneer family. He was fiercely independent and Nancy knew it.

"Charity!" she mocked. "No, old friend, this is business."

Terms and quantities were soon worked out in the warmth of the cabin where Nancy's quick thinking and fairness quickly became evident. The farmer puffed on his pipe and listened carefully to her plan, a grin spreading slowly across his face when his mind grasped the dual benefit to both buyer and seller.

"Hmm, you pay me more than wholesale," he mused, "and the Balmoral still saves on the retail."

"For the present, Meg can use some fresh vegetables so we'll take some of these off your hands right now, Tom," Nancy declared.

"Well, that one's easy!" Tom chuckled. "Take what you want, girl, or it's going to waste."

"None of it will go to waste, Tom. I'll send a truck out on Monday."

"Nan, I think if you're going to take some produce with you, we better do it in a hurry!" Dan announced. There was a note of urgency in his voice as he looked at the ominous-looking black clouds forming on the western horizon.

"Looks like we could be in for it today. Let's get loaded and we'll try to beat it home!" she exclaimed, running to the truck and starting it up. She pulled it into the barn and five minutes later they were loaded and saying their goodbyes.

Keeping a close watch on the skies, she drove as fast as she dared and it seemed like no time before they were nearing the city. They could hear the E&N train whistle in the distance as they pulled onto Bay Street and made their way toward Hillside. Heavy traffic slowed their progress as they reached the fountain intersection which was bedlam at this time of day with traffic going every which way.

"You're a good driver, love," Dan exclaimed, breaking the silence as she finally got herself onto Hillside and out of the way of a tram unloading its passengers at Quadra Street. "You must have had a good teacher!"

"Oh don't you believe it," she said, making a face at him. "The man who taught me left town, he was so afraid people would find out I was a better driver than him!"

"Cheeky brat!" he chuckled as she turned onto Cedar Hill Road.

As they drove across the top of the valley, they saw the first raindrops hit the windscreen and they both looked upwards.

"Come on, Nellie, get us home!" Nancy encouraged the vehicle as she gave it a bit more gas to get up the hill by St. Luke's Church.

Dark clouds were hanging low over the valley and thunder was beginning to ripple through the stillness of early evening. By the time they pulled into their drive, lightning was crashing about them.

"Oh, thank the Lord, they're home," Meg called to Jeb, in the other room.

"You have keen ears, woman, I can't hear anything!" Jebediah retorted, putting down the guitar he was strumming. Looking at his fingers he began rubbing them briskly, wincing as he stood up and went to the window.

"It's no wonder you can't hear with all that racket you're making!" she exclaimed.

Jebediah had seen the instrument that morning in a Government Street pawn shop and hadn't been able to resist when he saw the price. He'd always thought he'd enjoy playing a guitar but after plucking at the strings for the last hour he wasn't so sure anymore. He heard the door open and realizing they were loaded down with parcels he hurried over to help.

"Well, looks like they thought you needed some more work, Meg!" he called, noting the carrot tops sticking out of the bulging gunny sack and moving toward the kitchen.

"My gracious, have you been out to Tom's farm?" asked the Scot.

"Yes we were, and we've been just ahead of the storm all the way," retorted Nancy as she hung up her wet coat.

"What a terrible night it's turned into," declared Dan, wiping his feet and moving out to the kitchen to deliver his armload, "but Nan was determined to beat it!"

"Where did you get the guitar, Uncle Jeb? I didn't know you could play?" Nancy asked, seeing the instrument on the chair.

"He can't, it's barely tolerable!" Meg muttered, opening the door to the pantry for Dan. "It's surprising that Tom still had vegetables left this late in the season."

"The Chinamen hadn't called yet and he'd had no word from them so I told him he could supply the hotel. He said he had lots and wouldn't let us go home empty-handed," laughed Nancy. "We made a good deal for the hotel as well."

"He must have been happy then," said Meg, "and I certainly am!

After an early supper they gathered around the fire and Jeb amused them by trying out his newfound guitar-plucking skills. Nancy hummed along as she did some knitting, making a face each time he played a sour note. The storm passed and soon afterward they heard the sound of an automobile engine. Before anyone had a chance to investigate, running footsteps sounded on the porch and laughing voices were heard. They looked at each other in surprise.

"I wonder who that could be, on such a dreadful night, too!" said Meg, continuing with her knitting as Nancy went to the door.

The sound of a knock came as Nancy reached to open it.

Jack Duggan and his wife, Nellie, stood there along with another couple. Squealing, Nan flung the door open.

"Look who's here! Come in out of the cold," she cried, shutting the door and hugging her friends.

"Come in, come in!" Dan called, leaping to his feet to take their coats.

Nellie introduced Thomas Todd and his wife, Eva, as great friends of Jack's employers, the Parfitt brothers, and they all moved into the living room taking seats around the fire.

"Eva and Thomas are neighbours of yours!" Nellie explained. "We thought it was high time you met. We're sorry we didn't let you know. It wasn't really planned but we were nearby and thought we'd be sure to find you home on such a terrible night."

Thomas was a genial man of about thirty. He had bright red hair and stood well over six feet tall beside his petite, good-looking wife. He ushered her over to the chesterfield and sat down beside her. She untied her knitted bonnet and removed it carefully revealing her blonde hair pulled back into a bun.

Meg excused herself and went out to the kitchen to put on the tea kettle, quickly gathering a tray together with some of her freshly baked spice cookies. As they sipped their tea, conversation ranged from the weather to family history and the war. Eva was intrigued by this young couple whom Jack and Nellie had spoken of so glowingly. As the others talked, she and Nancy, sitting next to each other, got into their own conversation. The beginnings of a strong bond of friendship began to form as they spoke of their dreams and fears, pouring out their innermost thoughts and even comparing the hurt they'd experienced in their own lives. Nancy had never felt this comfortable talking with another woman.

Dan climbed to his feet and stoked the fire, sending a shower of sparks flying up the chimney and causing conversation to lapse for a minute.

"Do you play the guitar?" Eva asked, noticing the instrument beside Jebediah's chair.

"No, I'm just messing about with it. It's a new acquisition."

"They've got a piano, Eva!" Thomas interrupted, raising his eyebrows and grinning at her.

"Nellie told us that you sing, Nancy. I can play the piano," admitted Eva, looking hopefully at her new friend. "Shall we?"

"Oh, that would be wonderful, Eva. We don't often get to hear the piano as none of us play," said Nancy, getting up to find her small collection of music and passing it to Eva. Selecting three pieces, Eva sat down on the stool and lifted back the cover. Her long slender fingers began to move effortlessly across the keyboard. Thomas cocked his head and smiled as he watched his wife—his smile grew even broader when Nancy began to sing.

"You're wonderful," Eva whispered. "Let's do another."

Meg smiled when Nancy began to sing one of the Scottish songs, *Roamin in the Gloamin,* following it with the *Skye Boat Song*. Then, as Nancy liked to do when Jack was present, she sang an Irish song especially for him. Often he had sung with her but tonight he just sat back and smiled, his eyes closed, as his wife winked at the girls.

Thomas could feel his own heart pounding at Nancy's beautiful rendition of *Danny Boy*, imagining that Jack was living each word. He'd never heard such heart-wrenching singing before. As the song ended, the music stopped abruptly, though Eva kept her hands on the keyboard staring down at the piano. Jebediah broke the silence by clapping loudly and was quickly joined by the others.

Eva turned slowly from the piano. "My word, what a remarkable voice you have. You've been keeping it hidden from us! The Parfitt family will be very interested after I talk to them. Do you ever sing at concerts?"

Nancy shook her head. "No, I sang at a political meeting once."

"Oh my, I don't think we'll count that!" Eva said doubtfully.

"We warned you," said Nellie, standing up and going to hug the girls. "Her singing just tears at a body's soul and you are a wonderful pianist, Eva. Now, I think it's high time we were off home. Thank you for the lovely concert, girls."

"May we visit again?" Thomas asked. "We only live up on Tyndall. We have a little farm and a few cattle ... but no children, so Eva must find other activities to fill her day."

"Of course you may," Nancy replied, "but Danny is in the army. He's just home on leave. So he may not be here next time you come," she added sadly.

"I'm in the army, too," said Thomas. "I joined up about five years ago. Although I have a desk job now because of my eyesight, I expect I may be sent to England one day because of my experience."

Sunday's are the best," Meg called from the kitchen. "You come any Sunday afternoon. We always have the teapot on!"

They ran out to the car as it was pouring again, shouting goodbyes into the darkness. Once inside the car and knowing they only had a short distance to travel, Thomas eagerly asked questions about the young couple.

"Did you say Dan and Nancy were brother and sister, Jack?"

"I may have," replied Jack. "Why do you ask, Thomas?"

"They're unusually affectionate for siblings, don't you think?"

"That's because they're adopted siblings," explained Nellie. "They adopted each other many years ago."

"I thought there was something unusual. If you ask me, they're more than siblings, they're in love," said Eva. "It's obvious the way they look at each other and Nancy speaks of him so fondly."

"Hmm," grunted Jack, staring out at the darkness.

"Danny's a good lad," Nellie continued. "He's watched over that girl since she was 4-years-old. They're both orphans, you know, and now they share everything. Why, look how they took Meg into their home, and Jebediah, he's an American. They're building a family of their own. Jack and I believe they're just beginning to realize they have deep feelings for each other."

Thomas slipped his arm over his wife's shoulder in the darkness of the back seat and pulled her closer as they neared their home. His wife had known her own share of sadness and Thomas knew that life had not always been kind to his beautiful blonde wife.

Chapter 10

The next morning, just before sunrise, Dan was out on the cliff, a lonely figure watching the sun rise from behind Mount Baker. With the gentle breeze ruffling his dark hair, he watched the phenomenon that had taken his breath away every morning while out on the Pacific. As the light illuminated the many islands in the Strait he thought of his future and a cold chill went up his back.

I want to remember this picture forever, he thought, catching the movement of Sam's boat as it slid silently into the cove near the rocky shore. Almost invisible in the shadows, the boat moved closer to the dock and the old hermit climbed out. As Dan watched, he dragged two large salmon out of the boat, laying them on the jetty. Flash bounced about at his side whining softly as he looked up at the cliff, alerting the old man of his presence. Without reacting, Sam swung the fish onto his back and shuffled over to the stairs, slowly beginning the laborious climb to the top.

Intrigued by the Indian's performance, Dan remained perfectly still. When the dog reached the top, Dan noticed its tail was wagging furiously and it trotted away toward the kitchen, totally ignoring him. Sam's cursory nod acknowledged Dan but his dark, brooding eyes never wavered from Meg who stood waiting in the doorway. She held a parcel in her hand which she exchanged for one of the fish.

After breakfast, Nancy suggested they take a walk. "It's cool but such a lovely autumn day; let's go up the mountain, Danny. We'll be able to see the colours of the trees before they finish changing."

"Aye, what a splendid idea," said Meg. "If my legs could stand it, I'd come with you, lassie. You'll get a marvellous view today."

As they left the house, Meg watched happily as the young couple ran up the drive and disappeared from sight.

Jeb came up behind her and put his hands on her shoulders. "A penny for your thoughts, Aunt Meg?"

"Nay, you wouldn't want to hear them, Jebediah. I'm just so worried about those two. I pray their happiness will last forever."

Jeb took her by the shoulders and drew her away from the window. "Come on, let's clean up these dishes. I think a nice little walk through the farmlands, on level ground, might be in order for us oldies!"

At the gate, the young couple turned westward along Ash Road. Finding a well-marked cattle trail they made their way through the lush forest that led to the main road and were soon at the base of Mount Douglas. It was a small mountain, formerly called Cedar Hill after the Indian trail, although the tallest hill for miles. Dan located a rough path that seemed to lead upwards. They had often walked in the area but had never gone up the mountain—the thought of the marvellous view pressed them onward.

A snake slithered by, startling Nancy and she jumped out of the way. Dan laughed and took off after it but she managed to grab his arm. "Don't you dare!" she warned, making a face.

"What!" he said innocently, kissing her nose. "Come on, let's see where this trail leads."

Early colonists had cleared many of the giant cedars in spots and as they climbed higher they could see where farms were encroaching on the forests. But there still remained enough virgin land for a host of wild creatures and they met some of them, or signs of them, as they climbed upward under the towering canopy of branches and leaves.

Taking their time to follow the steep, winding trail, they took almost an hour to reach the summit. Coming out of the brush at the top, they stopped to look about and Nancy collapsed breathless on a rock.

"Oh my, we thought our view from the cove was nice, but this is spectacular!" she exclaimed, looking around in all directions. "You're not even breathing hard!"

Dan pointed out some islands not far away. "See that group of islands, Nan. Those are the San Juan Islands, they're in the USA."

"That's the way we go to Seattle, isn't it? They look so far away."

"That's probably because our little boat goes so fast. It tricks us into thinking these distances aren't as great as they are."

"Look Dan, through the trees, over there!" she exclaimed pointing excitedly. "I can see the smoke from our chimney!"

"Yes, it sure is. With so many leaves off the trees, it's easy to see," he mused, sitting down beside her. "I'm afraid you've missed most of the autumn colours though, honey."

"That's all right. It's still like a patchwork quilt down there. We'll have to come up here in the spring or summer. It would be so pretty. It sure gives you a different perspective seeing it all from up here. It makes one feel so small and unimportant."

They tried to figure out which farm belonged to whom but there were too many dotting the valley. They heard the shrill whistle of the V&S freight train and searching the area around Royal Oak a puff of smoke finally gave it away as it moved slowly toward the city.

The waters of the straits sparkled as the sun came out of the clouds, but a cold wind sweeping over the barren rocks quickly drove them back to the shelter of the trees. Halfway down the trail they met two young girls who politely identified themselves as Jean and Edith Dunnett from a farm on Tyndall Avenue.

"We grow sweet strawberries," little Edith quipped proudly.

"I know you," the older sister murmured looking at Nancy. "You live on the cliff and drive a funny little truck."

"Dorothy Poulton can drive," offered Edith. "Mr. Todd's teaching her."

Nancy and Dan looked at each other in surprise.

"Thomas Todd?" he asked.

"Yes, the Todds just live up the road from us," explained Jean.

Feeling deep in his pocket, Dan produced two of his favourite hard-boiled candies for the children, who timidly accepted his gift with well-mannered thanks.

"Nice children," Nancy whispered, waving goodbye to the young-sters as they went off in a different direction. "I guess this path *is* used by more than snakes!"

Walking back down the mountain, they took Cedar Hill through the trees and crossed over onto a little road called Cross Road. Nancy ran ahead onto the little wooden bridge, hanging over the side to look into the stream.

"Oh, look Dan," she cried, "there's fish in the stream today. Look, look, I see two of them ... they're quite large!"

"They're probably salmon," said Dan, hurrying over, but they had already disappeared in the murky water.

Taking a short cut into their yard, Dan raised his nose to the breeze. "Ah, I can smell the apples!"

"That's some imagination you've got, Dan Brown!" the redhead called over her shoulder as she ran away from him past the great heaps of ash from the burned-out roots. "I'll race you to the house!"

Dan took off after her. When they reached the porch, they were laughing and gasping for breath. After lunch Dan again broached the subject of the orchard getting out a notebook and drawing a plan.

"I'll talk to Ben Wall next time I see him. He told me he'd be glad to help us. We should be ready to start clearing in the spring. The war will be over by then," he said confidently.

"I hope you're right, lad," said Jeb doubtfully. Then he stood up and pushed his chair back. "We're going for a ride into town would you two like to come with us?"

"I don't think so, we've got some things to do around here," replied Dan, looking over at Nancy. "Such a nice day doesn't want to be wasted though— you two go and enjoy yourselves."

"You sure you don't want to come along, Nancy?" asked Meg.

Suddenly, the sound of a heavy vehicle brought Nancy to her feet, going to the window. Seeing Dan's uniformed friend, Percy, climb out of the army truck made her heart skip a beat.

"It's Percy, Dan," she said almost in a whisper.

"I wonder what he wants?" said Meg. "Strange he should come all the way out here on a Sunday."

Percy walked slowly up to the house where Dan was waiting.

"Hello, Captain," he said, as the others came to stand behind him.

"Excuse the intrusion, folks ... Nancy," he said. "I'm afraid you'll have to get your gear, Sergeant," he said solemnly. "Orders came down this morning, we have to be in Vancouver by morning."

"But he only just came home," Meg snapped.

"Orders, ma'am," Percy apologized. "We're soldiers. There's a war on and we just do what we're told." Then his voice softened slightly. "I'll wait for you outside, Dan."

"Will Dan be going to Europe now, captain?" Nancy asked as he turned to go down the stairs.

"I'm sorry, Nancy. I really don't know."

"But there is a possibility, isn't there?"

"Yes, there is. I would be lying if I said there wasn't. I'm sorry."

Nancy went inside and sat down on a chair listening as Dan's familiar footsteps climbed the stairs two at a time. Biting her lip, she kept repeating to herself, *Stay calm, please stay calm.*

Meg followed him, saying something about clothes and washing. In a daze, Nancy forced herself to get up and start the dishes, anything to keep busy. Jebediah took a tea towel off the rack by the stove and watched sadly as Nancy emptied the contents of the hot kettle into the sink. Meg returned and finished clearing the table.

Ten minutes later, Dan's boots sounded on the stairs. Resplendent in his army uniform and carrying his hat and kit bag, he entered the kitchen. A sigh escaped Meg's lips as Jebediah put down the plate he was drying and shook Dan's outstretched hand. He stooped to hug Meg.

"Take care of yourself, lad," she said softly, feeling a tightness in her chest. She took Jeb's arm and led him into the other room.

Dan stood looking at Nancy as she slowly dried her wet hands.

"Danny …," she began, looking up at him with a flushed face. He put his finger to her lips and grasped her arm.

"Come on, walk me to the car, love," he said softly, picking up his things. As they went out onto the porch, he stopped. "I guess that orchard is just gonna have to wait for a while after all."

"If I see Ben, I'll …," but the words stuck in her throat.

They stopped at the bottom of the steps and Dan put his bag down again with his hat balanced on top. He looked down at her lovely, sad face and brushed a tear from her cheek. Taking her in his arms, he kissed her gently on the tip of her nose, feeling the soft curves of her body under his hands. She turned her face upwards and, clasping her arms tightly around his neck, pulled him closer and kissed him with a fierceness born of desperation and fear and, he responded willingly.

Percy stood waiting beside the truck trying not to watch the touching scene but fascinated as he realized he had been right all along, these two were much more than siblings. He didn't know what it was like to love someone and have to leave them behind, but the heart-wrenching scene stabbed deeply at his heart. He briefly considered he was the cause for Nancy's sadness then reassured himself that it was the war and Dan would have left eventually anyway. They were walking arm-in-arm toward him now and he opened the back door. Taking Dan's bag, he stowed it away and closed the door again.

Dan turned to hug her once more and she melted into his arms, desperately trying not to cry. He stroked her hair and then her cheek, fleetingly thinking he wanted to remember her softness and then, taking her face in his hands he looked deeply into her eyes. It was at that moment he realized there was something … something his mind was telling him … these feelings were much more than brotherly love. From the moment they had found each other again he had wanted to be with her forever, but this was different.

He was unable to speak so he kissed her again on the lips. *Nancy, I love you,* his heart screamed. *I need you, but it's too damned late. I've been so blind!* He clasped her tightly to his chest. Swallowing hard, he desperately held his own emotions in check.

"We have to go, Dan," Percy quietly reminded him.

Then, kissing her forehead, he stepped back gripping her shoulders. Swallowing again, he solemnly took her hand and kissed her fingers not wanting to let her go. *Will I ever see you again, my beautiful Nancy,* he thought, blinking back a tear. "I love you, Nan," he said huskily. "I've always loved you." And, turning, he quickly strode toward the open door of the truck.

She shut her eyes desperately hoping this was all a bad dream. *Did he really mean he loved her ... really loved her?* She felt suddenly numb and light-headed. Then the truck door slammed and the engine started. She turned to watch the truck move away; she wanted to see Dan's face but everything was a blur. She wrapped her arms around herself as silent tears ran down her face. She willed her body to stay erect as she watched Dan's arm wave ... high in the air ... until they turned past the trees and disappeared. She felt two arms encircle her ... and she shut her eyes.

Chapter 11

Over the next three weeks everything seemed to fade into a blur. Nancy moved between home, office and Seattle dealing with each issue as it arrived, sometimes feeling she wasn't even aware of time passing. Each day on her half-hour lunch break, she made the short trek to the corner of Wharf and Government Street—the ornate sandstone structure that housed the post office becoming another part of her regular routine. The post office clerk no longer asked her name but each day she came away empty-handed adding to her growing distress.

Meanwhile, the regulars at the Balmoral were beginning to give her a dreaded feeling of hopelessness as they continually talked of the war and its disheartening news. One day the topic of conversation was a young local man named Herbert Boggs. Apparently the first Canadian casualty of the war, there had been an article in the paper about him. Forlornly, she had a talk with Waldo and he soon had the word out that they were upsetting their favourite waitress. This sort of talk ceased immediately, at least when she was nearby.

At last, her visits to the post office paid off. With fingers shaking so much she almost dropped the precious envelope, she stopped outside on the street to open it.

My dearest Nan; By the time you read this, my darling, I will be on my way to England aboard a troopship. Her throat went suddenly dry but she carried on. *We're leaving from Vancouver tomorrow morning.*

Her eyes flicked up to the top of the letter which was dated the 5th of November, 1914. *It's now the 25th*, she thought, breathing deeply. *The mail is so slow and he doesn't say if he was going by boat or train. He could be halfway there by now!*

A cold, sinking feeling hit the pit of her stomach and she leaned against the light standard for a moment. Then, gripping the letter tightly, she plunged it deep into her pocket and, head bowed, she walked back to work.

"Mr. Simpson wants to see you in his office," Katherine called, when she entered the kitchen. "Is something the matter, Nan?"

"Dan's on his way to England," she replied softly.

Kate's eyes flicked up to meet hers as she filled her order. "Oh golly, I'm sorry, Nan!" Then she was gone again.

Slipping out of her heavy coat, Nancy washed her hands and made her way upstairs to the general manager's office. Her light tap drew an instant call to enter.

"Sit down, Nancy," Mr. Simpson invited, never lifting his eyes from the papers he was reading, though his hand pointed to the chair on the other side of the desk.

She sat on the edge of the seat and waited. In a minute he looked up from his work, put his spectacles down on the desk, and turned to face her.

"Your supplies, Nancy," he began, showing little emotion so it was difficult to gauge his mood, "they appear to be costing us less money. I'd like to know why. Everywhere else in the city, prices are rising."

Cautiously at first, Nancy began by explaining her arrangement with Tom Irvine, adding, "The meat comes from Seattle at a really good price."

A moment of silence passed between them.

"Well," he said finally, "you have my blessing. We're delighted with the way you and Katherine are managing the restaurant." He stopped to study the girl's face. "Don't look so worried, Nancy, you girls are going an excellent job. Is there something you'd like to discuss with me?"

"No sir, nothing about the restaurant." She hesitated, then seeing his genuine interest, she carried on. It's my brother, sir. He's on his way to England. He's in the army. I just received his letter today."

"I understand it must be difficult for you, but be proud of him," he said kindly, rising from his desk. "He shows the spirit of a loyal Canadian."

Returning the way she had come along the dim corridors, Nancy thought hard on the general manager's words. Yes, she was proud of Dan and people should know it. *So darn it, stop moping,*" she told herself harshly. She stopped and began to talk aloud to herself. By the time she arrived back at the kitchen there was a smile on her lips and her eyes sparkled with determination.

Kate came through the door just as Nancy threw a wink at the cook telling them both that she was going to be all right.

On the way back to Gordon Head that evening, she stopped to buy fuel for the truck at Plimley's curbside pump. She talked to the young mechanic as he removed the seats to get to the gas tank. Remembering

Mr. Johnson's words, she forced herself to tell him about Dan and how he was sailing for England and the war.

The lad's reaction was instant. "Cor, I wish that were me!" he muttered, taking her money.

It wasn't exactly the reaction she had expected.

Light rain had begun to fall by the time she rounded the corner onto Hillside. A cold autumn breeze stirred up the fallen leaves and she began to sing, startling folks waiting for their streetcars. A lone dray moved slowly along Cedar Hill Road in front of her. She pipped her horn and passed, the driver's head jerked up in surprise when he heard a song coming from the Model T.

Meg and Jebediah knew they didn't have to worry about their girl anymore when she burst into the kitchen and happily exclaimed that she was home. Her beaming smile and the welcome sound of her laughter would bring the house back to life again. Over supper she told them of Dan's letter and they got to talking about his orchard. Her enthusiasm was infectious but tiring to the old folks who sighed with relief when she turned in for the night.

Climbing the stairs slowly, being careful not to extinguish her candle, Nancy looked across the landing at Dan's door and quickly went into her own room. Putting the candle on the night table near her bed, she went over to the window. She peered out into the darkness and listened to the wind blowing through the trees.

Shivering, she pulled down the blind and undressed quickly, getting into her long flannel nightgown. Draping her wool shawl about her shoulders, she sat down on the little stool in front of her dressing table. She picked up her brush and briskly applied it to her long hair until she had counted out 50 strokes. *I'm too tired to do 100 tonight, that will just have to do,* she chided herself, putting her brush down. She looked at herself in the mirror again and a worried frown came onto her face. *I wonder what Dan is doing right now*, she thought, and then before she could think any sad thoughts, she climbed into bed.

Crawling between the cold cotton sheets, she blew out the candle and settled into the softness of the flock mattress. Pulling the patchwork quilt Meg had made for her, up around her neck, she lay in the darkness conjuring up happy memories. Imagining Dan walking hand-in-hand with her in Beacon Hill Park, she drifted off to sleep.

Jebediah was still asleep when Meg waved goodbye to Nancy on Friday morning and watched the tail lights disappear into the darkness. The old Scot always hated to see Nancy go, she had grown so attached to the girl, yet she was grateful to have Jeb's company. *Without them it would be a lonely life,* she mused.

Nancy felt more rested this morning than any other since Dan had left. She was able to think more clearly now and knew she had to stop thinking of him so much. As her eyes searched the gloom, she drove as fast as she dared over the rutted country roads. She was almost at Hillside when she saw the dark shape of a man walking briskly toward the city.

Slowing the truck, she called to him. "Want a ride, mister?"

Smiling broadly, he wasted no time scrambling into the cab.

"Thank you, miss. It's a cool morning, I appreciate your kindness. My name is Dunnett, Malcolm Dunnett."

"I'm Nancy Wilson from Cunningham Manor off Ash Road. Do you live near here?"

"Just back a piece on Tyndall. My missus and I have a small farm and a large family." They chattered away until they reached the city and turned into Douglas Street. "It must have been you and your husband that our daughters met on Mt. Douglas some time back."

"Oh yes, delightful girls," she replied. "Dan's my brother. He's in the army and has just left to go overseas."

He looked sideways at her. "You know, my Jenny doesn't get out much with the young'uns keeping her busy. We'd be pleased if you came to visit us sometime ... you can drop me here at the corner."

Nancy nodded, keeping her eye on the traffic.

"You're a good driver," he murmured, as she pulled up to the curb at Store and Bay Streets and he climbed out. "Thanks for the ride, Nancy."

"See you again, Mr. Dunnett."

Delivery drays and early morning workers were the only movement along Wharf Street as she drove onto the boards in front of the Brown and Wilson dock and parked the truck. *This must be the coldest street in Victoria,* she thought with a shiver, thankful she'd worn her woollen bloomers. She hurried up the hill to Broughton pulling her skirts close as the chilling wind bit at her legs.

Dick was yelling more news of the war and she tried not to listen as a momentary feeling of dread surged through her body. *I hate this war already and Danny's barely gone.*

Thankfully, the morning passed quickly. Being one of the city's more popular restaurants, the Balmoral was always busy this time of

100

day, and she was grateful. There seemed to be a slightly new topic being bandied about today. It was centered on the Premier and his attempts to seek federal help in guarding their coastline from attack by the Germans. She found this surprising and wondered why the government would think the Germans were interested in a country so far away.

After lunch she was down at the dockside office trying to catch up on her bookwork and talking to Dumpy when Waldo walked in.

"Have you heard the rumours about prohibition?" he growled.

"Here?" both Dumpy and the redhead chorused.

"Yes, here!" Waldo scowled. "I just heard it from a freighter captain, who's been in Vancouver. He says it won't be long."

"I haven't heard the slightest whisper," said Nancy, closing her account book and coming to her feet, "but if there's talk of prohibition going around, I'm sure to hear of it soon."

Waldo was obviously concerned but Nancy didn't have time to get into a long conversation and he soon left. Needing the boat tonight for their Seattle run, she got it loaded with the shopping Meg had ordered, taking extra care with two big feather cushions from Spencer's. She wrapped the large oilskin tarpaulin around everything and, buttoning her coat, climbed aboard. Waving to Dumpy, she eased the craft away from the wharf and pointed it toward home.

Dumpy watched her with admiration as she manoeuvred around the many boats and obstacles in the harbour. *She's a tough one is our Nancy. I sure hope Dan will be all right.* Then he turned and went over to the shed where he had some equipment to repair.

Rounding the Ogden Point construction, Nancy sent the speedboat pounding through the waves speeded along by a brisk wind. Passing the snow-white buildings of the weather station atop Gonzales Hill, she marvelled aloud, "Sure is a fancy building just to monitor the weather. At least it will be a good landmark."

She loved this trip and the freedom she felt out on the water. Pushing the craft through the changing tides off Oak Bay, she gave a wide berth to the rocks at Ten Mile Point. Noticing the ominous yellow cloud hanging low over the gunpowder factory at Telegraph Bay she remembered Dan's urgent warning that she must never go near the factory's long jetty. She vaguely recalled a newspaper report of a small freighter exploding off Nanaimo early last year and wondered if it had something to do with munitions.

At the entrance to their cove, she saw Sam's little rowboat tied to a rock, but it was deserted and although she looked around, she was fully aware she would see nothing. Her three long blasts on the brass whistle were heard clearly in the kitchen bringing Jebediah to the edge of the cliff stairs. Seeing her load, he climbed down to meet her. When Meg looked out the kitchen window and saw them struggling across the grass loaded down with canvas bags and the two big cushions she had ordered, she couldn't help but giggle.

"Hmm, rabbit stew!" Nancy exclaimed, raising her nose to the delicious aroma. "Has Jeb been on the warpath against those poor little critters again?" She dropped her parcels on the table and went to hug Meg before heading out the door again.

"Dinner will be ready by the time you've loaded the boat," Meg promised. "Thanks for picking up my cushions, lassie."

True to her word, there were bowls of steaming rabbit stew and dumplings waiting on the table when they returned from loading the boat. Eating quickly, Nancy went upstairs to change into warmer clothes.

On the way down to the boat she suddenly stopped and turned to Jeb. "Do we have everything we need for the cannon?"

"Expecting trouble?" Jeb asked, climbing into the boat and pulling back the oilcloth that covered the little gun.

"No, just being prepared," she replied. "Waldo told me there's been some talk of prohibition locally. I'd rather be prepared than sorry."

It was already getting dark and the wind had picked up significantly as they slipped their mooring at 4 o'clock. The Scot listened until the roar of the engine disappeared down Haro Strait. Meg had a bad feeling about this trip but hadn't wanted to say anything. She felt better when she saw them check the cannon but as she turned back to the house a chill went through her body and she pulled her coat tightly around her.

Nancy's course took them sweeping past the Point No Point Lighthouse, making good time in spite of the weather. She eased back on the throttle as they passed Apple Cove. Since changing to Standard Time, most of their trip was now in darkness adding not only to the danger from the water but from hidden authorities watching for rum runners in American waters. She was heading for Ezekiel's hide-a-way and seeing his beacon she moving through the overhanging branches. Giving the signal, she listened intently before allowing the blue craft to slide into the cove. A lantern hanging on the bough of a tree threw its light in a limited arc as Ezekiel's voice rasped from the gloom.

"Welcome, Nancy. Step out and share a hot brew."

"You knew we were coming?" she asked, when the dark shape of the mountain man emerged from the undergrowth.

"I was lighting the lantern in me chimney and thought I saw you. You're one of the few boats that travel that fast. I hoped you would stop in," he said, leading them into the cabin, which Nancy noted was tidier than her last visit. "Where's Danny?"

Jeb came up beside him and beckoned him outside while Nancy was busy pouring tea. Quietly he told him of the developments of the past week warning him it was best not to talk about it around Nancy. A low grunt signified he understood.

Nancy asked what kind of tea it was and he explained that the hot peppermint brew was designed to keep out the cold, something the old folks at home had taught him. Sipping suspiciously on the dark-looking liquid, Nancy's eyes moved around the old man's home. Taking mental note at the absence of furniture and the animal skins covering the roughly boarded floor, she wondered how he had moved the large rock he used as a table, then she realized the cabin had probably been built around it. The top looked like it had been chiselled down until it was relatively flat. The stone fireplace threw out a generous share of heat from two large tree branches.

Not the Empress Hotel, she thought, *but certainly warm and adequate, and who am I to criticize?*

Ezekiel told them it had been quiet along the coast since their last visit. "I've had no trouble with intruders but on a trip to Kingston this week I stopped in a tavern and overheard some interesting talk."

"What sort of talk, Zeke?" asked Jeb, now all ears.

In a low secretive voice, the old man recounted what he could remember of the conversations—Coast Guard boats now regularly patrolling the inland waters, and now that Canada was at war, prohibition, on a national scale, was deemed imminent.

"With liquor loosening their tongues, there's much more talk about the Anti-Saloon League," said Zeke, still keeping his voice low. "It's gaining momentum as more and more precincts vote to rid themselves of the evil taverns! What about Victoria?" he asked suddenly, watching Nancy shake her head.

Allowing themselves an hour to complete the trip to Seattle, they said goodbye to their friend and got underway. Several large dark hulks, no doubt freighters, now moved slowly down Puget Sound. They were the only companions as cold spray stung their faces, keeping them alert.

A pinpoint of light flashed twice over at Skiff Point drawing Jebediah's attention; his experienced eyes swung quickly to the west to pick out the answering signal.

"Take her in fast, sweetheart," he called to the redhead, reaching for the Winchester.

Nancy threw open the throttle, sending the speedboat surging forward with a roar. A smile crossed the old man's face as his unusual partner made the speeding craft dance in and out of the freighters while using them to cover her movements.

Pacing the dock, Gus heard the powerful engine and strained his eyes across the black water.

"Easy boss, she's coming," Terry called, sending a shrill whistle of warning to his men.

Docking quickly, Nancy saw Gus when he stepped out of the shadows. She left the unloading to Terry and hurried over to see her friend. Noticing that he was smiling she was about to ask why when he took her hands and almost shouted at her in his excitement.

"My boys are alive, Nan! They're in hospital in England."

Relief swept across the girl's face as she looked up into the shipowner's dancing eyes. "But how?" she gasped, "why did it take so long to find out?"

"Don't know," Gus sighed. "We had a telegram from the British War Office this morning and Beth is so happy she can't sit still. I wish you could see her. Is Dan not with you?"

"No Gus, Dan's on his way to England," she said, a lump forming in her throat. "He had to leave earlier than we ever expected and I only found out from his last letter." Taking her arm, they walked along the dock talking softly as they found comfort from each other. What had started as a holiday friendship in Victoria between the two couples was quickly growing into a life-long bond.

"I'll go get Nancy," Jebediah growled, when Terry's men had finished their work and loaded Nancy's supply of meat now neatly packed in boxes.

"Leave her, they're all right for a few minutes." The Irish American's answer was spoken sharply, stopping Jebediah in his tracks. His natural instinct to protect his redhead rushed to the surface but then he realized Terry felt the same way.

"Ready to go, Uncle Jeb?" her voice came from the darkness as she and Gus came toward them.

"I'll keep you informed, honey," the shipowner assured her as she started the engine, sending them off into the night.

Meg had been standing on the clifftop for only five minutes when she heard the first distant sounds of their engine. Totally unaware that Sam was watching the glow of her lantern from the shelter of the trees, she left the light at the top of the stairs and made her way carefully back to the house to tend to their meal.

Three-quarters of an hour later, Jeb and Nancy dragged themselves up the stairs after stacking the boxes of meat in the cave and locking the ingenious door system that Jack had built. Nancy giggled as she watched him, instinctively reaching for the old man's hand as they moved toward the stairs.

"Gee Uncle Jeb, isn't life interesting?"

"Might be at your age, lass," he growled, squeezing her fingers affectionately, "but for me it's damned exhausting."

Chapter 12

It was dull and overcast Saturday morning as the speedboat moved past the Dallas Road waterfront toward the city. It was loaded, not only with boxes of meat, but Meg and Jebediah were along as passengers. As they approached the Ogden Point breakwater, the outer-harbour patrol boat, *Legal Limit* flagged them down and drew alongside.

"Good morning, Mr. Pease," Nancy called. "What's the problem?"

"Just checking you out," the patrol boat skipper laughed. "Who are those suspicious-looking passengers you're carrying?"

Algenon Henry Pease was the wealthy owner of the estate called *Hamsterley* on the top of Sinclair Hill. Offering his many talents to the military at the outbreak of war, he had been given the job of patrolling the waters off Victoria in his own sleek speedboat, *Legal Limit.*

Algy, as he was known to his many friends, was British and terribly patriotic, though prone to bouts of humorous behaviour now and then. He was well-known for the way he drove his thundering two-seater sports car, a Renault, through the streets of Victoria.

"Please sir, they forced me to bring them to Victoria from that foreign land called Gordon Head," Nancy replied, trying to keep a straight face.

"Better do as they say," Algy recoiled in mock horror. "They look mighty dangerous to me, girl!"

"Fool," Meg giggled, as the skipper peered at the old lady then waved and moved off.

Halfway up the harbour, the normally smooth-running engine began popping and banging.

"Sounds like trouble," Jebediah groaned, as Nancy pulled up to the Brown and Wilson jetty.

"SOUNDS LIKE WATER IN YOUR FUEL," Jim Goodwin shouted bringing *Ping Pong* alongside. "Unload and I'll take it up to Turpel's for you. Kenny Macpherson will have it fixed in no time."

Dumpy unloaded the boxes and, panting from exertion, threw a line to Jim. "Thanks Jim. Bring her back when she's done and I'll pay you."

"No you won't!" Jim exclaimed. "We owe Danny a few favours."

Warming herself in front of the stove and sipping on a mug of hot steaming tea, Nancy heard Fred talking to Dumpy outside.

"Do you know what he said?" Dumpy laughed, as the two men trooped in and shut the door. "A giant octopus grabbed one of the divers at Ogden Point."

"It's true, Nancy. I swear to God I only just heard it," Fred protested, knowing from her expression he wasn't being taken seriously.

"Well, did it eat him?" she asked, her eyes twinkling.

"All right you two, if you don't believe me, read the Times tomorrow. I'm not going to tell you any more. Have you heard from Danny, Nan?" he asked more quietly.

"Yes, I got a letter. Seems he left for England on the 5th of November."

Fred's eyes turned sad, his head dropping a little as he quietly reached out and touched Nancy's arm before turning and leaving the office.

"Bloody war," they heard him mutter under his breath as he pulled the door closed.

"Let's go make that delivery to the Balmoral," said Dumpy, interrupting her thoughts.

"You just have to learn how to drive, Dumpy. It would make life so much easier," Nancy scolded him as she drove up Broughton Street.

They had to stop at Government while they waited for a group of people alighting from a streetcar to clear. Horns honked madly and nasty tempers flared as she edged the truck through the melée. People were coming and going through the hotel doors and she knew the restaurant was going to be busy. Going into the kitchen, she looked out into the crowded room and was surprised to see people lined up in the foyer.

"Gosh, it's a madhouse around here," she commented. "What's happening, Mary? Even traffic is bad this morning!"

"Another troop ship is leaving," Mary said solemnly. "I think all their relatives want feeding!"

"See you tonight, Jack," Katherine called seeing Dumpy as she dashed through the kitchen.

Back out in the alley Dumpy shook his head. "Whew, that's a busy place today. What's going on?" he complained.

"Troopship leaving," Nancy replied, then slightly agitated she turned to him. "Are you really serious about Kate?"

Her question was met with dead silence as they climbed into the truck and she backed out to the road. Neither of them spoke a word until they were back at the office. He finally turned to her and she realized he was blushing.

"I love her, Nancy. I really love Kate," he whispered.

"Then ask her to marry you," she advised, "before somebody else runs off with her."

While Dumpy stoked the fire and put on a fresh pot of coffee, he seemed to grow more comfortable and began to talk about it. "We both have such heavy responsibilities," he explained, in a serious tone. "I have my mother and Kate has her grandparents."

"Then combine the families," she suggested, making it sound so simple. "But don't let Katherine escape you. She's a lovely girl."

At home later in the evening, she watched the flames burn brightly in the hearth and her mind turned to Dan, as was want to happen this time of day.

Far away out on the Atlantic Ocean, a troop ship bound for Liverpool steamed relentlessly toward its destination. A soldier, standing his duty watch in the darkness, suddenly swung his head around. *I hear you Nancy. I hear you,* his mind screamed into the inky black night.

Meg sat bolt upright in her chair.

"What's wrong?" Jebediah asked tiredly.

"I thought I heard Danny's voice," she whispered.

"And so did she," Jeb nodded toward Nancy, asleep in her chair, her face lit up by a happy smile.

Through November, the newspaper stories of the war seemed to grow more horrific with each passing day. The use of a new German weapon at the second battle of Ypres was finally being reported as the injured returned home telling of the terrors from poisonous gas. Hospital ships full of wounded began to arrive more regularly, bringing a strange toughness to the community.

With little time to spare from her arduous duties, Nancy chose to donate some of her savings to the hospitals and families of dead or wounded soldiers. On a suggestion from Jeb and Meg, she joined other well-meaning citizens in the cost of a new program for training amputees to become horticulturists at one of the nearby nurseries.

Mid-December brought the first snowfall to Victoria and hold-ups in the rail service to Sidney were experienced when ice on the track caused havoc on the Royal Oak Hill. There were some anxious moments, too, as weather created new problems for her and Jeb on their trips to Seattle, but she seemed to take them all in her stride.

The truck route along Cedar Hill Road was made even more challenging as rain and cold deepened the ruts and her trips into town and back became longer with each passing week. They were made only slightly less arduous due to the firm friendship which had now become established with Malcolm Dunnett whom she often drove into the city. She met his wife and family and often dropped in to see them when she had the time, taking Meg with her once.

She also enjoyed visiting Susan White and her children. They had become firm friends and she stopped often with treats for the youngsters while the women compared letters from their men who were both overseas. She learned that Susan, a trained singer, had gotten her start singing in Victoria's silent cinemas as the operators changed the reels of film. One day in early December she excitedly told Nancy that she had been asked to perform in a Christmas concert at the Royal Theatre.

A letter from Dan arrived on Friday, the 18th of December, sparking a rush of excitement as she was handed the precious envelope. She was so eager to read it she stood in the middle of the post office and people had to walk around her as she carefully tore it open.

My sweet Nancy,

All is going well over here. We're in a training camp on the Salisbury Plains of Southern England, my love. The comradeship and dedication of our Canadian soldiers is truly amazing. Richard McBride actually came here and toured the camp. I was so surprised to see him, Nan. He recognized me and we spoke briefly. Somehow it made you seem closer. I asked him to say hello to you and he assured me he would. I don't know when you will see him though.

Did you know there are many men over here who are from Seattle? We meet them sometimes when we go on leave for a day or two and visit the local pubs. They enlisted in the British army because they wanted to help. Imagine that. I guess that's all the news.

I love you, my darling, and I miss you like crazy.

Your favourite brother, Dan.

Dan's ending brought tears to her eyes as the words whispered deep into her brain. Then she smiled. *Your favourite brother!* she repeated.

Nancy felt an arm slip over her shoulder and looked up to see Mary Ellen Smith, Waldo's political friend.

"A letter from Dan, love? I know how you feel," she said sympathetically. "Mr. Smith is over there, too."

They walked arm-in-arm along Wharf Street and Mary Ellen told her how she was trying to complete her husband's government business and was going to talk to Waldo about it.

"You're in luck, there he is," Nancy pointed across the road. "He's just leaving our office."

"Oh, how fortunate! It was so nice seeing you, Nancy. Take care of yourself, dear," she called as she hurried away, calling to Waldo.

Nancy waved to them as they crossed at different sides of the street and she hurried down the boards to the office.

"What did Waldo want?" she asked, startling Dumpy who was busy writing notes on his pad.

"He has some goods for Sooke he wants delivered on Monday," Dumpy replied. "Oh, and Jim brought the boat back, it was water in the fuel line all right."

Half an hour later, dressed in new fancy oilskins, gloves and sowester hat, Dumpy had chosen for her, she turned the boat up the harbour. She was getting used to the winter seas now but each day brought new experiences and she remembered Dan's words, *Never trust the sea, just when you think you know it, it will turn on you.*

Cold winds and stinging wet spray beat on her face forcing tears from her eyes as she pushed through the choppy swells. Going only as fast as she dared, waves bashed at the sides of the sturdy little boat as spray made it almost impossible to see. Losing all sense of time, she thought momentarily of the letter tucked deep in her pocket, then put it from her mind and peered through the windscreen.

Dark rocks jutted from the water around Ten Mile Point—an accident waiting to happen that Dan had warned her about many times—then hidden as thundering whitecaps brushed over them. Not realizing she had gone so close to the shore she was upon them before she realized. Pouring on the power, she yanked the wheel hard holding her breath as the boat pushed frantically against the powerful waves that drove her toward the rocks. Letting her breath out slowly, she swung the boat northwards again searching through the salt-stained windscreen for the long jetty at the gunpowder factory. *I don't need anymore close calls,* she thought, finally seeing the jetty but realizing another boat was in her path and it had probably not seen her as it left

110

the dock. Knowing she could move quicker, she grimaced and pulled down on the throttle once again, leaving a narrow berth between them as they passed in the ripping current.

Cold, wet and feeling quite exhausted, she heaved a sigh of relief as she nosed the blue craft into the more protected waters beneath Cunningham Manor. It was 2:30 p.m. and she needed to eat before they started for Seattle.

"We're going early. I've rung Terry already," Jeb announced as they passed on the stairs. "I've already sent some boxes down. Give me ten minutes then throw the rest on the chute. I'll load while you're eating. I want to use all the daylight we can find."

Following his instructions, in ten minutes she was loading the chute. When she finished, she went into the house and found Meg warming her jacket in front of the kitchen stove. Sitting down heavily in her chair, she gratefully dug into the plate of sandwiches on the table gobbling them down with a cup of tea. Meg chattered brightly about seeing some neighbours when she walked out to the road this morning.

Her mind began to wander and she found herself reflecting on some more of Dan's wisdom, remembering his oft-made comment that *90% of your success at sea depends on preparation*. He had drilled it into her brain and she now knew he was right. Finishing her meal, she went to get dressed and Meg commented that she looked like a boy, causing them both to giggle as Jebediah's heavy feet sounded on the porch.

"Make us a bottle of that Scottish tea, love," he called as he burst through the door. "It's damn cold out there and we're gonna need it today."

Meg watched from an upstairs window as the little boat left the safe harbour and began to bounce like a cork in the waves. She knew it would be a wild ride until they were deep into Puget Sound where the American islands would give them some protection from the thundering sea. She tried not to worry and decided to go find some work to ease her mind. Hopefully it would be calmer when they returned.

"HOW MUCH LONGER?" Jeb screamed into the wind.

"TWENTY MINUTES, THAT WAS WEST POINT."

Moving between several anchored freighters gave them some protection from the waves and soon Nancy caught sight of the warehouses at Gus' dock. She could see the figure of Terry O'Reilly sitting cross-legged at the edge of the dock under a light. He was with another man and two trucks were already lined up behind them with the men standing nearby.

"SOMETHING'S WRONG," she snapped, unable to see Jeb in the dark so he wasn't able to see her worried look.

As they went into the shadows between two freighters she pulled back on the throttle until they were standing still. They bumped against an anchor chain and Jeb pulled out his field glasses. The old detective's trained eyes raked the scene, frowning but finding nothing suspicious.

"What is it, girl? What have you seen?"

"It's Terry. Look at him Jeb, who in their right mind would be sitting on a cold, stone dock at this time of year? He's never done that before. The other man is standing behind him and all the others are out of their trucks. I know something is wrong."

"Pull in quietly," replied Jeb, straining to see but it was too dark. Feeling the urgency, and long ago learning to trust the redhead's intuition, he checked the pistol tucked in his belt. He hadn't used it in some months but noticing it in his drawer that morning he decided to bring it. He reached for the Winchester. "Pull in close to the next dock and drop me off," he ordered into her ear.

"Right," said Nancy. "I'll give you five minutes to get behind them, and then I'll roar up to Jorgensen's dock. That'll draw their attention."

"Blast it," Jeb muttered, not quite loud enough for her to hear. "I'm getting too old for this foolishness."

With the engine just ticking over, she eased into the nearby jetty then swung quickly away when she heard him land on the boards. Keeping the freighters between her and the men on the dock, she went back the way they had come and waited.

Five minutes must be up by now, she thought to herself, pulling on the throttle. The engine roared into life sending the craft hurtling through the water toward the dock.

Just before she came in under the edge of the wharf, her eyes picked out some movement by one of the trucks and she recognized Jeb's slim shadow as he moved under a light and across the cobbles toward Terry. Making a mess of the docking, she made sure she held their attention.

"IS THAT OLD DICK WITH YOU, GIRL?" snarled an unfamiliar voice as a big man, holding a rifle, stepped out from behind Terry.

"NO," she shouted, leaving the engine running. "HE'S RIGHT BEHIND YOU!"

A curse was heard as Jebediah poked the Winchester hard into his ribs.

"Drop it, NOW!" Jeb ordered, and the rattle of the man's rifle on the cobblestones was heard. Jeb grabbed him by the arm. "Where's your partner?" he growled. "Tell me now or I'll shoot you right here and now!"

"Don't shoot, I'll tell ya where he is," the man gasped.

"Well, out with it then," Jeb prodded, poking him again with the rifle.

"He-he's over there behind the first truck."

"Is he armed?"

"Y-yes," stammered the young man, obviously an amateur and now showing it.

Jeb moved forward toward the truck. "Well let's us just see about this for ourselves," he said, pushing the man forward keeping his gun in his back. "I WANNA SEE THIS BIG MAN WHO HAS THE GUN?"

"Yeah, there's a man here with a gun," offered one of Terry's men. "Told us he'd shoot ya if we tried anything."

"Well, quit worrying about my hide. I can look after myself," called the old detective, now only 15 feet away. "Yer all acting like a bunch of scared rabbits. I'm gonna shoot this one if you have any trouble so what are you worried about. Can't you see you outnumber them, you fools!"

Terry's men looked from one to the other and one of them mumbled something.

"NOW!" ordered an authoritative voice and several of the men turned and jumped the unfortunate gunman—the sound of a fight was heard in the darkness.

Thinking they might kill the guy, Jebediah decided to step in. "All right … all right, enough already! Find some rope and tie them up!"

Meanwhile, Terry, seeing Jebediah had the situation in hand, leaned through the guardrails watching Nancy dock.

"How the hell did you know it was a set up, Nan?" he asked, when she had turned off the engine.

"That was easy, Terry. I didn't think any man in his right mind would be sitting on the cold ground in this kind of weather!" she laughed, climbing out of the boat.

Terry sprang to his feet, suddenly realizing she had a point. She laughed when he rubbed his behind then moved awkwardly toward the trucks. He began screaming abuse at his men who were standing around watching Jeb truss up the two prisoners with the help of one of their buddies.

"Get to work you lazy bastards. Do you want us to wipe your backsides, too?" he ranted. "I'll take care of these two from here on."

Unloading the cargo in record time, they soon had it replaced with boxes of meat and the oilskin tarp back in place. At the same time, Terry and Jeb loaded the two prisoners into the back of Terry's car and left them under the watchful eye of his driver, a burly black man.

"NOW, GET OUT OF HERE!" Terry snarled at his men and they quickly piled into the trucks and drove off with a squeal of engines and tires.

"So do you know who sent these two, O'Reilly?" asked Jeb.

"Yeah, I know who sent them. They're Roy Olmstead's men trying to cut in on the action," he sneered. "They won't play with us again."

"Wake up, kid," Jeb growled. "You're in a rough business and we might have saved your tail today. Nancy was the one who spotted it. She worked it out and damn your hide, she put herself in danger for a punk like you!" Jeb's temper was working up to a boil and there was no stopping him now. "And listen, sonny boy, if she had got hurt, I'd have killed you myself."

Jeb's harsh words stunned the young gangster and shocked Nancy who hadn't seen this side of him before. Terry sheepishly handed her the pay envelope.

"Thanks, Nan," he said meekly, and then he dropped his own bombshell. "Can you bring another load in tomorrow?"

"Not here," she said in a concerned tone. "Maybe at the Jorgensen's private jetty, but we might have trouble getting the stuff out of Victoria."

"We have it already, it's stacked in the back of the workshop," admitted Jeb. "And that SOB knows it!"

"All right, we'll do it," she said, without hesitation, laying a hand on Jeb's arm. "Terry, we'll need some directions to their private jetty."

"That's easy, I'll have Gus run up his Swedish flag on the flagpole," said Terry. "But there's more … Beth wants you to bring Meg and stay over for the night, says she wants to take you Christmas shopping and show you all the Christmas decorations!"

"How wonderful! Tell them we'll be there between twelve and one. It'll do Aunt Meg good to get some sea air and see some new faces. It will be a nice outing and wonderful to see them."

As they left the harbour, they noticed the Coast Guard boat slowly cutting across to the other shore using its searchlight, and again they threaded their way through the line of anchored freighters. The wind was still blowing, biting at their faces and Nancy pulled her scarf up over her mouth. Waves thudded against the hull and Nancy slowed down a bit. She easily found the beacon at Scatchet Head and they were soon roaring homeward. Nearing the cove, they happily spotted Meg's beacons and were soon looking forward to the warm fire and a hot meal.

As they ate a plateful of stew and dumplings, they told Meg of the Jorgensen's invitation.

"We'll be staying the night, too, Aunt Meg. It will be so nice to see Gus and Beth and spend some time with them."

"I'm not a very good sailor," Meg whispered hesitantly.

"You'll be all right," Jebediah interrupted. "The weather is going to be good and Nancy will take it easy," he said, looking over at the girl and winking. "We'll look after you, but we'll need an early start after breakfast. We still have to load up and deliver the meat to Victoria on the way."

"I think I had better get to bed," Nancy announced with a yawn. "I'll pack a few things before I turn in." Getting up, she stretched then changed her mind and went over to Meg, perching lightly on her knee.

Meg locked her arms around the girl's slim waist.

"We'll need to be up at dawn, Aunt Meg," she sighed, putting her cheek against the old lady's and hugging her. "It will be wonderful to see Beth again. At least they know the boys are alive now." She sighed, dropping her head onto Meg's shoulder.

"Go to bed my love, sleep well," Meg cooed, kissing her on the cheek. "You're trying to do too much and you need your rest. It will be very nice to see the Jorgensens again. I won't be long to bed myself."

Chapter 13

It was well before dawn the next morning when Nancy made her way down the cliff stairs with a lantern and waited for Jeb to send the boxes down the chute. Stacking them around her, she sat down and caught her breath, waiting for Jeb to follow the last box. Together they moved the boxes of meat out of the way and loaded up with the new shipment of liquor, putting the meat in last. It was a tight squeeze but the little boat had a surprising amount of room in its hold.

"Looks good, we'll make it," she announced, as they hurried back up the stairs eager for breakfast. She found herself quite excited about this unexpected visit to Seattle. She had been to the Jorgensen's home once before and was fascinated with how these wealthy people lived.

There was hardly a ripple on the water when they pulled out of the cove three-quarters of an hour later. It was a slower run than usual to Victoria with all the added weight and when they arrived Fred was with Dumpy. They were looking at something down the harbour.

"Man overboard," Fred laughed, his trained eyes noticing they were riding very low in the water. "What's in the boxes?"

"Meat!" Dumpy growled. He often got annoyed with Fred for being so nosy. "Give us a hand, will ya, Fred?"

"Did you say there was a man overboard? Is someone rescuing him?" asked Meg with concern in her voice.

"I wouldn't want to be in that cold water for very long," added Nancy.

"It's all right, they've got him. He fell off the tug. Silly bugger was probably celebrating Christmas already!" snickered Fred following Dumpy to the truck with two of the boxes.

It only took a few minutes to load up and Nancy and Dumpy left for the Balmoral. As she waited, Meg went inside out of the cold. Wandering around her old office, her mind conjured up images of the fun she used to have with the Joyce brothers. They had been such a big part of her life until six months ago. She could still hear Ned's soft laughter as he teased a tussle-haired kid named Dan Brown, and then there was the day she first met Nancy. *These rooms hold so many memories*, she mused, then hearing Jebediah shouting from outside, she went out to join him.

"They're back," he announced.

"Wrap up warmly," Nancy called as she ran toward them. "We're leaving right now!"

In no time they were underway, moving slowly down the busy harbour waving to the men aboard two small fishing boats and a tug pulling a log boom. As they went by, Nancy pointed out the soap works and the paint factory with its new coat of paint telling everyone it was now the Bapco company.

Just around the corner past Ogden Point, the magnificent Dallas Hotel stood proudly looking out over the Strait toward the Olympics. Always fighting for supremacy as the grandest hotel in Victoria now, along with the Driard, they found they had an even more impressive opponent in the more centrally located Empress Hotel.

"Brrr, it's cold! Come take the helm, Uncle Jeb," Nancy called. "I need to get into my heavy coat."

Jeb moved forward and she went to sit down beside Meg. She struggled into her sea coat, pulled on a woollen hat and slipped her hands into warm gloves.

Winking impishly at her aunt, she stood up and announced cockily, "Now we'll go for a ride!" Fortunately, Meg didn't hear her. Tapping him on the shoulder, Jeb slipped off the seat and grinned as she took over again. Her gloved hand reached for the throttle, resting lightly on the handle until he was sitting down. In an instant, the powerful engine surged forward.

Nancy looked back at Meg but Jeb had his arm protectively around her shoulders and she seemed to be enjoying herself as she watched the scenery, old fears forgotten. It was a clear, cold morning, almost as if the storm of the day before had swept all the clouds away so they could enjoy this extra excursion. She knew Meg would be enjoying the view of the magnificent snow-capped Olympics to starboard and as she turned south she pointed out Mount Baker, clear and majestic.

Even in winter, this area with its lush green forests of evergreens, mountains and wild coastline dotted with islands, made Nancy feel like she belonged here. It was the only home she remembered save for fragments of that frightful sea voyage she had begun as a 3-year-old when she and her father had come to Victoria so many years before. Her mind went back to the earliest years in Victoria when she and Dan had lived in the orphanage. She remembered vividly the day Dan went away and how much she had missed him and now he had gone away again. *Will history repeat itself? Will he come home to me again?* It was difficult not to think of him and she could almost feel his arms around her as she stood at the wheel. She shook off the thought and looked back at her passengers. *It's so nice to have daylight for a change. It's going to be a long winter with these trips every Friday but days like this don't make them so hard to take and the money is well worth it.*

The hours passed quickly and soon they were skimming past Edmonds and heading for Bainbridge Island. Nan's attention became riveted on the beacon at West Point and she cut her speed. As they rounded the familiar point, she called to Jeb and, using gestures, told him to get his field glasses. He knew what she meant; they were looking for the Jorgensen flag.

Meanwhile, Terry and his men had already arrived at the Jorgensen home and as requested by Nancy, he strung up Gus' flag. As she pulled up, he noted the lack of a name on her hull.

As she cut the engine, he called out to her. "You haven't given this piece of junk a name yet, captain!"

Ignoring him, their attention was drawn to the house and they saw Beth and Gus waving from the window. An Oriental manservant came hurrying down the path to meet them.

"Madam say Canadians must come in house, get warm velly quick," he said in almost perfect English.

Nancy, watched him pick up Meg and Jebediah's bags, then lead the way toward the house. When they had gone, she swung around to face Terry. "What do you mean, piece of junk?" she snapped fiercely. "That little beauty is the fastest boat in these waters!"

"No, it ain't," he chuckled, knowing he had gotten her attention. Calling for his men to begin unloading, he took her by the arm. "You just come with me, girl. I've got something to show you."

Following him across the wide jetty, Terry led her toward a large boathouse that looked brand new. She could hear the young Irishman chuckling to himself and her curiosity was becoming aroused.

"Take a good look at that!" he said and, with a superior smirk, he flung open the door.

Nancy's eyes widened at the sight of the red-and-gold monster boat, fully 40 feet long but with much more cabin space than her little 30 footer. Going inside, she moved carefully along the walkway, her mouth dropping open when she saw the two shiny engines gleaming with newness.

"Those are some engines!" she exclaimed, watching as Terry climbed aboard. Offering her his hand, he pulled her up beside him. Its roomy, fully enclosed cabin had plushly padded seats. On the dashboard was a compass and so many dials and gauges it made her head spin.

"A pretty little number, isn't she?" he asked, watching her curiously.

"Wow," she whispered, "this is real luxury. How fast will it go?"

"50 knots," he murmured reverently. "It'll do 35 knots with only one engine running."

"What's Gus going to do with it?"

"Don't know, says it's not ready yet anyway. I suppose you'd better go, they're waiting for you up at the house."

Hurrying up the dock, Nancy was surprised to find the servant still waiting patiently for her. Motioning her to follow, he led the way up the path and inside the house. Going up the staircase and along a corridor, he stopped outside a guest room where Beth was waiting for her.

"Hello dear, it's so nice to see you again," Beth welcomed her, moving forward eagerly to give her a hug. "I think a nice hot shower would feel wonderful about now. It must have been frightfully cold out on the water this morning especially at the hour you would have left.

"A shower … of water?" Nancy asked, frowning.

"Why yes," Beth laughed, realizing this was no doubt a new experience for her. "Here's a towel, love. Come on, I'll show you how it works. After that, we'll have some lunch, then we'll take you on a little tour of our city."

Nancy took the towel noticing how soft and plush it was. She'd never seen a towel like this before and she was most curious about the shower.

"I-I'll need to iron my other clothes first," she stammered, suddenly remembering her bag.

"No you won't, dear. I've already done some shopping for you!" Beth pointed toward the window. Nancy followed her gaze and was shocked to see the neatly laid out clothes that she hadn't even noticed. There were underclothes, stockings, and an attractive green dress, together with a beautiful woollen cardigan that looked suspiciously like cashmere—which she would never be so extravagant as to buy for

119

herself. Nearby, on the coat stand hung an exquisitely tailored long, tan-coloured wool coat, with fashionable matching boots.

"I hope you don't mind, Nancy. I have always wished for a girl to shop for and I just couldn't resist."

Nancy was speechless. She went over to the clothes and gently ran her hands over the soft fabrics. The dress was just like one she had seen in one of those fancy New York magazines the maids sometimes found at the hotel, left by a wealthy traveller.

"This ... is ... all ... for me?" she whispered, barely managing to get the words out.

Beth smiled. "Yes dear, they are all for you. First, let's get you out of those damp clothes before you catch your death of cold. I'll get Louie to wash them for you while we're out." She picked up Nancy's clothes and took them out into the hall returning immediately. Nancy was standing in her camisole and bloomers still looking quite overwhelmed. She had been holding the dress up in front of her and staring into the mirror but she put it back quickly on the stand.

Beth picked up the towel from where Nancy had dropped it and gave the girl a little push toward the bathroom. "Here's a nice cozy robe you can use," she added, taking it from a hook behind the door. Beth had never seen the girl so subdued. "Don't worry, darling, they're all the right size. Jebediah's a good, old detective!"

"He knew about this?"

"Yes, we both did," admitted Meg, who had come quietly to the door, already changed out of her boating clothes. "They're wonderful, aren't they?" Receiving only a slight smile, she continued, "Go on dear, you have your shower. It will do you a world of good. I'm going to try one later. We'll wait lunch for you."

Entering the luxurious bathroom that was almost as large as her bedroom at home, Nancy looked about her. She couldn't believe her eyes. She thought some of the bathrooms in the hotels were fancy but this was unbelievable. At Gordon Head their toilet was still outside!

She gently caressed the beautiful flocked wallpaper, shiny marble walls and matching counter. *Italian marble, I think they call it*, she thought as Beth followed her inside. Going over to the large bathtub, she realized there was a hose and an extra tap on the wall. First Beth explained how the taps and handle on the Swedish invention worked, then handed her a little towel in the shape of a hat.

"This will keep your hair dry. Just wrap it around your head and tuck it in. It's a marvellous little invention," Beth assured her. "We'll just be downstairs and there's no need to hurry. If you put the plug in you can even finish off with a bath! Enjoy yourself!"

Nancy heard the bathroom door click closed and slowly began to undress. Beth smiled at Meg who waited on the landing, took her arm and led her down the stairs. "She's going to enjoy this experience and when we come home it will be your turn, Aunt Meg!"

Nancy wrapped the large towel around her naked body feeling its luxurious softness. She picked up the funny little hair towel and following Beth's instruction wrapped it around her head as she looked in the mirror. She giggled. *If you have money you sure can buy some strange things these days!*

Next, she turned on the taps and adjusted the heat. Dropping her towel, she stepped under the warm spray and quickly pulled the curtain around herself so the water didn't spray everywhere.

An hour later, they were seated in the dining room and Gus turned to the attractive redhead sitting beside him. Her wind-burnt cheeks and red hair went remarkably well with the green dress, making her look fresh and lovely. *Beth did a nice job with the new clothes.* Then he thought of Dan and couldn't help but think what a lucky man he was. He leaned toward her and whispered, as if for her ears only.

"You're looking exceptionally beautiful today, young lady."

Sitting next to her, Meg beamed. A mother could not have been more proud. Her lifelong dream to be married and have her own daughter had never been realized but a strange twist of fate had brought her Dan and then Nancy.

"Thank you, Mr. Jorgensen," Nancy quipped impishly. "You must agree that your wife has good taste in clothes."

"My wife and I have good taste in friends!" he replied, winking.

The sound of metal being tapped lightly on glass turned their attention and they saw the others looking at them.

"If my husband will stop flirting with our guest, we'd like to share our wonderful news!" Seeing their expectant faces, she continued, "We've at last heard from the British authorities who have told us our boys are safe in two different English hospitals," she began, stopping briefly when Meg and Nancy clapped their hands happily. "Naturally, we are delighted. They haven't told us very much as yet so we are considering going over to England ourselves, although Gus is worried about travelling with war going on. I'm afraid I find it terribly difficult to be patient while waiting for news."

They all began to talk at once until Beth suddenly asked about Dan. Nancy felt a shiver run down her spine. She grew noticeably quieter and looked down at her dish suddenly unable to speak. Meg and Jebediah answered a few brief questions then they let the subject rest. When they finished eating the servants cleared the table and Beth explained where they were going for their outing.

"I have it all planned," she said excitedly. "We're going shopping first and then having dinner here later. We've invited a few friends to join us. I'm so eager for them to meet you all. And Nancy, we were hoping you might agree to sing for us tonight, dear. I know we didn't warn you but Meg said you often sing on the spur of the moment. We have a great stack of music you can look through. Nellie Cornish will be coming and she is a wonderful pianist. You will love her."

Nancy looked over at Meg who was nodding her head eagerly.

"It seems to have been decided then," she replied, grinning a bit self-consciously.

"Wonderful!" said Beth. "But right now we are going to take you downtown so we can show you our lovely James Moore Theatre. We won't be going in but James himself will be joining us for dinner later. He's a wonderful man and his theatre will make you positively swoon!"

Twenty minutes later they all climbed into the big green Chrysler. Following a short tour of downtown Seattle, Peter, their chauffeur, drove them up to the elegant Italian and Byzantine-styled front entrance of the James Moore Theatre on Second and Virginia.

"Don't be fooled by the simple exterior, because the inside, which you will see one day soon, will take your breath away!" warned Gus.

"What do you mean, simple?" asked Meg. "It looks like a palace to me!"

"It is rather nice, isn't it?" agreed Beth. "We are so familiar with it, we forget how unusual it appears to others."

They continued on to Pike Place Market which was pure bedlam as Peter skilfully avoided the streetcars, milling people and horse-drawn carts. It was the last Saturday before Christmas and the many street vendors were loudly bawling their wares.

"Looks like fun out there," Nancy laughed, as the car finally escaped the crowds and sped away.

Gus ordered his driver to show them the Hospital at Fifth and the City Hall on Yessler Way.

"My goodness they're big buildings," Meg gasped, "even larger than the Empress Hotel in Victoria!"

"Yes, you're absolutely right Meg, but just imagine that in New York City they are probably twice the size," laughed Beth.

"You may be exaggerating just a wee bit, darling," warned Gus as the women all giggled.

At the Bon Marché, one of the largest stores in the city, Jebediah took Meg's hand as they slowly walked down row after row of breathtakingly wonderful displays of all imaginable gifts. Assistants wrapped parcels in bright Christmas paper and, to Nancy's surprise, took no money when Gus handed them a card. He merely signed a paper and was given his card back. They went through three crowded floors of the huge store, gently urged on by Beth. Even with a limited amount of time, she made good use of the trip and, 2 hours later, Gus had an armful of packages to show for it.

Meg quietly mentioned she thought her legs were ready to give out and Gus took them over to the elevator that whisked them quickly back down to the main floor.

"My gracious!" Meg exclaimed when the doors opened. "These Seattle elevators don't waste any time do they? I think I left my heart up there somewhere!" she said, pointing upward and quickly taking Jeb's arm.

Peter was waiting outside and opened the door of the Chrysler as soon as they appeared. Darkness was settling in around them as he took them away from the bright lights of the bustling city. In a few minutes, the car was driving down a quiet country road with very few homes. Arriving at a set of decorative iron gates, they found them open inviting them to enter.

The butler opened the big oak door as soon as the car pulled under the porté cochére, welcoming them back. "Dinner will be served at seven, madam," he proclaimed, in a very correct English accent. He assisted them with their coats and Gus showed them into a small parlour.

"Thank you, Joseph," said Beth, dismissing the jovial man with a smile and joining the others. "Now, you all have time for a little rest in your rooms if you would like. Please make yourselves at home. We'll either be in our apartment or downstairs if you care to join us. Otherwise, just pull the bell string by your door and one of the servants will come to assist you."

Meg and Jebediah said they were going to rest for awhile and left the room together but Nancy, hearing the sounds of a piano, hung back. The butler suddenly reappeared.

"Miss Cornish is waiting, madam," he announced. "I have shown her into the music room."

"Joseph, please make sure our guests have everything they need," she told him, nodding up the stairs at Jeb and Meg, before turning to Nancy. "Come and meet Nellie," she said eagerly, taking her arm.

Gus followed them but knowing how much his wife had been looking forward to this day, he didn't want to interfere.

It was a large room with a highly polished wooden floor. A piano sat almost in the center and a dark-haired, plainly dressed young woman of about 30 years of age was playing the most wonderful music. Nellie Cornish stared off into space totally engrossed in the haunting music she was playing and it was obvious she hadn't noticed them enter.

"This room was specially built, so the acoustics are almost perfect," Beth whispered.

Nancy guessed the room probably doubled as a dancing area, though at the moment comfortable chairs were tastefully scattered about the area. Tall windows were heavily curtained against drafts and a magnificent white brick fireplace filled the end wall, adding a sense of splendour as it rose to the ceiling.

"NELLIE," Gus called, walking over to the piano and into her line of sight. "We want you to meet our Nancy. Nancy, this is Nellie Cornish. She knows absolutely everything about music and, as you have already heard, is an accomplished pianist."

Miss Cornish, the owner and operator of the Cornish School of Music, situated in the Booth Building at Broadway and East Pine Street, sat looking at the redhead for a moment before coming to her feet.

"I'm delighted, Nancy. Gus told me I would be able to meet you if I attended tonight's dinner," she said softly, holding out her hand. Her curiosity about this girl had been aroused ever since Gus had begun talking about her some months before.

Having her own music studio had given her much insight into the talented brand of student that was around today and she was well-known for being a good judge of character. Even at first glance Nellie liked the look of the unassuming redhead with the air of confidence.

124

Time and talent will tell, she thought, as she gripped the girl's firm hand and returned her smile.

"You're a singer, Gus tells me. Who trained you?"

"No one," replied Nancy, smiling sweetly. "I just do it."

"Do you dance?" Nellie continued, a frown creasing her brow. "Body rhythm and music all go together you know."

"No, I don't, but I'd like to. I've seen people dancing at the Empress Hotel in Victoria and thought it would be a pleasant thing to do."

"It's really very easy when you have rhythm. I'll teach you ... if you'll sing for me," she said boldly, moving her arms as if she was dancing a waltz.

"We'll teach you to dance, love," Gus quickly intervened, "but no singing, Nellie, not until later. Nancy has been persuaded to sing for us after dinner."

"Will you play for me, Miss Cornish?" Nancy asked.

"I'd be delighted, and please call me Nellie!" she insisted.

"Why don't you go get your dancing shoes on, Gus," suggested Beth, taking off her shoes and putting them out of the way. "I'll show Nancy a few steps right now if Nellie will play."

Nellie sat back down at the piano and her hands glided across the keys as the familiar strains of a Strauss waltz filled the room. Beth talked the steps out loud as she glided across the open floor by herself. Nancy began to copy her movements watching carefully as she walked alongside, then Beth took her hands and they moved across the floor together.

"See how easy it is," Nellie laughed. "You're a natural. You can feel the music, can't you?"

"Hold it, hold it," Gus called, coming through the door and gently pulling Nancy away from his wife's grasp. "Now it's our turn!"

Leading her out into the middle of the floor, he gave her instructions on how they would hold each other, and then nodded to Nellie. They had only taken a few steps when Beth began to clap gleefully at her husband's expression of surprise—as Nancy's feet followed him perfectly. Soon they were waltzing all around the room.

"You were fooling us," Gus grinned, "you've danced before!"

"Enough!" Beth announced a few minutes later, glancing at her watch. "Dinner's in less than an hour and you, young lady, will no doubt need a little help dressing."

"I'm already dressed," Nancy replied giddily, sorry they had to stop.

"Come with me," Beth whispered, conspiratorially. "We have another surprise for you."

Gus stayed behind to talk to Nellie as the women left the room and went quickly up the stairs. When they were out of earshot, Gus extracted a piece of paper from his breast pocket and handed it to the music teacher. It was a banker's draft for $2,000 and Nellie accepted it as if it were a common occurrence, which it actually was, as the Jorgensen Shipping Company was one of the main benefactors of her music school.

Upstairs, Beth was soon running between the two guest rooms as she organized Meg and Nancy showing them the gowns she'd had made especially for them. With flushed cheeks, the Scot fondled the soft wool of the floor-length MacDonald tartan kilt.

"Ach lassie, I've never felt anything as soft in my life!" she exclaimed, lifting it to her face and caressing her wrinkled cheek with the cloth.

Next door, Beth was showing the speechless redhead a lovely evening gown in light blue, shot-silk taffeta. Its form-hugging bodice and lightly gathered floor-length skirt were the height of fashion. Beth knew the girl's youthful figure was going to dazzle at least some of her guests.

"You will certainly be the envy of all my friends tonight, dear!" Beth tittered. "Try it on, love, let's make sure it fits. I've been dying to see it on you ever since it arrived on Wednesday."

"It's wonderful, Beth, but you shouldn't have spent all this money on me," said Nancy, almost in a whisper, as Beth unbuttoned the back of her dress for her.

"Don't you worry your pretty head; it really pleased me to do this shopping. You might say it helped to take my mind off the boys. Now, you start getting dressed and I'll be back in a few minutes," she said cheerily, shutting the door quietly behind her.

Nancy slipped out of her green dress and put on another new petticoat which Beth had laid out on the bed. This one was a slim-fitting petticoat trimmed with eyelet—a narrow blue ribbon threaded through the small holes around the hem. She looked in the mirror and smiled. She had never felt so beautiful as she did today. She sat down on the upholstered bench in front of the dresser and pulled on the finely woven, black silk stockings, rolling them over the elastic top to keep them in place.

There was a light tap at the door.

"Come in," she called.

Beth opened the door and slipped in. Seeing Nancy was ready for her dress, she took it off the hanger and held it while the girl plunged her arms into the long sleeves and wriggled it over her shoulders. She noticed that the sleeves ended in a 'v' at her wrist.

"Oh look, isn't that sweet. I've never seen a design like this before," Nancy gasped, as Beth began to button the tiny matching buttons that ran up the back of the gown.

"Aunt Meg! Look at you," she exclaimed as Meg opened the door and peeked in. "Come in, aren't you a grand Scottish lady tonight!"

But Meg didn't hear a word she said because the sight of the beautiful girl facing her had taken her breath away. Speechless, she watched as Nancy turned about in front of the mirror admiring her new dress. *She is stunning! Oh, how I wish Dan could see her tonight.*

"Look, Aunt Meg. Isn't my dress wonderful! I've never seen anything so lovely in my whole life!"

"Neither have I, lassie, and I'm noo talkin about the dress!" replied Meg, with a wink to Beth.

The women stood back and watched as the girl turned, first left and then right, causing the lovely blue dress to sparkle with streaks of pink as it caught the light.

"Let's do your hair, shall we?" Beth invited, showing Nancy how to sit down in the slim skirt. Beth picked up the brush and drew it through Nancy's long shimmering locks. She thought of her own daughter, lost to illness as a baby, and her eyes misted over. *They would have been very close in age*, she thought. She had often longed for those years of playing together with dolls and dressing her up in nice clothes, but it wasn't meant to be. Instead, she and Gus had two strapping boys and she wouldn't have traded them for anything even with the worry they had caused of late. But tonight, just for a few hours, Nancy was going to be that daughter.

Guests began arriving and the living room soon became filled with friendly laughter and chatter as Jebediah amused them with tales of his past. Meg went down to join them and Gus presented her to his friends as the Scottish-Canadian aunt of Nancy Wilson, causing a ripple of polite chatter to run through the room.

When Beth appeared in the doorway with the stunning redhead on her arm, the men all rose in awestruck silence. Beaming broadly, their host moved across the room to meet them.

"Friends," he said, reaching for Beth's and Nancy's hands to draw them closer, "I believe you all know the beautiful lady on my right is my wife, Beth, and this lovely creature is a remarkable young woman whom we met in Victoria sometime ago. Please welcome our good friend, Nancy Wilson."

Nancy knew she was already blushing and cursing her fair skin, tipped her head slightly and thanked them for the welcome, making a face at Gus. The dinner gong sounded faintly in the background, interrupting the group as they each moved forward to meet her. Meg moved closer to Jeb and their intertwined fingers gripped each other a little tighter as the Scot sighed audibly.

James Moore, the theatre owner, came up beside Meg as they moved toward the table. "My name is James Moore, Miss McDonald. It's a pleasure to meet you at last. Welcome to Seattle. Our Beth certainly knows how to make an entrance, doesn't she!" he whispered.

"Ach, you're the owner of that wonderful theatre we drove by this afternoon," cooed Meg.

"Yes, I am. I hope you will do me the honour of coming to one of our shows and seeing the inside of my little playhouse, perhaps next time you come to Seattle." Just then, someone called his name and he excused himself diplomatically, moving away.

Nellie Cornish, who always listened to her intuition, felt her finger-nails biting into her hand as she watched Nancy's confident presence. A thought flashed through her head. *She is no ordinary young woman. With the Jorgensens behind her she can't help but make an impression. I wonder if she can really sing?*

The butler, with only the slightest smile twitching at the side of his mouth, stood rigidly waiting as the guests sought out their place cards and sat at pre-designated seats. When everyone was sitting, he moved slowly around the table loudly introducing each person.

"Saves a lot of confusion," Beth whispered to Meg sitting beside her.

There was John Lamb, an old friend from the Seattle Water Department; James Moore, the owner of the James Moore Theatre; and Charles Blanc, a noted restaurateur, famous for his high-class cuisine.

Nellie Cornish had earned her place at the table this evening due to her talents as a pianist. She was well aware that she owed Gus Jorgensen a great many favours and was looking forward to accompanying Nancy when she sang later. Albert Rhodes and his wife, Hattie, ran a department store in the city, and last on the butler's list were Mr. and Mrs. Hiram Gill, the mayor and First Lady of Seattle. They were always looking for ways to foster good relations with the Jorgensens and Gus liked to hear Hiram's up-to-date information on local politics.

Borrowing Charles Blanc's chef to prepare the meal tonight had been a master stroke of planning by Beth. When the kitchen staff entered carrying large platters of turkey, ham and dishes of steaming food, the combined aromas brought smiles to everyone's faces.

John Lamb cocked an eyebrow but made no comment as the wine steward arrived with his trolley, inquiring of their preference for beverages. Smiling to himself, he watched the mayor's eager fingers reach for the glass of good Scottish whisky.

Chapter 14

The sumptuous Christmas meal at the Jorgensen's was like none other that Meg or Nancy had ever experienced before. The main course was followed by traditional English plum pudding, carried in and presented by the chef himself. Lavishly bathing it with rum, he set it ablaze, to the delight of the guests. After the servants had cleared the table, the wine steward appeared again taking orders from those who desired some liquid refreshment.

"What about prohibition, Mr. Mayor!" Nellie commented impishly.

"Private stock, little lady!" replied Hiram, grinning before he drained his glass for the third time. "Private stock, that's the difference." His hand shook slightly as he handed his empty glass to the steward.

"A toast, ladies and gentlemen," Gus proposed, rising with glass in hand, "success to our Canadian friends both here, at home, and in Europe."

They all rose, glasses clinked, and the Americans drank to their cross-border neighbours, never dreaming that their host's toast went much further than the two ladies at the end of the table.

All eyes shifted as Nancy stood up, looking radiant and confident. Silence enveloped the room.

"Friends," she said quietly, looking purposefully at Gus and Beth. "This has been a day I will remember forever. It has already been Christmas and still only the 19th of December! I offer you a toast to the men at war and our fervent hope that they will all come home safely." Her voice cracked a little but she squared her shoulders and with a toss of her head raised her glass of orange squash. Everyone rose and stood stiffly to attention, raising their glasses with murmured agreement, for although the United States had not entered the war yet, many of them knew boys who had gone overseas to help the cause, like the Jorgensens.

Now, that was dramatic, thought Nellie as Beth stood up and asked for quiet.

"Why don't we move across the hall and listen to some music. I'm sure if anyone would like to dance, Nellie would be happy to oblige with a suitable tune," laughed Beth.

"Thank you, sweetheart, your toast drove my point home," Gus whispered to Nancy as he took her arm and they followed the group.

Nellie was already seated at the grand piano when they entered and, as her fingers moved across the ivory keys, soft melodies gently interspersed with various conversations in the room. Two of the ladies questioned Meg on her Scottish heritage while off to one side, cigar smoke floated in blue clouds toward the ceiling as the men conversed on their favourite topic … politics.

"I'll soon put a stop to the operation of those evil saloons," Hiram boasted, gulping down another whisky.

Albert Rhodes, a forward-thinking man with a friendly disposition, shook his head in disagreement. "I can buy it," he murmured, "but the working man has to get his drink from the drug store. It won't work, Gill," he chuckled. "It's a prescription for trouble."

James Moore and Charles Blanc agreed with the department store owner but the mayor wouldn't be swayed from his line of thinking. He had reviewed and re-assessed his position many times following the devastating election in 1912 when he loudly promoted a wide-open city, and George Cotterill had beaten him for the top job.

At the piano, impatience was causing the pianist to look around the room eager to get on with the entertainment. Beth noticed and gave her a silent nod. Going to look for Nancy, she found her in the living room talking with Hattie Rhodes and Meg.

"Excuse me, ladies. Are you ready, Nancy?" she asked quietly. Receiving a nod from the girl, she took her by the arm and led her into the music room.

"What's happening, Miss McDonald?" asked Mrs. Rhodes.

"Come, let's go find out, shall we?" replied Meg, leading the way into the other room.

"Friends, can I have your attention," Beth was saying. "You've all heard me talk about Nancy and her wonderful voice. Well, she has agreed to sing for us, so if you will give her a few minutes to confer with Nellie, they will bring us some special entertainment."

Nancy looked around at the waiting faces and smiled. Walking over to the piano bench, she sat down beside Nellie. Thumbing through the music Nellie handed her, a thought suddenly struck the girl. *Nellie is a*

131

music teacher and an accomplished pianist, she must have a thousand songs in her head.

"Do you know *Men of Harlech?*" she whispered.

Nellie nodded.

"*Lili Marlene?*"

"How on earth do you know that one?" Nellie asked, looking startled. "It's a German love song!"

"We have a wonderful men's group called the Arion Choir in Victoria," Nancy replied. "One of the men taught it to me."

The room went quiet as Nellie began to play a thundering introduction to the Welsh fighting song Nancy had requested first.

As Nancy began to sing James Moore sat up straighter in his chair. He had a smattering of Welsh blood in his veins and he was most familiar with the history of this song. However, he had never heard it performed quite like this before. Nellie's rousing rendition and the depth of the girl's feeling sent shivers up his spine as the words tumbled from her lips.

"BRAVO, WELL DONE," he cried, even before the last note had ended, leaping to his feet in a sudden rush of excitement.

"Sit down, Jimmy, you're spoiling the show," Gus growled, winking at Nancy.

"I would like to dedicate a song," announced Nancy in a hushed tone, "to all those who are parted because of the war."

She looked over at Nellie but the woman's eyes had flicked up as the butler stepped into the room and stood quietly inside the door. Nancy nodded again to Nellie and she began her short introduction. As the words of the beautiful, but sad tune, *Lili Marlene*, floated gently through the air, men listened intently and one or two of the ladies reached hastily for their handkerchiefs.

"Glory be," Nellie gasped softly, when the song ended and her hands fell limply into her lap.

The guests clapped briefly as Nancy bowed. A hush came over the room as they waited to see what was coming next.

"*O Holy Night,* please Miss Cornish … Nellie," Nancy said quietly.

Nellie tried to raise her hands to the keyboard but they felt like pieces of lead. Her fingers simply wouldn't obey her command. She had never had an experience like this before and her mind was in turmoil. She'd searched for years for a natural talent like Nancy and, thanks to the Jorgensens, she had finally found her. She looked up at the girl with glazed eyes.

132

Nancy saw the woman's confusion and not knowing what else to do, simply began to sing. When Nellie heard the notes of *O Holy Night* begin without her she realized a person with this talent didn't really need her. Knowing it would spoil the song by coming in late, she sat back and savoured the moment. It was not often she had the chance to sit back and simply listen. Nancy had perfect pitch and her natural, untrained voice cut through the stillness of the room like a mesmerizing wand, transfixing them.

As the song came to a close, Nancy curtsied and the guests clapped wildly. Bravos flew from every corner.

Nancy turned to Nellie who was now smiling up at her. "I'm so sorry if I spoiled the song for you, Nellie," she whispered.

"No love, you didn't spoil anything at all. You have just given me an excellent reason to go on working."

"Need a job, Nancy?" James Moore's voice cut into their conversation. "You'd be a sensation at the playhouse. I'm sure Gus and Beth would be happy to see you more often!"

"Oh no, thank you," Nancy purred. "I have a job. I'm a waitress at the Balmoral Hotel in Victoria. They do see me often; I come to Seattle every Friday."

"Every Friday," the mayor repeated slowly. "Uh-huh, so that's where you get this good quality liquor, Jorgensen!"

Gus' brain snapped to attention as he scrambled for a reply, but it proved unnecessary.

"Idiot!" snapped Hattie Rhodes. "She's no rum runner, look at her. It's not possible!"

Stumbling for words, Hiram glanced at the ring of faces staring his way and quickly tried to make amends for his offensive suggestion.

"Humph! Well, you never can be too sure," he continued, watching Nancy carefully. "But if it were true, it would be within my power to give her special dispensation from Coast Guard interference!" He turned toward Gus and smiled slyly. "Naturally, I would require the name of your boat."

"It's the *Stockholm*," Gus offered quietly. "She's red-and-gold."

Nellie Cornish was nobody's fool, her brain always quick and alert. Her eyes flicked between their host and the girl noticing the barely discernible nod that passed between them. *Anyone who can sing like Nancy would have a soul for adventure,* she thought to herself. *There's more to this Canadian than one would think.* Dispelling the thought, she stood up and noisily closed the piano lid.

"This has been much too exciting a day for me," she announced, walking over to Beth. The women hugged and Nellie called her goodnights as the butler found her coat. A murmur of agreement erupted as many of the women followed her toward the foyer also seeking their coats, and it wasn't long before Nellie found herself a ride.

Fifteen minutes later, as the last car pulled away from the mansion, Nancy spun around to face the shipowner.

"I'm sorry …," she began.

"Not here," Gus quietly hissed, raising his eyebrows. "Upstairs."

Beth, back in her own private environment, busied herself making coffee telling the others to make themselves comfortable. She knew Gus had been taken by surprise by Nancy's admission and was eager to see what was going to happen next.

"It's all right, Nancy. You weren't to know, but I had to move faster than I expected," Gus chuckled, as he closed the door behind them. "It's obvious now, that the new boat is for you!" He held up his hand to stop her from speaking. "I have to admit that we've been testing you out, girl. I'm sorry but we had to be sure. That new boat is the finest in Swedish technology, faster than a speeding arrow and armed to the teeth. You'll love it!"

"But the cost must be enormous," she replied, having difficulty understanding it all as she followed his lead and sat down on the couch.

"And so are the profits," he grinned back. "The first boat has already paid its way, now we're really going to go into business. All the storage space in this boat is covered; nobody will know what you're carrying and that dispensation from the mayor is like a licence to print our own money."

"You mean he was really serious?" Meg asked.

Gus nodded.

"You still have a choice, love," Beth interceded gently. "Don't let him blind you with his enthusiasm. My husband loves a challenge."

"It's scary, but terribly exciting. I just wish Dan were here," she replied, lowering her eyes.

"What do you think, Jeb?" said Beth, turning to their friend who was sitting silent in the corner. "You've been very quiet tonight."

"Where she goes, so do I," he replied simply.

Beth smiled. She wouldn't have expected anything less.

Floating off to sleep between silken sheets that night, Nancy's thoughts turned to Dan, the war, and the terrible loneliness.

                              *   *   *

Thousands of miles away, Dan's patriotic eagerness has been dulled
slightly by a monotonous training schedule and bad weather conditions.
Arriving in England barely a month ago, he found himself, and many
thousands of other Canadians, occupying a huge tented camp on
Salisbury Plain. Here he spent his time training gunners for the arduous
task ahead of them. The consensus among the soldiers was that the war
would be over in a few short months. Eagerness to serve their country
was only slightly dulled by the censured reports coming from the
battlefront across the English Channel. In a few months, he and his
mates would face this cruel reality.

                              *   *   *

"You were whimpering, child," Meg murmured, sitting on the edge
of Nancy's bed as dawn broke. "Are you all right? I could hear you in
the hall when I got up."

Nancy sleepily opened her eyes and thought for a split second that
she was at Cunningham Manor. She noticed her surroundings and the
realization flooded back.

"I'm all right, Aunt Meg. I was just having a dream about Danny. I
miss him so much."

"I know you do, dear. Why don't you come down and have some
breakfast. Jeb thinks we might be running into a storm if we don't leave
soon. He wants to be off by 10 o'clock."

She pulled herself into a sitting position and hugged her aunt. "I'll
hurry," she promised.

"My word it's cold out there!" Gus announced as he entered the
kitchen half an hour later rubbing his hands together. "Morning Nancy,
the boat's been refuelled and the engines checked; your parcels are all
loaded. When you're ready, just leave your bag and Stanley will bring
it down to the wharf."

"Oh, all right. I won't take a minute, thank you, Gus," said Nancy,
pushing her chair back from the table. She looked at him thoughtfully.
"May I ask you a question that's been puzzling me since our shopping
trip?" Receiving a questioning smile from Gus, she continued, "When
we were in that department store yesterday, you gave the clerk a card
instead of money. How does that work?"

                                   135

"Oh that's just another American invention. We call it a charge card. They put it on an account then send us a bill at the end of the month. Only a couple of the large stores have it."

Nancy shook her head in amazement then, excusing herself, went off to finish her packing.

"You won't be long, will you lassie?" asked Meg.

"Aren't you coming up, Aunt Meg?" the girl asked.

"No dear, my bags are already on the boat."

"Oh my, everyone's way ahead of me this morning," she laughed, hurrying up the stairs. "I'll only be a few minutes."

At 10 o'clock they were all standing on the dock saying their farewells when Jeb pointed up to the dark clouds. After hugs all around, the threesome climbed into their boat and Nan soon had them underway. Waving one last time, she swung wide and opened the throttle. The engine burst into life and she felt suddenly exhilarated. She looked over at Jeb and grinned as they cut through the waves. Salty spray bit into her cheeks, soon turning them a fiery red.

"SHE LOVES THIS!" Jebediah yelled back to Meg as they flashed through the water. "Sometimes she scares the hell out of me, though!" he said as an afterthought, winking at Nancy as she grinned at him. *I hate to think what it's going to be like when we get a faster boat!*

They passed two fishing boats off the Wells Point Light and then a freighter chugging slowly toward the Strait.

"Want to meet Ezekiel Plunket, Aunt Meg?" Nancy called back to her aunt after looking up at the sky. Hearing no answer she made the decision and slowed down so she could find the entrance to his cove.

Taking the two whistles from her pocket, she nosed the craft through the trees. Making the secret call, she searched the beach for movement. Jeb saw him first, sitting between the logs with his back toward them. He was strangely motionless and Jeb called out to him. The slight movement of Zeke's arm holding his rifle was enough to tell Jeb there was something terribly wrong.

"Something's wrong, get in there fast, Nan!" He was already climbing forward onto the bow and preparing to jump.

Jebediah was into the water even before they touched bottom. Meg went to stand beside Nancy trying to see what was happening on shore.

Suddenly changing her mind, Nancy turned to her aunt and shouted, "HOLD ON TIGHT!" She threw the boat into reverse and pulled over to the dilapidated wharf searching for the safest position. Although they had never used it before, Nancy had a feeling it was going to be needed this time. She jumped out, tied up the boat and came to help Meg who was already climbing gingerly onto the rickety jetty.

When Jeb reached his friend, he was shocked at the sight which met his eyes. Ezekiel was covered in blood and his pants and shirt were almost torn into shreds. At first glance it appeared he was dead but hearing Jeb's voice, the old man tried to move. Quickly assessing the situation, Jeb realized he had lost a lot of blood and had probably been out here for some hours. His friend was definitely in bad shape.

"Don't move," warned Jeb, kneeling down beside him. Seeing the old man's bloodied knife lying in the sand, he picked it up and sliced some of the torn and soiled cloth away. Now better able to see the deep gashes on his chest and hip, he was shocked at the number of deep gashes. "We need to warm him up," Jeb growled, as the others arrived. He took off his jacket and laid it over Zeke, Nancy did the same. "Zeke, can you hear me? What the devil happened?"

Ezekiel stirred slightly and his eyes flicked open. "Big ... cat," he said weakly. "Surprised ... him ... this mor ...." then his body relaxed.

"Is he still alive? Does he live in that cabin?" Meg asked.

"He's passed out. We've got to get him out of here ... and warm."

"You're right. He must have some blankets, I'll go look," said Nan.

"I'm coming with you," exclaimed Meg, but she couldn't get her eyes off the injured man. "We need a needle and some fine twine. He's still bleeding. Should we light a fire?" she asked Jeb.

"No, we haven't time."

"Liquor," Meg murmured. "Jeb, you have a bottle of whisky in the boat, don't you?"

"He'll have some whisky in the house, his own personal brand!" said Jeb. "Go with Nancy and see what you can find. "Hold on, Ezekiel. Good thing we brought Meg, she'll know what to do."

Nancy and Meg returned a few minutes later with an armful of blankets and a whisky bottle. Meg sterilized the needle by pouring some liquor over it then poured whisky liberally over the raw flesh before passing the bottle over to Jeb. Zeke flinched slightly telling them he was coming back to consciousness.

"Open your mouth, you old bushwacker," Jeb ordered, prying his mouth open with his fingers. He poured a sizeable amount of fluid into the old man's mouth.

Nancy watched Ezekiel's face as Meg began to sew up the worst of the gaping wounds, but she had to turn away when he gritted his teeth and groaned a little. Jeb put a piece of driftwood between his teeth and held him still. Otherwise there was no sound out of the poor man and, when she was almost finished, they realized he had passed out again.

"We can't leave him here all alone," Nancy whispered.

"Nope, he's going home with us but he's not going to be very happy about it!" declared Jeb. "He wouldn't have a chance here on his own at this time of year. Matter of fact, he'd probably been dead if it had snowed last night. We better get him moved before he wakes up."

Getting a blanket under him, Jeb took one end and the women the other. Slowly, they dragged and carried him across the beach to the jetty. Then, carefully picking their way across the uneven and broken boards of the wharf, they finally reached the boat. Jeb jumped in and somehow they got Ezekiel over the side and onto the floor. Laying one of Zeke's dirty blankets on the floor, they piled their parcels and baggage around him making him as comfortable as possible. Jeb went back to the cabin, picking up Zeke's rifle from the sand and putting it by the door for his return. He closed the cabin door tightly, then went round and checked the windows. "That's the best I can do, old friend. Sure hope the Eggers don't notice you're missing. They'd be sure to find your still with enough time on their hands!"

When Nancy started the engine, Zeke opened his eyes briefly and asked haltingly for his gun. Jebediah looked over at Nancy and tucked his own rifle in beside him, gave him another drink of whisky and hoped he was too far gone to notice. He moved in behind the patient, wedged the injured man between his legs and Meg moved up beside him and pulled her blanket over them all.

Nancy pushed down on the throttle, eased the boat around, and soon they were out into open water. The race was now on to get Zeke home and in front of a warm fire. Nancy opened the throttle some more and, as the engines sprang into life, she looked up at the sky. Storm clouds had gathered and were getting darker and more ominous looking. *Thank goodness we have daylight*, she mused silently, adjusting her hat over her ears and peering across the white-capped waters. She'd have to be her own lookout this time so she took it a bit slower.

It was early afternoon when Sam heard them coming. Unafraid to be seen anymore, he watched curiously from the cliff. Jeb gave his patient another mouthful of whisky then, with the women's help, got him out of the boat and draped over his shoulder for the walk up the stairs.

"He's going to be awfully heavy, Jebediah," observed Meg.

Suddenly, Nancy ran partway up the stairs. "SAM, ARE YOU UP THERE. WE NEED YOUR HELP, she yelled.

"Too bad the slide can't be used in reverse!" Jebediah joked, watching Sam come down the stairs.

They put Zeke back down on the blanket and with Sam at his head and Jeb at his feet, the men moved slowly up the stairs. Stopping every few steps to catch their breath, they finally made it. At the top, they put him down and the women hurried ahead to get the fires lit. By the time the men arrived, Meg had some blankets on the floor near the fireplace. They lay him down and looking very ill-at-ease, Sam left quickly. Meg fussed around making Zeke more comfortable with pillows and the fire was soon roaring on the hearth.

Meg went to put some soup on and Nancy returned to the boat to get their bags. She was just coming up the stairs when Jeb appeared.

"Looks like you could use some help," he offered.

"No, I'm fine, Uncle Jeb. I have to go into town to get the truck so I didn't put the boat away," she called, breathlessly. "You stay there."

By the time they returned to the house, Meg was just beginning to feed Zeke some hot soup and Jeb sat down by the fire and took over. Colour was beginning to return to Ezekiel's cheeks as he lay back and closed his eyes again.

Meg brought Jebediah a bowl of soup and he moved slowly from the floor to a nearby chair.

"He's a tough old bird," Jeb muttered, looking down at his old friend. "I'm mighty glad he wasn't any bigger!"

Several taps on the door drew Meg's attention. "Come in," she called, but nothing happened. "Come in, Sam." Still nothing happened. Agitated, the Scot went over to the door and opened it. Sure enough, the hermit stood silently on the porch. In his hand he held a bottle which he held out to her as sorrowful dark eyes peered into the room.

"What is it, lad, are you hungry?" Meg asked, taking the bottle.

"Man hurt bad, Sam get sweet water from well, make him better."

"Well bless your heart," she sighed. "Thank you very much, Sam." Nancy came to see what was happening and they stood in the doorway as Sam hurried back to the safety of his forest.

"I've got to go," Nancy muttered finishing the last of her soup and going to get her coat, explaining to Meg where she was going.

"Do you want Jeb to go with you, lass?" Meg asked.

"No, no, I'll be fine. He'd better stay in case you need him for Zeke. I have to leave the boat for Dumpy anyway." Kissing her aunt on the cheek, she hurried back outside.

Chapter 15

Out in the Strait just beyond Clover Point a small patrol boat bobbed helplessly in the wind-whipped waves. Algy Pease had been checking an unidentified craft that seemed to be teasing him by criss-crossing the boundary, when his motor cut out. The strong tide caused him to drift eastward and, at the same time, with each swell the wave action dumped water into the helpless boat. He knew his bailing was futile and he was in grave danger of being swamped. To make matters worse, the craft had turned back and was closing in.

Nancy's attention was first drawn to the black boat thinking it looked familiar. Then she spotted the *Legal Limit* as it balanced on the crest of a wave leaning dangerously. *Jeepers, it's Algy,* she thought, immediately pouring on the power. It was then she realized why the other boat looked so familiar.

"It's the Eggers," she said aloud. "What are they doing—up to no good, I would think."

Without waiting to find out, she cut her engines and located the percussion caps for the cannon which she knew would be already loaded. Finding the hole under the hammer, Nancy primed her secret weapon. Now she was ready! With her temper rising, she roared in for the attack.

Algy watched in amazement as now two boats roared toward him. With his heart in his throat he hung on for dear life and watched the gap shorten. Suddenly, he realized the driver of the blue boat was Nancy. *No one else on these waters has such distinctive red hair! Whatever is she doing?* Seconds later, it came to him, she was trying to protect him, but why? *What can she do without getting herself hurt?* He began to wave at her frantically to go away but the gap kept closing.

Meanwhile in the Egger boat, the brothers were laughing crazily as they careened toward their enemy, a government boat. All of a sudden, one of the boys noticed they were being followed.

"We've got company, boys!" Milo called.

"Shit, it's that blue boat, again," cried Ted. "It's comin mighty fast. Think it's looking fer trouble?"

Ariel pushed him roughly away from the wheel. "It's a damn woman!"

"How do you know?"

"Look at the long hair. Never seen a man with hair like that. Let someone who knows how to drive deal with this one, Teddy boy."

"Well, ya better hurry up, 'cause she's gaining on us!" Milo cried.

Ariel had already pushed Ted out of the way and now opened the throttle turning southward toward their imagined safety zone. Close enough to see all three brothers, Nancy pulled back quickly on the throttle bringing her boat almost dead in the water. Tossing violently in the waves, she quickly stepped back to the cannon and pulled the trigger.

Flame and smoke belched from the muzzle. Hot buckshot screamed across the waves, rattling against the new metal plates on the black boat. Two of the boys stood up and waved their arms madly at her.

"All your cursing isn't going to help you boys!" she laughed.

The Eggers recovered quickly pouring on the power and hurtling toward the coast of Washington State.

Nancy now turned her attention on the next problem, helping Algy. As she got closer she realized the situation was worse than she had feared.

She can't get in close enough to throw me a line, thought Algy.

But the harbour patrolman was about to get a sample of the redhead's ingenuity. Nancy cut her power and quickly found her tow rope. It took a few minutes to jockey into position cautiously moving closer to *Legal Limit.*

"*ALGY ... CATCH THIS!*" she screamed.

He waved and instantly something flew through the air toward him. It was one of her bumpers attached to a length of rope. Landing in the water a few feet beyond his reach, she pulled it back, swung around and moved in a bit closer.

Coiling up the rope, she let the motorboat drift toward him then heaved with all her might. Again it landed in the water but, with a bit of help from a friendly wave, Algy was able to grab it. He untied the bumper and quickly went forward attaching the line to the bow. Breathing heavily, he sat down and waved to her that he was ready. Holding on with one hand, he used the other to massage his cold legs. He was mighty glad to be out of the frigid water that had risen almost to his knees. Feeling the jerk, he knew they were underway and he was going to be safe.

141

Hanging on for deal life, he looked toward the land and realized they weren't far from the breakwater. *I drifted farther than I thought.* Breathing easier now, he watched the girl. "That Nancy's a smart one," he mused aloud, as she skillfully cut through the waves at just the right speed to keep him afloat. He gratefully noticed she kept looking around to check on him.

Even before Nancy reached the Brown and Wilson jetty, Jim Goodwin aboard the *Ping Pong*, saw the familiar blue boat slowly coming up the harbour. When he realized it was towing a partially submerged boat, a grin creased his weather-beaten face. "By Jeez, it's Algy!" he exclaimed aloud, climbing down to a lower deck.

"I COULD USE SOME HELP, JIM," came the familiar voice, as the boat came closer.

"RIGHT-O!" he shouted back, jumping over the rail to the dock.

Nancy swung in close and he was able to leap aboard.

"Found yourself a little problem, did you girl!" he laughed, before going quickly to the stern. Heaving on the rope, he shouted some abuse to Algy as the nearly submerged boat came alongside.

Algy stood up on the bow and waited until he too was close enough to jump onto the dock. "DUMPY, HAVE YOU GOT A PUMP?" he yelled, spotting the lad coming out of the office.

Nancy was surprised to see Dumpy working on Sunday, but his help would certainly be useful. Another boat pulled up and Johnny Schnarr came to see what was happening. Johnny managed Fred Kerr's Empress Boathouse.

"YEAH, WE'VE GOT ONE," Dumpy hollered back heading toward the shed. When he appeared again he was pulling a large piece of equipment on his cart.

With Johnny's help they soon had it working and stood back to watch as the pump spat out the water in a steady stream. Johnny, an amiable young man of around 20, was well-known to the waterfront operators as a helpful and gifted mechanic, always eager to offer his assistance in times of emergency. He'd taken charge of the boathouse down on the mud flats just west of the CPR dock when its German proprietor, Fred Kerr, had been arrested as an alien and sent to the provincial prison at Vernon. Internment, the men had called it, when Nancy asked for an explanation.

"All these Germans could be spies," one of the other men had pompously declared that day, justifying the actions of the police.

"There's hundreds of the poor devils been spirited away," Waldo told her later. "I heard they're packed tight in Nanaimo and also out at the Colquitz Jail in Saanich."

Offering to drive Algenon home, he thanked her but declined, explaining that his car was over at the government wharf. She left him wrapped in a blanket and getting warm in front of their fire drinking a hot cup of coffee. Slipping away, she got into the truck and started for home eager to see how Meg and Jebediah were making out with Zeke. Nancy had told no one about Ezekiel or his injuries, though Dumpy had frowned when he saw her taking some bandages from the cupboard.

As she passed the Gordon Hotel on Johnson, she looked to see if the BC Drug Store was open so she could pick up some other medical supplies, but it was closed. She noticed several groups of men standing about outside the hotel. A bit farther down a loud argument had broken out on the sidewalk in front of the notorious Jubilee Saloon. She saw the window at Shotbolts, the Druggist, but it was also displaying a CLOSED sign.

That's no help either, it was a good thing I took some of the bandages from the office, she thought, carefully manoeuvring through the intersection at Government and waiting for the passing streetcar before turning left into Douglas. As she drove along, she thought of Dan. *Only four days to Christmas. It's going to be positively awful without you this year, Danny.*

Then her attention was taken up as it began pouring with rain and she turned on her wiper. It was raining so hard that it was difficult to see, and driving along hilly Cedar Hill Road became quite a challenge. Just past Cedar Hill Cross Road, she saw two small figures jumping puddles as they hurried to get out of her way. As she came abreast of them she realized it was Jean and Edith Dunnett and she stopped, beckoning to them.

"Come in out of the rain, girls," she called. "I'm going your way!"

Jean recognized her first and they piled into the back seat. Once they were moving again, the girls began to tell her that they had been visiting a sick friend after Sunday School at St Luke's.

"We had no sooner got outside when it begun to pour cats and dogs!" exclaimed little Edith.

"Mamma will be so glad you came by, Nancy," added Jean. "She's always afraid we're going to get putmonia."

"Well, we can't have that can we, Jean?" smiled Nancy, chuckling to herself over the girl's pronunciation.

Chattering away happily, they soon arrived at the corner of Tyndall. Turning the sharp corner, one of the bandages rolled out of Nancy's bag and onto the wet floor.

Picking it up quickly, Jean asked, "Is somebody sick at your place?"

"Sort of, but don't you worry about it, dear," Nancy replied, pulling up in front of the Dunnett house.

Jenny Dunnett came to the door and looked out, smiling when she saw her girls get out of the familiar-looking little truck.

"Thanks for bringing my girls home, Nancy, I was afraid they were going to be drowned!" she called, as she let them run by her into the house. "Can you come in?"

"Thanks, Jenny, but no I must get home today. If I don't see you, have a nice Christmas!" Nancy called back.

"Thanks Nancy. Merry Christmas to you, also," called Jenny, closing the door.

As she turned the truck around, Jean came running back out and handed Nancy two jars of homemade jam. "Mamma says, if you need some help with a sickness, please let us know. She'll come right away."

"Thank your mother, Jean," Nancy called, as the girl ran back into the warm house and the vehicle moved away. The rest of the way home Nancy thought about the Dunnett's considerate kindness and some of the things the girls had chattered about. Edith had mentioned their next-door neighbours, the Williamsons from Scotland. They had a little shop they ran in the front of their property. 'Edith really likes their daughter, Ruby,' Jean had said. 'She's the telephone switchboard operator and she lets us watch sometimes.'

Darkness was falling when she turned off Ash Road and into their drive. A startled deer jumped in front of her, bounding off into the trees. When she walked through the door and saw Zeke sitting up talking to Jebediah she was both surprised and pleased.

"He looks much brighter," she exclaimed to Meg, as she put the preserves down on the kitchen counter. "Your cooking must agree with him, Aunt Meg."

"He's tough as old boot leather!" Jebediah called from the other room.

"Dinner's ready, dear. Those preserves look lovely. Where did you get them?" asked Meg.

"From Jenny Dunnett, I found Jean and Edith walking home in the rain."

Jeb came up behind them with Zeke on his arm. "Are we going to Seattle on Friday?"

"Yes, we are!" interrupted Ezekiel. "I want to go home."

"You're not going anywhere, so just be quiet!" Meg sharply chastised the poor man.

During the meal, they talked of Christmas and what it was going to be like this year.

"It's going to be awfully hard for some folks," suggested Meg.

"I wonder what Danny is doing over there," Nancy said quietly. "I do hope they get to celebrate Christmas a little bit."

After the meal was finished, Meg said she had some mending to do and went and sat down at her new sewing machine in the corner of the living room.

"Have you got that thing figured out yet, Meg?" demanded Jeb.

"Heavens to Betsy, give me time, Jebediah. It only arrived this afternoon!"

"I'm sorry I couldn't keep it a secret until Christmas, Aunt Meg. It was a little large to hide! Jeb, you were asking about Christmas. I don't have to work on Christmas Day, so we can go to Seattle early and come home in daylight. It'll be a much easier trip and we'd be home for dinner."

Jeb mumbled something indiscernible but Nancy was too tired to care. It had been a long weekend and exhaustion had finally crept up on her. The warm fire and the drone of the sewing machine and their voices caused her eyelids' to flutter.

"Go to bed, love," Meg urged gently. "We all feel the same. I think we'll be turning in early tonight."

In the morning, Meg's humming and the sounds of breakfast soon awoke Jeb. Sleepy-eyed, he shuffled into the room and flopped on a chair.

"I'm too old to be sleeping in a chair," he groaned, rubbing his back.

"Ach, I thought you would have gone to your own bed. Zeke was feeling much better last night," said Meg.

"I wanted to make sure the fire stayed lit," he explained. "Morning Nancy," he greeted the girl as she came down the steps.

Light rain was still falling as Nancy turned the Model T up the drive and headed to town in the inky darkness. Malcolm heard her coming and waited under a tree by the church. Grinning, he climbed in beside her tipping the water from the brim of his hat.

"Blasted weather!" he grumbled.

"Don't you like Victoria's liquid sunshine, Malcolm?" she laughed.

They made good time into the city as they were earlier than most, even beating the first of the streetcars. A mix-up between two vehicles at the fountain was easily avoided but they could hear the drivers screaming abuse at each other. One of Waldo's trucks appeared on Store Street as she let Malcolm off. The truck stopped and the driver shouted a greeting to Nancy as Malcolm climbed in beside him and they took off again. *He must have a delivery at the dockyard,* she thought.

Dumpy had stoked the fire and was sitting down having his first cup of coffee when he heard Nancy's truck pull onto the dock. When she came through the door she felt the heat of the room and shivered as she hung up her raincoat.

"The whole waterfront is buzzing about you," he announced. "Algy did some talking after you left on Saturday, seems like you saved his life and his boat."

"I just did what anybody else would have done," she replied cautiously. "He's just lucky I was passing. Did he say anything particular?"

"No, what do you mean?"

"Oh, just wondered if he mentioned the cannon?"

"You used the cannon on them!" Dumpy sputtered.

"Shh, if Algy didn't say anything, it's best to keep it quiet, I think."

They checked their delivery schedule and Dumpy moaned that he had to go around to Sooke. "The weather is going to be lousy out there today."

"Be thankful you have a job," she admonished him. "You know there are hundreds of men out of work in Victoria."

He just looked at her with a woebegone expression and rolled his eyes. She grinned, put her wet coat back on and left for work. Hurrying up Fort Street through the rain, she heard the rattle of the first morning streetcars as they crossed the causeway in front of the Empress. Horses stood impatiently outside the Victoria Transfer stables, and motorized vehicles, puffing black smoke, moved off down Gordon Street toward the docks.

"Everyone is getting an automobile these days," she grumbled aloud.

Mary shouted a welcome when she entered the kitchen and stood just inside the door shaking the water from her coat. Changing quickly, she checked the dining room before turning back to have tea with the cook.

"Did you realize they're saying you're a hero?" asked Mary, sporting a big grin.

"Who says that?" Nancy mumbled through a mouthful of toast.

"Katherine said Algy Pease came in on Saturday with Jim Goodwin," Mary said quietly. "They were singing your praises to anyone who would listen."

The conversation ended abruptly when Nancy heard the clock begin to strike and ran to open the doors. A small but grateful group of dripping customers began to stream inside. As the day progressed, Nancy's gratuities almost doubled and the only explanation was that city businessmen were rewarding her for Algy's little adventure.

Algy himself came in on Wednesday and publicly thanked her in front of all the patrons. Then he made a big show of presenting her with a small silver medal he'd had made explaining that she was now an honourary member of Victoria's Coast Guard.

Christmas Day was spent on the water, thankfully just as she had told Jeb, during daylight hours. It rained for the whole trip so they were exceedingly happy to see the welcoming smoke curl from Cunningham Manor's chimney pot telling them Meg was cooking dinner.

Yes, Meg had their festive dinner ready … with Zeke's help she said, winking at him. He had become one of the family in the past few days and had seemed almost to forget about his desire to go home. Jeb got him talking about the old days and they soon had everyone in stitches over the antics they had gotten up to when they were sworn enemies.

Nancy was more quiet than usual so they mentioned Dan as little as possible. After dinner they went in to sit around the fire and enjoy the small evergreen tree Jeb had cut a few days before. Meg had been busy over the past weeks making popcorn garlands and paper links. She had them strung all about the room and over the tree. She had also used small fir branches to decorate the pictures on the walls, hanging strands of popcorn from them.

All in all, it was bright and festive, making the first Christmas in their new home something to be proud of. They each had a couple of presents to unwrap and, wanting Dan to know they were including him, had put his presents under the tree to give to him later. Jeb and Meg tried to keep the conversation cheerful although it was obvious they were all thinking of Dan.

147

Jeb got out his guitar and entertained them with some silly folk songs he had learned in his younger days trying to add the music to it. It was nice to hear Nancy singing even though her heart wasn't in it. Ezekiel glanced around at their faces, sensing the deep sadness this oddly matched family were feeling and was grateful they had taken him in.

New Year's Eve 1914 arrived too soon and a few revellers tried to revive the grief-stricken city but it was fruitless—bitterness had now taken the place of patriotic madness. Newspapers continued to deliver the depressing news from overseas and to make it worse they reported German U-boats were now sinking unarmed ships in the Atlantic. Friends had differing and often wild opinions and, frustration turned to despair when soldiers returned with more horrific stories of poisonous gas attacks, although now prepared, the soldiers' use of gas masks had drastically reduced the number of casualties from that source.

Leaving work one bitterly cold afternoon in early January 1915, she watched as the requisitioned CPR steamship *Charlotte* docked in the harbour. *Tomorrow it will be leaving full of vibrant young men eager to fight for their country,* she thought sadly.

On her regular visit to the post office that morning one of Dan's letters arrived telling her his unit was being moved out the next day. The date of the letter was December 6th. Conjuring up pictures of the battlefront and then seeing the injured men sent her frantic and she hurried down to the dockside office where she tried to engross herself in bookwork for the next two hours.

Ezekiel, now fully recovered and swearing it was because of Sam's magic water, accompanied Jeb and Nancy on their January 29th run to Seattle. The wind was rising as they entered the sound making it a bitterly cold day that felt like snow could be on the way. Gritting her teeth against the biting spray, she thought of Gus' new boat and how nice the luxury of a totally enclosed cabin would be.

As they entered Ezekiel's cove, the men were ready and Jebediah was out on the bow even before she touched bottom. Leaping onto the sand, Zeke was right behind him. Over his shoulder the hermit carried a sack of food put together by Meg, and in his hand was a large cloth bundle of clean clothes, mostly cast-offs from Jeb. They cautiously made their way to the door of the cabin.

Nancy followed, walking across the logs but always keeping an eye out toward the sound. In the dull light she was still able to see the dark bloodstain on one of the logs but all other signs of Zeke's struggle with the cougar had been washed away. A cold shiver went up her spine as she thought of how lucky it was they had stopped that day.

Thankfully finding everything as he had left it, Ezekiel stowed his supplies and picked up his trusty rifle, looking pleased to have it in his hand again. Outside, they stopped to say goodbye and he turned to Nancy. She looked into the sad eyes underneath the bushy grey eyebrows and grasped his hand.

"I owe you, girl," he said, voice cracking with emotion. Then he let go of her hand and strode off into the woods.

Chapter 16

"Here she comes," announced Terry to his companion standing in the shadows. Then he sauntered down the dark gangway to meet them.

Terry's men had the unloading timed to a slick operation and their truck was soon leaving the dock. He waved toward the warehouse and the man, who had remained hidden, stepped out of the shadows. Jebediah's Winchester was up and ready in an instant. Nancy heard the ominous click of the hammer as he moved in front of her.

"Easy, Uncle Jeb," she cautioned, grasping his arm. "Terry seems to know he's there."

An easy laugh was heard as the man came toward them.

"Well, I'll be damned," Jeb murmured, seeing the tall silhouette of the young policeman he'd met in Seattle a couple years back. Uncocking his gun, he turned toward Nancy. "This is Sergeant Roy Olmstead, Seattle Police Department!"

"Off duty!" Roy added, chuckling again as he took Jebediah's hand. "Relax, old friend. I'm here to buy some information."

Roy Olmstead, well respected and, with many friends in high places, had long been studying the possibilities of the rum running business and had now begun some serious planning.

Recently, at an informal City Hall gathering, Mayor Hiram Gill had told him about Nancy and her association with the Jorgensen family. As a lover of the arts, Roy had listened intently when the mayor raved about the girl's singing abilities—his suspicions becoming aroused when Hiram flippantly told him that the beautiful redhead visited Seattle each Friday. He made a mental note and having a long-time acquaintance with Terry O'Reilly, arranged for an introduction.

"I need somebody to check out a safe anchorage up near Victoria," he explained. "Can you do that and how much will it cost me?"

"Shipping what?" asked Nancy, cautiously.

Her question left the policeman scrambling for words as he considered how much he should tell her.

"Booze, Nancy. Booze in large quantities," Terry quietly interceded. "And he'll be no competition for you, don't worry."

Save for the sound of gentle waves lapping the dock, a quietness settled over the conversation. As Nancy considered her answer she felt Jebediah's gently reassuring hand on her back.

"You'll need a supplier, too," she whispered, still cautious. "I could get you some contacts."

Not an easy man to fool, Roy would have liked to read Nancy's facial expression but she was in the shadows. He felt a strange confidence in this slip of a girl whom Terry had warned was a thinking woman. *Loyal, brave and resourceful,* he had said. *I'd willingly stake my life on her reputation.*

Roy reached into his pocket and drew out his wallet. Searching an inner fold, he slowly extracted five one-hundred dollar bills and handed it to her. "Will 500 cover it?" he asked, knowing it was, when she took the money.

Lightning flashed overhead followed by rolling thunder and the lights on the dock blinked but stayed on as rain began to fall heavily. Quickly finishing their conversation, Jeb and Nancy returned to the boat and the men hurried back to their cars.

"It's going to be a bad one after all," Jebediah reasoned aloud as Nancy started the engine.

And he was right. Wind battered the speedboat from every direction and the next flash of lightning sent the city of Edmonds into darkness. Waves constantly crashed against the hull spraying them until the interior of the boat was drenched.

The waters of the sound were occasionally lit up by jagged flashes, giving them an amazing show but making Jebediah terribly nervous. He was grateful that they were able to see the lighthouses at Point No Point, Marrowstone and Admiralty as they found their way out to the open water of Juan de Fuca.

He silently marvelled at the girl's ability to stay calm, read the beacons and keep them on course despite the ferocity of the storm and waves. After what seemed like an eternity, he gratefully recognized the lights of the Oak Bay waterfront. Peering out into the pitch darkness, he knew that Meg's lights were going to be a mighty welcome sight on this night.

"WE'RE HOME, UNCLE JEB," he heard her shout on the wind about three-quarters of an hour later.

Rubbing his eyes, he felt the sting of salt on raw, windblown cheeks. He wondered how on earth she knew when he couldn't see a damn thing! But she was right and five minutes later he saw the tiny flicker of one of Meg's little lights up on the hill, the others had probably blown out.

Finally back in the safely of their cove, Nancy pulled into the boathouse and with cold fingers they found their emergency lamp and tied the boat securely. Closing the door, they knew the boxes of meat would be safe there until morning. Carrying the lamp, she pulled Jeb toward the stairs and they fought the wind together, dragging each other to the top. Checking the now dark cliffside for Meg's lights they found them where they had been blown and gathering them up dashed for the house.

The warm rush of air took their breath away as they opened the kitchen and stood dripping water onto the floor.

"Out of those clothes right now!" Meg reacted, without even a greeting. "You must be frozen."

A short time later, they were sitting at the kitchen table in dry clothes, wolfing down Meg's hot soup.

"You should have stayed over in Seattle," she chided. "You know how dangerous these winter storms can be. Neither of you have the sense you were born with!"

"Oh, stop your worrying," said Jebediah. "Nancy's a hell of a sailor."

"Taught by the best," the girl replied, her eyes fastening on the empty chair at the end of the table. Meg's eyes met Jeb's across the table and she abruptly changed the subject telling them of a visit she'd had from Eva Todd and young Dorothy Poulton.

"And it was 14-year-old Dorothy who was driving the Cadillac!" she exclaimed. "Thomas taught her so she could help Eva."

"What did she want?" asked Nancy.

"They were collecting for the Red Cross Society," replied Meg. "I've offered to knit socks for the wounded soldiers."

There was a faraway look in the redhead's eyes as she rose and went to her coat in the hallway. From the pocket she removed the envelope from Terry and the bills Roy Olmstead had given her.

"This," she said quietly, pushing the extra money across the table to Meg, "is to help the war widows."

Meg's hand flew to her mouth. Muttering almost inaudibly, she asked, "But how will we find them? I don't know many of them at all."

"Jeb can take you over to the Salvation Army, they'll know," Nancy suggested. "And don't tell them where you got it."

With the storm passing in the night, all Nancy's tension evaporated as she motored toward Victoria early the next morning in the boat. She wasn't in a rush so she sat back and, not minding the chilly breeze on her face, she began to sing. Feeling alive and refreshed by the time she swept up the harbour to within sight of their dock she could see Waldo and Dumpy talking at the end of the jetty. The men took her lines and she turned off the engine.

"I have a question for you two," she announced. "Do you know of a place where I could leave a boat away from prying eyes and curious busybodies?"

"Telegraph Bay," Dumpy replied without hesitation, climbing into the boat and beginning to unload the meat, "near the dynamite factory."

"Don't you go near that place, girl," Waldo snapped. "You've got a great little harbour at Cunningham Manor, that's all you need."

"It's not for me," she laughed.

A knowing grin creased Waldo's lips as he straightened his pipe and rubbed his chin, staring unwaveringly at the redhead. He considered his next question carefully. "Friends of yours?"

"No."

"Then it's behind D'Arcy Island leper colony," he growled.

Stunned by the stark reality of Waldo's answer, they watched as he swung on his heel and stomped off up the boardwalk.

"He's right," she said softly. "Come on, let's get this meat delivered."

As they drove to the Balmoral, Nancy churned Waldo's suggestion over in her mind and resolved to take a closer look at D'Arcy Island. She'd only ever heard it referred to by people with fear in their voice as 'that leper colony off Sidney.' A few minutes later, she was talking to Kate and Mary when they heard a loud bang in the restaurant.

"Oh dear," Katherine sighed. "He's back again!"

"Who's he?" asked Nancy.

"Mr. Oliver from Oak Bay. This war has him really edgy. He thinks all the foreigners should be locked up," Katherine explained, heading toward the door.

"Beef is 12 1/2¢ a pound in the city now," Mary sighed. "It's gotten really expensive and perhaps we should be serving something else."

Deep in thought, Nancy left her and went into the office, followed by Dumpy and Katherine. Without saying a word, she took her invoice from her pocket and changed the price of the beef to 9¢ a pound.

"Not high enough," her friend muttered glancing over Nancy's shoulder.

"Don't be greedy," Nancy admonished with a sly smile. "We can still do a lot of good for the wounded soldiers with that money."

"You mean you're giving it away?" Katherine gasped.

A call from Mary gave the redhead a chance to escape further questions as Kate hurried off again to deliver an order.

Mary sighed as she watched Nancy leave. She was most familiar with Nancy's generosity; she had experienced it first hand.

"I need the boat at Gordon Head for a quick run in the morning," she told Dumpy as they drove to the dockside office. "Can you bring it around for me?"

"Sure thing, Nan," he said, climbing out and waving as she turned the truck around.

"I'll be waiting for you at ten then."

She waved, stepped on the accelerator and took the truck out onto Wharf Street. Even from a block away she had warning of the black smoke as it covered the area near the E&N Railway Station. Choking, she turned up Cormorant Street. A crowd of unemployed men waiting for food handouts filled the area in front of the Salvation Army. Feeling their heartbreaking despair simply by looking at their faces, she felt even better about her own war efforts. However, it made her sad to think she couldn't possibly help everyone.

As she came up to the corner of Quadra and Hillside, she noticed someone in the street directing traffic and realized it was one of the streetcar drivers whose boat they had brought in. He saw her and waved, grinning broadly. *Nothing serious by the look of it*, she thought, seeing the 'No. 6' stopped in the middle of the street.

At last she reached Cedar Hill and going around the corner she met up with Susan White and her children walking toward home. She tooted her horn and stopped briefly to talk with them.

Although it was winter with the leaves off many of the trees, she still loved this time of year because she could see more of the valley. She marvelled at the tenacity of the old farmers and noticed several working on their properties as she passed. Too old to go to war they were oftentimes out in the fields even on the coldest days mending fences or doing other repairs. She had heard some wonderful stories of these older folk of late. Some of them had generously given of their time to help their younger neighbours—neighbours whose husbands had left them with all the responsibilities of home and children when they left for Europe.

As she drove up to the house, she thought of Dan's orchard and wondered if it would ever be a reality. She parked and Meg came out on the porch to meet her.

"I called Eva this morning and within an hour that industrious woman had Dorothy bring her around. She already had a list of needy war widows ... how she got it so quickly I'll never know!"

Showing her the paper, Nancy poured over the heartbreaking list. There were already 43 names and 28 of them had children to feed.

"We'll start here." The redhead pointed to a name. "This poor lady has four little ones."

"We need more money, lass," Jeb lamented, coming to join them.

"We'll find a way," Nancy muttered determinedly. "You can add the meat money to the pot, that's another fifty dollars."

"Wait a minute," said the old detective. "I've got an idea, but I need to be in Seattle."

"Use the telephone!" Meg snapped.

Clamping his teeth on the stem of his pipe, Jebediah winked mischievously at the redhead and went off to the hall.

"Now what's he up to?" she asked.

"I have no idea, lass," the Scot replied. "Did you bring a newspaper?"

Laying the Colonist out on the table, they both became engrossed in their reading, glancing up at each other when they heard Jebediah's comment from the hallway.

"Oh, I'm sure she will," Jeb was saying into the phone before they heard the sound of the phone being put back on the hook.

When he walked into the kitchen and sat down he had a smug look on his face. The women looked up from their paper and waited.

"We're staying over in Seattle on Friday night," he said, chuckling. "You'll get all the money you need."

"How ...?" Nancy began.

"Beth is going to arrange for a concert at the James Moore Theatre," he said casually, "and they'll take a collection for your widows and children. Of course, I volunteered you and your voice to be the stars!"

"What a wonderful idea! I'm coming too," Meg exclaimed, her arm moving around the surprised girl's waist and pulling her close. "If you're singing I want to be there."

"Well, it sounds to me like I have absolutely no say in the matter," Nancy said solemnly, then a grin brightened her face and she ran and hugged Jebediah. "It's a wonderful idea, Uncle Jeb."

The rest of the afternoon the women shared each other's excitement talking about the concert, what it would be like and, how much she might make. After dinner they tried to establish the needs of each family on Eva's list and found that their $554 wouldn't go very far, when it had to be shared by so many.

"We're still sixteen dollars short," Nancy sighed. "And we only gave ten dollars for the women and five for each child."

"It's better than a barrel of sympathy, sweetheart," Jebediah growled, flicking a twenty dollar gold piece onto the table. "Some of them need it desperately."

"You're taking on too big a job, love," Meg wailed. "Let Eva handle some of it."

"All right, after the concert," said Nancy quietly. "We have to try it and see how it works. I can't imagine the Americans wanting to help Canadian families, but I can still remember when I was destitute and Dan tried to take care of me. We have to try, there are so many children who are suffering, it breaks my heart." She paused to wipe a tear from her eye. "I know Dan would want me to do it." She hastily opened the door and walked out onto the porch. She stared out to sea, her heart suddenly torn by loneliness, and she began to sob.

Jebediah jumped to his feet but stopped when he heard Meg's voice.

"Leave her, Jeb, sometimes we need to be alone to feel our pain. It's a woman thing."

"But damnit she'll freeze out there," he objected, picking up her wool shawl from the chair by the fire.

Meg smiled and let him go.

Nancy's arms were wrapped around one of the posts when she felt the shawl go over her shoulders. She suddenly realized how cold she was. Meg had followed Jeb outside and, as the girl turned to accept the shawl, his strong arms encircled them both and the three of them stood hugging for a moment.

"My word it's cold out here," she shivered, laughing through her tears. "I think we'd better go inside before we all freeze!"

Jeb closed the door behind them and they watched her in silence. She walked to the stairs and turned around.

"Thank … you," was all she managed, then she hurried up the stairs.

Meg followed her a while later and found her red-faced, sitting on the stool in front of her mirror. She had changed into her night-gown but had her brush in hand as if she had run out of energy. Meg took the brush and gently stroked it through the girl's long hair a few times then led her toward the bed. Tucking her in, she pulled the covers up to her chin and kissed her lightly on the forehead.

"Things have a way of working out, lassie, you'll see," she promised, touching Nancy's cheek affectionately.

"Thanks, Aunt Meg." She shut her eyes and Meg quietly left the room closing the door behind her.

Watching Meg come down the stairs, Jebediah knew from her expression, they were both sharing Nancy's pain. He suddenly realized that he had become a family man at last—his wild, free spirit being curbed by the love he felt for these special people who had taken him into their home.

Chapter 17

A knock at the kitchen door brought Nancy to her feet and she found Sam standing in the doorway. He pointed toward the water.

"What is it, lad?" Meg asked.

"Boat come," the old hermit announced.

"I'll go look," said Nancy getting up and going for her coat. "I'm expecting Dumpy. You feed Sam."

Going to the edge of the cliff, she was just in time to see the *Legal Limit* before it disappeared around the corner. *What did he want?* she wondered, scanning the jetty. Her eyes found the coil of rope on the boards. *Algy's returned my rope. And his boat is back in order.*

"Who was it?" Jeb asked from the porch.

"It was Algy returning our rope, but I thought it might be Dumpy, he's bringing the boat at ten. I've decided to take a look at the area around D'arcy Island for Roy Olmstead," she said quietly.

Jebediah was heading into the house and stopped in his tracks. He turned, raised his eyebrows, then continued into the house. Just before 10 o'clock, armed with the names and addresses of the widows they were going to visit, he and Meg left on their latest mission of mercy. It wasn't long before Nancy heard the familiar sound of their boat and she went down to meet Dumpy.

That's a cold wind today," he muttered when she stepped into the boat beside him. "Where are we going?"

"D'Arcy Island."

Dumpy's mouth dropped open and his face turned white. "That's the leper colony. I'd rather not, Nan," he replied.

She ignored him and took the helm. Out on the open water the speedboat bounced over the waves toward the group of islands just south of Sidney. Nearing the leper colony, she cut the engines to half speed and made a circular tour around the dangerous rock-strewn coast. They were two islands, D'Arcy and Little D'Arcy, and it didn't take long for her to realize Waldo had been right; a boat could easily hide here.

Dumpy winced when Nancy cut between the two islands. *An ideal spot for Roy Olmstead,* she thought, *and so close to both Haro Strait and the San Juan Islands.* As they passed, they noticed several of the poor souls watching them from the beach.

Despite the light chop and a biting wind in their faces, the short run was a refreshing interlude for the redhead. She had developed such a keen affection for the sea and the adventure it held, she didn't even mind the bad weather and no one knew it more than Dumpy.

"There's someone in the timber on the clifftop," he told her, as they stepped onto the dock.

"It's only Sam, he's the Indian hermit we've told you about."

"Want me to stay around for a while?" he asked, his eyes darting suspiciously up at the cliff.

"No, no, you head back to Victoria. Thanks for bringing the boat out … it was a rather painless trip, don't you think?" she teased.

While she ate lunch, she found some notepaper and drew a map for Roy. When she was finished, she decided to write a letter to Dan. She was so involved in what she was doing she barely heard Jebediah's car on the driveway. She went to look out the window and was surprised to see how dark it was, suddenly realizing why she was feeling hungry. Meg's unmistakeable laughter preceded her through the door. She put a newspaper-wrapped parcel down on the counter and Nancy looked up and grinned, already guessing its contents.

"We brought a treat from the British Fish and Chip Shop," Meg announced. "We were over on Broad Street so decided to stop. They'll probably need to be warmed up now. Is the stove still going?"

Lifting one of the plates, the girl peered inside at the coals. "Goodness, I'm afraid I was so engrossed in my letter to Dan, it's almost gone out, but I'll have it going in a jiffy." She put several sticks of wood inside then bent down and slid the warming oven door open. Placing the still wrapped fish and chips into the drawer, she shut it.

Twenty minutes later they were all sitting down to enjoy their treat. Meg and Nancy splashed malt vinegar liberally over the fried morsels sending a distinctive aroma floating around the kitchen. They began to eat using their fingers, licking the salty-vinegar residue off of them intermittently, but Jeb frowned and used his knife and fork. He watched them with interest for a few moments before deciding to copy them, first pouring a little vinegar over top.

"Is the use of fingers supposed to make this English food taste better? Hmm, it is rather good," he murmured in surprise.

The women laughed at him but continued eating, then laughed even harder when Jeb cleaned up the leftover bits still in the paper.

"Did you find all the families?" Nancy asked quietly, as they sat around the fire after supper.

Meg related several heart-wrenching stories of the widows they'd met and of tearful children who had lost their fathers. One woman had really touched their hearts when she refused their help, donating a $10 bill for their cause.

"And we've more of them to find tomorrow," Jeb mumbled.

"It's a heartbreaking job," Meg said sadly. "But we know it's appreciated—we can see it in their eyes."

On Wednesday, a dusting of snow greeted early morning travellers and Nan was glad of Malcolm's company as she cautiously drove into the city.

On Friday, she found herself getting quite excited in anticipation of her concert that evening in Seattle. She brought the speedboat home early to find Jebediah had everything down on the dock ready to be loaded. He had also been to see Harry Maynard who willingly provided a list of liquor merchants for Roy Olmstead. By 2 o'clock they were loaded and Jeb went back to the house to help Meg down the stairs.

Terry and Roy were on the Seattle dock waiting for them. After tying up the boat and helping Meg disembark, Nancy went over to the men and handed the sergeant an envelope.

"I've drawn you a map of the location you were asking for and there's also a list of liquor suppliers," she explained.

He thanked her and left quickly. Terry herded them toward a waiting car assuring her his men would unload and bring the boat around to Gus' private dock. It was 5 o'clock when the car arrived at the Jorgensen's. Beth answered the door and enthusiastically greeted them calling Louie to deliver their bags to their rooms.

"Dinner is waiting in the dining room. It's only a light meal as we'll be eating at a reception after the concert. You eat what you feel like, dear. I know singers don't like to eat a lot before a performance. After dinner, you'll have time for a shower, if you like, and your clothes are in your room."

"I haven't seen Gus. Is he not at home?" asked Jebediah, as they entered the dining room.

"He had some business downtown so he'll meet us at the theatre," replied Beth.

After eating, Nancy and Meg immediately went upstairs to their rooms. This time, being familiar with the routine, Nancy's shower was much more relaxing and she truly enjoyed the luxury. Dressing again in

160

the beautiful gown Beth had bought her for Christmas she was brushing her hair when there was a tap at the door.

"You look stunning, dear," their hostess exclaimed. "How are you feeling, dear?"

"I'm feeling just fine ... a little excited though, I think," Nan replied.

Meg came in behind her and going over to the dresser took the brush from Nancy and finished brushing her hair, a job she loved but didn't often get the opportunity to do.

"We're expected at the theatre in 30 minutes. Are we ready to leave?" asked Beth.

"Yes, I'm ready," said Nancy, patting a bit of pink powder onto her cheeks and standing up.

"Me too," sang Meg, linking her arm. "Isn't this so exciting!"

In the foyer, Joseph, helped them into their coats and, noticing Beth's fur coat, Meg gently touched it commenting on its softness.

"It's mink," she explained. "Gus had one of his business colleagues bring it from New York. It's lovely and warm for winter."

Parked under the porté cochére, Peter was waiting and greeted them each by name as he helped them into the Chrysler. The short ride into the city through the gaudy fairyland of lights gave Meg another thrill, just like her first visit to Seattle only weeks before.

"I've never seen so many lights," she exclaimed, reading all the illuminated advertising boards along the way.

Pacing the foyer at the theatre, Gus waited impatiently for his wife and their guests to arrive.

"They're here, Mr. Jorgensen," the doorman announced from the curb.

"Take her through, Beth," Gus croaked with anticipation, giving Nancy a quick hug and wishing her luck. "Curtain's in 15 minutes and the place is packed."

After they had hurried away, he ushered Meg and Jebediah up the stairs to James Moore's private box. The vantage point was fabulous and the stage so close Meg stood mesmerized until Jeb took her arm and persuaded her to sit down. At center stage, behind a wispy white curtain, stood a magnificent, white grand piano. There was only a single muted light on the stage but below in the orchestra pit the small concert orchestra was tuning their instruments. Making some incredible sounds, they readied themselves under the watchful eye of a young man playing a violin. In a minute, he tapped his baton several times on the

161

music stand and the musicians put down their instruments. Noises in the theatre became hushed as the lights went down.

From the wings at stage left the maestro entered. Shaking hands with his assistant who handed him the baton and sat down, he bowed low to the crowd. Looking resplendent in a black tuxedo suit with tails, the audience greeted the popular conductor with enthusiastic applause.

Lights in the theatre dimmed and a spotlight shone onto the curtains. Another man also dressed in a tuxedo and tails walked out and stopped at center stage. Recognizing the owner of the theatre, the crowd again roared their approval.

"Good evening, friends and music lovers. I think you will agree we have a special treat for you tonight," he began. "For your pleasure, we have a young Canadian singer with us from Victoria. She is virtually unknown here in Seattle, but our highly esteemed pianist, Nellie Cornish, and I assure you she's one of the most refreshing and talented singers we have heard in recent years. At the intermission and after the concert, there will be a collection box in the foyer in aid of Victoria's war widows and orphans. Please show your appreciation and give generously."

James Moore paused and the audience waited expectantly. Then he flung his arm out toward the wing. "PLEASE WELCOME, NANCY WILSON."

A murmur ran through the audience as the redhead walked confidently onto the stage with Nellie close behind. Polite applause greeted them at first, swelling to a lively crescendo as everyone joined in encouraged by Mr. Moore who was still onstage.

They walked over to center stage, bowed to the audience, then made their way to the piano. Nellie spoke briefly to her as she set up her music and Nancy stood in the crook of the piano resting her arm on the gleaming white surface until the applause subsided. The conductor tapped the baton lightly on his lectern.

Nellie winked at Nancy and whispered, "Sing your heart out, love!" before beginning the short introduction to their first song.

And Nancy did … singing straight from her heart. As the lovely sounds of the attractive Canadian's voice shattered the stillness of the concert hall, the elite of Seattle sat up and took notice. After several songs, Nancy noticed the smile on the face of the conductor just before he turned around and held up his arms to get the attention of the audience.

"LIGHTS PLEASE," he called. "I think we should give this angel a rest."

The lights went up, the orchestra left their seats and, Nellie and Nancy went backstage as the clapping died away. Beth met them holding two cups of hot tea. In a moment, James Moore was also at Beth's elbow extolling the virtues of the performance causing Nancy to blush.

Meanwhile, trays of drinks were being brought down the aisle for those who remained in their seats but many decided to stretch their legs and moved out to the foyer. The noise level seemed to have risen to a feverish pitch as guests talked favourably of the girls' performance.

Ten minutes later, the lights dipped and James went out to center stage again.

"A MOMENT OF YOUR TIME, PLEASE, BEFORE WE CALL NANCY BACK," he called out as people returned to their seats. "Mrs. Albert Rhodes has offered a suggestion, but first, are you enjoying the performance tonight?"

No answer was necessary as many clapped and cheered.

"Thank you, I am so pleased and, since you are, Mrs. Rhodes thinks we should take up a collection right now, so we'll be passing around some containers in case you missed them in the foyer. Meanwhile," he said, pretending to be secretive, "I'll try to coax Nancy to sing a few more songs for us."

This last comment was met with laughter and scattered applause.

Nancy sang five more songs to an attentive audience before Nellie called a halt fearing the inexperienced singer would damage her voice. Holding hands, they stood side by side, to accept the appreciation and wild applause.

"You've made an impression on Seattle tonight, Nancy," Nellie told her as she led the way backstage. "But then I knew you would, I know Seattle!"

Leaving the theatre by the back door, the women were met by Peter with the car. Driving around to the front entrance they picked up the others and squished in like sardines, were whisked away to a restaurant owned by Charles Blanc. Here, Nancy was surprised by the sumptuous supper buffet, obviously laid on for the occasion. Nellie sat opposite Nancy who was placed beside James Moore. He laughingly admitted he'd made more money tonight than he had in the whole of January.

Gus noticed Nancy's startled expression and knew she had better manners than to ask.

"Alcohol!" he whispered, winking at her. "The crafty devil sold thousands of drinks tonight."

"It's a win-win situation," the theatre owner laughed. "When can we do it again?"

"Well, next month I suppose, on one condition," Nancy replied softly, looking at Beth across the table. "Each time I come and sing, I'd like a donation to be made to Nellie's school of music."

"How much?" asked James.

"Five hundred dollars," she said boldly.

"It's a deal," James replied, without hesitation.

Nellie looked shocked at the sudden turn of events. Her little school for the arts was always desperately short of money and this windfall would help immensely.

"Thank you, James ... and Nancy," said Nellie, feeling her colour rise. Giggling she added, "I hope you come often!" causing those nearby to laugh.

Terry O'Reilly suddenly appeared, going over to whisper in the ship owner's ear as he set a leather satchel at his feet. He nodded to the group and left quickly.

Later, when they were all relaxing over a cup of Beth's favourite tea blend in their private apartment, Gus casually handed the case to Nancy.

"Well, young lady, I'd say that your evening has been most rewarding."

"We got some donations?" Nancy asked wearily.

"Donations? I have six thousand, four hundred and forty-one dollars in donations for you, my dear!" the millionaire chuckled.

"What!" Nancy squealed, her eyes opening wide as she sat bolt upright. "Aunt Meg, we can help all those families now!"

"Nancy," Beth murmured from across the room. "We're so proud of you. Not many would be able to do what you have done tonight."

"Beth is right and we are all terribly proud of you, lassie," Meg whispered, holding out her arms as Nancy came to give her a hug. "You're my darling angel!" she said happily.

Winter sunshine streamed through the mansion windows the next morning and chatter at the breakfast table was all aimed at Nancy's next engagement at the James Moore Theatre.

"That's the 26th of February," Beth murmured as the Canadians prepared to leave. "You can leave your dress here, but I'll go shopping for a new one."

164

"No, you don't have to do that," Nancy objected.

"Oh yes she does. It's a wonderful excuse for shopping you know!" Gus chuckled. "You're going to become an institution in Seattle, my girl, one of our own homegrown stars and you can't wear the same dress twice in a row."

"But I'm a Canadian!" she replied.

"That doesn't matter. You started right here in Seattle," he laughed. "That makes you one of our own and the sooner people think that the better!"

Down at the dock, two servants were loading boxes of meat into the speedboat as the party walked down the path toward the water. Behind it stood the new boat *Stockholm,* its brightly painted red-and-gold paint shimmering in the winter sunshine.

"They're doing more trials today," Gus announced, "should be ready for you by April."

Walking over to take a closer look, Nancy began to talk to the two mechanics, deducing from their conversation they were trying to fit her with brakes … something never tried before on this type of engine.

"We call that an anchor in Victoria," she giggled.

"No, no," the Swedish technician wagged his finger. "It can be done, and it will give you a tremendous advantage if you have to suddenly stop moving."

You're darned right it will, Nancy thought to herself as she hurried back to the blue boat realizing they were waiting for her. She hugged the Jorgensens and went to take the satchel from Gus who had carried it down to the dock. She expected it to be heavy but it surprised her.

Gus grinned. "We changed the coin, and the paper into smaller denominations. It was awfully heavy and we didn't want Jeb to strain himself carrying it up your steps!"

They all laughed as she climbed into the boat and put on her heavy coat, glancing over at Meg who looked quite cozy in the back. Coat buttoned to the neck and hat pulled down over her ears, she slipped on her warm gloves and nodded to Gus and Beth who were waiting to cast off the lines. Jeb sat down beside her and she eased back on the throttle, waving to their special friends who stood arm-in-arm waving to them.

"That young lady is quite a sailor," exclaimed Hans, one of the technicians, watching her thread her way through the boating traffic until she was out of sight.

"Do you think she'll be able to handle it all right?" asked Beth.

165

"She'll be fine, Mrs. Jorgensen," Sven, his partner, replied. "We'll make sure she gets a few lessons before she takes it out alone. Don't worry, we've put the best of everything in that boat to protect her, just as you requested."

"Thanks, boys. I couldn't bear it if anything happened to that girl." Gus took his wife's arm and steered her toward the house.

A few weekend boaters were out on the water despite the cold, enjoying a break in the drab winter weather, as Nancy made her way down the sound to Zeke's cove. She blew the secret call and almost immediately he came out of his cabin and waved to them.

"He's still alive, Aunt Meg, despite your doctoring!"

Getting closer, Jeb stood up in the boat. "We're on our way home, old friend," he called. "We thought we'd come by and check on you."

Limping out into the shallow water in his gumboots and, despite their protestations, Ezekiel shook their hands and thanked them profusely. His pleasure at seeing them was unmistakable.

"We have to go," said Nancy. "Is there anything you need, Zeke?"

"Not a thing, love," he replied, "nice to see you though and I'll only ask that you keep coming back!" Then he waved and started back to shore. At the edge of the water he waved again, watching them until they went through the trees.

Back in the open waters Nancy sent the blue craft speeding up the Puget Sound then turned toward Victoria. When they entered the harbour, strains of a military band were heard coming from the lawn of the Parliament Buildings.

Dumpy was watching a troopship at the CPR dock when his gaze strayed to the Empress boathouse. *Strange*, he thought, i*t looks closed. Johnny Schnarr must have left for greener pastures like many others.* Hearing the familiar sound of Nancy's motor he realized they had come in without him noticing. Catching the lines from Jebediah, Dumpy tied the boat up and helped them unload the meat.

Meg followed Jebediah into the office. He had the satchel clutched firmly in his hand, stoically guarding Nancy's money. Dumpy and Nancy went to deliver the meat and when they returned they all climbed into the Model T leaving the boat with Dumpy.

As they left the city, they could see hundreds of people lined up along the harbour waving to the soldiers leaving on the troopship. A tearful young woman walked by, pushing a perambulator, as two older children walked beside her. Nancy sighed. *The reality of war has struck another family.*

Chapter 18

From a water-filled trench outside of Neuve Chapelle, France, Dan watched the team of horses approach as they pulled his big gun through the mire and into position. Mud and puddles were everywhere. It had been raining for days in this area but the Canadians had only arrived.

His men, and thousands of others, had grown used to the weather having just spent the last four months at the Salisbury Plains training camp in England. There, life had been unbelievably dismal, living in damp, mouldy tents and training on cold, rain-sodden ground, but the Canadians proved they had an unquenchable spirit of courage and willingness—fortunate, for this was pure luxury compared to that which they would experience in the next few hours.

As they had approached the outskirts of the once peaceful little village, Sgt. Dan Brown realized this was not going to be quite what they had expected. Fifteen battalions of British and Canadian soldiers now converged on this area across the English Channel. It appeared to be the edge of No Man's Land but nothing would daunt their spirits. They had been training for so long, both in Canada and England, these eager young men wanted to get on with their job so they could finish and go back home.

Dan pulled his helmet down over his eyes, fastening it under his chin. Grasping his rifle firmly he dragged his weary body out over the lip of the protective trench they had dug that morning from the remains of a previous battle. They would be calling this trench home for the next few days—those who survived that long.

A few yards farther, he leaned against the wheel of his division's cannon and looked through his glasses for the telltale flash of enemy guns. Across the flat wasteland pocked with shell holes and stark, vague reminders of fences and house foundations, he could see what he thought were German trenches—beyond were the houses of the village. He raked the nearby slits in the ground with his field glasses and saw a bayonet pop up with a dirty handkerchief tied to its tip. Lieutenant Bob Dolling, a special friend, was saying hello.

Two flashes suddenly rent the air through the morning fog, giving away the location of the German guns. The shells landed short but as they exploded they kicked up a great shower of mud covering everything in its path including some of his men. Not moving, Dan's gun crew waited for his orders. Their ex-whaler sergeant had impressed them all at Salisbury and now he was going to prove his worth.

By instinct Dan set the adjustments and lined up the target allowing for the weather. "ON MY SIGNAL ... LET HER FLY!"

Thirty seconds later, he lowered his arm and the boom told him the shell was on its way—the guns all around followed suit. With glasses fixed on his target he first heard the whine, then the explosion, followed quickly by a second explosion, a third .... he knew in his heart he'd killed for the first time and he tried not to think about it. There would be lots more killing before the day was over.

They moved forward inch by inch. This battle had only begun and Sgt. Brown's unit, like many others, would experience a true baptism of fire on this 10th day of March, 1915. They continued their relentless hammering at each other, loading and setting, shots rang all around them and several of his men were hit—medics running in with stretchers adding to the confusion. He wondered how the other divisions were doing.

Suddenly, he raised his head and listened carefully as a new sound penetrated his brain. It had an ominous whine and it was coming closer. He barely had time to yell, "TAKE COVER," as he flung himself into the nearest hollow in the ground ... no more than a dimple.

The next thing he saw was Nancy standing beside him holding his hand. He thought he was home but later when he regained consciousness he realized he was in a field hospital with many other wounded soldiers. Propped up on one side, a tremendous pain seared through his back as he tried to move. A medic told him he was the only one who had survived the direct hit on their gun emplacement.

"You're a lucky one, lad," the man quipped before hurrying away.

Apart from some shrapnel in his back he had sustained no other major injuries. He thought of his men and the families who would never see them again and then he remembered his friend, Bob Dolling, and feared he hadn't been so lucky. *Lucky,* he thought. *I'm the lucky devil who lives to go out there and kill again. Perhaps it was the others who were lucky!*

* * *

Dawn was breaking at Cunningham Manor when Nancy awoke. She groaned as a pain shot up her back even before she rolled over. Opening her eyes, a vision of Dan flashed on the ceiling above her. "He's been hurt," she whispered as the image changed and she watched spellbound as a soldier lay in the mud, his uniform in tatters and his back covered in blood. Suddenly, a ray of sunshine burst into the room from beneath a corner of the window shade, and the pain in her back floated away. Relief flooded through her as the picture faded, instinctively knowing Dan was all right.

Her hands shook a little while eating breakfast, not quite sure if she'd imagined it all. She couldn't help but wonder if Dan was sending these messages or …?

"Did you have a good night, lass, or were you dreaming again?" Meg asked softly.

"Dan's been hurt," she whispered. "He sent me a message."

Meg looked at her in surprise, wanting to ask more but knowing Nancy would tell her when she was ready. Long ago she'd had just such an experience and she knew it was private and personal.

The following Sunday afternoon, Eva Todd's black Cadillac came down the drive at Cunningham Manor. Dorothy was at the wheel. Nancy was now quite aware that her friend had a reputation of being a tireless worker when any good cause arose. Not having seen her for some weeks, Nancy suspected Eva would have found a way to continue her personal crusade. Since becoming involved in the war effort, her desire had been to help the needy women of Victoria who either had men overseas or had been widowed by the war and Nan suspected this had not changed.

"Haven't seen you all in awhile, but a couple of folks at church mentioned you on Sunday and I thought we should stop by," she began, giving the women a hug. "Yesterday I called on a Cedar Hill woman who'd been recently widowed and she told me in glowing terms how Meg and Jebediah's charitable contributions had helped her family. And they're not the only ones you're helping, are they?" said Eva, looking at them suspiciously. "But where in heaven's name are you suddenly finding all the money?"

"We'd better tell her," suggested Jeb, "this thing's getting too big for us, Nancy."

Over tea, they told their visitors the story of Nancy's singing for the elite of Seattle. When they explained how the collection was taken for

Victoria's widows and orphans, Eva dabbed at her eyes with her handkerchief.

"I had no idea," she gasped, "although Algy Pearce did tell me you go to Seattle every Friday."

"How does he know?" Nancy asked, catching Jebediah's eye.

"It's his job to watch the shipping, he works for the military," Eva replied, shrugging her shoulders. "Now, how can I help?"

Over the next few years, the close association that developed between Eva Todd and the family at Cunningham Manor became legendary among the growing list of widows and wounded soldiers— their humanitarian efforts spreading a much-appreciated measure of comfort to Victoria's needy. Even though Nancy's voice provided the revenue, in the early days this fact remained a closely guarded secret among a trusted few in Victoria.

At lunch on the 22nd day of March, Nancy's daily visit to the post office finally brought her some news of Dan … although it wasn't quite what she was expecting. As the clerk handed her the envelope she saw the dreaded military insignia in the left corner rather than Dan's handwriting. Glancing up at the clerk she saw the sad look in the woman's eyes and she grabbed the letter and ran from the building.

She didn't stop running until she reached the top of the boardwalk at Wharf Street, her heart was beating fearfully. She stopped, knowing she had to calm herself before seeing Dumpy. She looked down at the envelope. There were no other markings on it. *How could the clerk know it was bad news? It can't be bad news. Dan would have sent me a message … or had he?*

Gathering her courage, she put her little finger into the small open corner and ripped. It was a single sheet of folded paper. It looked very official because it was typewritten. Her heart was beating so hard she thought it was going to pop out of her chest.

Dear Miss Wilson,

This letter is to inform you, as next of kin to Sergeant Daniel Brown, that Sergeant Brown recently sustained an injury and is convalescing in hospital. These injuries are not life threatening and he is expected to return to his duties in approximately six weeks.

The rest of the letter was a blur as she slumped against the railing and took a deep breath. Looking out over the harbour at the view she and Dan had shared so many times, she wondered what sort of injuries could keep him out of action for six weeks. Then she quickly shook herself. *I can't possibly imagine what they are so there is no use making myself sick about it. They said he will be back to his duties, which means he will be writing to me soon. I know he will.*

She slipped the letter into her pocket and carried on down to the office deciding not to say anything to anyone for the time being.

The following Tuesday, as she had fervently hoped, a letter from Dan arrived. It had been the worst week of her life, waiting without telling anyone of her fears. Opening the envelope shakily, she first noticed how illegible Dan's writing was. Her heart skipped a beat as she again imagined all the terrible things that could have happened to him. Hardly having the courage to read she wondered if the military had lied to her. Her eyes scanned the page quickly for key words ... *pieces of metal ... lodged in my back ... bedridden ... not able to feed myself ... frustrating ... friends dead ... sat up yesterday ... hold a pen ... miss you ... going back ... two more weeks ... love you ... miss you.*

The words jumped off the page at her but she knew now that he was all right. The worst of it was that they had been right, he wasn't coming home. She read it more carefully this time.

The pieces of metal lodged in his back had all been successfully removed. A wry smile crossed her face as she realized she had been right that cold frosty morning when she awoke with searing pain in her back. She knew that her subconscious lifeline to Dan was still working.

By the time the daffodils bloomed in early April, the gardens of Victoria were producing a wonderful carpet of colour which added to the welcome displays of snowdrops and crocuses. Gardeners emerged from their homes and everyone knew that spring had come at last. Nancy welcomed the breathtaking sight of nature's beauty. She felt her spirits lift as the warmer weather and longer hours of daylight helped to make her long drive back and forth to town more enjoyable.

Jack Duggan was sitting in his truck waiting for her after work one evening.

"Hi Nan, have you given any more thought to that orchard of yours?"

"I'm afraid not, Jack, Danny mentions it once in a while in his letters though. I think it will have to wait until he returns."

"I could finish the clearing for you—I seem to remember that many of the trees were removed when we built the house," he continued. "The big job will be getting the roots out."

"Are you not working?"

"Oh sure, love, Parfitt Brothers is building the new Armoury on Bay Street, but they won't need me for a couple of weeks later on in the month and that will be plenty of time to get the boys onto it."

"Oh Jack, that would be wonderful. I could write to Dan and tell him. He'd be so pleased."

"Good, I need some exercise," lied the Irishman, "so you just leave it up to me. I'll arrange the men and horses. You just tell me where you want it and how big. We'll worry about payment later."

"Thanks Jack, you're a good friend. Why don't you and Nellie come for dinner on Sunday? It's been too long since we've seen you."

"I know Nellie would like that," he grinned.

"See you at 5 o'clock then and thanks, Jack."

Tipping his hat, he started his engine. *Nellie will be pleased,* he thought as he waved and the truck bounced off the dock.

Dumpy, hearing the noise came out of the office. "You're late tonight, Nan," he exclaimed, then before she could reply he began to grumble that they needed another boat to take advantage of the weekend trade which was growing with the warm weather.

A thought suddenly struck her. Gus had been quite evasive when she asked about the new boat and she couldn't seem to get them off her mind this week. *I wonder if they're planning a visit?* "Quit your moaning, Dumpy. It's surprising how things work out. You'll see," she said. "Now be a good man and give the T a crank for me, will you?"

All the way home her thoughts tumbled about in her mind. The strange feeling persisted that Beth and Gus were either close at hand or soon would be.

Deep in thought, she almost missed Malcolm as he stepped from the 'No. 6' streetcar on Hillside—if their schedules coincided, she often gave him a lift home at night. Climbing in beside her, he chatted enthusiastically of his strawberry plants, farming, and his dreams of giving up the back-breaking work at the shipyard. He loved to work the land and dearly wanted to do it fulltime. He asked of Dan's welfare and generously offered to help Jack with the clearing for the orchard.

"You haven't got time to spit with your workload," Nancy laughed, as she stopped at Feltham to let him out. With the warmer weather, he now insisted on walking partway home. "Thanks for your kind offer

172

though, Malcolm. You're a good man. Jack says he'll have no trouble finding the necessary workers." She pipped the horn and moved off.

A chilly wind was blowing down the drive and in the shade of the trees the lights of the house were a welcome sight.

Meg's keen ears heard the truck and she put her finger to her lips. "She's home, stand over there out of the light," she instructed her guests.

Quick steps sounded on the porch just before the redhead stepped inside and banged the door behind her. A faint but familiar odour of perfume drifted out to meet her. She hung up her coat in the hall and dashed into the kitchen.

"They're here! I know they're here," she squealed. "I can smell them!"

"Smell who?" Jeb asked, frowning and trying hard to look surprised.

"GUS AND BETH!" she screeched, racing into the living room. Finding them standing quietly in the corner, she embraced them fiercely and began to chatter excitedly about her premonition. "You've brought the new boat, haven't you?" she asked expectantly.

"Yes, we have," Beth laughed, "and the expert to show you how to run it. You remember Sven Sorensen, Nan?"

It was then Nancy realized that sitting off to one side in the darkened room was the man who had talked to her about the boat that night on the Seattle dock. She welcomed him warmly, then answering Meg's call, she led them into the dining room. Meg had put a leaf in the large table tonight and there was still plenty of room.

Over dinner, Mr. Sorensen went into great detail on the *Stockholm*'s secret features—its four powerful and secret cannons that worked with a flick of a switch to spray buckshot over a great distance.

"We got that idea from your little boat," the engineer said with a grin. "But then we refined it and put two on each side. The *Stockholm*, my girl, is one of a kind. It's also got brakes that will stop you on a button, although it has no propeller or rudder."

"Then how does it drive forward or turn?" Jeb snorted.

"Water power," the Swede grinned, "and a swivelling nozzle."

"Leave it alone, Jeb," Gus laughed. "It's a totally new concept and it takes a bit of understanding. We'll show you tomorrow."

That evening Cunningham Manor rocked with laughter for the first time in months as the men traded hilarious stories of boating experiences. Just before they retired to their rooms, Beth modelled her new winter coat, quilted inside with the down of a goose.

"It's wonderfully warm and so cozy and light," she told them, hugging the coat around her causing a ripple of admiration from the women. "My fur is so heavy."

Nancy had trouble sleeping that night and, as she drove into the city next morning, her mind was still full of exciting thoughts between Dan's news, the new boat, and her next trip to Seattle. As she turned into Store Street, the truck skidded on the tramlines damp with dew. She heard the rattle of the rice mill and knew that they had been working through the night again. Heavy smoke, from two railway engines standing at the Johnson Street station, made her sneeze as sulphur-laden clouds filled the car.

Dumpy, seeing her go by as he walked to work, yelled and she waved him to hurry. She parked the truck and got out as he ran down to meet her.

"You're early, is something wrong?" he asked.

"No, something is right!" she exclaimed as they went into the office. "I have a new boat. It's out at the cove. You can keep the blue one here from now on. I told you things would work out."

"You must have known about it. Where did it come from?" he asked eagerly, stirring up the stove's few red embers causing them to burst into flame when he added a bit of kindling.

"It's a runabout," she answered coyly. "You'll see it one of these days."

"Well I've some news of my own," Dumpy muttered. "I think you'd better sit down."

Nancy looked at him doubtfully but did as she was told.

"Katherine and me ... are getting married."

"When?" she gasped.

"Last day in July. I think it's the 31st. Can Dan get home?"

Shaking her head, Nancy now fumbled for words. "That's wonderful, Dumpy. I'm so glad you decided not to wait." She was both glad and envious of her friends. Redfern's clock began to strike the hour, reminding her she had to get going. "I've got to go," she exclaimed, jumping to her feet. "I'm really happy for you." As she hurried toward work, a smile lit up her face. *I can't wait to see Kate!*

It was young Dick, the newspaper vendor, who almost wiped the smile from her face with his news of the latest mayhem in Europe. She ran quickly by arriving at the back door of the hotel breathing hard.

174

Seeing Mary and Katherine soon put the smile back on her face when she joyously hugged her friends.

"Dumpy just told me your news! Has she told you, Mary? They're getting married!" she cried, joyously.

"There have been no firm arrangements made yet," Katherine retorted, blushing a little. "There's his mum and my grandparents to consider."

"Easy," Nancy chortled. "Get one big house and all live together!"

Kate frowned and ran off to serve her customers.

All morning Nancy watched the glum faces of city traders as they trooped in and out of the restaurant. Overhearing snippets of their conversations, she realized that business was not looking good in Victoria. Groups of disgruntled workers, now on strike, roamed the streets adding to the city's feeling of uncertainty. One voice even suggested he could feel violence in the air.

The unpopular conservative government of Sir Richard McBride was being loudly blamed for all the trouble. Passing more legislation on concentration camps for enemy aliens and seemingly endless talk about prohibition only added to the public's frustration. The premier was often absent and left the running of the province to Bowser, his deputy—Bowser, who had become a vocal proponent of liquor restrictions for the many freewheeling saloons in the city.

"Food prices are rising and the city's almost bankrupt," Sergeant Walker commented. "There's bound to be trouble."

Nancy's mind refused to dwell on the unhappy situation, choosing to think more of her new boat and her friends' engagement. The office was empty and Dumpy had left a note on the table for her. *We got a new customer and I had to go out to Metchosin. Lock up when you leave.*

It was Friday so she decided to leave immediately thinking about the evening ahead of her. They were taking the Jorgensens back home tonight but the real exciting part was that she was going to get her first chance to try out the new boat. She checked the fire, locked up and went out to the truck. Cranking the handle, the truck coughed briefly but refused to start. She turned the crank again and again, to no avail.

"Darn it anyway," she muttered in frustration, kicking a tyre before resetting the controls and trying again. This time the Model T sputtered with life and she let out a sigh of relief. "Don't you dare quit on me," she threatened, pounding the steering wheel as she climbed in.

Calling at Plimley's curbside pump for gasoline, she told the mechanic her problem. She got out and watched as he lifted the engine hoods and tinkered for a moment on each side. Then he went into the shop and came back with a brush and told her he was cleaning the spark plugs. Pulling the covers back in place he grinned at her.

"The engine will be fine for a while now, Nancy. Go on, get yourself home," he said kindly, holding the door open.

"Thanks Gordon, see you next time," she said, as the engine started easily.

"I hope it won't be too soon," he teased, patting the fender.

At home, Jebediah and Gus had increased the load of liquor she usually carried, stowing it all out of sight in the roomy, specially designed hold of the *Stockholm*. Sven tried to explain to Jeb some of the features he'd built into the new boat, but Jeb waved him away with a scowl.

"Don't tell me," he growled, "you'd better save it for Nancy."

Excitement began to overtake the redhead as the truck reached their gate and bounced along the drive up to the house. Her eyes roamed over the tall stand of trees behind the house that Jack would soon be removing. Beth came to meet her at the door. Hugs were exchanged and Meg announced that the meal was going on the table.

"Jeb, would you please go call the men. They may not have heard Nancy arrive," asked Meg.

A few minutes later all three of them appeared. Sven took his seat opposite Nancy eager to talk to her about the new boat.

At last dinner was over and they were ready to leave. They said their goodbyes and the group headed down the stairs to the dock. Meg's proud, but lonely figure, stood on the cliff and waved as Nancy stood at the helm.

The first thing Nan noticed was that there was room for all four of them in the cabin and they didn't have to yell to talk to each other anymore. As they sailed through the open waters to Port Townsend she put the sleek craft through its paces. With Sven beside her, she marvelled at its instant response to her touch. She tried out the guns on a deadhead floating dangerously low in the water, instantly blowing it to pieces with buckshot. Sven clapped his hands and grinned. Then he alerted the passengers to hold on.

"Try your brakes!" he commanded.

Bracing herself, she threw the brake and felt a tremendous shudder run through the vessel as the forward motion stopped dead.

"Holy hell!" Jebediah cried as his body squashed tight to the back of the cabin.

"Wow!" Nancy exclaimed, glancing at the Swede.

"If you want to go backwards now," he added, "you simply use your throttle. To go forward, take the brake off and use everything as normal."

"You're a genius," Nancy whispered, laughing when Sven nodded his agreement.

"Take us home, love," the shipowner murmured, "and tuck it away in the boathouse."

Nancy was elated. She was not only thrilled with the power of the large speedboat, she now felt a lot safer.

"Easy girl," Gus murmured as they neared home.

"I've got brakes!" she chuckled, slowing down and easing around the pilings.

Accepting a hand down from Gus, Nancy following Beth onto the jetty and the women walked hand-in-hand to the edge of the lawn happily discussing Nancy's next performance on the 23rd of April.

"James tells me people are scrambling for seats," Beth giggled. "You've become quite the celebrity, dear."

"What about your boys, Beth?" asked Nancy, stopping to look squarely at her. "You haven't mentioned them. Are they still in England?"

"Yes, still in hospital, love, but we've booked our passage to Britain to see them. We'll be travelling on the *Lusitania* on the 1st of May. I simply can't wait. We've been frightfully worried about them."

Servants came hurrying from the house and were put to work emptying the boat of its illicit cargo and stacking it on the dock under cover. Beth went on into the house and Nancy went back to see how the men were making out. When she saw the number of boxes being unloaded, her eyes widened with surprise.

"There are 160 cases here," Gus told her, chuckling at her expression. Then, hearing footsteps, they all turned to see Terry coming toward them.

"That's two thousand dollars!" Nancy whispered.

"That's right love," Gus agreed. "Pay her," he said to the gangster, "and remember what you said."

Cocking an eyebrow, Terry had a mischievous glint in his eyes as he produced an envelope, thick with money, and handed it to her. On top, under his thumb, were two $50 bills.

177

"What's that for?" she asked.

"My personal contribution to your widows' fund," he murmured.

"If there's anything I can't stand, it's a reformed crook," laughed Jebediah. "See the effect you have on some men, Nancy!"

Terry looked so crestfallen by Jeb's comment they all burst into laughter. Then the noise of a battered old fishing boat coming toward them caught their attention.

"Here comes your meat," Terry announced.

"My word, is this your new undercover boat?" asked Gus incredulously, shaking his head.

"Well ya gotta admit it had you fooled, didn't it, boss!" the gangster replied, grinning.

When the boat pulled up to the dock, two burly men in sleeveless singlets appeared—their bulging muscles and almost naked upper torsos making Nancy blush, having rarely seen men without their shirts on. One man jumped onto the dock nearby and she scurried out of his way. He easily tossed the heavy boxes to his partner and in no time the 160 cases were neatly stacked and covered aboard the fishing boat.

Gus went over to talk to Terry's man briefly then, with a grin, he saluted his boss and jumped back aboard the vessel. His partner started the engine and with a loud wheezing and popping, the boat turned around and went back the way it had come.

"Come on, Terry, help me with these boxes," called Jeb, grabbing a box of meat and disappearing into the boathouse.

"Leave them, that's what servants are for," he retorted.

"Not when you need some exercise, they're not!" replied Gus, winking at Jeb as he picked up a box and handed it to O'Reilly.

"Jeez!" complained the gangster, taking the box and heading into the boathouse.

When they were finished Terry left and the men were standing talking on the jetty when Nancy reappeared with Beth, a maid at her heels. Between them they were carrying a picnic basket and a tray with cups and saucers as well as a hot bottle of tea wrapped in a towel.

"You're not going away from here hungry," Beth exclaimed, leading the way into the boathouse. Handing the basket to Jeb, she climbed aboard and took the tray from the maid, dismissing her. Then she began to lay out the cups and saucers. "Come on in, it's warmer in here," she ordered, pouring them each a cup of tea. Passing a plate of sandwiches to Jeb and Nancy, she slapped her husband's hand when he reached for one. "They're not for us. We're going to have dinner soon!"

Sipping his tea instead, Gus sat down and began to elaborate on their forthcoming trip in the *Lusitania*. "They're saying it's the world's most luxurious passenger liner," he said. "We're expecting it will be quite a trip!

"To say nothing of the long train ride beforehand!" added Beth. "I've never been so far on a train and I'm rather looking forward to it. We'll be gone about 6 weeks."

"But aren't you concerned about the war?" asked Nancy.

"No, the United States isn't at war and this ship is leaving from an American port. Besides it's a passenger ship not a troopship, the Germans won't be bothered with us," said Gus.

Fifteen minutes later, the Jorgensens said their farewells and returned to the dock.

"You're sure you're going to be all right with the boat, Nancy?" asked Beth, with a concerned expression.

"Of course, she's all right dear. It still works basically the same as the other one. It's just bigger. Enjoy your ride, kids!" Gus grinned.

"We'll take it easy," Nancy promised, waving one last time before backing out of the boathouse.

"It's a wonderful view from up here, isn't it Uncle Jeb?" she declared as she settled into her seat. "It's so warm and quiet; I can hardly believe the difference."

"This is pure luxury, Nan, but don't kid yourself, girl, we're going to earn it and those Eggers won't give up easily!"

Nancy looked at him briefly and frowned, then a little smile crinkled the corners of her mouth as she realized how comfortable she was feeling. "Let's surprise Meg and try to make it home before dark," she said, winking at the old detective.

She pulled on the throttle, her attention totally on her job as she peered ahead. Skirting fishing boats and avoiding freighters, they thundered up Puget Sound. The light was fading as they crossed the Strait of Juan de Fuca and slid up the side of the Oak Bay coastline.

As she scanned the water, her thoughts returned to Gus' comments about their planned trip to England. *How can they be so sure that the Lusitania is going to be safe? I wouldn't want to be travelling over there right now. I'll be mighty relieved when they arrive home safely.*

The last rays of sunshine bounced off the light ripple of Haro Strait creating a dazzling effect as they entered the deep shadows of the cove.

"We can leave the meat in the hold," said Jebediah, jumping onto the dock and giving Nancy a hand. "It's still cold enough at night and it's well protected now."

Meg and Eva Todd were startled when Nancy burst through the door, quickly followed by Jeb. Nancy noticed the worried look on their faces as she gave her aunt a hug.

"You two are early tonight! I didn't even hear you!" she exclaimed.

"We were being extra quiet to surprise you," Nancy admitted grinning, as Jeb also gave her a little hug. "So what have you ladies been up to today?"

Eva looked over at Meg who was now looking off into space. "I received an urgent phone call from one of our ladies this morning. She'd heard about a newly widowed woman who lived down at the bottom of Cook Street. She has a houseful of children and desperately needs some help. Her rent's unpaid and she's hardly been able to feed the little souls as it is. Now she's beside herself with grief and we want to help her. The problem is there's no money left in the kitty," Eva sighed. "Meg and I were just trying to work out what could be done."

"Hush, love, it's all right. I can help," replied Nancy, putting her arm around her aunt then going over to her coat and reaching into the pocket. "Someone made a contribution to our fund just this afternoon." She placed Terry's two fifty dollar bills on the table.

"Bless them!" Eva gasped.

"I don't think anyone will ever do that!" the redhead chuckled, raising her eyebrows at Jebediah.

"You certainly are a marvel at finding these donations, Nancy," Eva sighed. "Now, I must get home and deliver this before it gets too dark."

"Well, its almost dark now. How did you get here?" asked Jebediah. "I didn't see the car."

"I walked, it's not so far," she replied. "Dorothy was in town but she'll be back now. I just had to get out of the house and couldn't wait."

"Come on then," said Jeb. "Let's get you home, Mrs. Todd. We mustn't hold up your mission of mercy any longer."

Chapter 19

Spring rain lashed the clifftops the next morning as the redhead left the safety and warmth of the manor. The white-capped waves whipped the water into a wild sea that crashed against the rocks below as she carefully made her way down the steep stairs.

A strange thrill ran through her body as she untied the mooring lines and climbed aboard the *Stockholm*. Engines growling, as if welcoming the oncoming fight of two powerful and opposing forces, Nancy shot the speedboat forward into the storm.

"Now we'll see what you're made of," she hissed aloud, clutching the wheel as she increased the power. Warm and dry in the cabin, she fought her way around the rugged coastline, but was much relieved when she entered Victoria harbour.

"Strange weather, but I don't suppose it gave *you* much trouble," Dumpy grumbled sarcastically as his eyes ran over the *Stockholm*. "So this is your new runabout is it?"

Nancy just grinned as she moved aft to open the lower compartment.

"Holy hell! Look at all that space, quite a ship this *Stockholm*," he grinned, now a lot more interested.

"Yes, and you just keep quiet about it. Word will get around fast enough!" Hearing her name being called, she turned to see Waldo and Harry Maynard striding toward them. "See, what did I tell you!" she whispered.

"New boat, lass?" Waldo growled, walking past and surveying the new craft. "B&W must be doing well."

"B&W?" she asked, frowning.

"Brown and Wilson," said Harry. "Take no notice of him, he likes abbreviations."

"Hmm, I sort of like it!" she returned, looking at him curiously. "What's the problem Waldo? You have something on your mind, I can tell. Spit it out!"

Waldo moved in closer, bushy eyebrows twitching as his hand ran across the mahogany woodwork. "I hope you never get caught, lass," he muttered softly, then turned away quickly.

Harry grinned, watching his old friend stomp off the dock. He knew what a soft spot the haulier had for the redhead and he had often made his concerns clear about prohibition. On the other hand, they all knew there would be hell to pay if anyone hurt her and thankfully they knew Gus Jorgensen felt the same.

"What brings you here, Harry?" asked Nancy.

He placed his hand on her elbow and steered her toward the office. "I have to talk to you."

"About what?" she asked, looking at him curiously as they went inside and sat down at the table.

"I've heard that you're singing at the James Moore Theatre. Millie and I are going to be there come the 23rd!"

A look of anxiety came over the redhead's face knowing her activities were no longer a secret.

As if reading her thoughts, the brewer continued, "It's all right, lass. I was down to Seattle recently and one of my business acquaintances told me of a wonderful singer he'd heard. Seems she had red hair and came from Victoria. Oh course, my interest was peaked immediately but I couldn't imagine it was you. He told me this girl sang at Moore's theatre every month in aid of Canadian war widows. He couldn't remember her name though."

"So how did you know it was me?"

"Well, my Millie put the puzzle together. She said there couldn't be another girl like you in Victoria so it had to be you and it was just like you to want to help someone. I thought you might be trying to do it on the sly as we hadn't seen anything in the local papers. So I contacted Gus Jorgensen and he confirmed our suspicions. He swore us to secrecy and invited us to your next performance."

Sighing with relief, Nancy's eyes spoke volumes to her friend across the table. He knew of her humble and sad beginnings and he also knew of the inseparable bond between her and Dan that had started in the orphanage. The relationship which had developed between the young people was unlike anything he and Millie had ever witnessed before. Reaching out he took her hand and felt the ring he and Millie had given her a few years before. He spoke quickly as he heard Dumpy's loud footsteps coming.

"Don't worry, your secret's safe with us, honey."

"How are we going to get these boxes to the Balmoral, the truck's not here?" Dumpy called through the open door.

"I can take them for you," Harry offered.

"Thanks Harry, that would be most appreciated," she said.

"It'll only take a few minutes for me to load them if you want to get on your way, Mr. Maynard," advised Dumpy. "I'll come with you. I can walk back."

"No need to hurry, Dumpy, I don't think Nancy is trying to get rid of me yet!"

A smile strayed across her face as she watched them drive away ten minutes later. She walked back into the office and went to look out the window that faced the Parliament Buildings. The harbour was quite tranquil-looking today as there had been no troopships arrive this week. A flag fluttered near the entrance to the CPR Ticket Office and one of the old paddle-wheel steamers rested quietly at the dock. *Gives one a false sense of peace,* she marvelled, knowing the heartaches and unhappiness that surrounded her.

Leaving a note for her dock manager, she returned to the boat and headed up the harbour to the Turpel shipyard for fuel not wanting to use their limited supply in Gordon Head. Kenneth Macpherson watched with interest as she cruised toward him. He walked over to greet her, casually inspecting the *Stockholm* as a dock worker began to pump gasoline into its tank.

"Nice boat," he murmured, noting the strong, clean lines. "Looks powerful and fast." Pensively, he lifted his cap and scratched his head. "But what are those two small holes for?" he asked, pointing to the gun holes in the side.

Turning away so he didn't see her smile, she ignored his question and signed the docket for the pump attendant. "Thanks! See you later, Mister Macpherson!"

Scowling fiercely, the superintendent watched her go. *She's being evasive, but why?* There was something different about that boat but he just couldn't put his finger on it. He listened carefully to the noise of the engine and noticed an unusual gurgling sound. *No matter, I'll find out soon enough.*

Calling back at the office, Nancy found Dumpy reading the Saturday Colonist on the table.

"Have you seen this about those miners trapped below ground in Nanaimo?"

"No, I haven't!" she snapped. "Why do they always have to print that stuff about somebody's pain and sorrow?"

"It's news I guess," Dumpy mumbled, realizing he'd hit a soft spot again.

The wind had dropped and a ray of sunshine was trying to force its way through the clouds as Nancy took the *Stockholm* out of the harbour. She slowed to take a look at the breakwater construction. *It's amazing how they can lift those huge pieces of granite and place them in just the right spot.*

There was no urgency now so she kept her speed down enjoying the warm spring weather. Following the coastline toward Trial Island, her eyes scanned the skyline resting briefly on the Dallas Hotel and wondering how business was doing as recent newspaper reports had reported they, along with many other businesses, were in financial trouble. Her gaze moved along the coast noting the number of people walking along the seafront near Beacon Hill Park. Children could be seen running on the beaches, climbing over the piles of logs thrown up by winter seas. *You could almost believe life was normal,* she thought.

On past the familiar outcroppings, bays and islands she went, taking more notice of her surroundings than she had in months. Passing the Chinese Cemetery, she looked upward at the house sitting high above the water on its great rocky bluff. *What a view they must have.*

She tried to make out some of the larger buildings as she rounded the corner and went past Oak Bay with its pretty little bays, the golf course, and many larger homes sprinkled along the landscape amongst the trees. Seeing the white sandy beach near the Willows Fairgrounds she remembered the day she had taken Dan there when he joined the army. It seemed so long ago.

She passed the grand houses of the area that had become known as the Uplands, an area where the wealthy of Victoria were building homes on very large lots with seafront and sea views. As she passed Cadboro Bay, Algenon Pease and his wife Lolitia Jean, were just mooring the *Legal Limit* and she waved, wondering if they would know who it was. They waved back and Algy stood up and watched the unusual craft. He'd seen it the day it arrived and he dearly wanted a closer look. Rumour had it that Nancy was rum running and although she wasn't doing anything illegal in Canada, he was concerned about her involvement.

"Why don't we drop over and see Nancy for a minute, Algenon," his wife suggested. "You've been saying that you wanted to thank her. This might be the perfect opportunity, dear, and I'd love to meet her."

Wondering if his wife had been reading his mind again, he untied the boat and they climbed back in. Knowing they would have to hurry if they were going to catch her on the dock, he poured on the power.

Nancy took a wider berth around Cadboro Point, remembering her experience in the winter storm. This time she was extra careful to avoid the dark shadows having been warned by Gus that her keel was longer in the new boat. Sending the *Stockholm* out into the quickly flowing current, she turned on the power and soon came within sight of her own coastline.

As she secured the last of the lines, Nancy heard a boat cut its engine behind her. It was the *Legal Limit*. "Hello Algy," she called brightly. "What brings you to our cove on this beautiful day?"

"Nancy, I want you to meet my wife, Lolitia Jean. We saw you go by and decided to catch you up."

He began showering her with questions about the new boat but she laughed and held up her hand so she could greet his wife.

"It's wonderful to meet you at last, Nancy. I haven't expressed my gratitude for the time you assisted my husband. He didn't tell me much about that day but he seemed mighty happy you came along!"

This was the first time Nancy had even seen Mrs. Pease, although Eva had often mentioned their neighbours in conversation. Reddish hair, neatly pulled back under her bonnet, surrounded a pleasant, round face. Her strong body was well-dressed and she wore a shawl which she had pulled about her as the wind whipped around the boathouse.

"Please call me Jean. I feel like I know you already, dear. Eva Todd thinks you're an angel!"

"Why don't you come up to the house and have a cup of tea with us?" Nancy invited. "If you don't mind the stairs, that is! You must meet my Aunt Meg and Uncle Jeb."

"We don't mind at all, the exercise will be good for us," said Jean, frowning at her husband.

They noticed the tone of Nancy's voice change as she led the way up the cliff stairs. "You won't be able to meet my Danny as he's away in the war."

"Your brother ... yes, we know dear, Eva told us. You must miss him terribly," said Jean.

As they reached the path to the house, they noticed Old Sam shuffling away into the trees carrying a small bag. When Jean saw him she touched her husband's arm and Nancy caught the gentle look that crossed their faces though neither made the slightest comment.

During introductions, Meg learned that their neighbours were from Hamsterley Farm on Sinclair Hill. She fussed around making the visitors welcome and offering tea and cakes. As they sat chatting at the kitchen table, Jebediah encouraged Algenon to talk about his job. In no time the cunning old Pinkerton man had the information he wanted. Firmly engrained in his mind was a map of the area near the harbour entrance surveyed by Algy and his navy patrol vessels.

An hour later, the Peases took their leave.

"My, what a nice couple they are. I'm so glad you invited them to join us, Nancy," declared Meg, when they were out of earshot.

"Yes, it was a pleasant way to spend the afternoon wasn't it?" she agreed, helping Meg clean up the tea dishes.

That evening, as they sat around the fire, Jeb watched Meg as she knit yet another pair of socks.

"Are you still knitting socks, Meg? Gracious, you must have outfitted every one of our Canadian lads by now!" He took a deep puff on his pipe and smiled as he blew the smoke into the air. He looked over at Nancy curled up in her overstuffed armchair studying her music, a usual position for her these days. She had been spending every spare minute memorizing several new songs for her concerts.

Fog was thick on the water Sunday morning, slowing her progress as she took the *Stockholm* up the coast to Salt Spring Island to pay a visit on Ben Wall and his wife. It had been almost a year since she and Dan had taken them to the island to meet their family and wondered how the orchard grower and his wife were getting on. She was hoping Ben would be willing to help her if she told him the land was soon to be cleared.

The mist was lifting quickly as the bright sun worked its way through the clouds. A stiff breeze pushed the waves into tumbling rollers and she slowed a bit to make the ride smoother. By the time she pulled into the dock at the north end of the island it was almost 11 o'clock. A boy was fishing nearby and, when she asked for directions to the Wall farm, he offered to lead her there.

It was only a short walk through a wooded area, when they came upon a small log house. Thanking the boy, she knocked on the door. Nancy recognized Asha immediately and was surprised that the woman recognized her also. Obviously pleased to see her, she opened the door wide and invited her in.

"Land sakes, it's Miss Nancy! Come in! Come in!" she cried. "Nathan, run and get your uncle," she ordered a boy of about eight who was playing on the floor. "Tell him Miss Nancy is here from Victoria, quickly now."

He ran shyly past her, slamming the door. It was only minutes and he was back accompanied by an older man.

"This is a joy, Miss Nancy," the familiar deep voice boomed as he burst through the door.

If she wasn't sure of his face, she certainly recognized that wonderful voice.

"We feel honoured that you come to visit poor folks like us."

"Hello Ben," she murmured, embarrassed by the dark-skinned man's enthusiastic greeting. "I came to offer you a job."

He sat down and his wife poured them both a cup of tea giving Nancy the fanciest cup which had a cracked handle. Asha timidly offered the cup to the redhead, smiling gratefully when Nancy graciously accepted it.

"A job, Miss Nancy?" he asked, looking at her curiously.

"Apples, remember?" she laughed. "Dan spoke to you about always wanting an apple orchard. Well, he's overseas now and a friend has offered to clear the land for us. It will be ready in 2-3 weeks and I need someone to do the planting and teach us how to look after it. Can you help us?"

"I can start on the tenth of May," he replied, "but how do I get over there and back each day?"

"Don't you have a boat?"

"Yes, I have a rowboat."

"Then I'll send somebody for you on the Sunday and you can stay with us during the week for as long as it takes. I'll bring you home on the weekend."

Ben's eyes opened wide and looked like they were going to pop right out of his head. "You mean ... stay with white folk?"

Asha's hand began to tremble, rattling her cup on its saucer. She quickly put it down.

Nancy looked from one to the other. "Of course you'll stay with us. We wouldn't have it any other way." It took a while for her to settle the couple down and assure them that her family wouldn't object. There was still a sense of insecurity about the couple when they walked her back to the dock. Standing close together they waved as the fancy red boat pulled away and was soon in the channel with Nancy waving goodbye.

Asha instinctively reached for her husband's hand as they watched the disappearing craft. "That young lady is a mighty fine person," she whispered. "That's a bigger boat than Dan had when he brought us here. They must be rich, Ben!" Ben tightened his grip on her hand and smiled down at her.

A light rain mixed with spring sunshine made the trip home through Sansum Narrows a most enjoyable experience for Nancy. She watched the progress of a rail barge up ahead and, as she rounded Piers Island, she heard a little toot from the tugboat in the lead. It was the *Earl* and Nancy knew it was Mr. Van Saint, the owner and captain of the former lighthouse tender. He was waving from the tug's bridge. She stepped outside and waved back.

As she entered the cove, Sam's rowboat came out of its hiding place to meet her. The only time he had done this before was when he had given her a fish. As she slowed, the old hermit came alongside and held up a nice salmon. She was so grateful Gus had thought to put a fishing net on board. It had already come in handy a couple of times … although she had not even had the experience of fishing yet. Sam grinned and dropped the fish carefully into the net then quickly turned away.

Calling her thanks, she pulled the net aboard and lay it on the floor. "It's a beauty," she exclaimed, looking down at the fish as she brought the boat alongside the dock. *Meg will be pleased to have fresh salmon for dinner. Jack and Nellie are coming tonight.*

"Oh wonderful, we'll have fresh salmon for our dinner!" Meg exclaimed, when the girl dropped the paper-wrapped package of fish on the kitchen counter. "Have you had any lunch, lass?"

"No, but I'm not really hungry, I had tea with the Wall's. I'll have a couple of your cookies to hold me to dinner. It will be nice to see Jack and Nellie again. Where's Uncle Jeb?"

"Oh, outside somewhere," Meg murmured, pausing to glance through the window. "How did you make out with Ben Wall?"

"Really well, he's going to help us. He starts on the 10th. I'll tell you all about it when Uncle Jeb comes in."

Thirty minutes later Jebediah came into the house and they sat and had a cup of tea. He, too, was eager to hear of Ben's reaction to the orchard plans.

"He wasn't very comfortable when I told him he could stay over with us," said Nancy, "but I think it will work out fine. He said he only had a rowboat or he could go home each evening."

"Oh, I could probably run him home every couple of days if it was important to him," replied Jebediah.

Nancy got up and began to set the table in the dining room. "We'll just have to see what happens. I might need the boat elsewhere and it wouldn't be convenient to ferry him back and forth. They're a nice couple and he'll be fine after he gets to know us. They'll just have to get used to the idea they are just like the rest of us white folk."

Jeb raised his eyebrows. "That might take some …," he began.

"There's a truck coming up the drive," Meg interrupted, turning from the window.

Going out onto the porch, they realized it wasn't the Duggans but one of the Harvey and Briggs delivery trucks, the liquor merchants from Wharf Street. The driver must have been here before as he proceeded to turn around and in reverse backed up to the doors of the workshop. Nancy watched from the porch and heard the driver talking to Jebediah as they off-loaded the shipment of 80 cases of Scotch whisky.

"Can't think what you do out here with all this booze," the driver rambled. "I come every week and your orders are just getting bigger."

"We drink it," the old detective growled. "What the hell do ya think we do with it … bath in it!"

This stopped the driver's questions and he just looked around as if he was checking to see who the big drinker might be, but a thought was now festering in the American's brain. It was a warning and Jeb saw it clearly. As he watched the truck drive away he decided he'd have to talk to Nancy and they would need to make some other arrangements … and soon.

A few minutes later, Nancy heard the sound of another vehicle and pulled the curtain back on the window. Jack Duggan's truck was slowly making its way down the drive.

"Jack and Nellie are here!" she called, going quickly to the door.

Nellie Duggan giggled as she hugged Nancy, and arm-in-arm they made their way into the house to find Meg.

"We met the wholesaler's truck up on Cedar Hill and figured it had been here, but thought it strange he was working on a Sunday," Jack said quietly to Jeb as they stood talking.

"Said he lived near here and didn't get finished yesterday."

"Ah. That chute working all right for you, Jebediah?" Jack asked as they walked over to the cliff stairs.

"Perfect," Jeb said in a faraway voice. "You knew the lad was wounded, didn't you?" he murmured.

"No," Jack sighed. "We haven't seen much of Nancy lately."

"He's all right though. Don't mention it, she'll tell you when she's ready."

A shout from the porch calling them inside, interrupted their conversation, although Jack would have liked to question Jeb some more about Dan. Going in, they found the women in the parlour. Jack raised the topic of the new orchard suggesting that Nancy talk with Emil Layritz at his nursery and tree farm on Wilkinson Road.

"Oh, I have an apple grower of my own," Nancy smiled. "But I guess he'll need to buy the seedlings."

"Saplings they're called, honey," corrected the builder. "Who have you got?"

Ben Wall from Salt Spring Island," she replied. "He's a Negro."

Jack's jaw dropped. "A black man ... an apple grower?"

"He's going to plant all the trees and train someone to look after them for us," Nancy replied proudly.

"Darn it, lass," Jack chuckled. "You're full of surprises, but if that's what you have in mind, we'll cut the bill in half as my contribution."

"Right, if that's what you're going to do, old friend," she purred, looking over at Nellie. 'I'll sing just for you, after supper!"

Nellie looked at her husband. His eyes were sparkling as he watched Nancy. Nellie knew how much her husband enjoyed this girl. Dan had introduced them many years before and they had become great friends. *This girl always seems to bring out the best in people,* she thought.

The meal of fresh salmon went down well until Meg told them Sam, the hermit, had brought it as a gift. Nellie's face turned visibly pale.

"What's the matter, Nellie?" asked Nancy.

"You're not afraid of him, Meg, a hermit wandering around about your property? Good gracious me."

"Oh no, he's harmless," the Scot laughed. "He's just a lonely old man and he watches out for us."

After supper Nellie insisted she help with cleaning up the dishes and Nancy mentioned receiving a letter from Dan but she didn't elaborate and Nellie didn't want to pry. Jeb went into the parlour to light the fire. He and Jack sat talking politics and smoking their pipes until the ladies joined them. Jeb pulled out his guitar and quietly began strumming.

"Is that a hint, Uncle Jeb?" Nancy smiled, ruffling his hair. She went to look out the window. "I have an idea. It's been such a nice day and still not quite dark. Let's you and I go down to the dock and the others can sit on the cliff steps, just like at a theatre!"

"That's different," Nellie murmured, as they all gathered their coats and went outside.

Jeb and Nancy went on ahead, each taking a lantern with them. Once down at the dock, they set their lanterns up and perched on the edge of the *Stockholm*.

Jeb began strumming on the guitar. "What are you going to sing?"

"Why? Does it make any difference to the tune you're going to play, Uncle Jeb?" she teased.

Blushing, he kept his mouth shut and waited.

When she began there was no doubt in anyone's mind who she was singing to. *My Bonny Lies Over the Ocean*, began as a whisper but, in the stillness of the night air, it reverberated around the cove, as Nancy turned toward the cliff.

Tears welled in Meg's eyes as she whispered, "Oh please Lord, send Danny home safe to us soon."

Sitting behind Meg, Jack wrapped his arm around his wife and she dropped her head on his shoulder. They really enjoyed Nancy's singing and it had been a while since they had heard her—even the work-hardened builder was touched. Three more songs rose up to meet them and when they applauded it sounded as if a much larger audience was present. The cove was the perfect amphitheatre, one of nature's beautiful natural settings with its gentle slapping of tidal waves and it was perfect for a concert.

Chapter 20

Monday, the 19th of April, saw the cliffside property abuzz with activity as Jack Duggan arrived at 8 a.m. with two men and a truck full of equipment. Minutes later four more men arrived with several large workhorses. All day they climbed, cut, roped and felled trees. A large pile of scrub and tree branches began to take shape in the middle of the clearing and dust was settling on everything despite the overnight rain.

Meg and Jebediah watched in wonder as several tall firs went tumbling to the ground. Worried they might fall onto the house, Meg took up her vantage point on the cliff stairs, barely able to contain her concern. But the men knew what they were doing. By the end of the second day several monstrous roots, left behind before the building of the house, as well as many smaller ones, had been torn from the ground and added to the growing pile.

Meg fed them all sandwiches and tea and, in the afternoon, Jack set the fire ablaze making sure they had a hose connected just in case any sparks got away from them. Fuelled by dry tree branches, great plumes of smoke and flames roared skyward. The smell of burning soil and timber would hang for days over Gordon Head even after the billowing clouds dissipated.

By Thursday, the weather cooperated adding just enough dampness to clear the air and water down the soil. The 5-acre orchard behind the house was beginning to take shape.

This was also the week Dumpy finally took some lessons and learned how to drive a car after admitting to Nan how inconvenient it was that he didn't drive. Nancy teased him ruthlessly, saying he was scaring the living daylights out of half the drivers and pedestrians in Victoria. Kate mentioned they were talking about purchasing a vehicle of their own and how much she, too, wanted to drive. As a result, Nancy found herself organizing her time to fit in some lessons for her friend the following week.

On Friday before she headed home, she called in at the post office and was rewarded with a small yellow envelope with Dan's name on the corner. She stopped outside to eagerly tear it open.

Hello my darling, his words whispered from the page, as her lips gently kissed the letter. *I'm at Ypres, all mended and back in fighting form again. It's not fun anymore, as it was at the beginning. The Canadians are fighting like devils, in mud up to our ankles and each one of us is intent on surviving this hell. I wish it would stop raining though, perhaps you could send me an umbrella!* Dan's attempt at humour caused a tear to run down her face. She read the rest of his letter as she walked.

That same day, Eva, driving her buggy with a shiny black, high-stepping horse in front, called at Cunningham Manor. She had been watching the smoke clouds all week and decided to investigate. She found the property abuzz with men and equipment, but Meg and Jebediah were inside out of the dust.

Nancy hadn't told her about the plans for the orchard and Eva found herself concerned for her friend. *I wonder if she's even considered that Dan might never come home,* she thought sadly, thinking of her own Thomas who was now also in England, albeit at a desk job in relative safety.

Eating lunch with the older couple, Eva waited for Nancy to arrive home from town so she could give her an accounting of the money she had spent helping the needy families. She also had several new stories to tell of the hardships of some of the young families in the area.

"You know, it's dreadfully difficult having to keep Nancy's part in this a secret," she admitted to the older couple.

The sound of the Model T brought Jebediah to his feet. Excusing himself, he said he had work to do and went outside. Eva talked with Nancy while she ate her lunch and Nancy soon found they had much more in common now that Thomas' unit was overseas. They soon found themselves comparing news and discussing Eva's conversations with the wounded soldiers at the local hospitals.

"It's so frightfully sad," Eva murmured, as they went out onto the porch.

Nancy hugged her goodbye. "It should be over soon, Eva. We must keep doing what we can and it helps to pass the time more quickly. It's all we can do. See you next time."

"We're ready, lass," announced Jeb from behind them, as they waved goodbye to her.

"I haven't had a chance to tell you that I got a letter from Dan today. He's at a place called Ypres in Belgium. It's really wet but he's feeling great, all healed and eager again by the sound of it," she said, trying to hide her concern.

"That's wonderful news, lass. Now you two better go," said Meg hurrying them out the door. "You be careful tonight."

Since using the new boat, they had found that the *Stockholm*'s cabin not only kept them warmer but it also gave them the opportunity to talk as they travelled. Nancy told Jeb more about Dan's letter voicing her concern. He listened but didn't say a lot. Then he remembered the truck driver's comments about the liquor and mentioned them to Nancy.

"This has me concerned, honey. I think time has come to split up the order to prevent any further suspicions. You know how people talk."

"You might have a good thought there, Uncle Jeb. We could have it delivered to the dock in town, even if we did that twice a month it would help allay suspicion. I can bring it home in the truck but it would take several trips or, we could send the boat around. It might be worth the effort."

Jeb nodded as he took another look through his field glasses. His attention was taken by a small freighter with several small boats tied up alongside.

"Slow down, I want to see this," he said quickly, pointing to them.

"Do you think there's a problem?" she asked, pushing back on the throttle.

As they slowed she kept her distance and Jeb again lifted his glasses. He turned and slowly searched the shoreline at the entrance to Lake Union.

"Move away slowly and head straight over there." He pointed to a black launch, almost invisible as it stood at a small jetty.

Warily, Nancy obeyed, her eyes darting left and right as she watched for trouble and searched for her quickest escape route. She tucked into another small jetty some distance away and cut her engines.

"It's the Coast Guard," explained Jebediah, pointing to the black launch and handing her the glasses.

Fifteen minutes passed, then suddenly in a flurry of activity, the freighter started its engines and all the boats scattered before the freighter began to move. The Coast Guard cutter slipped her mooring and, hugging the coast, slowly made her way toward Elliot Bay. Ten minutes more they sat in silence before Jebediah gave the order to go.

"What was that all about?" she asked, scooting around West Point and heading for the Jorgensen estate.

"I'll tell you when we get to the boathouse," Jeb growled.

Terry glanced at his watch for a second time, then smiled to himself when he heard the sound of the distinctive engines, quite sure it was the *Stockholm*. Helping hands were waiting when Nan backed into the boathouse and shut down the engines. Terry was there to meet her with his men right behind.

"You run into the Coast Guard?" he asked with a chuckle, handing her the envelope.

"Not quite," Jeb replied. "They seemed to be on a surveillance mission. Who owns that small freighter we saw just down by Lake Union?"

"Doc Hamilton, Roy's competitor."

"Then who owns the Coast Guard?"

"Roy, of course, he's the law!"

A sudden burst of laughter escaped the old detective, seeing the picture more clearly. He turned to explain it to Nancy who had a confused look on her face. "Roy Olmstead is using his position on the police force to find out who runs booze for Doc Hamilton, then he leans on them." He glanced over at Terry. "What about us?"

"Almost immune," he replied. "Doc doesn't know about us and Gus Jorgensen's too powerful for Roy. It's the independents you have to be wary of, like the Eggers." He stopped, his eyes fastening on Nancy. He tapped the gun in his shoulder holster. "But then you have me."

"But you're not on the boat," Nancy pointed out.

"That's why you have the *Stockholm*, girl!" Terry growled. "That boat is as safe as Fort Knox!"

"Where's Gus?" she asked brushing off his comment as she watched the men load the meat.

"Out of town," Terry replied, "but they'll be back for your concert next Friday."

Finishing their business, they waved goodbye and pulled back out into the channel. They rode in silence up through the islands, both of them immersed in their own thoughts as the sun dipped behind the layers of hills.

They were passing Oak Bay when the redhead finally spoke. "I've got a strange feeling about Gus and Beth, Uncle Jeb, almost as if they're in danger."

"You're tired and thinking way too hard," Jeb teased. "You'll feel better in the morning."

Meg was sitting on the porch waiting patiently. She had already lit the lamps a half hour ago and was beginning to feel a bit apprehensive.

Sighing with relief when she heard the *Stockholm's* engines, she went inside to set out a light snack for her weary charges. She hated it when they were late but not being familiar yet with how long the trip took in the new boat she had tried to keep herself busy rather than worrying.

Nancy mentioned her uneasy feelings regarding the Jorgensens to Meg but Jeb dispelled her fears once again. Meg, however, wasn't going to dismiss the thought so easily and after Nancy went off to bed she sat staring into the fire. She remembered very clearly the morning Nan had awoken with a terrible pain in her back only to find out later that Dan had been wounded.

The beautiful weather on Saturday morning made travelling to the city an adventure for the threesome. It seemed everyone was hard at work in their fields, young and old, and many of them women. It was a time of new crops and everywhere green shoots were rising from the ground and gardens, with many trees beginning to sport their new leaves. They all loved this time of year for another reason, too. They got to actually see their neighbours and Nancy loved the friendly camaraderie, waving to many as she chugged by.

After making their delivery at the Balmoral, Jeb saw some men he knew and went into the dining room for a cup of coffee while Meg and Nancy visited in the kitchen. A bit later, they collected Jeb to go shopping and found Government Street bustling with activity as the warm weather enticed reticent Victorians from their homes.

They stopped in at the Rogers' grocery store and purchased a few of their chocolates for a special treat, then on to Campbell and Angus to get a new corset for Meg. Jebediah declined their invitation to enter the ladies' wear store and instead eagerly escaped across the road to have a beer at the Brown Jug Saloon.

Despite the war, Woolworths still seemed able to attract a lot of shoppers with its five and dime prices and neither of the women could resist a walk through its gaudy interior. When they came out they found Jeb waiting patiently on the sidewalk with a box of Cuban cigars, tucked under his arm, acquired from nearby E.A. Morris Tobacconist.

"Come on, let's go," he urged them. "I'll buy you both lunch at the Poodle Dog Cafe."

The last time I came here, Nancy thought, as they entered the popular restaurant, *was with Dan, more than a year ago.*

During lunch, she suggested a trip out to Wilkinson Road to find the Layritz Nursery that Jack Duggan had told her about.

They found the place after a nightmarish drive, for Wilkinson Road was little more than a rough track through the forest. Its only connection with civilization was the BC Electric Railway track, known as the Interurban Line. This railway crossed the valley on its way to Saanichton and Patricia Bay. When they passed the castle-like structure of the Colquitz Jail standing starkly beautiful in its clearing, a shiver went up Meg's spine.

"Isn't that the place where they're holding all those poor European people because of the war?" she asked.

"Oh my, you're right, Aunt Meg. They call them enemy aliens. What a strange name to use."

"It sounds better than spy!" grunted Jebediah.

"I don't understand why the government would think these people are all spies just because there is a war on," clucked Meg.

"What about their children, are they imprisoned, too?" asked Nancy.

"Eva told me some time ago that her ladies' group had talked about this. One of the ladies, a Mrs. Brown, whose cousin works for the government, said they had found out that some of the … ah aliens, were spies and that's why they arrested everyone. I suppose the younger children would go to an orphanage if there was no one to look after them."

"Orphanage … oh my word, that's dreadful, but I guess the government knows what they are doing. I feel so sorry for them," said Nancy, seeing a sign and turning into the nursery yard.

As they entered the yard a middle-aged man hurried over to greet them even before they were all out of the truck. Emil Layritz was a friendly man of small stature; his strong work ethic and high energy levels were admired by all who knew him. They introduced themselves and he greeted them warmly, leading them toward the house. From the large porch Nancy noticed what looked like a huge garden with hundreds of little trees growing in long rows. There were many different kinds each in various stages of growth.

"This is my wife, Eliece," Mr. Layritz was saying as an attractive blonde-haired woman came outside to join them. "Eliece, this is Nancy Wilson, she's the young lady the Gunters told us about—the redhead who drives the little Model T. This is her aunt, Miss McDonald, who used to work for the Joyce boys down at the harbour."

"Pleased to meet you both," Eliece replied, her German accent making her a bit difficult to understand. "Oh yes, Miss McDonald, I remember we met the day Emil and I came to buy fish at the dock. That was a long time ago," she added, looking inquiringly at Jebediah.

"This is my uncle, Jebediah Judd, Mrs. Layritz," Nancy added.

Handshakes were exchanged and Eliece shepherded Meg and Jebediah over to the sheltered corner of the porch. "We'll have some tea while Nancy talks to my husband about trees! It's so nice to have company."

The nurseryman took Nancy down to the garden and as they walked between the rows of plants and trees he made suggestions. He proffered a great deal of helpful advice and within half an hour Nancy had decided on the Newton Pipin as her main choice and the Goldridge for a variation. She arranged a delivery date for the 10th of May and they went to join the others.

When they were leaving, Eliece walked out to the truck with them. "Please don't wait until you need trees next time," she declared. We are quite isolated away out here and Emil's visitors are more often men— all they seem to talk about are gardens and soil! Please bring your aunt and uncle and come again, Nancy."

"We will, Mrs. Layritz," the girl promised. "Thank you for tea."

The following week the Colonist newspaper headlines again upset Nancy as they published more pictures and accounts of the war and lists of the dead and wounded. Stories of hardship from frontline soldiers were also featured along with glowing reports of the advance of allied armies.

Tom Irvine and Billy called in to see Nancy one morning while delivering farm produce to the Balmoral. The old man was looking tired and acting more subdued than she remembered and she watched him with concern. As they were leaving, Tom lingered behind Billy and stopped as he and Nancy reached the door. Taking a long puff on his pipe he held out an envelope.

"Keep this safe, lassie," he mumbled. "You're the only one I trust. You're to open it after I die."

"Don't be foolish, Tom," Nancy whispered, taken aback by her old friend's statement. "You're that bad-tempered, you'll go on forever!"

But he insisted and left quickly before Nancy could argue with him. She found it difficult to rid herself of the nagging feeling that something was going to happen to Tom, although she realized he was no longer a young man; then the lunch crowd poured in and it finally slipped from her mind.

Conversations seemed more heated than normal today as men argued between tables about the conservative government and Premier McBride's constant absence from the province, presently in far-off London. Meanwhile, it appeared Acting-Premier Bowser's actions were beginning to cause panic amongst the saloon keepers. She frowned as she listened to the raging discussion thinking of her own profits. The strange foreboding feeling of disaster flitted across her mind once again but this time it was not Tom Irvine or the Jorgensens who caused it.

On Friday the 23rd of April, Terry was already at the boathouse when the three of them arrived in Seattle. "They're waiting for you up at the house," he said, sporting a big grin as he gave her the envelope.

Beth hurried in from the kitchen to meet them when she heard their voices. "You are probably starving. Come, dinner is ready. I have some wonderful news to tell you."

"Let them get their coats off first, Beth," Gus scolded his wife. "You can tell them your news after dinner."

She ignored him and continued to chat as they stowed their bags and were led into the dining room.

"Seattle is abuzz about your single-handed war effort, Nan. Tickets were sold out a week ago," she said excitedly. "Hattie Rhodes donated a new gown for the occasion. You're going to love it!"

Twenty minutes later, Gus cocked an eyebrow as the ladies excused themselves and, giggling, hurried from the room. At last he could talk to Jeb about an issue he found difficult to discuss with his wife.

"Have you heard the news that our German embassy has issued a warning to shipping in the Atlantic?" he began quietly, leaning toward his friend. He saw he had Jeb's attention and continued. "They say they're ready to torpedo any ships going to England."

"But you're booked on the *Lusitania*, aren't you?"

"Exactly. I know they're capable of it, even if Wilson thinks it's a bluff. Beth wants to see the boys so badly but I must admit I'm a bit nervous."

"The war is heating up," Jeb offered, in a warning tone. "I saw in yesterday's newspaper that they're threatening to bomb London from those large zeppelin balloons."

"The British won't stand for it!" Gus answered sharply, looking toward the doorway as one of the servants entered and came toward them.

"Madam asked me to convey to you the time, sir," he said slowly, then bowing, left as quietly as he had entered.

"I guess we had best take the subtle hint, Jebediah. These women don't like to be kept waiting." The men stood up and moved toward the door. Putting his hand on Jeb's arm, he held him back for a moment. "I'll give this trip some more thought. Perhaps I should talk to Beth."

Jeb nodded solemnly but he felt a slight feeling of relief as they moved toward the stairs.

Chapter 21

James Moore was waiting in the lobby when the car pulled up in front of the theatre. "Well Nancy, are you ready to meet your public?" he asked jovially, welcoming her like an old friend and kissing her on the cheek. "By the noise level here tonight, it sounds as if all of Seattle is awaiting your arrival!"

Nancy greeted him with an excited giggle accepting hugs and best wishes from the others.

"You'll have to excuse us now," he interrupted. "The show must go on and the star seems to be missing!" Taking her gently by the arm, he quickly whisked her away. "You look radiant tonight, my dear, and not a bit nervous. Would you like to powder your nose before meeting Nellie? She's waiting backstage."

"No, I'm fine thank you, Mr. Moore. I'm quite eager to talk with Nellie before we go on."

"Well, here we are then," he said as he opened a door and they entered the dark confines of the backstage area. "Derek," he called to one of the stagehands who immediately approached them. "Take Miss Wilson's belongings to her dressing room, please."

Nancy slipped out of her coat with James' assistance and handed it to the young man, then carefully removed her hat. Again, James took her elbow and steered her across the cables and around staff and obstacles until she realized they were on stage behind thick black velvet curtains. Then she saw the familiar white grand piano. Nellie was sitting on the bench studying her music and playing quietly when she noticed them.

Not giving the woman a chance to speak, James led Nancy to the bench and prodded her in beside Nellie. "I leave you in good hands, my dear. The curtain rises in 15 minutes."

The women grinned at each other then Nancy turned to thank him but he had already disappeared.

"You look stunning, Nancy," Nellie murmured as they hugged briefly. "I received this piece of music just two hours ago when Terry O'Reilly delivered it. We're going to make this a night to remember, love! You just keep your eyes on me and don't even worry about the orchestra. They just add a bit of fluff and the patrons pay you more!"

True to his word, exactly 15 minutes later they were suddenly aware that the noise level had dropped in the theatre followed by some loud clapping. When the applause stopped they could hear James' voice on the other side of the curtain performing his usual dissertation on the purpose of the evening's entertainment. Before he finished, he reminded the packed audience to give generously to the cause they had come to support.

Up in the owner's private box above stage right, Meg, Jebediah, Harry and Nellie Maynard, and the Jorgensens, expectantly awaited Nancy's entrance. When James finished, he went backstage, waving to Nancy and Nellie before hurrying off to join his guests.

The lights dimmed and, from the orchestra pit, the conductor appeared. The audience clapped a warm welcome to their local maestro, Bruce Winters and, he smiled, bowing low with an exaggerated flourish. Turning around, he picked up his baton tapping it lightly on his music stand. Looking down at his musicians, he said a few quick words to them and raised his arms. With a flick of his wrist, the baton was in motion and the orchestra began to play the National Anthem.

Everyone stood and sang, even Nellie and Nancy, the latter having now learned the song with her friend's help. When it was over the audience sat down and the curtain slowly rose revealing the performers. When the audience saw Nancy standing beside the elegant grand piano, they exploded into applause. And it was no wonder. On this night, she was a vision of complete loveliness, truly angelic-like in a striking yellow dress with a scoop-necked bodice. Her hair, cascading over her slim, white shoulders, sparkled like a thousand rubies as the spotlight enfolded her. Hattie Rhodes had chosen her dress well.

Nellie's fingers began to fly across the keyboard and a hush fell over the audience as she played the introduction to the first song. Nancy's performance that night, many claimed later, was the best they had ever heard her sing. After each of her numbers the theatre erupted in rapturous applause finally coming to an end when the curtain fell, announcing the intermission.

Backstage, the two young women were having a hot cup of tea in their dressing room and discussing the second half of their program, when there was a tap on the door.

"Come," called Nellie, regretting her reply when she saw Bruce standing in the doorway.

"Hello Nellie," the conductor said haughtily, brushing past her to stand before Nancy. Taking her by the shoulders, Bruce Winters stood at arm's length as his handsome face broke into a patronizing smile. "Nancy, my dear, I could make you a star in an instant, if you would allow me," he gushed loudly.

"She *is* a star, with or without you!" interrupted Nellie, her temper rising as colour rushed to her face. She had to put up with this pompous man far too often and tonight she wasn't going to allow him to spoil Nancy's triumph.

Terry O'Reilly also heard the conductor's loud proposition as he walked past the partially open door. He stopped as a sinister smile twisted his lips. He went over to the door and opened it.

"Mister!" he growled, moving into the room. His tone of voice coupled with quick action were everything he intended as his hand flashed out and gripped the maestro's coat collar. "If you annoy these ladies again, I will put a permanent bend in your baton and possibly you as well!"

The young Irish gangster's reputation was well-known and this threat was not lost on Winters. Visibly shaken, he pulled himself away from Terry's grasp. Groaning quietly, he hurried from the room.

"What a stupid man," Nellie muttered, as the bell rang indicating five minutes to show time.

"Nice singing, Nancy. If I didn't know better, I'd think you were trying to reform me!" said Terry, winking to her before he turned to leave.

"Here we go again, dear. You've got them in the palm of your hands and it doesn't seem to matter what you sing tonight," tittered Nellie as she took Nancy's arm and they headed back to the stage.

Nellie was right. Years later, this performance would be long-remembered in Seattle musical circles. Taking her bows to thunderous applause, they were convinced to perform two encores before the audience would let her stop ... and then only when Nellie came to stand beside her, gently ushering her off the stage.

Peter was standing just offstage waiting for them and he stepped forward as they came toward him, with the applause still ringing in the background.

"The car is waiting at the back door, ladies. Come when you're ready," he announced.

Hurrying to the dressing room to collect their belongings, they were stopped many times to be congratulated as people rushed by them toward the exit. Nellie gently eased her toward the back door and finally got her outside. Peter helped get their long skirts safely into the car before closing the door.

"Where are the others, Peter?" Nancy asked as she settled back into the soft leather seats and he pulled the car into traffic.

"Mr. O'Reilly has already taken Mr. and Mrs. Jorgensen home, Miss Nancy," he replied, drawing into the late evening traffic. "I only arrived at the very end of your performance but I gather from the noise the crowd was making you were a resounding success again."

"Thank you, Peter," she murmured. *Gus and Beth were in a hurry!* She put her head back against the coolness of the leather upholstery and sighed happily. *What a wonderful evening.*

Beside her, Nellie smiled but kept silent. Nancy deserved her moment to savour her success. Nancy was surprised that she had such a wonderful feeling of contentment as she watched the nightlife of the bustling city flash by. She didn't think she had felt so relaxed since Dan had left.

Ten minutes later, they pulled in under the mansion's porté cochére and Peter got out quickly and assisted them from the car. Nellie noticed a number of cars already parked in the driveway.

"When you are ready to leave, Miss Cornish, I will be happy to take you home, ma'am," he said quietly, as Nancy went ahead. "Don't worry about the time."

"Thank you, Peter. It probably won't be necessary. There should be others going in my direction."

Nancy, wanting to share her entrance with Nellie, stood outside the door and waited. Reaching for the doorknob, the big door opened from inside and the grinning faces of Gus and Beth greeted them, hugging and congratulating them. Nancy could hear the din of voices in the background as she moved inside. She looked tentatively toward the living room, noticing the French doors were closed. Taking off their coats, they handed them to Joseph, the butler.

"You were wonderful, honey. We thought you wouldn't want this night to end so quickly so we invited a few of our friends to join us for a nightcap," Gus said slyly. He winked at the other women as he took Nancy by the arm and steered her toward the closed doors.

"I knew you were up to something," she giggled, looking up at him as he reached out to open the door. "Thank you, Gus ...," and the rest of her comment was obliterated by the cheering and clapping coming from inside the room.

Meg and Jebediah were the first to join them, both giving her a huge hug of congratulation. For the next hour and a half, Nancy mingled with the guests as servants passed around sandwiches and cakes. She received many compliments from what she knew to be the influential of Seattle. Gus made a short speech thanking Nancy and Nellie for their entertaining performance, then he made a stunning announcement.

"Beth and I have some exciting news of our own. We will be leaving tomorrow for New York where we will be boarding that wonderful cruise liner, the *Lusitania.* We're finally going to see our boys. We sail for England on the 1st of May."

A concerned buzz moved about the room and he exchanged a quick glance with Jeb.

It was well after midnight when Nancy dragged her weary body into the luxurious bed and pulled the soft quilt up around her neck. Sleep didn't come easy though as thoughts of Dan, Gus and Beth, tumbled through her mind.

When she awoke there was sunlight streaming through the window because she had forgotten to pull the blind. Meg was sitting on the bed beside her.

"You were dreaming again, love," the older woman murmured.

"I guess it was all the excitement, Aunt Meg," she said sleepily, sitting up and rubbing her eyes. "When do Gus and Beth leave?"

"Not until later today. Why don't you have a shower before you come down, breakfast is almost ready," said her aunt, as she started toward the door.

Nancy stretched her arms over her head and nodded her agreement.

At breakfast, Gus and Beth talked excitedly of their trip to England making light of the warning that German U-Boats were patrolling the Atlantic.

"They've already sunk several merchant ships," said Jebediah, his voice laced with concern.

"The *Lusitania* is a passenger liner," Gus replied, sounding to Jeb like he was still trying to convince himself.

"They wouldn't dare," Beth added, her voice catching as desperation to see her sons fought with common sense. She was finally beginning to understand that there was the possibility of grave danger. "That would most certainly bring America into the war," she said.

Realizing what she had said, a chill ran up her spine and she looked over at her husband.

"And so we should be!" Jeb murmured under his breath as he stood up and pushed his chair in.

Jeb's comment did not go unnoticed by the shipowner, but he stood up and quickly changed the subject as he went to pick up the satchel over by the door. "Nancy, I don't imagine you've been told that your fans gave so generously last night your proceeds topped $7,000! This should keep you going for awhile, young lady."

"So much?" Meg exclaimed, looking over at Nancy who had a shocked look on her face as she reached for the case. "That's wonderful! So many families have been affected by this war already."

"Including our own," interrupted Beth, looking over at her husband.

Awhile later, walking down the pathway to the dock, the group was unusually quiet. Nancy felt herself drawn toward the water at the side of the jetty and stared down at her reflection. Thoughts tumbled about her head as a nauseous feeling consumed her body. *The sea! It's something to do with the sea.*

"What's wrong love?" Beth asked, coming up behind her and sliding her arm around her waist. "You're awfully quiet."

"Please don't laugh at what I am going to say, Beth," Nancy begged. "I can feel danger in the water and I've been right before, that's what scares me. Please don't take that ship to England."

"Woman's intuition!" chuckled Gus, giving her a hug. "Off you go now, we'll see you in June."

Nancy sighed heavily, looking over at her friends with panic-stricken eyes. *At least I've told them the rest is up to them.* "Please be careful," she whispered.

By Thursday, the orchard was almost finished. After the men had gone home for the day, Nancy went outside for a walk around the freshly ploughed plot. They had all been surprised at how quickly Jack and his men managed to clear the land. Tomorrow they would be finished. She stopped, looking over the almost flat, neat lines of dirt, and the one remaining pile of still-burning scrub, trying to imagine an orchard in full bloom.

All of a sudden, the sound of Dan's laughter whispered through the trees behind her. She smiled and turned automatically to look. A cool breeze whipped at her hair and a few drops of rain splashed on her face. Thunder crashed overhead, sending her scurrying for the house, while out on the strait a distant flash of lightning lit up the eastern sky.

The storm continued into Sunday bringing with it a torrent of rain.

"Too bad we didn't have the seedlings in," she commented later as her knitting needles clicked busily and she relaxed in front of the fire.

"Not sure about that!" exclaimed Jeb, from behind his newspaper. "This storm might have washed them all away by now!"

"At least the soil will be nice and wet for them when they come," added Meg, looking up at Nancy even though the click of her knitting needles continued their steady rhythm.

Having taught Nancy to knit when they lived in town, the girl now found she often liked to sit by the fire and knit for awhile before she went to bed. Since the call had come for socks and warm sweaters for the men out in the field, it had also spurred Meg on and now she seemed to be knitting socks all the time.

*   *   *

That same day, the Jorgensens arrived in New York City. They were exhausted from their long train trip but nonetheless met with some friends for dinner. On Friday, Gus decided to visit several of his competitors in the shipping industry. Leaving Beth to go shopping, he set out alone by taxi. Over the next 36 hours he gained a much better picture of the dangers lurking in the Atlantic.

On Saturday they excitedly embarked on their journey. Standing on deck watching the Statue of Liberty disappear into the early morning mist, Beth and Gus clasped hands and took a deep breath; their fingers tightened as they looked back at the fading New York skyline.

*   *   *

A week later, Nancy was enjoying a relaxing morning after another trip to Seattle. Not needing to deliver the meat as Dumpy was going by on an errand to Salt Spring, she decided to take the truck and go into town with Meg. Jeb went out to start the truck for them but 15 minutes later they had still not heard the sound of the engine. She looked out the window to see him fiddling with something under the hood.

Jebediah was growing agitated with his limited knowledge of the new-fangled motorcars, but knowing Nancy and Meg were looking forward to their shopping trip, he worked on the engine for two hours without any success. By lunchtime, and in complete frustration, he was ready to admit defeat and was going into the house to call one of Plimley's mechanics when Jack Duggan's truck came up the drive.

"What's your problem, Jebediah?" he asked, climbing out of his truck and going over to investigate. "You look about ready to shoot someone, or something!"

"Think I need a lesson on these here engines, Jack. This one has me beat today."

"Let's have a look. It's the little things that usually cause the most problems." He fiddled with some wires, looked at the battery, then reset the controls, all the while Jebediah was watching closely. "Give it a little gas if it needs it, Jeb. I'll crank her up." Going to the front of the car, Jack heaved on the starting crank and the engine burst into life.

"You make it look so easy. I'm mighty obliged, Jack."

"Glad I was here to help, Jebediah."

Nancy had been watching from the window and now appeared on the porch.

"Is it fixed, Uncle Jeb?" she called. "Hello, Jack."

"Right as rain, thanks to Jack's magic touch!"

Scolding the truck as she drove, Nancy and Meg chattered happily as they enjoyed the pleasant drive even though they were late. The early afternoon sun was a delightful change from her usual morning trip and it seemed to lift her spirits. Meg was always happy for a change to her routine and looked forward to her Saturday outings.

Before they reached the corner of Douglas and Pandora they were surprised to see a noisy crowd gathered in front of City Hall. It was so large they were spilling out onto the road, totally oblivious to the traffic.

"I wonder what's going on?" Meg mused.

Nancy noticed an unusual number of people milling about town in groups and she was glad to turn up Douglas and get away from them. Many of them seemed to be yelling, but she couldn't make out what was being said. She decided to go to the hotel to see if Dumpy had delivered the meat.

"What's happening up town?" she asked Kate when she entered the back door.

"Go look at the Colonist on our desk," Katherine said quietly. Everyone is hopping mad at the Germans now."

She disappeared into the dining room as Nancy went into her office, picking up the paper from the desk. Even before she read the headline, a cold chill went up her spine as she saw the picture of the *Lusitania* filling the top portion of the front page. Mesmerized, she picked up the paper and read the words in the headline, GERMANS TORPEDO LUSITANIA.

"Oh God no, please!" she said aloud, with sinking heart, quickly scanning the newspaper article. *German submarine sinks Lusitania ... 1,400 passengers lost at sea.* The faces of the Jorgensens flashed across her mind and all the energy drained from her body. She grasped the desk and slumped into the nearest chair. *I was right, it was the sea!*

She forced herself to read the list of Victoria's known casualties, noting the familiar name of the prominent family of Dunsmuir ... Lieut. James. She gasped. Even the heir to the wealthy Victoria family whose grandfather had built Craigdarroch Castle had not escaped the ire of the German Navy.

"They say there's a screaming mob gathering in front of the German Club," Kate called from out in the kitchen, even before she came to the office door. "Nancy, will you tell Dumpy to come get me at six. You'll not find me walking the streets on my own tonight ... are you all right?"

"Beth and Gus ... I think they were on board the *Lusitania.*"

Kate came over to her and put her arm around her shoulders. "What do you mean you 'think they were,' Nan? Don't you know for sure?"

"That's the trouble, I don't know," she cried, covering her face with her hands. "We were trying to talk them out of it after all the warnings in the news, but they left anyway. Beth wanted to see the boys so badly. I can only assume they were on board."

"Can't you phone someone to find out ...?" Kate moved toward the door when Mary called from the kitchen.

"You're right. I'll call their house. One of the servants should be able to tell me something. Or I could contact Terry, surely he would know," she muttered, continuing to talk to herself after Kate had gone. "Thanks Kate!" she called after her friend who had disappeared into the dining room.

Just then, Meg appeared at the back door.

"Nancy's in her office, Miss McDonald," called Mary.

Hearing her name, Nancy looked up.

"We won't be going shopping today, Aunt Meg, we need to get home," she said quickly, folding up the newspaper and tucking it under her arm. "I'll explain as we drive. Goodbye Mary," she called as she opened the door and followed Meg outside.

It took patience to push the truck through the crowd but Nancy made a determined effort to cross Douglas and, achieving that, they moved slowly down Broughton Street. Shops were closing and shutters were being hastily erected as traders prepared for trouble from the angry mob.

Meg had immediately noticed Nancy's change of mood. *Something has happened and I hope she tells me soon or I'm going to burst!*

Dumpy was standing guard near the road, swinging a club in his hand and scowling fiercely. His almost six-foot broad frame made him a menacing figure and he was hoping to deter any intrusion. Pulling alongside the walkway, Nancy shouted Katherine's message, seeing him wave before driving away. She worried about leaving him alone but knew he'd be leaving in a couple hours. Her mind in turmoil, she completely forgot that her aunt didn't yet know what was going on.

Angry yelling could be heard uptown in the direction of the German Club and then the crashing of glass, but she breathed a sigh of relief as it faded into the distance. By the time they turned onto Hillside from Quadra Street it all seemed like a bad dream. The stillness of the Cedar Hill countryside made her feel like she was in another world where only beauty and solitude prevailed.

Nancy had gone so quiet, Meg looked over at her. "Nancy, are you all right, lass? Do you know what the riot is all about?"

"Oh gosh, I'm sorry, Aunt Meg. Yes, actually I do know. Take a look at that paper I picked up at the hotel but, be prepared, it's a distressing story," she fought back tears as the torrent of words tumbled out.

The old lady looked over at her in surprise then reached for the paper. She had only seen Nancy act like this when worried about Dan. *What has happened?* Opening the paper, she soon understood.

"But weren't the Jorgensens ...?" she began, glancing over at the girl. Realizing she was thinking similar thoughts, her hand holding the paper began to tremble violently.

"They were supposed to be," Nancy reluctantly agreed, wiping her eyes with her hand and staring out at the road as she tried not to think about her friends. "I'm going to make a phone call to Seattle as soon as we get home."

Turning into the drive at Cunningham Manor all thoughts of the *Lusitania* disappeared momentarily as they were met by a strange sight. Jebediah and Sam were in the middle of the large, newly cleared and, now quite muddy area, that was to be their orchard. Sam seemed to be shuffling around in a circle as he waved a long-feathered staff in the air. Jeb moved to the side out of the mud but was watching Sam closely and mimicking some of his actions.

"Whatever are they doing?" Meg asked, echoing Nancy's own thoughts as they stepped out of the truck and heard the Indian chanting.

"I don't know but Uncle Jeb seems to be enjoying himself!"

"You're back early," he panted, coming over to meet them. "Sam decided it was necessary to bless the new orchard lands, asking his ancestors to send their favour and a plentiful harvest. Seems quite silly to me when it isn't even planted yet!"

"They sunk the *Lusitania*, Uncle Jeb," Nancy blurted out, unable to contain herself as they went up the steps to the house.

"They did what?" he gasped, his dirty hand flying to his mouth as he looked from one to the other with an incredulous expression. He sat down on the chair outside the door and began to pull off his boots. "How do you know?"

"It's all over the newspapers," she began, hanging up her jacket and handing him the paper.

Taking it from her, he looked into her eyes seeing her fear and his heart sank. "Do we know if they were aboard?" he asked, at the same time quickly scanning the page for information. Then he suddenly stopped and turned to face them. "Gus and Beth weren't on that ship."

"How do you know that?" she gasped, sagging into the other chair.

Suddenly the phone began to ring, startling the two women. Jebediah cocked an eyebrow and walked inside to answer it.

"Cunningham Manor," he growled into the mouthpiece.

"I have a long distance call from Seattle. Hold the line, please," Ruby Williamson, the telephone operator's familiar voice came into his ear.

"Who's that?" a familiar male voice asked abruptly on the other end.

"Jebediah Judd, you fool! What's your problem, Mr. O'Reilly?"

"Have you seen the newspapers?" Terry asked, then not waiting for an answer continued, "Thought you might like to know, Gus and Beth weren't on board the *Lusitania*. They went to England on a private ...." There was a hissing of static and the line went dead.

Ruby's voice was the next thing Jeb heard.

"Sorry Mr. Judd, we're having trouble with some of the lines today. Your party's gone, sir. Goodbye."

"What did he say?" Nancy asked fearfully, standing at his elbow.

"What did I tell you," the old man smiled. "Gus and Beth weren't on the *Lusitania*. We were cut off but I heard enough to know they must have heeded our warnings."

Meg sighed with relief, stopping to dab her eyes with her apron as she stood at the sink. Nancy slumped into a nearby chair. Crossing her hands over her heart, she closed her eyes and exhaled deeply.

Sunday afternoon they all climbed aboard the *Stockholm* and motored over to Salt Spring Island, keeping the redhead's promise to provide transport for Ben Wall. Having sent a message to him the week before via one of the local farmers, she hoped he would be waiting.

On the way, they pointed out some of the landmarks to Meg. At Sidney's rail terminal, two engines puffing black smoke, stood waiting for Captain Van Saint's barge which was just docking.

Jebediah also noticed the Saanich Canning Company's barge tied up at the dock. It was piled high with snow-white clam shells. "What the devil do they do with that lot?" he asked.

"Dan told me they go to Bellingham, but he didn't know what they did with them."

Meg gazed around her. "What a beautiful place!"

"You haven't been up the Sansum Narrows before have you, Aunt Meg?"

"No, it's the first time I've been so far north on this side of the island. You know how fond I am of boats, so I never wanted to go even if the Joyces had the time to take me."

"Hold on, now!" Nancy warned, opening the throttle as they entered the light chop in the channel. She slowed as they turned into Vesuvius Bay and they could see Ben and Asha waiting on the small dock.

"Hello Ben, Asha, everything is on schedule and the saplings arrive in the morning," she informed the coloured man, when she stepped onto the jetty. "Can you have them all planted by lunch time?"

"Tomorrow?" he asked, rolling his eyes in dismay then glancing at his wife.

Asha smiled then threw up her hands and burst out laughing.

"Miss Nancy's just funning you, Ben, just funning! These your folks, missy?" she murmured shyly, staying close to her husband.

Yes, this is my Aunt Meg and my Uncle Jebediah," Nancy said proudly. "They live with me at Cunningham manor."

Ben gave his wife a quick kiss on the cheek and they all climbed aboard. As they pulled away from the dock, Asha stood waving until they were out of sight. *She looks so forlorn and alone*, thought Nancy.

212

This was a feeling she knew all too well of late. Ben paced the outside deck interested in everything around him. As they slowed a bit to go through the tidal pools, they could hear him singing softly.

Listening intently, Nancy turned the wheel over to Jeb and went outside to join him quietly humming the melody as he sang. A log boom entering Cowichan Bay slowed their progress as two tugs toiled against the tide manoeuvring the boom toward a nearby sawmill.

Ben's eyes opened wide when Nancy pointed to Cunningham Manor up on the cliff. *It might take more effort than I thought to prove to him we're just normal folk!*

When they entered the house, she showed him to Dan's room and the coloured man shuffled nervously in the doorway.

"B-but, I can't stay here," he stammered.

"Oh yes you can, and you'll be eating with us as well," she insisted in a kindly tone.

"Could I see the new orchard, Miss Nancy?" he asked, trying desperately to hide his discomfort.

"Come down when you're ready, Ben. Uncle Jeb will show you."

Setting his case on the floor, Ben let his gaze wander slowly about the room. His eyes came to rest on the life-like picture of Nancy, hanging prominently on one wall. Sketched in brilliant colour it was enclosed in a handmade wooden frame. He could feel the warmth of her smile and he moved across the room. On a shelf by the window was an intricate model of a whaling boat. He stood admiring it for a few minutes but didn't touch it. He drew the curtains back. This room faced the side of the house and he was pleased to see he had a view of a corner of the newly cleared land. He stood looking at it for a long time before he turned and walked to the door.

Jebediah took him outside and they walked around the perimeter of the 5-acre plot. The old detective laughed as the coloured man picked up a handful of the damp soil and lifted it to his nose. Then he rubbed his fingers together letting the soil run between his fingers. All the while he muttered to himself. Lastly, he licked some of the dirt from his hand then spit it out, grinning at Jebediah's expression of revulsion.

Chapter 22

Dan sat in the cramped and muddy trench with ten other soldiers trying desperately to read Nancy's last letter without getting it wet from the rain which had been inflicting misery continuously on them for days. Some of the words were smudged now but he knew them by heart so it didn't really matter. He tried to imagine her voice as he read it for probably the fiftieth time.

Here in Flanders it had been raining for eight days with sporadic hard fighting and the men were exhausted from lack of sleep and sickness. There had been no mail in weeks in this God-forsaken area of Belgium and they were all so tired, restless and desperate for word from home—anything to help them forget what was going on around them.

The day before there had been a lull in the fighting as the enemy retreated, but they knew that wouldn't last. The Canadian artillery line had struggled to move forward through the mire worried the guns would catch them unprotected in no-man's-land. The screaming of terrified horses was indelibly etched on his mind and, in frustration, he folded the letter and tucked it safely back into his pocket. Then, off to the east, the guns began their incessant booming all over again.

Adjusting his helmet, he leaned against the side of the hole and cautiously looked over the top as he waited for orders. His eyes darted about barely noticing the flat landscape interrupted only by an occasional burnt-out tree and remnants of a stone wall. He had often tried to imagine how it would have looked … someone's home and garden … children playing not so long ago … but today he had his own survival on his mind.

From the corner of his eye he caught the single flash of light and signalled his men to readiness. Furtively he viewed the scene around him, barked another order and, together they scrambled over the walls to their new gun placements. This time there were only three others with him as they waited for replacements. Two of them were young, inexperienced and scared.

He set the measurements into the cannon and took one last visual measurement before giving his men the command. The shell was sent on its way. He listened for the explosion as they readied another shell.

He'd grown used to the killing after three months of hell watching his comrades die all around him. He just wanted it to be over and to be alive. His only solace was his thoughts of Nancy, Meg and Jeb ... and their orchard.

*   *   *

"Darn this war anyway," Nancy muttered to herself as she chugged past the noisy rice mill on Store Street on her first day back to work after the *Lusitania* sinking. She told herself she should change her route if the noise bothered her so much. *Maybe I'll do just that tomorrow,* she vowed. *I suppose as long as the war is on I'll have to put up with it.* She wondered how anyone living nearby, especially in Chinatown, could possibly sleep.

She thought about how happy she'd been this morning seeing Ben working outside on the land, then realized how quickly her mood had changed. She thought how unhappy many Victorians were getting as worry permeated their lives. *You've become positively grumpy, Nancy. Buck up, girl! This will never do.*

Trains belching smoke and steam waited at the E&N Railway Station and traffic blocked her way. Turning up Fisgard, she noticed the unusual presence of police and soldiers patrolling the streets.

It was then she noticed the damage. Shop windows were broken and walkways littered with debris. Passing the German Club, she caught her breath when she realized nearly all of the windows had been broken and piles of smashed furniture lay on the sidewalk. It gave her an uneasy feeling as she moved down Broughton and onto the B&W dock.

"Did you see all the mess?" Dumpy asked from the doorway. "That mob sure went on a rampage Saturday night, they virtually destroyed the old Kaiserhof Hotel. I guess changing the name to the Blanshard Hotel didn't save them after all!"

Nancy shook her head in dismay as she read the Sunday newspaper that Dumpy had left open on the table. It told the sad story of how many respected businesses had suffered wanton damage because they were owned by men of German extraction. She gasped when she read the unbelievable news of the complete demolition of the old Kaiserhof Hotel; and banged her fist on the table when she read about the looting of Simon Leisers. She remembered him as the kindly grocer on Yates who, Waldo had told her recently, had lived here for 35 years and had the largest wholesale grocery and liquor business in the province.

"Those poor people," she said sadly, looking up at Dumpy. "This war is affecting more people than we thought possible. Harry Tabour was right. It was a good thing he left when he did. Where is it all going to end?"

"We can only hope soon. This is getting out of control. Can you imagine, if it's happening here, it must be happening elsewhere, too? Come on, I'll walk you over to the hotel," said Dumpy, opening the door for her.

As they passed Government Street, they saw city crews were still cleaning up the mess, and nearby, several armed militiamen stood keeping a watchful eye. Called in by Acting Premier Bowser at the height of the riot, even their presence, along with many local soldiers, had been unable to prevent the worst of the damage which went on into the night.

All morning, the buzz in the restaurant naturally centered on the Saturday riots and now that more information was available on the *Lusitania* sinking, it became public knowledge that 14 Victorians were among the dead. Bitter arguments erupted between tables as men voiced their opinions as to why the riot had gotten so out of hand. Some agreed with the intolerance of the government while others blamed the saloons and taverns with their free-flowing liquor.

As each day went by, she looked forward to going home to see Ben's progress and, each night, after driving home past neighbouring orchards, often getting a whiff of the wonderful scent, she was pleased to see how much work had been accomplished. She tried not to think of Dan but there had been no letter for over two weeks and she ached at the thought of him. She desperately needed to know that he was all right although she felt sure he was for there hadn't been any other bad dreams or premonitions in weeks.

She took note of Jebediah's interest and involvement with the orchard, arranging with local farmers to buy load after load of manure which he helped Ben spread on the soil. He also acquired a regular worker in Kent McLeod, an amputee soldier trained by Emil Layritz. Kent lived nearby in Gordon Head and it was quite convenient for him, riding his horse over each day. Ben accepted him eagerly and they seemed to work well together.

Jeb told her that Kent was a jovial soul who made light of his injury, a leg blown off below the knee, and rarely talked of the war. He used both a stick and a pegleg but told Jeb his stump got so blistered with chaffing he preferred to hobble around on his stick.

"That kid has more guts than I would have under the circumstances," said Jeb one evening over dinner.

"Kid? Is he so young?" asked Nancy.

"Told me he was 21-years-old last month," replied Meg. "He's such a nice boy, too. It's a real shame what this war is doing to our young men."

Nancy had been thinking an awful lot about the Jorgensens since the news of the *Lusitania* and as she and Jeb made their way to Seattle that week she felt a real need to speak to Terry. Jeb trained his glasses on the Jorgensen's dock and for some reason she felt quite relieved when he announced he could see Terry waiting for them. As soon as she had the *Stockholm* berthed, she leapt over the side.

Terry welcomed her with an unexpected hug and arm-in-arm they walked up to the garden. When questioned, he told her that the house had initially received a call from New York saying only that Gus and Beth were not travelling on the *Lusitania*. They didn't think much of it until they read the news of the disaster, upon which they contacted him. Later, when the Jorgensens landed in Southampton and heard the terrible news, Gus called him directly.

"I ain't never had a phone call from England before," he laughed, handing the redhead her envelope. "Gus asked me to make sure you knew they were safe and to say 'thank you'. What did he mean by that?"

"I guess we'll find out when they get back," she replied, swallowing a lump in her throat. Did he say anything else?"

"He said they'll be back before your next concert on the 25th of June ... but I've heard something else," he continued, a serious tone creeping into his voice. "You better watch out on your way home, word is out that the Eggers have a new boat and they're itching for revenge on the monster boat that blew them out of the water!"

Heeding Terry's warning, she told Jeb as they were leaving and, once out in the sound, they watched every boat with renewed interest. Turning toward the coastal town of Kingston, her eyes fixed on a group of small fishing boats. She smiled when she spotted the old Kentuckian, pointing him out to Jeb. His little boat was bouncing in the swell just north of the entrance to his cove.

Jebediah swung round peering intently through his field glasses. Tapping Nancy on the shoulder as they pulled in near Zeke's boat, he pointed out the Coast Guard cutter as it raced across the sound from Edmonds.

Nancy invited Ezekiel to climb aboard and showing a broad grin he climbed up and tied his rope to the *Stockholm's* rail. He touched the woodwork and looked all around him, his face showing a look of absolute wonder at the sight of the new boat.

At the same time she noticed the Coast Guard cutter had changed direction and was now heading straight toward them. Nancy let the *Stockholm* move forward slowly until the gun ports faced directly into their woodwork. Jebediah smiled wryly, cradling his Winchester in the crook of his arm.

"Are you Canadians?" the officer called to them. "We're trying to find Nancy Wilson from Victoria."

"So you found her," Jebediah growled, cradling his Winchester in plain view.

"E-easy now," the Coast Guard officer stammered. "We have a message from Fred Barrett in Victoria. He says there's a storm blowing into Juan de Fuca and wanted to warn you. He thought you'd be in the area!"

"But Fred's in Victoria, did you talk to him by phone?" Nancy asked suspiciously.

"Nope ... by radio," the officer replied, waving as the cutter pulled away.

"Radio?" she muttered, turning toward Ezekiel's cove. "Radio ... what the devil is radio?"

As Ezekiel disembarked and untied his boat, he grinned at his old friend who was scratching his head and looking puzzled.

"Well?" demanded Nancy, looking from one to the other. "Are you going to tell me?"

"Don't ask me," Zeke replied. "I ain't never heard of a radio."

"It's a sort of telegraph without wires," Jeb mumbled. "Oh, I don't know, ask Fred Barrett. Let's get home."

Laughing, Nancy waved to Zeke and they were soon back out in the channel. Embarrassed, the old detective picked up his glasses and searched the coastline. Nancy sent the *Stockholm* hurtling toward the top end of Whidbey Island and soon realized the wind was rising, and quickly, whipping the sea into a raging tempest.

"Think we should go back to the cove?" Jeb asked.

Nancy shook her head stubbornly.

218

As they entered the open waters of Juan de Fuca the sight that greeted them left no doubt that Fred had been right. *We're in for it this time*, she thought looking over at Jeb who appeared to be holding on for dear life as he looked straight ahead into the storm. She knew that a spring storm off the Pacific could be treacherous but she also knew that the *Stockholm* was a much stronger boat than any built in these parts. Treated right, it would get them through it. Gus had planned this boat for every situation. She hoped she wasn't merely being foolish this time.

Sheltered somewhat from the elements, in their cabin, she peered ahead barely able to see 20 feet in front of her. It had begun to rain and the increasing darkness enfolded them as they ploughed through the waves. Sinking into each trough, they were blinded by the spray as the *Stockholm* rose to take another battering.

Then, with a strange suddenness, the wind dropped and rain pelted down, so hard it looked like hail. Finally able to get her bearings and realizing they were closer to the coastline than they should have been, Nancy looked over at Jeb and grabbed his arm.

"Hold on, Uncle Jeb!" she cried as she cranked the wheel into a full 90-degree turn, at the same time pulling down on the throttle.

"Holy hell!" Jebediah exclaimed, as he watched the foam-swept rocks of Ten Mile Point slide safely by their portside.

Ten minutes later they entered the cove and, as she slowed the engines, she began to laugh. "What a treasure!" she exclaimed, patting the woodwork in front of her.

"You love it don't you?" Jebediah retorted with mock disgust, jumping onto the dock with rope in hand. "This boat and you belong together," he cried, pulling his hat down over his eyes to keep the rain off. "Danny sure had you figured out when he thought you could handle this job!"

"Oh quit your complaining. Let's get the cover on and get up to the house. I'm starving!" she exclaimed, wringing the water from her hair. "Aunt Meg's going to be mighty relieved to see us, I think."

When they wearily reached the top of the slippery stairs, Jeb headed immediately toward the house. Reaching the porch, he looked back and realized Nancy was still over at the stairs. Watching, he saw her turn back toward the water spreading her arms wide. He knew how much she loved the wild unpredictable seas and seemed to gain strength from them. She and Danny had an affinity with the ocean and having it at their doorstep beside the wind-swept cliffs of Gordon Head couldn't be more appropriate. Cunningham Manor was definitely home for this redhead.

"COME INSIDE, NANCY!" Meg called from the doorway, shaking him from his thoughts. "And you too, Jebediah, you'll both catch your death of cold!"

A minute later, the door slammed as Nancy came in and pulled off her dripping coat. Meg rushed to help her, handing her a warm towel for her hair. Nancy wound it around her head and then wrapped her arms gently around the old lady. Resting her head affectionately on Meg's shoulder, she sighed deeply.

Fully understanding the girl's thoughts, she patted her back affectionately and led her toward the warm kitchen. "He'll be home one day soon, love, I feel it in me bones."

"Oh, do you really think so, Aunt Meg?"

Meg looked over at Jeb and raised her eyebrows.

"Come child, let's have some supper and tell us your news. Ben had to finish early due to the rain so he's sitting in the other room enjoying the fire. We've waited our meal for you."

The wind and rain continued intermittently all day Saturday so Ben stayed for the weekend knowing he would be going home sometime the next week anyway. By Wednesday afternoon he and Kent finished planting the saplings. All that was left was to leave instructions for the lad in the art of taking care of them. Kent promised he'd care for the orchard as if it were his own … until Dan arrived home.

The earlier suspicions, seen in both men, had given way to a gentle friendship and when the two men parted it was obvious they had a new respect for each other and their lingering handshake told the story. Ben had grown much more comfortable at Cunningham Manor, now considering these 'white folks' his friends. When Nancy took him home that evening, she suggested he should bring Asha to visit them some weekend. He grinned broadly.

Chapter 23

A letter arrived from Dan on May 20th and he apologized for the dirt-splattered pages. *I'm now in a place call Flanders and I'm sending some of our mud home to you, honey. I have lots to share!* But Nancy could feel his fear and frustration and her heart ached for him.

More hospital ships arrived that month and the shortage of beds in local hospitals caused many generous Victorians to open their doors and hearts to convalescing soldiers. Work opportunities increased at the shipyards as war orders slowly filtered in finally bringing work for thousands of local men.

At public meetings, Acting Premier Bowser angered hotel owners and saloon keepers by continually suggesting that he was contemplating liquor control. At month end, Nancy, Jebediah and Meg went to Seattle for Nancy's regular concert. James Moore expressed his pleasure with Nancy's latest performance, while Terry O'Reilly impressed them all by dressing in his best black suit and acting as their host at the mansion.

Nancy's 19th birthday on the 10th of June was a quiet mid-week affair held at Cunningham Manor and attended by the Skillings, Maynards and Duggans, along with Eva, Kate and Dumpy. Waldo tried to keep the mood light by amusing everyone with rousing tales of his younger days as a stagecoach driver in the Interior of BC. His stories of robbers and highwaymen, heat waves and blizzards, vividly illustrated the unbelievable hardships of life on the trail in bye-gone days.

"What year was it that Nancy came to live with you on the dock, Meg?" asked Millie Maynard.

"That was back in March 1913. It seems so long ago," mused Meg."

"Gosh, Aunt Meg, how can you remember so well?" Nancy asked.

"It was a very special day when I met you, lassie!"

"It was special for me, too. I was so lonely living in my little room under the stairs at the Occidental Hotel. It does seem a long time ago."

"And look where it got you both!" Waldo chuckled.

"Aye lad," Meg sighed. "This lassie has brought me more joy than I ever deserved."

Nancy looked over at her and silently raised her eyebrows.

"Nancy," interjected Jebediah softly, going over to stand beside her. "Why don't you and Millie give us some entertainment? It's not very often we have a pianist available and a piano needs to be played, especially when they helped buy it for your last birthday!"

Nancy grinned and looked over at Millie who winked, nodding toward the instrument. Katherine's hand found Dumpy's. She had only heard Nancy sing once before and she had almost forgotten that magical night on the clifftop one year ago.

"Do you think she will, Jack?" she whispered hopefully.

"Hush, love," her husband-to-be scolded.

Millie moved to the piano and Meg got up and pulled off the dust cover. Millie sat down on the stool and reached for the small pile of music on the nearby shelf. She made several choices and set them up on the music rack as Nancy watched over her shoulder. As she began to play the first introduction, Nancy turned to face their guests.

Nancy sang three songs and her audience clapped joyously after each one. Following the third number, she suddenly left the room and went outside and over to the clifftop. In the quietness, they could hear her voice as it floated back to them on the still evening air.

"She's singing to Dan," whispered Meg, in reply to the question in Katherine's eyes.

*   *   *

Dawn was breaking and an ominous stillness hung over the trenches as Sgt. Dan Brown scanned the terrain with his powerful field glasses. British soldiers were beginning to appear and take their positions, some still chewing on their breakfast rations. But the enemy had apparently retreated under cover of darkness and all was quiet.

"Come on, lad, move that gun up," the frustrated voice of his commanding officer sounded nearby as the gun crews readied their horses. "Damnit, where's that singing coming from?"

Straining against the weight of the great guns bogged down in the mire, the screaming animals pulled, then slipped back again, before each gun was finally rolled slowly into position.

Dan's voice calmly shouted orders to his crew while his commanding officer rode by trying to keep his own terrified steed under control.

"Well done, lad, but what on earth is that singing? Can you hear it or am I going loony?" he cried.

222

The light mist was lifting from the battle-worn plains as the horse and rider went by. Dan cocked his ear to the breeze. "What's the date, soldier?" he asked the man beside him.

"11th of June, Sergeant."

"It's Nancy," he whispered, "my beautiful Nancy."

Then the enemy guns began firing in the distance.

* * *

Nancy stopped singing and Eva went out to join her. Katherine also moved toward the door until Meg's voice gently stopped her.

"Leave them be, dear," she whispered hoarsely, watching as the girls embraced on the clifftop. "Those two girls have much in common with both their men at war. Let's let them have their moment together."

"He heard me, Eva," Nancy murmured, fighting to hold back her tears. "I felt him touch my cheek. I know he's still alive!"

The Maynards were the last to leave, having offered to drop Katherine and Jack home on the way back to the city. Eva, fearless and strong-willed as ever, refused all offers for a ride and strode off through the forest alone with her thoughts. Taken aback with Nancy's perceived ability to feel Dan's presence, she needed some time to calm her nerves.

On June 23rd the phone rang at Cunningham Manor and Beth Jorgensen's voice announced they were home and had good news of their sons.

"They're still in hospital, Nan, but they're on the mend from their terrible injuries."

"I can't wait to hear all about them and especially your unexpected ride over there. We were so worried about you two."

"We appreciate your concern, dear. We're so happy we made it back in time for your concert. We'll see you all on Friday," and with that the line clicked.

Nancy slowly hung up the receiver and turned to Meg who was standing by the sink watching her.

"Well, we can stop worrying about them now," she sighed.

"Thank goodness for that!" retorted Meg.

Beth and Gus were waiting on the dock Friday afternoon. Nancy and Meg were nearly bursting; they were so eager to hear all their news. Once in the house and with a cup of tea in front of her, Nancy blurted out the question she had been waiting to ask for weeks.

"How on earth did you get to England if you weren't on board the *Lusitania*?"

"I think I should let Gus answer that one, dear," Beth replied, smiling coyly as the servants began to serve supper.

"The day before leaving New York," Gus began, "I looked up an old friend named Eric Burton. He's also a shipbuilder and he offered us his cabin to sail as a guest on his new motor yacht, the *Ballywho*. He was leaving for England the next morning, the same day as the *Lusitania*. It didn't leave us time to contact anyone except the shipping company. However, we asked our friends to phone home for us and tell them of our change of plans. I guess the servants never thought to tell anyone until they heard about the sinking."

"Personally, I think you wanted us to sweat for awhile, just so we'd appreciate you more when you returned," Nancy laughed, wiping her mouth on her linen napkin.

"Well, I admit Gus mentioned you might think that, but it was totally unplanned, honest!" objected Beth, her face growing serious. "We were shocked beyond words when we heard the news soon after our arrival in England. We had seen the *Lusitania* in New York and although we thought it seemed inconceivable that the Germans would attack it, you had all made us realize we were taking a deadly and unnecessary chance. We were horrified when we heard the news— unbelievable that one so large could go down so easily." Standing up, she quickly changed the subject. "Now, I think we had better get changed or the star performer is going to be making a not-so-grand entrance!"

They all trooped upstairs to their rooms. Beth followed Nancy, standing in the doorway while the girl entered.

"Oh my ... Beth, it's remarkable!" exclaimed Nancy, moving quickly to the other side of the room where her clothes were displayed. Hanging on its hanger was a new, emerald green evening gown with accessories. Even in the low light of the bedroom, the rhinestone-studded bodice sparkled brilliantly.

"I'm so pleased you like it, dear. When I saw it hanging in the window of that little shop in London I knew it would be perfect for you. Have a quick shower and let's see how it fits," chirped Beth, fussing around to get her a towel. "I do hope I guessed your size correctly."

After the concert, Peter quickly whisked them away to Charles Blanc's restaurant where a huge reception was held to celebrate the Jorgensens' safe return.

Nancy, now the darling of Seattle's concert-going crowd, which included a large portion of the city's elite, looked radiant in her floor-length, emerald green chiffon over taffeta evening gown with its bejewelled low-cut neckline. It had fit perfectly, of course, as she had the perfect figure and Beth had always kept careful note of her sizes for shoes and gloves. The matching shoes were not too high but had thick soles and block heels, a favourite item with stylish young women. Many came over to touch and admire her beautiful Chinese shawl of pure silk.

It was well after midnight when the limousine left the party, driving through a city still at play despite the hour. Nancy stared through the car window surprised at the number of people still milling about, coming and going from the many taverns. She loved the vibrant ambiance of Seattle.

She soon realized her eyes were fluttering with tiredness as she relaxed in the back seat. When they arrived back at the mansion Beth quickly led the women upstairs.

"It's so nice to be home again," she commented, but I'm exhausted and the rest of you must be as well." Hugging them goodnight, she told them not to rush in the morning, knowing full well Meg would be up early.

Sleep came easily to the redhead that night and for the first time since visiting Seattle she wasn't disturbed by one of her dreams.

At breakfast the Jorgensens drew graphic pictures of an England at war. They were quick to express their admiration, however, for the resolve and determination of the ordinary British citizen in the face of all the hardship.

"We're so glad the boys were taken to a British hospital. We wouldn't have been able to see them if they were still in the war zone. The care of the hospital staff was truly remarkable considering the number of patients they have. It was such a pitiful sight to see all the beds lined up in the hallway full of wounded soldiers and civilians. The British have already paid an unbelievable price for this horrid war. You simply can't imagine it without being there," Beth sighed.

Before climbing aboard the *Stockholm* later that morning, Beth hugged all of them.

"We're so proud of you, Nancy," she whispered. "And you, Jebediah, are doing a wonderful job of looking after her ... and Meg. Thank goodness for the care Gus put into the *Stockholm*. One day soon our boys will be coming home to us and we can't wait for you all to meet them."

"Beth has told them so much about you they said they feel like they know you already," Gus quipped, handing over the satchel to Jeb. "Don't forget this. I think you have some people waiting for it."

"Yes, let's go home," Jebediah growled impatiently.

"You are home, you old fool," Gus laughed.

"No, I ain't," the old detective replied, reaching for Meg's hand and smiling up at her. "Cunningham Manor is my home now, Gus, and these two ... and Dan, are my family."

The Jorgensens waved from the dock as the *Stockholm* swept out into the sound and quickly disappeared.

Walking back toward the mansion with her husband, Beth murmured almost to herself. "It's strange how much of an impact Nancy has on other people's lives."

"Not strange at all," Gus replied, pulling his wife closer. "Nancy Wilson is a very special person ... as you are, my darling."

Chapter 24

By July, Katherine and Jack's wedding plans were in full swing having arranged with the Reverend Robert Cornell to officiate over the afternoon ceremony on the 21st of August at St. Saviour's Church. They had found a nice 2-storey home in Esquimalt close by the church on Wilson Street and with their combined incomes it wasn't such a hardship to make the payments. It was large enough to accommodate Dumpy's mother and Katherine's grandparents, easing the problem of keeping an eye on everyone. Fortunately, their relations had now met each other many times and being eager to help the young couple who were trying so hard to make a life for themselves, their families had accepted the arrangement without argument.

Nancy sang at the wedding thrilling the small congregation of friends, many whom had never heard her sing before. The redhead felt a twinge of envy run through her as Dumpy placed the ring on his bride's finger and they looked at each other with such love and affection. Meg took care of the bridegroom's mother, a sickly old lady, who smiled bravely as her son walked his bride down the aisle.

At the reception in the newlyweds' home, Katherine's folks, who were here from Seattle, engaged Jebediah and Nancy in a long conversation. Her father, Jim Flounder, worked on the docks and said that the American port was roaring with trade. Knowing a bit about their trips south, he told them he knew many of the liquor smugglers including Doc Hamilton, Jack Marquett, an ex-police officer, and the villainous Egger brothers. A smile creased Jebediah's face and he slyly winked at Nancy as Jim described the Egger's new craft.

"Looks like a sailboat," he chuckled, "but don't be fooled, there's a big engine tucked out of sight and it's very fast."

Fred Barrett joined the conversation, presenting the perfect opportunity for Nan to ask him about radio.

"You want me to explain radio to you," Fred laughed. "All I know is that the voices travel on air waves."

"You're pulling my leg, Fred Barrett!" she scoffed. "Telephones use wires. What's an airwave and where do you get them from?"

"It's new," he tried to explain. "I don't know how they do it. It used to be Morse code but now we can hear voices." He watched Nancy shake her head. "That's how I warned you about the storm when you were down in Seattle?"

Still unconvinced, Nancy wandered amongst the guests until she finally got the chance to talk to the bride.

"Well, you've really gone and done it this time," she murmured as the two girls hugged each other, "but I'm so happy for you."

"So am I," Kate whispered, "because I'm two months pregnant!"

Startled by the sudden revelation, Nan stepped back to gather her thoughts. Then, eyes sparkling with excitement, she murmured almost inaudibly. "You mean I'm going to be an auntie?"

Katherine nodded, pressing her finger to her lips for secrecy. Nancy knew what a horrifyingly embarrassing scandal this could be for their family so she nodded secretively. It would come out some day but until then she would happily keep the secret.

An hour later almost everyone had left when Nancy gathered up Meg and Jebediah and they, too, said their goodbyes and headed down Esquimalt Road in Jeb's car. He slowed to cross the Point Ellice Bridge and they followed a 'No. 6' streetcar up Government to the fountain. Here it stopped and they were able to pass. Stepping on the gas, in a fit of unusual exuberance, Jeb tore up Hillside at 25 miles an hour.

"Slow down!" Meg cried. "You're driving too fast, Jebediah!"

"Sorry, love. I guess I'm eager to get home," he grunted, winking at Nancy.

All along the Shelbourne Valley people were outside working or playing and many waved to them as they passed. They slowed as they went down the drive, admiring the new orchard with the little trees standing straight and tall in their neat rows.

"They're home," Eva murmured to Dorothy as they sat on the cliff stairs enjoying the sunshine and the view. She glanced over her shoulder and noticed Sam still watching them from the tree line.

"Old Sam still makes me nervous," Dorothy complained, getting up and running down the stairs to meet them.

Over a cup of tea, Eva produced a letter received from her husband. Thomas was stationed in an administrative post in the south of England a long way from the fighting. She said he indicated he was very unhappy with the non-combative role he'd been given. She read Nancy an excerpt: *Tell Nancy, her Danny is making quite a name for himself amongst the frontline soldiers. News of his uncanny accuracy with the big guns has been mentioned in dispatches to London. It wouldn't surprise me if they didn't give the lad a medal.*

"Have you heard from him lately?" Eva asked, watching as the redhead shook her head.

"I don't want a medal, Eva, I want Danny home again," said Nancy with a deep sigh.

The conversation took a lighter note when the three women discussed the money earned from Nancy's concerts.

"We still have a surplus," announced Meg, who acted as their book-keeper. She went to a drawer and took out a ledger book. Checking it, she frowned. "There are three ladies here," she said, pointing to some names. "They don't seem to have been contacted this month."

"Widow Jones from Cook Street got married again," said Eva, with a smile. "She took a fancy to one of the neighbourhood boys who couldn't go overseas due to a minor disability." Reaching into her bag she found a piece of notepaper. "The other two went back to their families in Alberta and the Okanagan. We paid their fares," she added, holding up a piece of paper before passing it across the table to Meg.

Marking the figures diligently into her book, the Scot looked at Nancy with a question in her eyes. Jebediah, who rarely took part in the women's conversations, spoke up from the other room.

"Maybe it's time you visited the hospitals, Nan. Then you'd really get a picture of what this damned conflict is causing."

"You're right, Jeb," Eva said quietly. "I've been several times and they really do appreciate seeing people. Many of them have no families around here. Would you like to go with me, Nancy?"

"Not really, but I will," she said slowly.

Over the next few weeks, Nancy would find herself even busier than she had planned as events took shape in Victoria.

Before their wedding, Nancy had purchased the little house Dumpy's father had built on Mason Street; she was quietly making plans to house another war-torn family that couldn't afford their own accommodation.

Many local church ministers were now stirring up the public, preaching temperance and social reform from their pulpits, as the government went from scandal to scandal after newspapers announced some startling revelations.

Attorney-General Bowser began enforcing legislation limiting liquor sales to hotels, and the breweries began a massive upgrading of facilities to comply with the law. There was talk of elections from

Richard McBride when he returned home from London and still the capital city floundered in turmoil as angry mobs jeered.

One evening that same week, Nancy toured the Jubilee Hospital with Eva, talking to many wounded soldiers and listening intently to their stories of hardship. For the first time she saw the graphic results of the war and found out what living on a battlefield was like. She watched the dedicated ladies of the Red Cross and the Hospital Society as they moved about the wards trying to bring a moment of happiness to brave young men with broken bodies.

As they left, Nancy descended into silence as a feeling of helplessness gripped her. Her mind raced with terrible thoughts of the battlefront in Europe. She looked over at Eva and their eyes met.

"When will it all end?" she asked forlornly, feeling a new sense of despair.

"I don't know, Nan, but it can't be too soon."

As they bounced along Richmond Road, Eva sensed her friend's mood and understood perfectly. When she had begun her campaign to help the local families, she had felt it, too. Now she realized you just had to work through it and she knew Nancy would.

They cut through to Cedar Hill Road over one of the rough tracks and saw where the new road construction was beginning along what would be a continuation of Shelbourne Street. Presently ending at Hillside, this street was now planned to run right out to Mount Douglas Park. It was going to make their drive back and forth to town much easier. Newspaper headlines had earlier announced that this project was going to be a boom for jobless local workmen. Using horse-drawn road-building equipment, the road was anticipated to take approximately a year to complete.

The hospital visit was weighing heavily on Nancy's mind as she slowed to turn into the driveway at Cunningham Manor.

"You go ahead, Nancy. I'll walk home from here," said Eva, reaching for the door handle.

"I'm sorry, Eva. I wasn't thinking. Let me take you home." Nan stopped the truck but she gazed pensively over at the new orchard.

"Oh no! I enjoy the walk and it only takes a few minutes," her friend replied, climbing out quickly. "I see your orchard is coming along nicely."

Nancy nodded silently then watched her friend disappear into the trees. *What an indomitable lady*, she thought. *Few know what a driving force she is. I wish I could be more like her.*

Nancy had realized some weeks earlier that it was Eva who was giving her much of her will to carry on. With the widows and family project now involving her more, she found herself thinking less of Dan, and the days were going by more quickly. She was even sleeping better. But today the visit to the hospital had thrown her mind into turmoil again. After talking with the wounded soldiers she was better able to understand what Dan was doing in Europe and it horrified her.

Summer went by too quickly and soon autumn arrived. There was a definite chill in the air and the residents of Cunningham Manor began preparations for another winter without Dan. Trips to Seattle were becoming quite hazardous not only due to poor weather conditions but also the number of freighters making their way down Puget Sound to the bustling American port had increased substantially. In stark contrast was the commerce-starved port of Victoria.

Newspapers continually reported chilling news of a war accumulating astronomical numbers of casualties. Nancy's heightened awareness made her now realize there was no end in sight to this dreadful battle playing itself out so far from home. She searched the post every day for Dan's letters, going for weeks without news, then one day receiving several having accumulated it seemed in some army postal center.

Seattle's industry was benefiting greatly from its state of neutrality in the European war, although many internal conflicts were raging through local levels of government. Reform took the shape of a referendum on prohibition and only six counties voted 'wet' for the freedom of the drinking establishments.

Liquor became a much-sought-after commodity as saloons closed and the underworld element moved in. Rivalries developed and turned into violent confrontations as booze-laden trucks roared over state borders shrouded by night. Vancouver Island, though itself facing the threat of prohibition, was quickly becoming a water-borne supply route.

Late in December 1915, Premier Richard McBride announced his resignation and William Bowser at last took full control as premier. Newspapers called him the "Little Czar" or the "New Brunswicker" and Nancy's patrons all agreed that the popular vote would desert the new premier in the upcoming elections.

But she soon found she had little time to care about politics as Katherine became violently ill one day while at work. Rushed to St.

Joseph's Hospital by her deeply concerned husband, sadly she suffered a miscarriage and went home to recuperate.

Aware of the situation, the owners of the Balmoral talked with Nancy and decided to hire a new restaurant manager. A month later, both girls terminated their employment deciding the time was right to open their own restaurant sometime in the New Year.

Jebediah and Nancy took on two extra liquor runs to Seattle for Christmas and on December 22nd, the three of them arrived at the Jorgensen mansion for Christmas dinner. Nancy had earlier agreed to sing for two holiday concerts at the James Moore Theatre, again receiving the proceeds for her cause.

In January, with more free time on her hands, she saw Kate often as they visited back and forth, helping her deal with the loss of her child while they made plans for their new business.

She visited the Royal Theatre for the first time and marvelled at its lavish interior. Attending one evening with Meg and Eva, they watched top-line American artists perform an opera to a small but appreciative audience.

"This place was built in 1913," Eva explained in a whisper. "It's such a shame it's not a success."

At intermission they were approached by a well-dressed old gentleman, who apologized for his interruption and introduced himself as Colonel Meyer from Virginia.

"Don't I know you, young lady?" he asked, looking at Nancy.

"How do you know her?" Eva asked, as Nancy shook her head.

"I'm sorry, ladies, an honest mistake," the colonel assured them with a flourish. "But you certainly look like the young woman I heard singing in the James Moore Theatre in Seattle at Christmas."

Quick glances flashed between them as Nancy's face turned several shades of crimson. The colonel, noticing their reaction, smiled with satisfaction.

"You are Nancy Wilson, aren't you?"

"Yes, she certainly is, Colonel Meyer," Meg retorted proudly.

In the next few minutes Colonel Meyer begged, then cajoled her to sing at the end of the opera performance, explaining he had some clout with the organizers. Urged on by her two companions, Nancy finally gave in and they had a quick discussion about what she would sing.

"Follow me," he insisted as the bell rang for the second half of the performance "You can use my box, it's at stage right." Leading them backstage through a group of artists waiting for the next act, he opened a door and soon had them all seated in the prime location. "I'll join you in a moment," he whispered, leaving them quickly.

Nancy was surprised to see Colonel Meyer appear on stage shortly after. He walked boldly to center stage in front of the curtains and began to address the audience in a loud penetrating voice. The noise level dropped but the audience continued returning to their seats obviously wondering what was going on.

"Ladies and Gentlemen, may I have your attention, please. I beg your indulgence to remain in your seats for a few minutes following the performance. I have a special treat for you which I don't believe you will want to miss. Now, please enjoy the opera."

There was a buzz of puzzled conversation but it soon stopped when the orchestra began to play. True to his word, when the opera was over, the colonel appeared again, with Nancy beside him.

"This young lady, whom many of you will recognize, is Nancy Wilson," his voice boomed. "Nancy is one of your own citizens, but few of you realize, I'm sure, that she is Seattle's favourite singer. I leave her with you to be the judge." Under his breath, he whispered, "You show 'em girl!" as he moved offstage.

There was a doubtful look on the conductor's face as he stared at Nancy thinking she was hardly dressed for a performance. Taken by surprise at the turn of events, he watched to see if she desired their accompaniment. The redhead, however, did not look his way. She simply stepped closer to the footlights and began to sing.

The conductor instantly recognized the song, *My Home Is In The Highlands* and, after speaking softly to the musicians, those who knew the piece began to play. The sounds of her magical voice filled the theatre despite the lack of a full orchestra and the audience was spellbound. Someone dimmed the lights and a spotlight was flicked back on. Suddenly, the sound of soft humming voices came from behind her as the opera chorus and cast moved back onstage and the curtains opened.

The conductor couldn't help but smile. This young woman sang with such clarity and feeling she could easily have been one of the soloists tonight. He remembered a comment made by a friend who had heard her perform in Seattle some months before. *The voice of an angel and the looks to go with it*, he had said. More of the orchestra was playing now and he kept the music toned down so Nancy's voice could rise above them.

"MORE!" yelled someone from the dark recesses of the theatre as the number ended, many others clapped their agreement.

As if it were the most natural thing to do, Nancy looked down at the orchestra and asked if they knew *Lily Marlene.* The conductor nodded, announcing her choice to the orchestra. Playing from memory, the orchestra swung straight into the popular soldier's song, followed quickly by her own favourite *My Bonny Lies Over The Ocean.*

Wild cheering erupted and the audience, led by the colonel, rose to their feet as Nancy finished her song. She curtsied gratefully, nodded to the orchestra and chorus, and quickly left the stage. Eva and Meg were waiting for her in the wings along with the colonel. They hugged her jubilantly and helped her on with her coat while the colonel wished her well assuring her they would meet again some day. Then the women made a hurried exit out of a side door onto Blanshard Street. Mingling with the crowd, they escaped unnoticed.

A few days later, Waldo brought news of the perfect location for their restaurant. He said it was on a corner at Richmond across from the Jubilee Hospital. A burned-out shell of a house was all that remained on the lot when Nancy bought it cheaply, coaxing Jack Duggan into rebuilding it for them.

On the last Friday in January, an unknown boat appeared from Keystone Harbor and followed them down Puget Sound as the weather took a turn for the worse and storm clouds gathered to the south. Meg was with them and Jebediah didn't want any surprises—worrying about the weather would be enough on this trip. He said nothing to Nancy but he watched them through his field glasses, failing to identify the boat.

"Pull over toward Maxwelton," he ordered taking her by surprise. "Slow down, but don't pull right in."

"Don't worry, I'll soon lose them!" she exclaimed, seeing the snowstorm coming at them behind the three freighters looming off their portside. "Hold on!" she cried as the *Stockholm's* engines burst into life.

Too late he grabbed for support but losing his balance went crashing against the back wall of the cabin. Crying out in alarm and gasping for breath he cursed as he sat down heavily beside Meg who held onto him protectively.

Foghorns sounded and their distinctive notes whispered on the wind from the Edmond's headland. *That's probably West Point Lighthouse,* Nancy thought as she adjusted her course unaware of Jeb's difficulty.

Her evasive action seemed to have worked but the snowstorm was closing in around them and she couldn't be sure. At this point, she was mighty grateful to hear the foghorns and catch short glimpses of the coastline.

West Point, with its small square lighthouse and several white-painted outbuildings, appeared like magic as the weather began to break up. Jebediah breathed a sigh of relief as the hills of Magnolia went by on the portside and the Jorgensen boathouse loomed into view. Men on the dock looked startled as the *Stockholm* raced toward them, but the redhead's control was perfect. Brakes were applied and the stern swung around in one confident motion before sending the red-and-gold craft shooting backwards into the boathouse and out of sight.

Jebediah leapt over the side rail and hurried to the end of the dock sweeping the water with his field glasses.

"What's happening out there?" Terry growled, helping the women alight.

"Uncle Jeb's watching for the boat that followed us down the coast," she laughed, "but I gave them the slip."

Snow turned to rain before the detective's eyes picked out the first of the freighters, moving slowly down the waterway. As the last one passed, he focused his glasses on the dark-coloured speedboat following closely behind, centering his attention on the two men on deck.

"Let me see!" Terry snapped, taking the glasses from Jeb. "They're Billingsley's men," he hissed into the wind. "A word in Jack Marquett's ear will soon take care of them!"

"That's scary," Jebediah muttered, taking back the glasses and staring at the young gangster through pinched-up eyes.

"You ain't scared of nothing, you old coot," Terry retorted.

"I am when punks like you start using their brains," Jeb replied with a chuckle. "That *is* scary!"

A grin creased the young man's face as Jebediah strode back toward the boathouse. He admired and respected this old man's courage. There was a fire in his eyes that was not to be ignored and during those times he moved with the confidence of a much younger man. Servants came out to look after their luggage and Jebediah took Meg's arm and escorted her along the path.

Gus and Beth were overjoyed to see them and Beth immediately led her toward the stairs, eager to show her the dress Hattie Rhodes had sent over for the concert. A car door banged and Nellie rushed through the door.

"I need to run through these songs with you, Nancy," she called. "I'll be waiting at the piano."

The women went up the stairs and Beth led the way to the guest room that had become Nancy's own.

"There," Beth purred, pointing to the turquoise satin gown trimmed with matching lace. "Isn't it magnificent?"

Speechless, Nancy moved across the room and her hands caressed the shiny turquoise garment, gently touching her cheek to the silky smooth fabric. Beth smiled as she saw the stunning effect the colour was going to have with the girl's red hair. "It's luxurious," Nancy whispered, picking up the silver shoes that completed the outfit.

"I really need you now, Nancy!" Nellie called frantically from the bottom of the stairs.

Nellie was sitting at the piano and frowning at the music she was playing when Nancy appeared. Reaching for the sheet of handwritten notes, Nancy scanned the page then put it back on the music stand. As Nellie began to play Nancy picked up the tune and followed over her friend's shoulder.

Nellie's head began to nod as her hands flashed over the keyboard. *That's it, that's it! I knew something was wrong*, she thought, relieved with her discovery. "Thanks love," she said, making some adjustments with a pencil. "I must have made a mistake in the key when I copied it. Let's quickly go over the two new songs, *There's A Long, Long Trail* and *Keep the Home Fires Burning*, then we'll just have time to eat.

The James Moore Theatre had a *Sold Out* sign posted at the box office when the Jorgensen car pulled up to the main entrance half an hour before curtain time. Although it was a cool evening, it did little to dampen the enthusiasm of the theatregoers who savoured every moment of Nancy's performance.

Nan also found she was enjoying these concerts more and more as Seattle audiences welcomed her as one of their own. At the after-party she was feted as the toast of the town and basked in the luxury of her own popularity.

Rising late on Saturday morning, she was still eating when Gus came in greeting her with news that a new storm was coming in over the Cascades.

"Better make a dash for it," he advised.

"You could stay, dear," Beth pleaded, patting Nancy's hand.

236

With no guarantee of when the weather would clear, they decided unanimously to leave immediately so Nancy finished her breakfast hurriedly. Jeb had the *Stockholm's* motor already running when she and Meg arrived at the boathouse and goodbyes were said once again, promising to phone when they arrived home. Bundled up against the cold, Gus and Beth stood at the end of the dock and waved until the boat disappeared into the rainy haze. Knowing his wife was feeling a great deal of concern for their safety, he drew her closer.

"The *Stockholm* was especially designed to cope with these storms, Beth. Nancy has already proven she's as good as any captain that sails these waters. Come on, you're shivering, let's go sit by the fire with a nice cup of tea."

Out in the sound, the powerful boat was tossed about like a cork in a bathtub but they hung on for dear life as they fought their way up the inside passage. Not yet as tumultuous as their trip several weeks before, it was nonetheless a scary experience, especially for Meg, who tried bravely not to show her apprehension. Before reaching the strait, the rain turned to wet snow making visibility even more difficult. Three hours later they all breathed a sigh of relief when they saw the familiar landmarks that told them they were almost home.

Strong winds and sleet beat down on Gordon Head all weekend, as the storm virtually closed down the Pacific Northwest. A drop in temperature on Monday afternoon warned of worse to come and, by Tuesday noon a heavy snowfall brought Victoria to a standstill. Soldiers were called out to help overworked city crews dig walkways along main streets in a desperate effort to keep traffic and people moving.

Relieved that she didn't have to go into town, Nancy talked with Dumpy on the phone at the office. She was shocked when he announced that trams were littering the downtown streets as snow-drifts hampered their movement.

"Many people are leaving their cars on the side of the road. I imagine there'll be a lot of unexpected visitors in hotels tonight! I've secured the boat and equipment as best I can, Nancy, and I'm going to walk home before it gets any worse. Our phone is out so I can't call Kate, but we'll try to phone you later."

By the next day, Victorians were complaining it was the worst snow storm they had ever experienced and abandoned motor vehicles littered the city with only their roofs showing as stark evidence of their drivers' frustration. The Victoria Fire Department, with snow drifting to their rooftop, was rendered totally inoperative. Many small boats sank under the weight of the snow but Dumpy struggled into town wearing homemade snowshoes and shovelled out the little blue boat before it became overwhelmed by the white blanket.

On Friday morning, Nancy and Jebediah took Meg with them when they went to load the *Stockholm* in town. Having been cooped up inside for a week, Meg was glad to escape for a few hours.

"How the hell did you get here?" Waldo exclaimed in surprise when he saw her. "There ain't nothin moving outside the city."

"By boat," she laughed. "I had to come and load up, but my shipment hasn't arrived at the dock yet!"

"By George, even a snowstorm won't stop you … I'll go call Harvey and Briggs for you!" The haulier shook his head muttering to himself, then disappeared inside the warehouse.

A train whistle sounded as one of the E&N locomotives chugged into the station at the bottom of Johnson Street.

"I thought you said nothing was moving!" she called after him.

Meg, meanwhile, deciding the street was too slippery for her, sent Jebediah to do her shopping at Spencer's. She stayed inside the office, only venturing out after Dumpy had cleared the walkway. Looking about her, she knew she had not seen anything like this since leaving Nova Scotia many years before. Shivering, she went back inside, poured a cup of coffee and went over to the window. Looking over toward Laurel Point she noticed the paint factory roof looked rather odd compared to all the others around it covered with white.

"Must be very hot in that building," she declared, pointing across the harbour as Nancy came up beside her.

"Yes, it might have saved them from a nasty accident," mused the girl, still finding it hard to believe the sights she was seeing around the city. "It's not exactly the weather Victoria wants to become known for is it, Aunt Meg? It's a good thing it doesn't happen when all the tourists are here!"

"Oh look," exclaimed Meg. "They're dumping snow into the harbour."

"Yes, they have a lot of soldiers out clearing streets and loading drays with the pesky stuff. It must be awfully cold for the poor horses."

"Everything looks so pretty in the snow," Meg said thoughtfully, looking out the window again. "Look at the lawns over at the Empress and the Parliament Buildings. It's such a shame it creates such havoc."

The door opened and Dumpy came in stomping his feet and blowing on his red hands. "The shipment is here. Oh, and I have some good news for you, Nan," he said brightly. "Kate is eager to get started on the new restaurant!"

"All right! That's the best news I've heard for awhile," she replied.

Half an hour later, they were back on the water pushing through great lumps of snow that floated in the harbour as Nancy manoeuvred the *Stockholm* out into the strait. From the east, a naval vessel was coming toward them at a fair speed and Jeb pulled out his field glasses to make the identification.

"It's the *Galiano*," he muttered, holding the wheel as he handed the glasses to Nancy.

HMCS Galiano, the ex-fishery patrol vessel commanded by Robert Pope, a good friend of the Joyce brothers and Dan, had been requisitioned for war service recently. They all waved and the vessel tooted its horn. As they went by Gonzales Bay, they saw two sailing boats up on the rocks. Jeb groaned as he put the glasses to his face.

"Looks bad, Uncle Jeb?"

"Not good, that's for sure. I don't think the owners will find much to salvage there."

All along the shore they noticed piles of logs flung onto the beaches by the storm.

"Ach, that must have been a terribly fierce storm," declared Meg. "I don't remember seeing this happen very often."

"It was only beginning when we came home on Sunday," Jeb reminded her. "Those waves can toss logs around like matchsticks."

Meg looked concernedly over at Nancy as her thoughts flashed back to her father and brothers who had been swallowed by the sea many years before. "Don't take any chances this trip, please lassie," she begged as they turned toward home.

Later, as stories circulated about the snowstorm, one that surfaced in the newspapers was of an ingenious method of transport devised by their friend and neighbour, Algenon Pease. Apparently he had built a sleigh with a rowboat on top, filled it with the regular supply of cream for the Union Club and had his horse pull it all the way into town.

Chapter 25

Winter turned to spring but the doldrums of war and depression still hung heavy over the capital city. By April the early flowers were blooming once again and the new orchard was springing into life with the first blossoms showing on the earlier variety of the little trees.

Premier Bowser's inability to bring the good times back to the province angered the public and talk began to center on the November election of a new government.

More sadness came into Jack and Katherine's life when Jack's mother passed away peacefully in her sleep. Though not unexpected, coming so soon after the loss of their unborn child, the shock drew the young couple closer. The service was held at Hayward's, BC Funeral Parlour.

Kate and Nancy's plans to open their restaurant were finally coming to fruition with Kate deciding to take the initiative in planning a fabulous grand opening that would keep her mind on business. Jack Duggan was putting the finishing touches to the building at the end of May and although they opened the doors on May 31st, Nan wanted the advertised opening to be for mid-June, after they got the kinks out.

Unbeknownst to Nancy, Kate was planning the real grand opening for her birthday. It became an instant success with the convalescing soldiers from the Jubilee Hospital who, once they were able, came across the street to get a decent meal, or just enjoyed each other's camaraderie over a coffee.

Nancy's next trip to the post office was joyous, for a moment, receiving a letter for the first time in months. She had stopped her daily visits because the disappointment was too hard to bear over the winter. Then in early June her pleasure turned to dismay when she realized the letter wasn't from Dan but had the dreaded British War Office insignia on the corner.

With trembling hand, she carried it back to the B&W office then sat staring at it on the desk unable to summon the courage to open it. Her mind was running wild with all the worst things that could have happened to Dan. Shaking herself, she finally picked up the envelope and slit it open with the letter opener. Inside were a very official-looking letter and the grimy remains of another. Trembling, she began to read.

Dear Miss Wilson: We are truly sorry for the unsightly mess you find the enclosed correspondence, ascertained to be addressed to you. A shell destroyed one of our mail boxes and this is all that remains of your letter from Sgt. Brown.

She sighed in relief and dropped her head into her hands. Heavy footsteps sounded outside and the door opened. A voice began to speak, then stopped abruptly, seeing the opened letter on the table. Waldo moved quickly in behind her, resting a hand lightly on her shoulder as he reached for the official-looking letter.

"You had a scare didn't you, love?" He gently pulled her to her feet and wrapped his arms around her. Dropping her head onto his chest she began to sob. Waldo had watched Nancy grow from a homeless child to a successful business woman and being told by his wife he could be a softy when required, he recognized this as being one of those moments. He'd always had a soft spot for Nancy, ever since that day many years ago when he watched the 15-year-old waiting on tables at the Occidental. Her determination had gained his admiration and respect, often reminding him of a much younger man he had known intimately … himself.

That evening Nancy and Meg put the pieces of Dan's letter dated May 8th together. Copying it meticulously they tried to fill in the missing words. It was typical Dan with light-hearted comments on the countryside and unending wet weather. He talked of being at the battlefront at St. Eloi and seeing Paris while on leave for a few days but longed to be home. The contents, combined with his now bold pen strokes, left Nancy in no doubt that he was healthy and strong or, at least, that's what he wanted her to believe.

However, unbeknownst to her, at this very moment, Dan's unit is fighting for their lives in an area not far from St. Eloi and Ypres. Horrendous numbers of casualties have already been reported but Dan has so far managed to elude the ultimate sacrifice, although hundreds of his men haven't been so lucky. Now an experienced battle-hardened soldier, Sgt. Brown feels no emotion as their shells hit multiple targets and the Canadians inch forward day after day, sometimes being driven back to where they began. His tears dried long ago as his men fell and dicd about him   now only a cold emptiness envelops him during his darkest moments.

In moments of danger, he draws strength from his thoughts of Nancy, often praying that his life will be spared and he can spend the rest of his days with her. Having had much time to think over the past two years since he had said goodbye to her that day at Cunningham Manor, he aches to hold her in his arms again. *I have to live,* he tells himself fiercely. *She's the only one who can possibly be the mother of my children.*

On the 9th of June, the day before Nancy's 20th birthday, James Moore prepared a surprise after the popular redhead's performance at his playhouse. As she took her bows, Maestro Winters turned to the audience and coming to their feet the crowd sang a pre-arranged *Happy Birthday*. Beth and Hattie Rhodes appeared on stage presenting her with a huge bouquet of spring flowers.

Later, Gus and Beth hosted a large cocktail party in her honour and she was thrilled to see the Maynards who had come over from Victoria to be there for this special event. But it was Nellie Cornish's gift that she would cherish the most for years to come—a tiny silver brooch with the initials of Nancy and Dan interlocked. She felt the slightest wisp of a kiss on her cheek as she left the party at midnight. Believing Dan had sent his birthday wishes from the battlefields of Europe she slept peacefully that night.

Warm sunshine greeted them the next morning as they made their way home across the unusually mirror-smooth waters of Puget Sound. It was a trip of relaxation and boating pleasure for Meg and Jebediah, still lounging on the deck when the *Stockholm* came to rest at its dock in Gordon Head.

"Don't just sit there," Nancy laughed. "Kate wants us to drop over to the restaurant for lunch."

"You go, love, you don't need us old folk," Meg sighed, as a grinning Jebediah helped her onto the dock both knowing full well about Kate's party and planning to drive there themselves.

"No!" Nancy called stubbornly from halfway up the stairs. "It's my birthday and you two are going to be there."

Bundling into Jebediah's car half an hour later, they made their way over to the restaurant and entered from the back lane.

"She's here!" Kate and Eva squealed, hearing the car arrive.

When Nancy came through the back door, Kate and Eva led everyone in a shouted, "SURPRISE!" Nancy was stunned to see all the people inside now cheering wildly with many shouts of "Happy Birthday." Eva grabbed her hand and pulled her through the crowd to the front door. As they stepped outside, the sun momentarily blinded them so Nancy was not aware of the crowd filling the sidewalk out in front. Loud cheers deafened her as a large group of soldiers on the sidewalk joined the others across the street in shouting, "HAPPY BIRTHDAY, NANCY!"

Nancy shielded her eyes and gazed open-mouthed around at the crowd, too stunned to speak. A crowd of people and many convalescing soldiers lay about or sat in wheelchairs on the lawn across the street at the Jubilee Hospital. Then from her right, a group of musicians began to play, one had a harmonica, another a clarinet, and there were two fiddlers. Nancy glanced around at the faces and, grinning, gave them an exaggerated curtsy. Then she shouted her thanks, but another cheer rose as all inside now came out to join them. Someone called, "Sing for us, Nancy."

The crowd took up the request. "SING NANCY! SING NANCY! SING NANCY!"

She raised her hand and went to talk to the musicians. Already prepared by Eva, they named several songs familiar to her and as they began to play she joined them. As the melody drifted over the crowd the men listened in silence, watching her every movement. Nancy tried not to notice the missing limbs and bandages thinking only of the smiles on their faces as they moved or clapped with the music. For the next hour, she walked amongst them sometimes singing, sometimes just talking to them.

Kate came outside with a drink of ginger beer for her. "That's all, boys," she called. "This songbird needs to have her lunch." She took Nancy by the arm and gently pulled her into the restaurant amid loud exclamations of disappointment from the crowd.

"Don't leave us, Nancy!"

"We'll wait for you, Nancy!"

"Come back later, Nancy!"

The crowd slowly dispersed and nurses arrived to help those who couldn't get back on their own accord. But this day would be well remembered as Nancy's Day—a day when the beautiful redhead had sung her heart out just for them. The restaurant had been aptly named, The Wounded Soldier, and on that sun-drenched day in 1916 she had stamped her image forever on the memories of all present.

Even the newspapers carried the story of Nancy's unselfish performance. It was written up by an enthusiastic reporter who just happened to be visiting someone at the Jubilee Hospital. He knew a human interest story when he saw it.

Offers would soon pour in for Nancy to sing, but few invitations were actually accepted, limiting her visits to the Naval Hospital in Esquimalt, Resthaven in Sidney and Stadacona Convalescent Hospital for the Volunteer Aid Detachment. She also made time one Sunday afternoon to visit the army camp at Willows Fairground and the barracks not far from home at Gordon Head.

Excitement filled the Wharf Street waterfront on the 15th, when the Langley Rooms burst into flames, spreading quickly to the Angel Hotel next door. Nancy and Dumpy watched from a safe distance as the city's horse-drawn pumper trucks arrived and scores of soldiers came running from all directions to help quell the blaze.

"It's the Lord's justice!" yelled a Bible thumping minister. He was referring to the hotel's recently tarnished image when the local magistrate had sent the lady operator to prison for selling strong liquor, contrary to Premier Bowser's new law on limited prohibition.

Dumpy and Nancy joined Waldo and Tom Ben from E. A. Morris, and many other concerned businessmen who remembered the damage from previous fires. They wanted to help knowing their own businesses might suffer if they didn't. Starting two separate bucket brigades, within two hours the worst was over and everyone was exhausted. Invited to Waldo's for a desperately needed drink, the four of them sat around his office talking.

Dumpy suddenly remembered something. "I've taken three groups of Japanese people to Nanaimo this week, Nan. They go ten at a time," he exclaimed, obviously puzzled. "We've two more trips booked for tomorrow and Monday!"

"Ten at a time!" the redhead moaned, cocking an eye at him. "That's too many."

"Hold on, love," Waldo interrupted. "I saw them. They're only as big as children."

"Why Nanaimo?" she asked.

"They're labour for the lumber mills," Tom asserted, pleased to be able to display his knowledge. "The women are wives for the men who are already there."

"Know it all," Waldo growled, getting up and refilling his tankard.

Richard McBride made one last headline when he publicly gave over $1,000 to the Jubilee Hospital just before sailing for England. This was the amount collected from his colleagues in the Civil Service as a going-away present. At about the same time, the provincial government passed the War Relief Act, effectively protecting servicemen's families from unscrupulous debt collection agencies.

Each day Nan continued to scan the long list of injured soldiers in the Colonist, reading with fear that another terrible conflict had begun at Ypres. She fervently hoped his unit had been moved to a safer place but she wondered if such a place would be possible to find.

Many a night she tossed and turned as she thought of the lack of letters from Dan. Then, one night she woke up in a hot sweat, shaking violently, but couldn't remember if it was because of a dream she'd had. This worried her terribly for a few days but eventually she dismissed it telling herself his previous messages had been much more obvious.

The Gordon Head valley was now producing mountains of berries, apples and pears, along with many varieties of flowers. Each Saturday in the summer the neighbouring farmers loaded up their wagons and struggled along the rutted and dusty Cedar Hill Road to take their wares to the Farmer's Market in town. This was the time of year they were able to scrape together a meagre living from the soil. As a result, the residents of Cunningham Manor made this trip to Victoria one of their regular Saturday outings.

Shelbourne Street was nearing completion and would soon make the trip to town much easier for everyone. It would also allow easier access to the streetcars that went up Lansdowne to the housing development of Victoria's elite, known as The Uplands. There, the trams negotiated a circle, The Loop, allowing them to easily return to the city.

Election fever began to influence the daily life of Victoria. Brewster's threat of prohibition was to be included on the upcoming ballot for the 22nd of November. It would be a referendum to the people, along with the question of the emancipation of women. Strangely, the referendum didn't close until the 31st of December.

At the end of July, they travelled to Seattle for yet another concert. But this time a surprise awaited them when they arrived. As soon as they entered the house, Nancy knew something was happening by Beth's excited manner.

From the living room, Gus appeared, smiling broadly. Two young men were with him. One had a patch over his eye and was pushing the other in a wheelchair. Nancy knew instantly it was their sons, home from England at last.

Introducing their boys, Beth made no excuses, smiling proudly as Nancy hugged each one of them and they shook hands with Meg and Jebediah.

Christopher, the youngest, had lost the sight of one eye and his left arm hung useless by his side. But even with one arm the affection between him and his brother, Bill, was obvious as he helped him with his wheelchair.

"So you're our new sister!" Bill said mischievously. "I wonder if she's got a temper to go with that red hair, Chris?"

Nancy's eyes sparkled, but Chris interrupted, admonishing his older brother. "Be nice, Bill, let the poor girl get to know us first."

"Don't you worry," Nancy laughed. "If he messes with me, I'll thump him!" Flexing her bare arms she showed off her muscles and, moving cat-like, reached for the wheelchair.

Bill showed his manoeuvrability by shooting across the room out of her reach, then spinning around and going over to his mother.

"Mom, Mom, save me!" he cried, hiding behind her.

But Nancy moved in and began flailing playfully on his broad shoulders. He reached out and grabbed her with both hands, sweeping her off her feet and onto his knee before she could stop him.

"Hold on!" he announced, pushing hard on the wheels while Nancy, screaming with laughter, clung tightly to him.

Beth, standing close to her husband, linked her arm through his as they watched. She remembered their initial reaction when arriving in England and they were informed by the doctors that their eldest son was doomed to a wheelchair for the rest of his life. "Look at them, Gus. I knew they'd like each other; you'd think they've always been together and I was afraid the idea of a sister would revolt them!"

The meal was announced and Bill rolled on through the dining room doors with Nancy still on his knee. The others followed and when they were all seated, Gus rapped his knuckles on the table.

"I expect you two to act like gentlemen tonight!" he warned, trying to keep a straight face as he looked proudly at his sons.

Bill winked at Nancy and pointed to his brother. "I always get the blame. He used to do that all the time when we were kids. He loved to kick my shins under the table, too!" He looked over at his brother and they made a face at each other. "But he won't do that anymore 'cause he knows I've no feeling in my shins now!"

It was a touching scene and Beth smiled sadly. Then realizing Billy had not lost his silly sense of humour, she laughed with him.

Nellie Cornish arrived as dinner was ending and Nancy went to talk to her. "I've picked out some more new songs but I think you'll know them," she announced. "I'd like to go over them, if we could, as well as the two new ones for tonight. It'll be a good warm-up for you, Nan."

"All right, but first you must come and meet the boys, Nellie."

After introductions were made, they went into the music room and closed the door. After 20 minutes, Nellie put down the piano lid. "Time to get changed now, young lady," she announced. "You are such a quick learner, I'm not worried in the least."

Just then there was a light knock on the door. "Nancy, you'd better come and get ready, lassie," called Meg.

Nancy went to the door noticing the Jorgensen boys were nearby and looking so sheepish she suspected they had been listening at the doorway. She grinned blowing them a kiss as she hurried by.

"My word, can she ever sing, Billy," Chris muttered to his brother as they moved away.

Nellie heard them as she collected her belongings, understanding only too well her own first reaction on hearing Nancy sing. Lifting the piano lid once again, there was a sense of joy in her fingers as they danced across the keyboard. "You haven't heard anything yet, boys. Wait until tonight, she's magnificent!"

Separate cars were used to get them all to the theatre and the boys saw no more of Nancy until they were settled into the owner's box and the curtains opened. They looked at each other in the dimly lit box, each thinking the same. She was certainly stunning. Meg smiled as she glanced over at them, both now leaning over the rail of the box.

Gus was heard to whisper. "That's shut them up!" as the orchestra began to play.

Nancy made a quick visit up to the box at intermission, receiving compliment after compliment from the boys until their mother told them to quit embarrassing her.

"*My nightingale's wings are broken but he still sings sweetly for me*," recited Chris, in a sensitive whisper, repeating a line from Nancy's last song. "You were singing that to us, weren't you Nancy?"

He reached out with his good arm and took her hand, their eyes locking for a moment as Beth watched with glazed eyes. A bell was heard in the background causing the redhead to excuse herself, scurrying away through the drapes.

247

Thundcrous applause greeted the end of the performance as Nellie joined her in the spotlight. The two young women linked hands and took call after call from the appreciative audience. A curious stillness settled over the theatre when heavy footsteps sounded behind them and Christopher stepped forward.

Holding up his good arm for quiet, he spoke as one comfortable with being in the spotlight. "Ladies and gentlemen," his voice boomed out across the now quiet theatre. "Many of you know me as Christopher Jorgensen, but what you don't know is that this is my little sister, my new little sister! Our parents seem to have acquired her in our absence and Bill and I are absolutely delighted!"

Many of the audience looked over at the Jorgensens as others began to clap. But the clapping died away and was replaced by a hushed whisper as they watched Nancy take Chris' useless left hand and kiss it tenderly. He coughed slightly keeping his eyes fixed on the audience.

"My brother, Bill, and I are just back from the war in Belgium and we bare our scars proudly," he said passionately. "But I'm damned if I know why we can't go help the Limeys; they're fighting for our freedom, too, not just for theirs!"

There was a moment of stunned silence when he finished as everyone seemed to be digesting his emotion-filled words. He was a young man, but his passionate plea had struck the audience like a thunderbolt and someone started the chant which soon filled the theatre.

"HELP THE LIMEYS! HELP THE LIMEYS!"

"You tell 'em, little brother," Bill Jorgensen yelled, dragging his wheelchair closer to the rail and raising his fist into the air.

"Holy cow," Gus moaned, "now we've got a politician in the family!"

The party following was a riot of laughter as the two girls shared the limelight with the Jorgensen boys. Beth's eyes shone with pride watching her younger son corner the politicians and win them over with his articulate arguments, only stepping away when they agreed to take his plea to President Woodrow Wilson in the capital.

A strong bond began to develop between old Jebediah and Bill, as Jeb looked after him, pushing him around in his wheelchair and telling him stories of his colourful past. Gus had apparently told the boys, when they were children, of his friend who was this legendary Pinkerton man, but Bill had thought the old detective was a figment of his father's imagination.

"I never thought you were real," the young man admitted, grinning at his new-found hero.

In the morning, Terry O'Reilly arrived at the Jorgensen's dock as the Canadians were preparing to leave. Instead of giving the satchel to Jeb, he purposely went over to Nancy.

"Word is that the cops are chasing a vicious, mystery hijacker who's working the straits," he told her in a secretive voice. "You be careful, and listen to that old coot."

Nancy's expression turned serious, fully appreciating the warning. She climbed aboard and, making sure everyone was settled, waved her goodbyes.

"We're off!" she called, moving the *Stockholm* out, and they were soon enjoying the warm breezes of Puget Sound. They called to see Ezekiel who greeted them warmly not having seen them for sometime. He offered peppermint tea to the ladies and a sample of his latest batch of home brew for Jebediah. They questioned him about any new craft he might have seen running the coast but the old man merely scratched his beard.

"Only them damned Eggers," he growled. "They're always sniffing around like a dog in heat."

The sun was directly overhead as they left Zeke. Passing Keystone, Nancy steered for Lopez and the channel to Friday Harbor before swinging past the white-stained cliffs of the San Juan Islands. Meg, enjoying the trip and delighted with the scenery, shielded her eyes from the glare as she watched a sailboat some distance ahead.

"Strange," she said aloud. "They've no sails, but they're moving!"

Jeb looked over at her and she pointed to the boat. He swung his field glasses around and trained them on the black sailboat thinking what an unusual colour it was. He leapt to his feet going to stand beside Nancy.

"Problem?" she asked, following his arm and taking the field glasses.

Meg sat with bated breath knowing Jeb was concerned about the boat but not understanding why. Jeb told Nancy what Meg had said and watched the concerned frown crease her forehead as she handed back the glasses.

"Better get Meg below deck," she suggested.

"Hell no! She won't want to miss this." Jeb turned to Meg who was watching them carefully. "Hold on tight!" he warned her, putting the glasses up to his eyes again. "Speed up and aim right for them," he ordered.

Trusting him implicitly, her hand obediently found the lever and eased the throttle open another notch. The *Stockholm* roared into life, leaping forward as the captain poured on the power, her eyes glued to the target.

"AH-HA!" Jeb shouted, watching the foam boil behind the sailboat as they, too, poured on the power. "We found 'em!"

Nancy glanced over at Jeb feeling his excitement but he motioned for her to slow down. "It's the Eggers and their new boat. No wonder they painted it black again, makes it awful difficult to see. Remember, Jim Flounder told us about it at the wedding? They've been in no hurry to show themselves to us."

Nodding, she winked at him and a wicked smile flashed across her face. "HOLD ON!" she shouted, so Meg could hear. She opened the throttle again and the *Stockholm* tore past the sailboat in the direction of home. Meg squealed as spray flew all around her. Jeb grabbed for the dashboard.

"What's that all about?" he shouted.

"Now they know this monster boat is the fastest one on the water!"

Standing on the clifftop at Cunningham Manor, Sam watched in amazement as the boat literally flew past the cove entrance, barely hitting the tops of the waves as it took a wide arc and came toward him. His mouth dropped open when the *Stockholm* suddenly slowed almost to a stop and eased gently into her berth. Nancy waved from the jetty, but received no acknowledgement as the old hermit turned away.

On Wednesday the 16th of August, Nancy appeared at the post office window and was solemnly handed another letter with the War Office insignia stamped in the left hand corner. With trembling hands and her heart feeling like it was going to jump from her chest, she forced her legs to take her outside where Jeb and Meg were waiting. Seeing her come through the door, he knew instantly something was wrong and moved toward her. She was holding her arms around her body and in her right hand she was clutching an envelope to her chest.

"A letter from Dan?" he asked, putting his arm over her shoulder.

"No, from the War Office. I-I can't open it, Uncle Jeb. Y-you do it, please," she begged, choking on the words as Meg came to join them.

"Nancy, you mustn't imagine the worst. Come on, let's get away from here," he suggested quickly, moving them along the street toward the B&W office. When they reached the boardwalk overlooking the dock, he stopped and took out his pocket knife. Neatly slitting the envelope open, he handed it to her. She shook her head and he extracted a single piece of paper. Unfolding the sheet, he held it up so they could all read it together.

Dear Miss Wilson, We regret to inform you that your brother, Sergeant Daniel Brown, has been wounded and is being treated for his injuries. These injuries are of a relatively minor nature and are not life threatening. Further communication will be issued in three to four weeks. Yours truly.

It was short, to the point and signed by a colonel. Nancy held her hand over her mouth as silent rivers of tears rolled down her cheeks.

"He's alive, honey. That's what *is* important," Meg murmured, gripping her arm firmly. "They said the injuries are not serious."

"They said they are relatively minor—that could mean anything!" she wailed.

"You must remember he's alive," Jeb added, "and he's relying on you to hold things together for him, love."

The strength of the old detective's words filtered through her tears. He was right and she knew it. She looked out over the harbour and then turned to face them.

"Help me, please," she pleaded. "I need you both now more than ever. I have to be strong and I don't think I can do it on my own."

"Yes, you can, lassie, but we'll be here whenever you need us," Meg assured her taking out her handkerchief and wiping the girl's tears.

Chapter 26

Meg and Jeb could hear Nancy's heart-rending sobs as they went upstairs to bed that night. They felt helpless but knew there was nothing more they could do to comfort her. She cried until it seemed her tears were all used up and then she drifted into a fitful sleep, imagining Dan on the battlefield, and seeing him fall to the ground again and again.

At breakfast, despite the sadness in her swollen eyes, the stubborn set of her jaw told them she was coming to terms with the news as they knew she would.

Dan's name appeared in the newspaper's casualty list that week, alerting neighbours and friends that he'd been injured. Eva and Dorothy dropped by to offer their support. Kate told her to stay home for a few days which she declined, knowing it best to keep busy. Many of her sympathetic friends sent their good wishes and regular patrons at the restaurant smiled knowingly.

Jebediah told Terry the news on their first trip to Seattle, noting the instant look of concern that flashed into the young gangster's eyes. Gone was his brashness and hard-nosed exterior, as he offered his genuine sympathy. He quietly assured Jeb he would inform the Jorgensens who had gone with the boys to their horse ranch in California.

Nancy continued to check the post office every day hoping for a letter from Dan or at least more news on his condition. Eva and Kate gave their full support and slowly laughter returned to the redhead's life as she resolved to make the best of a bad situation, praying this was the worst news she would receive.

Harry Maynard called in at the Wounded Soldier Restaurant for a late afternoon coffee one day and spoke of the upcoming election. "It's become a one-horse race," he grouched. "Brewster's Liberals are going to walk in and so will prohibition."

Arriving just ahead of him, Waldo was sitting at his usual corner table—missing the girls at the Balmoral, he often stopped in on his way home from work. Hearing Harry's comment, he chuckled out loud.

252

"Prohibition won't last a week," he forecast, "and if it does, we can all become Nancy's customers."

"Quiet man!" Harry chastised, going to sit with him. "You never know who's listening these days."

"She's not illegal at the present time here in Canada," Waldo asserted, "but if they bring restrictions in, all she needs is an export licence and then she can buy all she needs." He looked right at Harry and whispered, "Legally!"

As the men left the restaurant together 20 minutes later, they shouted their goodbyes. Nancy smiled coyly at Katherine. She had overheard part of the men's conversation and realized Waldo had just given the answer to a question that had been concerning her.

"They can't stop people drinking, can they?" Kate asked her.

"No, they can't stop them drinking, but they sure can make it illegal, if they want to!"

Leaving early that night, Nancy made her way home up Richmond, stopping occasionally to look across the farmland to where workmen were busy putting the finishing touches on the new Shelbourne Street. She turned down Cedar Hill Cross Road, intent on trying the new smooth surface. Once the Model T reached the new road it actually seemed to purr as they raced along toward Mount Douglas. Suddenly, she had to slow down as the new surface ended, dropping back onto the old pothole-strewn lane before turning onto Cross Road.

At home, Meg and Jebediah told her of the constant activity out in Haro Strait noticing many loaded barges going by of late. "Mr. Peterson called to see us today in his launch *Island Bell*," Jeb announced.

"We saw him coming and wondered who on earth it was," added Meg. "He told us the explosive works are moving to James Island."

"They desperately need the industry over in Sidney," Nancy commented. "Right now there's only the Rubber Roofing Company employing anyone. You know the one I mean Uncle Jeb ... where that big tank is on the coast? I also heard that the sawmill is beginning to run again, but the Sidney brickworks are gone forever."

Rain clouds hugged the surface of the water as the *Stockholm*, loaded with liquor, left the cove on the 25th of August. Nancy had waited impatiently for the last two weeks for further word on Dan's condition. It was growing increasingly more difficult to keep her mind from imagining the worst.

253

Raindrops began to beat on the windscreen as the speedboat flashed past the lighthouse at Port Townsend. She caught sight of the Egger's sailboat in one of the little bays and almost wished they would attack, to ease her frustration.

* * *

In a small hospital about 15 miles southwest of Ypres, Dan lay unconscious in a ward filled with injured French soldiers. Causing some concern amongst the staff at the little hospital, although they now realized his head injuries were not life-threatening, they could only hope that he would wake up soon with no ill effects.

Early on the 6th day, a young local girl doing volunteer work, came into the ward to open the curtains just as she had for the past four days of her shift. The man in the bed next to her was already awake and reached out and touched her, mumbling something in English. Turning around, she was startled when she realized it was the Canadian, Sgt. Brown. Being unable to understand English and not knowing what to do, she ran from the room to find help.

Fortunately, one of the orderlies on duty that morning was an Englishman. Going to talk with the patient, he soon ascertained that Sgt. Brown did not even remember his own name and would not be able to give them any more information than what they already knew.

Some days later, military officials came to talk with him and they tried to explain that his battalion had been caught in the German push which had killed hundreds of his men, he being one of the few survivors. Without his memory, he was not able to relate to the extent of this loss, therefore he did not ask about his friend Percy Neville who had also been on the field that day.

* * *

Rubbing the pain on her brow, Nancy skillfully manoeuvred the *Stockholm* down Puget Sound amongst a variety of other craft. Sunshine broke through the clouds as they neared Seattle, producing a beautiful rainbow that helped to lift her spirits. As they slid into the Jorgensen boathouse, Terry was there to meet them. His men took care of the unloading and refuelling and he informed them the Jorgensens were up at the house.

Entering the mansion, Nancy gripped Meg's hand but determination shone in her eyes leaving no one in doubt she was going to put on a good front tonight. Nellie took her into the music room and they had a quick rehearsal. The pianist bit her lip as she tried to control her own emotions wondering how Nancy could possibly sing when her mind was in such turmoil.

She gave no hint of her suffering as they ate dinner, then Beth and Meg took her upstairs and helped her get dressed. Nancy's spirits began to lift when she stepped from the limousine, feeling the thrilling hum of the audience as Mr. Moore led her backstage.

There was just one moment in the redhead's near flawless performance when Nellie heard her voice catch as she sang her hallmark number, *My Bonnie Lies Over The Ocean*. Sharing her pain, Nellie was momentarily afraid her own calm was going to crumble.

On Saturday morning, they left quietly before the boys were up. As they watched the boat disappear out of sight, Gus slipped his arm over Beth's shoulder. "She'll be fine, love. Our Nancy is a tough one."

At the end of September, the City Market re-opened following a period of dwindling support from farmers. Thanks to the efforts of neighbours George McConnell and Algenon Pease, fresh produce once again became available in downtown Victoria. On Fisgard Street, city workers had been busy removing the Victoria to Sidney railway tracks, the station being relocated up to Blanshard Street.

Nancy finally received a second letter from the War Office, giving more details of Dan's confinement. It said he had been moved to a hospital in the north of England. *Sgt. Brown is recovering well from his injuries*. This comment left her frustrated and fuming.

"Why can't they just tell me what his injuries are?" she exclaimed in frustration. "Do they do this to all the families? What torture!"

Soliciting help from every corner, she tried to contact Richard McBride but there seemed no way to find the answer. Waldo also tried, using his private connections, as did Harry Maynard, until finally an unexpected source provided an answer.

Eva had quietly contacted her husband, who was able to make some discreet inquiries sending his findings to Eva at the beginning of November.

Dan, he wrote, *apparently has amnesia, after being struck in the head by several pieces of metal from an exploding shell. He has no memory of anything before the 8th of July and is confined to a convalescence hospital in Whitby, Northern Yorkshire.*

"I want him home," Nancy stated fiercely when Eva read the letter.

"Honey, don't you realize how hard that will be for you if he doesn't remember?" Eva gently reminded her.

"I don't care," Nan responded stubbornly. "I'll help him remember. He *has* to remember." *Otherwise, I'll die!* she thought forlornly.

Together, they formed a plan, and in the weeks that followed she pestered the politicians with her problem wherever she could find them, sometimes in the restaurant and sometimes out on the street or at the hospitals. At the official opening of Shelbourne Street on the 18th of November, she took her plea to Mayor Stewart of Victoria and the dignitaries of Saanich. But her moment of triumph came in Esquimalt at the Naval Hospital when she sang for the wounded soldiers. Meg, who had accompanied her, was having a chat with a kindly old vicar who she discovered was leaving for England with his son, an army surgeon. She explained Nancy's plight and called the girl over to meet him.

"Nancy, I'll explain your problem to my son. Being a colonel, he may be able to do something for you," the religious man said gently, gripping his Bible tightly to his chest. "Have faith, my child, the Lord will provide."

"I try to, sir, but sometimes it is most difficult."

The vicar, Thomas William Burton, a retired clergyman from the prairies, was for the first time in years, a minister without a ministry. He had listened intently to Meg MacDonald's story, having heard Nancy sing many times as she gave her time freely to the soldiers. Before they left, he had already decided that if need be, he would move heaven and earth to reunite the two orphans.

Confidence in the old vicar's ability gave Nancy her first glimmer of hope, and Meg noticed the smile had returned to her lips. As they headed home it became quite obvious some of her old spunk had returned. Rain began to fall as they came up Hillside and turned onto Cedar Hill. When they reached North Dairy, Nancy turned off onto the bumpy old road that led to Shelbourne. Black storm clouds rolled in and a light rain had begun to fall making it difficult to see as they drove through the valley.

"I'm sure glad the new road is finished," Nancy told Eva as she drove cautiously, well under the speed limit of 20 mph.

The 22nd of November was again wet and dismal as a massive turnout of voters made sure Premier Bowser's Conservative Government was swept out of office. Brewster's Liberals were installed with an overwhelming majority just as Harry Maynard had predicted. Many believed prohibition was now imminent.

Rife with rumours, Victoria brewery operators and tavern keepers held their breath while British Columbia waited tensely for results of the referendum on prohibition and the rights of women.

Lightly dusting the landscape with snow, Christmas came to Cunningham Manor amidst a flurry of activity as Nancy continued her schedule of singing at hospitals and army camps. A festive dinner was held at Jack Duggan's in Fernwood and Nancy entertained their friends with a medley of Yuletide numbers, accompanied on the piano by Millie Maynard.

Fans in Seattle showed lively appreciation when Nancy finally gave her Christmas performance on the 29th of December. Brimming with confidence, she chatted happily with guests at the after-party, her mind full of hope that Dan would soon be coming home.

Through January and February 1917, the redhead waited for news from England. Seattle's liquor demands continued to grow helping to fill her time and occupy her mind. Meanwhile, in Puget Sound, violence often erupted in the darkness of night caused by the conflicting participants in the liquor running business.

Victoria staggered under rising food costs, lack of employment and scandals surrounding the building of a national railway to link east to west. A hot topic at The Wounded Soldier Restaurant was the announcement from the federal government, who were considering military conscription. Rumours were rampant on both sides of the border as American shipping continued to suffer huge losses at the hands of the German U-boats. Canadian newspapers urged President Wilson to join the war and fight their common enemy.

Vicar Burton's letter arrived near the middle of March. It contained the long-awaited news—Dan was coming home at last. *He's on a hospital ship which is expected to arrive in Victoria at the beginning of April,* she read. Looking at the date of the letter, she realized he was already well on his way, perhaps as far as the Panama Canal. He warned her that Dan did have amnesia and would require constant care in the beginning. *My son assured his doctors you would be up to it!*

Nancy sighed with relief.

Two days later an army vehicle rolled up the drive and pulled to a stop near the house. Jebediah was in the orchard showing it off to their visitors, Billy and Tom Irvine. Seeing the military truck, he hurried over to investigate. As the uniformed man stepped from the passenger seat, he introduced himself.

"Captain Hugo Jennings of the Medical Corps, sir. I understand Miss Nancy Wilson lives here."

"Follow me," Jeb growled suspiciously, as the driver got out and also joined them. Leading them over to the edge of the cliff, Jebediah pointed down to the dock below and called Nancy's name.

Nancy came out of the boathouse and, seeing them, excitedly raced up the cliff stairs.

"You have news of Dan?" she gasped breathlessly.

"Yes ma'am," the captain answered crisply. "If you can prove you *are* Miss Wilson."

His reply startled the old Pinkerton detective, whose temper now exploded. "Damnit, just tell her!"

Before he could answer, Billy's voice floated menacingly across the clearing as he stood with Tom Irvine at the corner of the house. His Winchester was balanced ominously on his arm, pointing at the soldiers.

"Are you having trouble with these men, Nancy?"

Taken aback by the sudden confrontation, Captain Jennings stumbled backwards throwing up his arms.

"Don't shoot! We're friends."

"Say yer piece soldier!" Jebediah growled.

Captain Jennings, a recently arrived career soldier from England who lived by the rules, told himself these were just backwoods colonials and nothing to concern himself about. He rendered a half-hearted apology to the girl, but the casual way Billy held his rifle made him uneasy and he became even more eager to deliver his message.

"Miss Wilson," he said quietly, "Sgt. Brown, is aboard a hospital liner due to dock in Victoria next week on the 2nd of April. Commander Jackson, the Chief Medical Officer at Esquimalt would like to speak with you before the ship arrives, ma'am."

Nancy nodded, but found herself so overwhelmed, she was unable to speak. The captain bowed, turned quickly on his heel, and strode back to his car. Grinning mischievously at Jebediah, Billy lowered his rifle remembering a few years back when Jeb had rewarded him with a brown top hat for capturing an outlaw.

"You always need my help, lawman," the Indian murmured, his black eyes twinkling with devilment as he walked over to Nancy.

"I didn't realize you two were here. What are you doing so far from home?" Nancy asked, hugging her child-hood friend.

Tom came over to greet her and was beginning to explain when Meg appeared in the doorway, calling them all inside. Once seated in the kitchen, with a cup of tea in front of them, Tom began again.

"We were delivering produce to Katherine at the restaurant when she told us Dan was coming home. We wanted to see the new Shelbourne Street, so we came out this way to see you."

"That's a long way by horse and cart," Meg chuckled. "You'll be late getting home."

Tom and Billy's eyes met across the table as they both burst into laughter. Tom's pipe wobbled precariously in his mouth and he pulled it out and pointed it at his young Indian friend.

"He drives," the old man gasped. "We have a new fangled gasoline truck. Didn't you see it out there?"

"I guess I didn't notice. What's so funny about that?" Nancy asked.

"Truck too fast," Billy grinned, "sometimes I bump into things!"

"Like what?" she asked.

Billy looked pensive for a moment. "Fence posts, barrels, and a cow once! They just jump out in front of me," he replied solemnly.

"And the barn door!" Tom spluttered.

As the merriment evaporated, Nancy told them why the army had visited. She told them about Dan and how Vicar Burton had helped them. Billy reached across the table to take Nancy's hand, his gentle eyes looking deep within hers and they remembered the sadness of long ago when Nancy had first met Dan at the orphanage. She had met Billy and his sister, Rose, during those first days at the orphanage when she was only four years old.

"Anything we can do to help?"

"Thanks Billy, you've always been there when I needed you, but I think this I have to do on my own."

"You're strong, Nancy. You'll be all right and so will Danny," Billy quietly assured her.

Watching them leave, Jebediah winced when the young Indian stepped on the gas sending up a cloud of smoke and dust as the vehicle jerked forward. Wobbling from side to side, it made its way up the driveway.

"Tom Irvine's a brave man to ride with that lad," Meg muttered as she returned to the house.

"We've three trips to Seattle this weekend," Jebediah reminded her, slipping an arm over her shoulder and leading her to the edge of the cliff. "We'd better order more supplies."

"We need gasoline, too," she added, staring out across the strait to look at Mt. Baker, almost hidden by clouds. Then suddenly she let out a deep sigh and turned to face the old detective. "Uncle Jeb, we've got things to do. Danny's coming home!" she said excitedly.

Over the next two days Nancy's exuberance returned and she and Meg prepared Dan's room for his homecoming. Clothes were washed, the bedroom aired, and her spirits soared. Now knowing what Dan's injury was they talked about what they could do to help him gain back his memory. The first thing was to make sure all his favourite items were visible around the house.

On Monday, Nancy took Meg and Eva to Sidney with her when she sang for the soldiers at Resthaven. The kindly matron introduced her to a visitor who was the Chief Medical Officer at Esquimalt.

"Commander Jackson! I was coming to see you tomorrow," Nancy informed the surprised man.

"About what, my dear?" he asked, frowning.

"My brother, Sgt. Daniel Brown. I'm Nancy Wilson."

Puckering his eyebrows at the instant recognition of Dan's name, the military man took Nancy's arm and led her across the hallway to the matron's office.

"Please sit down, Miss Wilson," he urged, offering her a chair. He perched on the corner of the matron's desk and nervously adjusted his spectacles. "I have orders from the highest authority to release Sgt. Brown into your care, but I must admit I am somewhat concerned." He folded his arms and frowned deeply. "Miss Wilson, you're only a slip of a girl, do you think ...?"

Her eyes flashed and she came quickly to her feet. "He's my brother and I want him home! We own land at Gordon Head and we've a pile of money in the bank. If you try to keep him from me, I'll give you a fight you'll never forget."

A smile crossed the medical officer's face as he eased himself off the desk.

"Thank you," he said, grinning at her. "You've just confirmed everything I've heard about you!"

"From whom?" she asked defiantly.

"Harry Maynard, Waldo Skillings, Tom Ben and none other than Sir Richard McBride," he said, pausing to look at her with penetrating eyes. "I will need to examine him when he arrives and then I promise he's all yours!"

"How long will that take?"

"Two days at most."

A tap sounded at the door. "Your help has arrived, if I don't miss my guess," the officer chuckled as he opened the door revealing Eva and Meg. "There, what did I tell you," he laughed.

"Is everything all right?" Eva asked.

"Yes it is," the chief medical officer replied. "Dan Brown will be home on Wednesday afternoon, I can almost guarantee it. Now ladies, if you'll excuse me."

Nancy's body tingled as she watched the tall military doctor stride away. She felt Meg's reassuring hand on her arm but her body began to shake and Meg pushed her gently back into the chair.

"Our waiting is almost over, Aunt Meg."

Chapter 27

On the hospital ship *Empress of Russia*, a CPR liner pressed into war service, Dan Brown stood gazing out across the unfamiliar scenery of the Panama Canal. The once beautiful ship had been converted from luxury liner to troop carrier and now carried many more troops than originally planned for. As it slid through the last of the locks, the orderly told him they would now be heading north into the Pacific Ocean and home ... a home he couldn't remember.

"We'll be home in a week, mate," the medical orderly announced at his shoulder, resting a firm but gentle hand on his arm.

"I can hear someone singing," Dan whispered. "Am I hearing angels or am I going crazy?"

"No lad, you're beginning to remember, that singing is stuck deep in your mind. It's trying to tell you something."

"Do you think so?" Dan asked. "Is Victoria my home? Will there be someone to meet me? Will I know them?"

"Easy lad," the orderly's voice soothed the frustrated soldier. "Someday you'll remember it all, but first you'll be visiting the hospital in Victoria. The doctor there will brief you a bit about your family and what to expect. You'll be seeing them very soon."

Family! thought Dan. *I wonder what they're like.*

* * *

Nancy was in high spirits as she, Meg and Jebediah called in at the B&W dock Friday morning to load the *Stockholm*. Once on their way again, the unusually calm water made short work of the trip as she sent the red-and-gold craft speeding across the straits.

Scanning the coastline through his field glasses, Jebediah tapped the redhead's shoulder, pointing to the grey Coast Guard cutter leaving the harbour at Port Townsend. Several freighters slowly moved toward their destination at the booming port of Seattle. A second urgent tap on her shoulder drew her eyes to a point on the coast and there, moving ever so slowly was the black sailboat.

"So, they're back!" Jebediah growled more to himself than anyone. Glancing over his shoulder, he noticed the Coast Guard cutter running a little behind them and off to one side.

"I think we have an escort," he chuckled. "Now, who set this up I wonder?"

A deserted dock greeted their arrival but Meg and Nancy were halfway up the garden path when the door burst open and Beth rushed out to meet them.

"You're early," she called with delight, "but I'm so glad you're here. Terry just pulled into the drive and Gus isn't home yet."

When Gus arrived home minutes later, he went to the window and stood gazing out over the water, then he turned his head sideways and listened. He opened the window.

"Terry, where are you?" he called. "I thought I heard Nancy's voice."

"Jeepers, boss, they arrived about twenty minutes ago! The girls are up at the house."

The shipowner shut the window, spun on his heel and listened again. *Yes, that was her voice. They're upstairs!* Hurrying to the foyer, he stopped and listened again, then taking the first four stairs two at a time, he hurried up the grand staircase. Now he could easily hear the merry tinkle of the redhead's happy laughter and when he entered their apartment Nancy came instantly to her feet, running to hug him.

"There's my beautiful sweetheart. Why so happy? What's happened, honey?"

She repeated the news of Dan's homecoming, explaining about his memory.

"Do you need any help?" Gus offered.

"No thanks, I just need Dan home," she said quietly. Then the story came tumbling out and Nancy's happiness became infectious.

"Billy and Christopher will be so pleased for you," said Gus. "They'll be meeting us at the concert."

Nellie arrived and Nancy went into the music room with her. The pianist was looking very frustrated as she searched through her satchel.

"Have you lost something, Nellie?"

"Oh gracious, I seem to have misplaced a sheet of music," her friend exclaimed, looking quite worried, "and I don't know this one well."

"Then why don't we sing it as a duet, unaccompanied. Come on, let's try it," Nancy said eagerly.

Nellie looked up at her. "We couldn't do that," she whispered.

"Sure we can, let's try it. We'll run through them in order."

Nellie quickly sorted the music and began to play. Meg and Beth quietly entered the room and sat down by the door. When the girls reached the last song, Nellie stood up beside her and they sang, *Pack Up Your Troubles* in perfect harmony, and they knew it.

"Wow," cried Beth, as she and Meg clapped enthusiastically. "That was terrific!"

"Are you going to do that at the concert?" asked Meg.

"We're not sure yet," replied Nellie, smiling doubtfully at Nancy. "Nancy thinks we should."

"Well, I think you should, too," agreed Meg.

"I agree. The audience will absolutely love it!" cried Beth.

At the dining table, the discussion centered for a few minutes on the subject of the girl's singing together. Beth described what she and Meg had heard and was adamant they should go ahead with their plans. Nellie's doubts at last faded away when they all assured her it would add an unexpected highlight to the performance.

Arriving at the theatre a bit earlier than usual, the Chrysler was met by a crowd of theatre-goers hanging about outside enjoying an unusually warm evening. The Jorgensen group climbed out and someone was heard announcing that it was Nancy. It almost caused a riot as many pushed forward eager to touch the young Canadian as Jeb eased them through the crowd.

Once inside the theatre, Nancy and Nellie, giggling hysterically, went off by themselves. The others made their way to the owner's box. They found the boys already there deep in conversation.

"Where's Dad?" asked Christopher, hugging his mother.

"Talking to James in the lobby," she replied, giving Bill a hug and taking her seat.

In the foyer, James Moore had taken Gus aside and they were talking quietly.

"Have you heard the rumour?" James whispered. "It's said America is going to declare war on Germany in April. Do you think it's true?"

"I don't know." Gus frowned. "Where did you get your information?"

"Your son, Christopher, but President Wilson ran for office on a 'Keep Out of the War Ticket'."

"Damn, it's high time we helped the Brits," the shipowner snapped. "The Germans have sunk thousands of tons of American shipping. Think of the *Lusitania*, and Beth and I should have been on her."

"I know, I know," James replied. "Rumours are flying everywhere, but is it true?"

"The lights suddenly dimmed and the men dashed for the stairs.

"We'll soon find out, it's April next week," whispered Gus, as they opened the heavy curtain and entered the box.

At the intermission Nancy paid them a quick visit until the bell rang. Soon afterwards, the program resumed. The rest of the concert was flawless, thrilling the audience … and then they came to the last number. Alarm swept across Maestro Winters' face when Nellie stood up and joined the redhead at center stage. Receiving their nod to begin, the sound of the girls' voices blending in perfect harmony soon told him they knew what they were doing. As expected, their surprise astounded everyone, even James Moore. The amazed expression on his face was priceless.

When *Pack Up Your Troubles* ended, with one tumultuous roar, the audience came to their feet, applauding wildly. James stared wide-eyed at the two young women. "Bravo! Bravo!" he called, jumping to his feet. Turning to Beth he added, "A nice touch … they're wonderful together. I didn't even realize Nellie was a singer!"

Nancy grasped Nellie's hand and whispered something to her as they took their bows. Nellie returned to the piano smiling broadly. Waiting for the crowd to settle down and return to their seats, Nancy held up her hand.

"We have a special song to end our program tonight," she announced. "This one is for a very special person in my life, my brother, who arrives home from Europe next week." She turned to the pianist and took a deep breath.

Nellie began to play the introduction, praying that Nancy could pull this off. The orchestra, being previously warned this might occur, joined in and the audience recognized the tune immediately. At first they began to clap enthusiastically then the clapping slowly died away as Nancy's magical voice put them under her spell. The old Scottish song heralding the return of a warrior was now received by a hushed and almost mesmerized audience. The beautiful words were wrapped in a wonderfully simple melody and Nancy's voice tugged at their emotions allowing them to experience their own joy and pain.

As the last notes faded away and Nancy took a deep, emotional curtsy, the thunderous applause reached a deafening crescendo, easily heard by passersby out on the street. Nellie came up beside her. Taking her hand she pressed it tightly and the applause continued even after the curtain came down.

As Peter drove them toward the party at the Jorgensens, Nancy looked out at the twinkling lights on Elliot Bay and her eyes misted over. *Where is he right now? What will he think when he sees me? Will he remember my singing?*

The party tonight was a lively affair buzzing with political rhetoric, especially after word got around of Christopher's prediction.

"They have a mighty peculiar way of voting on prohibition in some of our counties," someone said loudly.

"Already there's no liquor allowed in the army camps in Washington," Christopher informed those standing nearby.

"Hey, quit it with that serious political crap," Bill whispered to his brother. "This is a party and I want to dance with Nancy! Nancy where are you?" he called, his voice growing louder. "Can I have this dance, Nancy?"

This will be interesting, thought Nellie, finishing the song she was playing and beginning a slow waltz. The dancers who stayed on the floor began to move back when they saw Nancy and the wheelchair coming toward them. They curiously opened a circle for the young people and Nancy moved into the center.

Her body gently swayed to the music as she untied the sash from her gown, flicking the end to Bill. Slowly, she pulled him around the circle as she dipped and swayed to the music, turning under her sash, their eyes never left each other's faces as they laughed and giggled.

Someone alerted Beth and she came to the door, gasping as she gripped Meg's arm. Everyone watched in fascination at the display of courage and affection from the odd-looking dancers. As the music stopped Nancy went over and kissed Bill's cheek whispering into his ear.

"You're quite a man, Billy Jorgensen!"

He pulled the redhead onto his lap and the guests cheered them on. With Nancy giggling uncontrollably, he transported her out into the hallway.

Soon afterwards, Nellie closed the piano and went to join the others now graciously accepting her own accolades. By midnight, the last of the revellers were leaving the mansion and Nancy tumbled into her bed. The silken sheets caressed her body into welcome slumber as soon as her eyes closed.

Meg came in quietly to say goodnight and found the girl already asleep. She gently kissing Nancy's brow, thinking how proud she was. Her wrinkled old hands straightened the luxurious sheets about the girl's face and then she went out and quietly closed the door.

After breakfast, Terry waited on the dock as the family accompanied the Canadians down the garden path to see them off.

"Take care out there," the young gangster muttered to Jebediah, as he handed him the satchel. "The Eggers have been getting bolder and causing some trouble lately."

Jebediah nodded his thanks.

"Go on, get off with you," Gus laughed, hugging the redhead. "You've only two days more to wait. Give our love to Dan even if he can't remember us. See you soon, honey."

Waving, they watched the red-and-gold boat move away from the dock. Beth sighed and looked up at her husband. "Maybe we should go up to Victoria next week and be there when she meets him."

"No, love," Gus frowned. "She has to face this on her own but we will make sure to visit them soon. Perhaps he'll be able to travel with her. That would be something, wouldn't it?"

"She's some gal is that Nancy," commented Bill. "Such a shame I don't have legs anymore."

"You wouldn't have a chance, brother. That girl is madly in love with someone else and he comes home in two days!"

Moving quickly along the waterway, Nancy smiled as she thought of old Ezekiel, turning the *Stockholm* toward the hidden entrance. She gave the signal, taking the craft through the trees.

"No one is here!" called Jebediah, as he leapt onto the jetty.

"OH YES THERE IS!" Ezekiel's voice rang out from behind some boulders to their left. "And I have you trespassers in my sights!" Crashing noisily through the bushes a wild-looking figure appeared surprising Meg for an instant. His ancient hunting rifle was in one hand and field glasses bounced on his chest as he ran toward them.

"Been hunting?" Jebediah smirked.

Completely ignoring his old adversary, Ezekiel came toward the boat, grinning at Meg and Nancy. He turned his head and spat a stream of tobacco in the general direction of Jebediah.

"I've got some news, Miss Nancy," he muttered. "Them Eggers and two other boats are sneakin up and down the coast. Do you want me to shoot 'em."

"Hell no, you crazy old coot!" cried Jebediah, coming over to join them. "You'll just open a kettle of worms."

"Can you describe the boats, Zeke," asked Nancy.

"Well now," Ezekiel muttered, thoughtfully scratching his scraggly beard. "Let me think, they all have a tatty red flag flying at half mast."

"Signals," said Jebediah confidently, climbing back aboard the *Stockholm*. "The position of the flag tells the others something."

"Doesn't matter," the redhead chuckled. "Just so we know who they are. Dan will be home soon—he'll deal with them." She paused for a moment, her lips tightening. "Or I will!"

A quick glance flashed between Meg and Jebediah.

"Dan's home?" asked Ezekiel.

"He will be on Wednesday," replied the grinning redhead.

A few minutes later, they left the little cove with Jebediah keeping a close watch on the coastline. Seeing nothing, they shot off into the open water and turned for home. Brisk winds blew the waves into whitecaps as the *Stockholm* sped past Port Townsend.

Meg pointed out the Bell Tower rising from the bluff. "Looks like there are some pretty nice homes over there," she commented. "They must have a marvellous view."

"Be mighty cold in the winter, too," Jeb growled, and Meg grasped his arm playfully.

As they pulled into the cove, Nancy cut the engines and turned back to the older couple. "He'll remember this, won't he?" Nancy asked hopefully, looking around the dock.

"I don't know, love," the Scot replied, shaking her head. "You'll have to be patient."

The next day Jebediah found Nancy walking in the orchard and together they marvelled at the developing fruit on trees that were so small. The noise of a car turning into the drive disturbed her thoughts and her heart skipped a beat. Looking over at Jeb, he raised his eyebrows, and they started toward the house.

Fred Barrett, Dan's longtime friend and mentor, stepped from the car, groaned as he straightened his back, and greeted Meg on the porch.

"Blasted gardening," he complained. "I'm not getting any younger, I suppose."

"You just need to do more of it, Fred," Meg chastised him. "Nancy and Jeb are out back in the orchard, but they'll have heard you. Come on in, it's almost tea time."

As they went toward the kitchen, Nancy burst through the back door. Seeing Fred she began to ask him questions, hardly pausing for breath.

"Have you heard from the ship? Where are they? What time will they be in?"

"Slow down! Slow down!" Fred chuckled. "Yes, we've made contact with the hospital ship. It docks at noon tomorrow."

"He's almost home," she whispered reverently, turning to Jeb who had followed her inside.

"I thought you'd want to know, but it's confidential information, and you're not to tell anyone," Fred cautioned her.

"How fast does the hospital ship go?" Jebediah asked casually.

"Oh they'll come up the straits at about 15 knots but they'll run in open water at 30," he replied.

It was almost four in the afternoon when Fred left, never suspecting he'd given Jebediah the location of the ship as it made its way toward Victoria.

"Nancy," said Jeb, looking over at the girl who couldn't seem to keep still and had been pacing the floor ever since Fred had gone. "Danny will be coming down the Straits of Juan De Fuca at nine in the morning. Do you want to drive over to Esquimalt to watch him come in?"

"Oh yes please, Uncle Jeb," she replied, stopping her pacing.

"Nancy, come sit down. You're beginning to make me nervous," Meg pleaded.

Another car arrived and Nancy went quickly to the window.

"It's Eva and Dorothy!"

Meg went to get her account books from a drawer, while Nancy brought out the satchel of money and dropped it by her chair.

Eva knocked lightly on the door, then pushed it open and entered the kitchen with Dorothy close behind her.

"Hello folks. It's month end again," she exclaimed sadly.

"Thank goodness for the donations from Nancy's concerts," the old Scot said quietly, marking her book as she counted out a large sum of American dollars from the bag.

"Have you heard from Tom?" Nancy asked.

"Yes," Eva sighed. "He says the Germans are retreating and the war's nearly over, but there's a terrible shortage of food in England now. They're on rations over there. It must be so hard for everyone."

Over a cup of tea, they swapped observations of the goings on about Victoria and Nancy told her of Bill Jorgensen's prediction of America entering the war.

"If they do," Eva retorted, "it would soon be over with their enormous resources and it wouldn't be soon enough as far as I'm concerned."

There was little sleep for Nancy that night tossing and turning until she finally got up and wandered about the dark house with a candle. She tried to read, then finally lay down on the chesterfield and fell asleep. Just before dawn broke she awoke and went outside. She loved to watch the sun rise as it threw its first light across the islands highlighting every little indentation and hill. Today, as was quite usual, there was a bit of fog hanging almost to the water, making the islands look quite mysterious but breathtaking.

When Meg came down to the kitchen, she opened the curtains and saw Nancy standing at the clifftop staring out to sea. *I do hope her happiness isn't spoiled today. I wonder if we'll be able to see Dan amongst the crowd.*

Nancy sat down on the stairs and pulled her heavy woollen housecoat about her. She was beginning to feel the cold but she felt so at peace out here she didn't want to leave. The fog began to dissipate over the water and the hills beyond and the sun slid slowly from its night-time cavern of darkness. She shivered again and, pulling herself to her feet, she walked quickly back to the house.

Meg heard the door. "Breakfast is ready, lassie. Come have a bowl of hot porridge, it will help to warm your soul."

Nancy half-heartedly hugged her aunt and silently sat down. Sprinkling some sugar on top, she then poured cream over the steaming oats. She picked up her spoon. Meg watched her eat a few mouthfuls then put the spoon down.

"You have to eat, lass," she clucked. "You need your strength."

"I know, Aunt Meg, but it feels like my stomach is in knots." She tried another spoonful and looked up helplessly.

Meg went over and hugged her. Kissing the top of her head, she cleared the half-full dish away.

At 7:30, they got into the car and Jeb drove them over to Esquimalt. From a hill overlooking the sea, they watched as the *Empress of Russia* grew from a speck in the distance trailing black smoke. Ever so slowly it moved toward them. Nancy sat down on a rock and brought out the field glasses she had thankfully remembered to bring. Training it on the decks of the ship, she soon realized they were still too far away. *Perhaps if I concentrate hard enough, Dan will hear me!*

Meg and Jeb jabbered away trying desperately to break Nancy's silence, to no avail, and they soon decided to ignore her.

"I think we'd better drive around to the harbour now," Jeb suggested, when the liner came level with them.

"I've never seen her like this before, Jeb," said Meg as he offered her a hand up the hill to the car.

"She'll be all right. I think it's Dan we should be worrying about."

Meg looked up at him and nodded as Nancy caught up to them.

Jebediah parked the car at the B&W dock then they walked down to the inner harbour and over the bridge to the CPR terminal building. Dumpy and Fred had decided to join them even though they realized they may not even see Dan. The two men got separated from the others in the crowds so they stopped to watch the band playing in front of the Buildings. Rows of ambulances and army trucks lined the nearby streets and walkways.

Meg noticed few happy faces amongst the watchers and wondered if many of them hadn't been as lucky as Nancy to learn that their loved one was on the ship.

Slowly the big liner moved into its berth helped along by two harbour tugs. Using the field glasses, Nancy frantically searched the rows of faces that stared out from the deck; pitifully thin men in mismatched uniforms many with bandaged heads and arms appeared on deck as the boat docked. Stretchers were carried ashore, loading ambulances that quickly left for hospital destinations. Then came the more seriously walking wounded, proudly staggering on crutches or the arms of attendants.

Nancy finally spotted him. He was amongst this sad-looking group moving slowly down the gangway. Although he looked remarkably well considering how thin he was, he had a dazed expression and his eyes looked straight ahead. One of the nursing sisters from St. Ann's took his arm as he landed on the dock. She spoke to him briefly and led him toward one of the army trucks.

"DANNY!" Nancy cried, desperately pushing her way through the crowd.

His step faltered for a moment. A frown swept over his face but he stared blankly at those around him. She waved and repeated his name. He turned and seemed to look right at her. Her heart stopped as they stood looking at each other for a brief moment and then someone gently pushed him forward.

"He didn't recognize me!" she whispered forlornly.

Jeb put his arm around her and led her away.

"Danny didn't recognize me, Uncle Jeb," she said incredulously.

"Remember what your aunt told you yesterday, honey. You're going to need to have patience. Miracles happen when you least expect them, they say."

It was Monday evening before she was able to calm herself enough to stop weeping whenever she thought of Dan's face and his vague expression. On Tuesday afternoon, she sat alone on the cliff stairs staring down at the *Stockholm,* when suddenly a thought came to her. Closing her eyes, she started singing, softly at first. As the warm glow ran though her body she stood up and pretended she was in Seattle on the stage at the James Moore Theatre.

Meg and Jebediah heard her from the house.

"It's a wonder that girl can sing at all in her state," clucked Meg.

"Singing makes her happy," replied Jeb. "Maybe she's finally remembering that."

"I think she might be doing it for a different reason," Meg said softly.

Jeb just looked at her and frowned.

*   *   *

At Esquimalt Naval Hospital, Dan sat listening to the orderly as he told him a bit about the city. The man was carefully watching the soldier's eyes for any show of recognition.

"There it is again!" Dan interrupted, a look of frustration on his face as his hand flew to his forehead. "I can hear someone singing."

"Easy lad," the orderly said gently, knowing Nancy was a singer. "Perhaps it's your memory trying to come through, don't fight it."

*   *   *

She didn't sleep at all well those two nights knowing Dan was so near, yet so far away. Dreams disturbed her sleep as her mind took her back to their childhood when she had first met him at the orphanage. She felt the touch of Dan's warm, friendly hand. Waking with a start, she sat bolt upright in bed sure that she heard his voice calling for help. She listened to the silence for a few minutes then settled back onto the pillow. She had forgotten to pull the curtains when she retired and now noticed the moon shining through the trees. She tried to count the stars hoping it would put her back to sleep.

Sleeping fitfully, she awoke again as dawn broke and heard Meg's footsteps as she went downstairs to light the stove. Minutes later, there was a clatter of pans, and she decided to get up and get dressed. It was cold in the room, but she opened the window even wider so she could hear the birds chirping. She stood there for a minute watching the sun rise and listening. *How can I be so miserable when I have so much to be grateful for?* Realizing she felt better already, she closed the window and dressed quickly. Meg was busy and didn't notice her, so she grabbed her coat and went outside.

Chapter 28

Wednesday morning she found it impossible to keep still, knowing this was the day Commander Jackson had promised Dan would come home. She walked around and around the property all morning checking each apple tree and noticing how much they had grown. *Was he going to remember how much he wanted an orchard,* she wondered. Her blood raced with nervous apprehension.

At 11:30 she heard a vehicle and knew it was an army truck. Racing over to the house, she threw the door open calling excitedly, "Aunt Meg! Jebediah! They're here! Dan's home!"

The truck came to a stop not far away from the house and the uniformed driver and an orderly, dressed in white, got out of the front seat. The orderly opened the back door and Dan stepped down. Dressed in civilian issue, the ex-whaler looked totally out of character in his new blue suit, stiff-collared shirt, and a tie, which he fiddled with nervously.

We'll leave him with you, Miss Wilson," the orderly said firmly. "There's no medication, he's perfectly normal except for his memory." He handed her an envelope full of papers. "Good luck, sergeant," he said shaking Dan's hand before climbing back into the truck.

Nancy stood as if nailed to the ground, her mind only seeing her Danny standing there looking so pitifully lost. "Danny," she whispered. Willing her legs to move toward him, she self-consciously wrapped her arms around his shoulders and hugged him. "You're with your family now. Do you ...?" she began, but her voice would not allow her to continue. She felt his arms go gently around her and she began to sob.

"Please don't cry, Nancy," he said gruffly. "I know I belong to you but I don't understand it all. The doctor in Victoria told me about you and that we're not really brother and sister; yet he thought we'd been together most of our lives. You'll have to help me remember."

Stepping back, she looked up at him, swallowing hard as she tried to smile. "You won't need this here," she said, reaching forward and loosening his necktie until it came off. "You rarely wear a tie. You never liked them."

"I'm glad of that," he grinned. "I hate it already!"

She cleared her throat and took him by the arm. "Come meet our Aunt Meg and Uncle Jeb. None of us are blood, but we'll explain to you later how we all came to be together as a family."

Walking toward the house where Jeb and Meg were waiting, Dan held out his hand, but Meg brushed it away, hugging him instead.

"No handshakes for me, son," she cried. "I've been the only mother you've known since Ned Joyce brought you home to the whaling boat as a lad."

Dan noticed the handshake with Jebediah was firm and the man's smile genuine, making him feel much more comfortable. *I like this man already, Nancy called him Uncle Jeb.* "So I worked on the sea, did I?" he asked, walking toward the cliff. He paused and turned back. "That's why I feel so comfortable on the water. It was a long trip here but I quite enjoyed it."

The next day Nancy took Dan for a walk that took them over almost every inch of the Gordon Head property. She showed him the orchard and watched the joy on his face as he gently touched the new-forming leaves of the little trees.

"How long have I been away? These are new trees, did you plant them?" he asked.

"You always wanted to have an orchard here, Dan. Our friend, Jack Duggan and some of his men prepared the land and a man named Ben Wall did the rest."

She told him the whole story and he was amazed that his friend would do that for him. She told Dan how he knew Jack and how Dan had introduced her to Jack and his wife, Nellie, so many years ago. She showed him Jack's hidden chute that sometimes still fed cases of liquor from the shed down onto the dock. Dan found this highly amusing and laughed heartily especially when she told him how Jebediah sometimes used it to transport himself down to the dock. She took him for a short ride in the *Stockholm* proving he was right at home on the boat.

When they took to sea on Friday afternoon, Dan was a willing part of the crew. *Almost like old times,* thought Nancy as she watched him looking about and wished she could read his mind. As they sailed past Oak Bay and turned westward toward Victoria, he came forward to stand between her and Jeb.

"This area is so beautiful," he said passionately, as if seeing it for the first time. "It's so hard to believe I can't remember it."

"You will, lad," said Jeb, patting Dan's shoulder. "Give it time."

"But I want to remember, Jeb. It's so terribly frustrating that I can't."

"You know, Dan. I once lost my memory for 24 hours after I drank some bad liquor. My friends told me it messed up my head pretty badly. When my memory returned, I couldn't remember much about it. Our mind has an amazing capability to look after us when we can't do it ourselves. Just give it time. You'll see what I mean someday."

Dan looked at him with a wan smile. "Thanks, Jeb."

"Look, Dan," cried Nancy, "that's our dock, see the names above it. Those are our names. This is our business. Jack Dumpford is our manager and you used to work with him on the whaling ship, *Belfast*. He's going to be mighty pleased to see you. We all call him Dumpy."

"Jack Dumpford ... Dumpy, eh?" Dan repeated slowly.

"Yes, Dumpy," reiterated Nancy. "Oh, it looks like Fred Barrett is with him. See those two men over there. Fred is an old friend of yours as well," she continued, deciding not to confuse the issue by telling him that Fred had saved his life many, many years ago.

Shaking hands with Fred and Dumpy who were obviously very glad to see him, Nancy thought he was doing a great job pretending he knew them. They loaded the boat and within 45 minutes were on their way again.

Jebediah scanned the water ahead, alert for the troublesome Egger brothers. She slowed at Port Townsend, pointing out the mansions that stood majestically on the headland, before weaving through the freighters and charging down Puget Sound to the Jorgensen dock. She looked back at Dan and was particularly pleased to see how relaxed he appeared. Like her, he was completely at home on the sea.

Sitting in the sunshine, Terry waved his hat in the air when he noticed they had an extra passenger and surmised it was Dan. She introduced the two young men, smiling as the gangster lied, telling Dan he was a business man from Seattle. Linking arms, she walked Dan slowly up the garden path letting him take it all in. Dan's eyes darted from side to side before settling on the huge house.

"Do I know this place?" he asked.

"No, you've never been here before, but you know the people who live here."

The door opened and Gus and Beth came out to meet them. Beth welcomed Dan with a hug and Gus shook his hand. As they went inside they could hear a piano playing quietly in the background.

"That's Nellie playing," Nancy laughed. "I'll just go say hello."

Dan watched as she disappeared into another room and he and Jeb were led into the living room where a cup of coffee and some cakes were waiting. He became most interested in the Jorgensen's description of how they'd met at the Gorge Park a few years ago.

In the music room, Nellie frowned as she struggled with the difficult piece of music she was playing. Looking up as the girl entered, her frown slipped away and her fingers quickly flew across the keyboard, playing the redhead's favourite song.

"Sing for me, Nan," she pleaded. "I'm so frustrated!"

Nancy smiled at her friend before bursting into song, her voice filling the room and carrying across the hall to the living room. Dan, sitting on the sofa, suddenly covered his ears, moaning as he hung his head rocking back and forth.

"What's wrong, Dan?" Beth cried, rushing over to sit beside him.

"It's that singing in my head again," Dan cried, continuing his rocking.

Beth gently took his hands away from his ears and looked into his eyes. That's not in your head, son," she whispered, shakily. "It's Nancy singing!"

Sitting up with a start, Dan looked at her incredulously. "Are you sure?" he asked, looking around at the others who were grinning broadly. He looked toward the door and smiled as a new awareness swept over him. He sat back and listened closing his eyes. He had been hearing Nancy sing for months without realizing what it was. *The orderlies were right,* he thought joyously. *Maybe my memory is coming back.*

"What's happened?" Nancy asked worriedly as she came into the room to see Dan's relaxed expression and tears being hastily wiped by the others.

"We've just solved one of Dan's problems," said Gus, gruffly. "Seems his memory is still there, it just needs awakening."

Nancy looked puzzled, until Beth explained Dan's reaction to her singing.

"I could hear you singing in England," he said excitedly, interrupting them. "Even on the ship as we were coming home. Others heard you, too."

Beth shook her head. "I've heard of telepathy before," she whispered, "but always crossed it off as bunkum. Now I'm not so sure."

Dan glowed as Nancy reached for his hand and pulled him to his feet.

"Come here you big lug and let me hug you," she said giddily, shaking off her tears of joy. "Now you know for sure where you belong, we just have to find that memory of yours!"

They were a happy, noisy group that walked back down to the dock a bit later. Beth had invited them to stay for dinner but they insisted they must get Dan back before he got overtired. The boat was gassed up and ready to go and Jebediah stood talking to Terry. Beth had the kitchen staff pack them some sandwiches and she handed them over to Jebediah just before they left.

"Do you know your way home from here?" Nancy asked Dan as they climbed aboard.

"No, I don't believe so," he chuckled.

"Then come sit up here and watch," she invited, patting the seat beside her.

"I'll stand here behind you, if that's all right," he said shyly, placing his hands on her shoulders.

Jebediah watched fascinated as Dan moved to the exact position he used to take. He saw Nancy turn and look at him and he winked at her.

It was coming on five o'clock when Jebediah pointed out the lineup of freighters in Admiralty Inlet, just south of Keystone Lighthouse. There appeared to be an American Naval gunboat and two Coast Guard vessels blocking their passage.

"What the devil's going on?" the detective growled, peering through the field glasses.

Nancy slowed the *Stockholm*, easing back on the throttle as she came opposite the first of the freighters. One of the Coast Guard craft pulled out from the line, shooting across the water toward them.

"HI NANCY," yelled a peak-capped sailor. "WE'RE AT WAR WITH GERMANY. IT JUST CAME IN OVER THE RADIO. WE'RE SEIZING THEIR FREIGHTERS."

"HOW DO YOU KNOW ME?" she shouted back.

"I BROUGHT YOU FRED BARRETT'S MESSAGE ABOUT THE STORM, DON'T YOU REMEMBER?"

Dan's hands tightened on her shoulder. She could feel the tension in his fingers and she reached up to pat his hand reassuringly. She strained to catch the last of the Coast Guardsman's comments, but they were drowned out as the vessel pulled quickly away.

"What did he say?" Nancy asked Jebediah.

Grinning, the detective shook his head. "He said all the Coast Guard boys know the *Stockholm* belongs to Nancy Wilson, the singer."

Smiling to herself, she opened the throttle sending the speedboat hurtling toward the Straits of Juan de Fuca. When they reached Gordon Head an hour later, she cut back on the power before entering their peaceful cove.

"I've seen this place before," Dan murmured, as if in a daze. "I thought it was a figment of my imagination."

"When?" asked Jebediah, watching him closely.

"I slipped on the rocks at Whidbey and banged my head one day when we were out for a walk," he said, pausing for a moment to gather his thoughts. "Later, I dreamed vividly of this scene but I never told anyone."

Nancy squealed, throwing her arms around him and kissing him on the cheek. Then she raced up the stairs, eager to tell Meg of their day. Bursting into the kitchen, she stopped suddenly when she saw Eva.

"Dan's starting to remember," the words came tumbling out anyway. "He knew he'd seen the cove and Cunningham Manor before."

"That's marvellous," Meg beamed, giving her a hug, "but don't get too hopeful."

"We've got some news, too," announced Eva, as Jeb and Dan came through the door. "The phone lines have been buzzing all afternoon. America has declared war on Germany."

"We know," replied Jeb. "The Coast Guard told us at Keystone."

"It'll soon be over now," Eva continued, noticing Dan was watching her closely. "Then my Thomas can come home, too. Welcome home, Dan."

"I assume I know you, but I'm afraid I don't remember."

"Yes, you do know her, Danny, but only slightly. Eva and I have become good friends while you've been away," explained Nancy, taking his arm and moving toward the girl. "This is Eva Todd, her husband, Thomas, is in the army, too. He helped you get home. They're neighbours up the hill. They visited us once before you went away. Tom has been an army man for years."

"I'm so glad Tom was able to help," said Eva, shaking his hand. "Now, I must be off. See you again soon, Dan, and good luck with the memory."

After dinner, Nancy got up to help Meg with the dishes but she shooed her away, pointing out the window. "Look at that beautiful sunset. Why don't you and Dan go out and enjoy it—it's a perfect evening."

Taking Dan's hand, Nancy pulled him toward the door, kissing Meg as she went by. Dan noticed their comfortable interaction as he had several times before. *These people have a wonderful sense of family and yet they aren't even related. It's nice belonging to them. I hope my memory comes back soon.*

They walked over to the stairs and sat down overlooking the dock.

"Do you get sunsets like this very often, Nancy?" Dan asked, looking up at the beautiful pink-streaked, sky.

"Not often enough, but we do get some lovely sunrises. The days are getting longer now so if you wake early enough, you'll see one."

They quietly watched the waves beat lazily on the rocks below. Nancy treasured these moments when she could be so close to Dan yet she realized she mustn't push him into remembering their special relationship. He had loved her once and, in time would again, no matter how difficult it was for her in the meantime.

Suddenly, her eye caught a movement amongst the rocks below and she touched Dan's arm and pointed. "Look, Danny. The seal has come back," she whispered excitedly. "It's just like he knows you're home again! We haven't seen him for a very long time."

"How do you know it's a he?" he teased.

"Well," she said, giggling, "it's the boys who go away, isn't it?"

"My word, look at that. There are two of them!" Dan interrupted. "Now, we know why he's back. He's brought his lady friend home for your approval!"

"Aren't they so cute!" she exclaimed.

"You're pretty cute yourself, you know." He slipped his arm around her shoulder. "It seems so natural to be close to you. I'm so glad you're my sister." He went quiet again as they watched the seals jumping from the rocks into the water. Darkness closed in around them even without their noticing.

"Would you like me to sing for you, Danny? We used to sit out here often and you liked it when I sang to you."

"Well then, I'm sure I'd like it now," he said, taking his arm away and moving slightly so he could watch her.

Meg and Jebediah had come out to the porch to watch the sunset, too. When Nancy began to sing they weren't surprised in the least.

"Look at them," said Meg, tucking the blanket tighter around her legs. "Dan seems so comfortable with her. Do you think he'll fall in love with her again, Jeb?"

"Let's hope it doesn't take so long this time!" he grunted, patting her hand. "Come on, let's go in. This is a night for the young'uns, my dear."

Nancy's voice rose above the clifftop and seemed to echo amongst the stillness of the trees. She sang two songs then an involuntary shiver went through her body.

Dan put his arm around her shoulder again. "I can see why I liked that," he said, pulling her closer.

In the darkness, she turned to face him, kissing him on the cheek. "I think we'd better go in, Danny, we don't want you catching pneumonia."

"Or you either," he exclaimed, offering her a hand.

Chapter 29

A cool breeze swept over the cliff as Dan and Nancy left home the next morning. She took the old route along Cedar Hill Road, deliberately bouncing through some of the ruts and potholes as she pointed out places he might remember. Dan was getting more comfortable every day, but she could still see the anxiety on his face as he tried hard to remember things.

As they passed neighbouring farms, they often saw friends out in their fields and she tooted her horn explaining to Dan who they were and what crops they were tending. They waved back, many of them shouting greetings to him by name. When they came to Hillside, he asked her about the streetcars, having seen them the day he arrived. He said he had also seen similar conveyances in England.

Looking around with inquisitive wonder, he began to ask more questions especially when they reached the junction where several of the main streets converged at the fountain. He was fascinated by the large black watertrough and drinking fountain and she explained its history and how the streets had changed around it.

Turning down Government, a startled expression crept over his face and she noticed he was clenching his hands so tightly the knuckles had turned white.

"What's the matter, Dan?" she asked, looking over at him quickly as she manoeuvred through traffic.

"That awful smell, what is it?" he asked, noticing his body was beginning to twitch.

"It's awful isn't it? It's from the Albion Iron Works," she explained, keeping her eyes on the road.

Totally unaware that the stench had triggered a memory from the battlefield, she continued up Government toward the foundry. But Dan's mind had already taken him back to Belgium and the muddy trenches where the Germans had used the poisonous gas. Re-living the horror, Dan saw his comrades writhe on the ground as they gasped for air, falling back into the puddles. Many managed to climb over the top of the trench escaping the fumes, only to be shot as they entered No Man's Land. He now remembered it all too clearly, as the sulphur-

282

laden smoke stung his eyes, his body began to shake and he thought he was going to be sick.

Nancy, still busy watching traffic, failed to notice the terror he was experiencing. Finally glancing over at her passenger, she waved her hand in front of her face to try clear the air.

"Dan! What's the matter," she cried, seeing his difficulty. She yanked on the wheel and moved off the road.

"Don't ... stop! Get me ... out of ... here," he wheezed. "I ... I can't ... breathe."

Alarmed almost to a state of panic and realizing it was the smell that was bothering him, she stepped on the accelerator. The little Ford raced up Government Street away from the offending smell. Turning left onto Herald, she looked about for clear air and turned again onto Douglas. She looked over at Dan and slowed as they passed the still-derelict Hudson Bay building. Thankfully, he was beginning to breathe more normally.

Stopping the car, she threw open the door and ran around to the other side helping him out. She led him over to a low wall and gasping for breath he sat down.

"I'm so sorry, Dan," she exclaimed, gently rubbing his back.

He shook his head. "It's not your fault, Nancy, I'll tell you about it later," he said hoarsely, pulling out his handkerchief and breaking into a series of body-wracking coughs.

When they got going again, they noticed a crowd milling about up ahead.

"I wonder what's going on now," she said, realizing where they were. "People usually gather at the City Hall only when there's a problem.

Dan watched the crowd with interest. All the way down Douglas, he stared at the boarded-up shop fronts until Nancy turned right onto Broughton, guiding the Model T through the congestion of rushing shoppers and clanking streetcars.

"You're a good driver, Nancy," he commented, as she stopped suddenly at the corner of Wharf Street to allow the right-of-way to a horse-drawn conveyance.

"I suppose I could blame it on my teacher," she said coyly, looking straight ahead. "That was you, Dan."

"Oh, well I guess I can take some of the credit then," he said solemnly. "I look forward to the day I remember that."

"I don't know. It might be one of those memories best forgotten!" she giggled, as they bounced onto the boards that led to the Brown and Wilson office.

"We've been here before," he said confidently, as Dumpy appeared at the door.

"Hello Dan, I'm just leaving for Sooke, come see me off. I've got a surprise for you two."

"A surprise?" Nancy repeated.

They walked around the building to the end of the dock where the blue boat was tied up.

"You've given her a name, Dumpy!" she exclaimed. "*Highliner,* how appropriate. Well done. One day, Danny, you will understand. You explain it, Dumpy."

"Danny, when we were whalers," Dumpy began, "we were the best and got the name *highliners.* Nancy had never given the blue boat a name and with your homecoming it just came to me. I thought it was right and knew Nancy wouldn't mind."

"Mind? I'm so glad you thought of it. Well, we better let Dumpy be on his way," she said quickly, turning back to the office. "Have a good trip."

As Dumpy untied the *Highliner,* he explained to Dan what he was doing and where he was going, pointing to the barge tied behind. He climbed aboard and started the powerful engine. With a roar, it pulled smoothly away from the dock with the barge on tow. Waving, he made his way out into the harbour.

"His tow rope's too long," Dan muttered as he stood watching.

"What did you say?" Nancy gasped, coming up beside him.

Looking puzzled, Dan turned to face her.

She reached for his hand. "How did you know that, love?"

"I don't know. It just popped into my head."

Heavy footsteps sounded behind them as Waldo strode across the dock. Puffing hard on his heat-blackened pipe, he had a merry twinkle in his eyes when he stuck out his hand to greet Dan.

"Do you know me, lad?" he growled. "I still owe you ten dollars!"

"No, you don't!" Nancy laughed. "Dan, this is Waldo Skillings, a very good friend."

"Don't you remember, Dan?" Waldo continued, pulling a ten dollar bill from his pocket and putting it into Dan's hand. "Most men remember when someone owes them money," he chuckled, "long after they forget everything else!" The haulier turned to leave. "One day you'll remember so you better keep it. Have a drink on me, son," he called back. "I think your lad's a damned hero, Nancy!"

Taking Dan's arm, she led him into the office. "Believe it or not, Meg and I used to sleep in those two rooms," she said, pointing toward the two closed doors. "And this old stove has stood here forever." She watched him closely but there appeared no glimmer of recollection. "This is your chair, Dan," she murmured, pulling it out from the table. He sat down. "Let's see, Dumpy usually makes a big pot of coffee. Like a cup?" He nodded and she got out two cups and filled them.

"You were a whaler on a ship named, *Belfast*, owned by Tim and Ned Joyce. This was their office and more or less their home, when they weren't on the boat. As long as I've known you, you and the Joyces always slept on the boat even when it was tied up at the dock outside. People said you were the best gunner on the West Coast. I'm rambling aren't I? I'm sorry, Dan."

"It's all right. I don't remember any of that," he muttered, hanging his head. "You know, sometimes I get strange thoughts of children. I'm almost sure it's me, and there's also a tiny little girl. She's always holding my hand and looking up at me with sad eyes."

"That's you … and me!" she said softly, barely able to speak. "It was almost 20 years ago in the orphanage."

"DAMN, IT'S FRUSTRATING!" he said suddenly, banging his fist on the table.

An engine had stopped out on the dock and at that moment Harry Maynard's body framed the open doorway.

"What's this I hear you shouting, son?" the brewery owner laughed. "I've heard all about your memory and I bet it's bloody murder not knowing. I'm Harry Maynard," he said. I don't expect you'll remember me either right now. I own one of the local breweries and my wife plays piano for Nancy sometimes."

He joined them at the table. Nancy poured him a coffee and they talked for a while about Dan's problem.

"Walk the streets with him, Nancy," he suggested, finishing his drink. "Something might click in his mind." Harry got up and walked slowly toward the door. "You'd better sort out your liquor supply, young lady. This province is heading for prohibition under Brewster."

After Harry had gone, Nancy brought out the sandwiches Meg had packed for them. She thought Dan seemed a lot more relaxed.

"When you've got time, Nancy, I'd really like to do as Harry suggested," Dan said suddenly.

"That's a great idea. I'm finished here, why don't we go right now?" Seeing his smile, she opened the door and they went outside. Taking his arm, they headed up the boardwalk and they turned southward toward the inner harbour. Dan's eyes took in everything. He asked questions, too, about the huge Empress Hotel, the Causeway Boathouse, Evans' wharf and the offices of the Grand Pacific Steamship Company.

She answered his questions but was concerned that she was confusing him and told him so.

"I feel like a ... tourist ... is it called? You're doing a great job."

Pleased that he seemed so happy, they turned back crossing to the other side of the road. Stopping in front of the Empress, she pointed ahead to the post office building that straddled the corner of Government and Wharf.

They went past the now vacant Harper and Wells automobile showroom and she told him this was where Brian Harper had sold them the truck. Behind them, a voice called out a greeting, and they saw Fred Barrett leaning against the door of the Harbour Master's office.

"Are you two playing tourist?" Fred asked.

"Sort of, trying to jog Dan's memory," she explained as they continued on up Wharf.

They walked past the Brown and Wilson dock and she pointed to the wharf next door telling him it was run by a nice family called Guthrie. She pointed across the road to Pither and Leiser's large liquor store. Dan looked up Fort and commented on the large number of shoppers about. They walked by the dull, uninteresting front of the Hudson Bay warehouse and peered through the dusty windows of Kelly Douglas, the wholesale provisioners.

Dan cast his eyes across the street at a vacant storefront with cobwebs in the windows. It stood forlornly between Rithet's and the BC Sugar Refinery offices.

"Seems to be a lot of empty stores around," commented Dan.

"Yes, it's been a really hard time for people around here with the war and men out of work."

The ring of a hammer on steel drew their attention to Jim Morrison's smithy. Inside, a horse stood waiting and the old blacksmith pulled a glowing horseshoe from the fire. A second later a loud hiss was heard and a cloud of steam filled the air.

Carrying on their way, Nancy took them past the Hudson Bay liquor store, Marvin's, the ship's chandler, and the Columbia Paper office before arriving in front of Peter McQuade's busy store. At each shop she tried to find something personal to relate to Dan, something he might remember.

In the background, the thunder of a steam engine told them a train was arriving at the E&N railyard. They quickly crossed the street to escape the smoke.

"Come on, let's go inside. This is the Occidental Hotel, Dan. I used to work here."

They entered the noisy restaurant and found a table. Selecting their food from a well-thumbed menu, Nancy noted the unfamiliar waitress in her gaudy, wrinkled uniform. The girl came over to them and when told they were not ready, she showed her impatience as she waited. The interior of the once-proud hotel was terribly run down, with flaking paint and a smoke-blackened ceiling.

They ordered some soup and as they were waiting the noise level increased to an alarming pitch. They soon realized it was coming from the crowded bar room next door where an argument seemed to have erupted. Loud voices calling obscenities became so obvious even out in the restaurant, it became very distracting. However, no one appeared to be particularly disturbed by it, except Nancy.

"Doesn't that racket bother you, Dan?" she asked curiously, her eyes continually flicking to the doorway.

"It's a bit disconcerting while we are eating, but I suppose I've gotten used to so much noise I hardly hear it!"

Dan finished eating and put down his spoon. He watched her carefully fold her napkin, placing it neatly on the table next to her bowl of half-eaten soup. He could see that she was agitated and obviously wanted to leave. She paid the bill and quickly led the way outside.

"That's the last time we'll ever come here for a meal!" she exclaimed fiercely. "It's sure gone downhill since I worked there, but that was years ago now."

A few raindrops splashed onto their faces and they noticed the dark cloud overhead. As they hurried back up Wharf Street, it began to rain harder. The drops were huge and they, and several other shoppers, sought shelter underneath a store canopy. The shower passed over quickly and Dan pointed to a large rainbow which had appeared over the harbour.

"Rainbows!" he mused, with a far-off note in his voice.

Nancy watched him as he looked at the pretty phenomenon and scratched his head.

"I remember rainbows," he said slowly. "There was so much mud around and rain ... it seemed to rain all the time." He stopped and closed his eyes as if conjuring up an image. "When a rainbow came out I remember that men cheered. It was a glorious sight!"

"Oh Danny, you're remembering! You told me about the rain. In one of your letters, you asked me to send you an umbrella. The paper even had some watermarks on it. I'll have to show them to you."

They walked down the boardwalk to their office, but Nancy led him past the building out to the farthest jetty. Staring out across the water, she slipped her arm through his and pointed to the smokestack puffing white vapour at Laurel Point.

"That's the soap works," she informed him, "and next door is the paint factory." Her finger rose again, pointing to the steamship at the CPR terminal. "Do you know what that is?"

"A troopship," he replied, without a moment's hesitation.

Nancy turned to face him. "And that?" She pointed toward the Empress.

"The Empress Hotel."

"Now where have we been, can you remember?"

"Along Wharf Street to the Occidental Cafe and you said we're not going there again."

"Well done, love," Nancy laughed. "You're picking it up fast."

"Listen, Nancy," Dan frowned, "my memory for the present is fine. I can remember everything since I came out of hospital in England ... but nothing before. Perhaps some of that is good. Strangely enough, the soldiers at the hospital in England envied me."

"I'm sure they have their reasons and it would be nice to be able to be selective," she agreed. Changing the subject, she announced, "I think we'll stop in at our new restaurant now so you can meet Kate. You knew her when we worked together at the Balmoral restaurant. Now she's my business partner and Dumpy's new wife."

They went into the B&W office, checking to see if anyone had left a message on their notepad. Finding none, she locked the door behind them. Climbing into the truck, they headed slowly up Fort Street, waiting behind a streetcar as it dropped off their passengers near Cook. Going up the hill, she pointed to Craigdarroch Castle and told him a bit about its fascinating history and the Dunsmuir family who built it.

She pointed out the street that would take them to Jack and Nellie Duggan's home and Dan noticed a sign telling them the Jubilee Hospital was ahead. He looked up at the mansions on the hill overlooking Victoria and Nancy pointed out the fork in the road which would take them to Oak Bay. However, she continued to go straight and they picked up speed as they went down the slight incline to Richmond Road. Making a left turn, she pulled into the lane behind the restaurant.

"Let's walk around to the front," she suggested, taking his arm. "Kate and I are very proud of our new business. She works here much more than I do but she really enjoys it."

As they rounded the side of the building, Dan was surprised to see many soldiers congregated at the small tables set at the edge of the sidewalk. Some were in uniform, or partial uniform, and they seemed to have an amazing assortment of injuries. Nancy led him past a man with crutches and another very young soldier with walking sticks propped up against the wall. As they went inside, he noticed another with a patch over one eye and an empty sleeve tucked into his waist band.

Dan stopped, squaring his shoulders, and Nan heard his sharp intake of breath. His eyes moved over the faces, some looking at him curiously.

"Hello boys, I want you to meet my brother, Dan," she said proudly. "He's back from the war, too. He's lost his memory from a head injury and like you, he's trying to adjust."

"Hell, that must be annoying," a young, ginger-haired soldier with only one arm and terrible scars on his face, sympathized.

Kate appeared in the doorway. Stopping to sweep a wisp of hair from her face, she squealed with delight when she saw Nancy and Dan throwing her arms around him.

"Golly it's so good to see you, Dan." When the soldiers cheered her on she put her finger to her lips. "I know you don't remember me, Dan, but I'm Katherine. I'm sure Nan has told you all about me. Are you going to sing for us today, Nan?" she called over her shoulder as she headed back into the kitchen.

A violin began to play a few notes and Nancy recognized Bobby Dunn, an amputee from the Boer War. He was a regular customer who often tried to persuade Nancy to sing by stroking his bow across the strings and grinning foolishly.

"Look after him, please Kate, we've already eaten," Nancy called to her friend. Turning to the fiddle-playing old soldier, she grinned and started clapping her hands. "Right Bobby, follow me!" she called, moving outside.

Dan watched in amazement as Bobby hobbled outside on a crutch, carrying his fiddle. He found a chair and sat down. Nancy's voice rang through the air and people on the other side of the street stopped and turned to look. Soon the lawns in front of the hospital began to fill with people. There were dressing gowns, wheelchairs, uniformed soldiers and white-coated attendants. Windows popped up in the hospital building, and heads leaned out to listen to the music with only the strains of a single violin and the rustle of a breeze for accompaniment. She sang two more songs and, with the audience cheering and whistling, she curtsied coyly, waved and disappeared into the restaurant.

"Wonderful," Kate beamed. "You've made their day. Are you staying for awhile?"

"No, we were on our way home," Nancy replied, looking over at Dan who seemed happy talking with a group of soldiers. "He seems so happy though, I don't think I'll drag him away just yet. Can I help with something?"

As the women went out to the kitchen, Dan listened intently as the men tried to help him remember telling him of the horrors of war—violent explosions, gas attacks and the searing pain of being wounded. He vaguely remembered the day the smoke of the iron foundry had triggered some horrible memories but it was fleeting and he was almost relieved when their efforts, too, failed.

Katherine's arm found its way around the redhead's waist and, watching him from the kitchen, they could feel Dan's frustration. However, despite this, Nancy was noticing a subtle change in him for as his confidence grew, he was learning to laugh at himself again.

Leaving the restaurant half an hour later, they went along dusty Richmond Road, passing the dairy farm of Arthur Lambrick near Kings Road where cows were grazing peacefully in a pasture.

"Hey, those are cows!" Dan laughed, looking pleased with himself.

Nancy laughed with him as she turned west on Cedar Hill Cross Road stopping at Shelbourne. A mischievous smile suddenly crossed her face. "Hold onto your hat, mister," she warned him as she took a right turn. "We're going for a ride!"

Swinging the Model T onto Shelbourne, almost deserted of traffic, she clutched the steering wheel tightly and pressed down on the accelerator. Getting her speed up to a mind-shattering 30 mph, they tore along the new flat surface flashing by the intersections of Feltham, then Kenmore, before slowing down where the bumpy park road began.

Glancing over at her passenger she noticed his face was glowing. She stuck her arm out the window and slowed for the right turn onto Cross Road and the quick left to Ash.

"We're almost home," she exclaimed, pointing to the open gate a little way up the road.

"I like the orchard," he commented, as they came slowly down the drive and Nancy stopped the car. He got out and stood staring at the rows of evenly spaced trees.

"It's yours, you started it," she reminded him.

"Look's like I made a good job of it!" he chuckled.

"Did you bring a newspaper?" Jebediah's voice came from around the corner as they met on the porch.

"We sure did," she replied, handing it to him.

Meg, busying herself with supper, glanced up from the stove and wiped her hands on her apron. "See anything you recognize, lad?" she asked, casting a disapproving look at Jebediah who was spreading his newspaper out on the table. Noting Dan's negative headshake, she rounded on the old detective. "Get that paper off my table, it's almost time to eat."

Teeth gripping hard on his pipe Jeb peered over his glasses. "Blasted bad-tempered women!" Winking at Dan, he refolded the newspaper. "Come on, lad, we know when we're not wanted."

Before Meg called them for supper, the men had time to scan the front few pages with Jebediah explaining many of the news stories to Dan. Supper was almost over when Jeb remembered to tell Nancy that Algy Pease had called in at the cove and had left a message for her.

"He said the sawmill in Sidney is operating again and to watch out for log booms up this way."

Dan's eyes flashed from one to the other as Nancy's cup slowly settled onto its saucer.

"Their log booms would come down from up-island, Cowichan way, wouldn't they, Uncle Jeb?"

"Don't know, love," he replied. "Algy mentioned they were going to get the CP to put a railway connection to Patricia Bay."

"Show me, please," Dan pleaded. "Draw me a map. Let me see these places. Maybe I can build a new memory."

"He's right you know," Meg sighed. "Dan's life was the sea; he once knew this coastline like the back of his hand."

Nodding, Nancy agreed and went to find the maps. For the next three hours, the two of them discussed the prominent features of the island coastline as she tried to re-teach Dan all the things he had learned from years of experience.

Cold winds blew down from the north on Sunday and continued into Monday, whipping the waves into frothy whitecaps as the two young people went out in the *Stockholm* to do some exploring. She pointed to the buildings being erected on James Island and told Dan stories of the great powder factory still operating at Telegraph Bay. The Rubber Roofing Company's huge water tank at Sidney and the government wharf jutting out into the bay were prominent landmarks and behind they could see a railway engine, puffing black smoke as it left the station. Powerful saw blades screamed as they tore through heavy lumber alerting Nan to the newly reinstated saw mill that Algy Pease had mentioned to Jebediah.

It was late in the afternoon when Nancy swung the *Stockholm* around behind the leper colony. It was the masts that caught her attention first, then two craft rocking in the tide. They were sitting close together transferring a load that looked like gunnysacks.

"Booze," she muttered, looking through the glasses. Then she noticed the small red flag on the mast of the black sailboat. "Darn, it's the Eggers; they're a bit out of their area!"

Scanning the nearby waters adjacent to Sidney Island, she searched for their lookouts. Dan tapped her shoulder, pointing toward Henry Island, on the American side, from which a boat was now moving on a straight line toward them. Zeroing in on them with her glasses, she quickly picked out another red flag and issued a sharp warning.

"Hang on tight, Dan, we could be in for trouble."

Hands clasping her shoulders, he remained behind her. She could feel the tension in his fingers but with no time to explain, she threw open the throttle. Engine roaring, the *Stockholm* lurched violently forward, screaming with power as it flew across the water. A rifle barked several times as the other boat changed direction and turned toward them. She twisted and turned avoiding rocky outcrops as they sped through the familiar waters, but no bullets came near them. As they arrived at the northern end of Cordova Bay, the other boat dropped back and she continued to Gordon Head.

"They're getting bolder," was Jebediah's only comment when Nancy told him of the incident.

All week Nancy helped Dan increase his knowledge of the coastline and, with his confidence growing, she gave him some basic instructions on handling the speedboat for their next trip south. Also, now realizing

Dan needed little care, she made the decision to return to her own schedule where she had obligations to fulfill, missing her visits to the hospitals. She hated to have to leave Dan behind but it wasn't a good place to take him under the circumstances.

On Tuesday afternoon, she and Meg went to pick up Eva on their way to Esquimalt. Nancy's unusual approach to Dan's problem had already come to the attention of Commander Jackson and she expected she would see him at the hospital today. Following her afternoon concert, she sought him out finding him just coming out of a meeting with the matron.

His eyebrows rose with interest when she told him her plan and the success she was having at refurbishing Dan's memory. "I had my doubts about trusting you with Sergeant Brown's condition, but you seem to be quite a remarkable young lady." He paused, and a trace of a smile crossed his tired face. "Keep me informed, Miss Wilson," he added, before turning on his heel and striding down the corridor.

Over the next few weeks Dan learned the route to Seattle, becoming totally comfortable with old Ezekiel, Terry O'Reilly, Nellie, and the Jorgensen family, spending many hours listening with rapt attention to tales of the war from Bill Jorgensen as he pushed him around the garden in his wheelchair. He attended one of Nancy's concerts and he tried to hide his tears when she sang the songs he had heard so often in his head.

Americans, now in the war, scrambled to meet him and shake his hand, treating him like a hero. On May 4th at the Jorgensen party following their concert, Nellie found Dan looking totally lost as a group of admirers gathered around him. Taking his arm, she excused them and found a quiet corner in the parlour. She sat him down and took his hand.

"Dan, I know this is very difficult for you but you have to believe that you are going to get your memory back," she said softly, seeing his sad expression. "Nancy won't rest until you do. She's a wonderful girl and I admire you both for your tenacity." Then changing the subject, she asked, "Would you like to dance with me?"

"I don't think I know how," he replied.

"Then I'll teach you," she chuckled. She again took his hand pulling him to his feet and they made their way down the hall to the ballroom.

A group of local musicians were playing a slow waltz as several couples moved around the floor. Nancy was standing by the piano looking through some music when she saw Nellie and Dan enter. She pretended not to notice, wondering what they were up to. It soon became apparent as Dan clumsily followed Nellie's steps, his hands on her shoulders.

Years of teaching had given Nellie Cornish a wonderful gift—the ability to make people comfortable as she imparted her knowledge. It was soon evident that she had this same affect on Dan by the way his body was interpreting the music—his feet moving smoothly through each new step.

Envy welled up in Nancy as she watched the now lone dancers on the floor, their bodies moving closer and closer as Dan gained his confidence. Nellie skilfully manoeuvred her partner across the open floor, coming to stop in front of Nancy. She took his hand and placed it in hers, then stepped away.

"Nancy, now it's your turn!" she declared, grinning.

Word quickly passed between the guests and soon a group had formed at the door, several coming onto the dance floor to join them. Whispers of approval were heard as Nancy and Dan moved around the dance floor with such ease it was as if they had been dancing with each other forever.

Despite the recent changeable weather, sunshine streamed through the curtains the next morning at breakfast. The evening had been a tremendous success and the morning banter between the three young men, caused ripples of laughter to run through the room.

"Jeepers you're clumsy," Bill chuckled. "You must have two left feet."

"I'd like to see you try that dancing stuff," Dan replied.

"I don't have any trouble with my feet," Bill laughed.

Looking out the window, Jebediah saw Terry standing at the end of the dock. Excusing himself, he collected his bag and made his way down to the boathouse.

"Need to talk to you, lad," the old detective growled as he came toward him. "Them damned Eggers are straying right up into Canada."

"I heard, Nancy told me last night."

"Then you and Roy Olmstead had better do something about it!"

Their conversation ended abruptly as voices were heard up by the house and the rest of the group came down the garden path. An urgent call for Gus quelled the chatter as the shipowner turned back inside.

"DON'T LEAVE YET," he shouted after them. "I WON'T BE A MINUTE!"

Meg and Jebediah settled into the long seat at the back of the *Stockholm*, wrapping a blanket around their legs, obviously intending to enjoy their trip home in comfort.

Suddenly, they heard Gus shouting to them as he rushed down the path. "Wow, have you had a proposition, young lady!" he gasped excitedly, his face flushed. "That was Major General Greene, Commander at Camp Lewis. That's the big army base south of Tacoma," he panted, trying to catch his breath.

"Gus, slow down, dear. They're not in that much of a hurry to leave," Beth said calmly, although her face showed deep concern for her husband.

"I'm all right, Beth. This is important. He wants Nancy to sing for the soldiers at the Camp on the 16th of June ... as the star of the show!"

"Tell him yes," Nancy replied, "but with one condition. I want all of you there, including him." She pointed her finger at Terry.

"That's basically what I told him!" beamed Gus, throwing his arms into the air. Looking over at Terry he saw the young man turn away, and suspected this man who pretended to be harder than nails, had actually been deeply touched by the girl's generous consideration.

Nancy climbed into her seat as Dan cast off the last of the mooring lines and, with engines growling, the boat slid away from the dock. Waving, she turned northward and opened the throttle.

"Mother dearest," Bill said quietly, his eyes following the speeding *Stockholm* until it disappeared amongst the freighters. "You did a great job picking us a little sister. I just wish you'd done it earlier!"

Chapter 30

Nancy handed over the controls to Dan as they roared past Useless Bay and two German freighters still held by the American Navy. Several boats, their sails billowing in the wind, appeared out in the strait ahead of them as they passed Port Townsend. Nancy was standing on the portside when a sudden unexpected movement caused her to snatch up the field glasses.

"Trouble ahead, Dan!" she called pointing to the northeast.

Dan changed their direction, trying to see what was going on. Nancy found the capsized boat and noticed another sailboat was trying to reach it but they would get their first. They were about 500 yards away when she noticed several figures in the water desperately trying to scramble back aboard the badly listing boat. Despite the fact it was almost May, the water would be deathly cold and she shivered.

Easing off on the throttle as they approached, Dan cruised slowly alongside. "IS EVERYONE ACCOUNTED FOR?"

Three men, now clinging to the rigging, waved to them as the water lapped ferociously at the overturned hull beneath them. "NO … HELP HIM … OVER THERE," they yelled, pointing to their shipmate who had just bobbed to the surface off the *Stockholm's* bow. Nancy threw out a life preserver and although he was obviously having some difficulty he managed to grasp it and hold on long enough for them to get closer. Realizing the man wouldn't be able to climb aboard unassisted, Dan threw their rope ladder over the side and climbed out onto it. He managed to get hold of the man just before he let go. As Jeb helped him pull the exhausted man over the side, two of his friends swam toward them. They climbed unassisted up the ladder as, finally, the last man set out heaving a sigh of relief as he, too, climbed over the side, his teeth chattering uncontrollably.

One of the others shared a blanket with him and they all stood watching helplessly as the foundering craft turned onto its side amongst the tangled wreckage of its broken mast and torn sails. Meg had put on the kerosene heater and made some tea which she handed to one of the men. She was particularly concerned about the first man they had brought aboard as he seemed to be suffering more than the others.

"If we could get those lines cut before the canvas pulls her under, you might have a chance of saving her," Dan was saying. "Have you got a knife? You'll have to be fast!"

The authoritative tone of his voice caused two of the sailors to exchange quick furtive glances and, without hesitation they dropped their blankets and dove back into the frigid water. With knives slashing at the rigging, they yelled orders back and forth to each other with Dan shouting instructions from above. One of the men dove under the surface disappearing momentarily. Meg grabbed Jeb's arm as they watched. Finally, with a groan the tangled mass floated free and the diver bobbed gasping to the surface.

"HOLD HER STEADY, SIS. DO WE HAVE A TOW ROPE?"

"Under the back seat, Jeb," she called, enthralled at the way Dan had taken control.

With Dan's instructions, it was barely more than a minute before the men had the rope in place attached to the broken mast. She was watching the men closely now for she worried they had been in the water too long.

Dan took the rope from one of the men before he climbed aboard, tying it to the tow ring on the *Stockholm*. Then, as if reading her mind, he gave his next order. "TAKE UP THE SLACK, NAN ... EASY, WE'LL GET THESE MEN ON BOARD FIRST." The rope twanged tight as the first sailor fell exhausted over the side. "A FEW DEGREES TO THE NORTH, NAN, THEN GIVE HER SOME POWER." Pulling the second man over the side, he added, "Good job, men!"

With the rope lifting out of the water and tightening again like a bow string, the blanket-wrapped 4-man crew watched in awe as the *Stockholm*'s stern dipped into the waves. Biting fiercely into the water, the speedboat began its battle against the sea as it fought to claim the foundering vessel. Nancy carefully adjusted her tension on the line until with one loud groan the boat heaved upward; the water released its grip and the hull rolled suddenly upright.

A half-hearted cheer rose from the shivering and exhausted sailors as Meg bustled them into the cabin where they gratefully accepted another cup of hot tea.

"WHERE ARE WE TAKING YOU?" she called.

"KEYSTONE," called one of the men, poking his head out of the cabin.

Nan turned the *Stockholm* into the wind feeling it tug laboriously on its half-submerged load as she headed back to Keystone Harbor, less than two nautical miles away.

Being warned by the other boat, which had already reached port ahead of them, many eager hands were waiting on the Keystone dock when they arrived. Nancy pulled the boat up to the dock. One of the two sailors who had saved the boat was a hardy, bearded man of about 50 years. Having been the person who had done most of the talking, Dan suspected he was the owner. Handing his blanket to Meg, he thanked the ladies and Jeb profusely and, jumping nimbly over the side, landed heavily on the dock. He was immediately handed a steaming tankard of hot coffee laced with rum, which he accepted gratefully.

"The rest of you go get into dry clothes," he growled, as his companions dropped onto the deck beside him and were hurried away. He gulped down the liquid, rubbed on his beard and asked for more. Equipment was being placed on board the sinking boat and the noise of pumps made it difficult to hear. "ARE YOU GOING TO CLAIM SALVAGE, YOUNG MAN?" the seaman asked Dan in a well-cultured voice.

Glancing up from coiling his rope, Dan smiled slightly. He turned to Nancy who he knew had been listening.

Seeing his questioning look, she took up the conversation. "We're Canadians, sir. We're your neighbours and this is your boat. However, I think you could say that you owe us one now, mister!"

Squaring his shoulders the bearded yachtsman smiled. "My name is Morgan Tyler, I'm senior surgeon at Providence Hospital in Seattle, and you're absolutely right, I owe you a big favour!" he paused, eyes fastened on Nancy as he rubbed his beard again. "I've been thinking that I should know you from somewhere."

"Take your hat off, girl," Jebediah chuckled, coming up beside them and hearing Dr. Tyler's comment.

The woollen scarf holding her hat had slipped loosely about her neck and she uncoiled it removing her hat. Red hair cascaded about her shoulders.

"My word!" Dr. Tyler gasped. "You're Nancy Wilson—I was at your concert at Christmas! I knew I recognized you. We thoroughly enjoyed your singing. I see your talents include being a sailor!"

A light suddenly flashed in the redhead's eyes. "Thank you, doctor, but could we talk to you for a moment about a medical matter … when you're finished here?"

"Certainly," he replied, quite used to giving out free medical information. "Just give me a few minutes to check on my boat and get some clothes on!"

While he was away, Nancy moved the boat and they had no sooner turned off the engine when he returned, climbing back aboard the *Stockholm* and joining them in the cabin. Dr. Tyler listened intently as the girl described Dan's memory loss. She explained how he had heard her singing in his head and, of the moment, only days before, when he knew Dumpy's tow rope was too long.

"You've just had a perfect example of what I mean," she explained, "when he rescued you and righted your yacht. He's really a very skilled seaman and quite respected on this coast although he doesn't remember any of it."

Dr. Tyler reached for her hand. "The singing in his head is easy, my dear," he explained gently. "His whole life has been linked to you one way or another, it's called love."

"That's true," Meg added, "from childhood until now, she's been the first thought on his mind."

"It's not unusual between brother and sister," the doctor reflected.

"Brother and sister, be damned!" Jebediah snapped. "We're all orphans from different families, all four of us." His eyes flashed with fire. "And we're a blasted fine family together, too!"

Startled by Jebediah's revelation, the doctor's eyes swept across their faces with renewed interest. "My apologies, folks, I just assumed," he murmured. "Please, let me carry on. Your second love must be the sea, Dan. I'll wager you come from these parts and have spent most of your life here. Every now and then, when you least expect it, you'll find a door opens and memories flood out, then quick as a flash it's gone again. But don't worry, son, one day that door is going to swing wide open and stay that way. The signs are all there. Now give me a pencil and paper, I'm going to give you my personal phone number. Feel free to call me any time." He stood up to leave and they all thanked him profusely, shaking hands before he left.

Nancy followed him outside.

"I wish you all the best, Nancy," he said quietly, shaking her hand once again. "This is going to be a difficult time for you." Climbing out of the boat, he smiled encouragingly. "If anything concerns you, anything at all, please call." As he walked away, he glanced back over his shoulder and realized she was still watching him. A strange feeling of guilt ran through his cold body. He realized he'd given some hope

299

to his Canadian rescuers when he knew from experience the true fact of Dan ever recovering his memory was slim to none.

Humbled by some of the comments he had heard in the cabin, Dan followed Nancy outside and went to stand behind her at the wheel.

"Is that all true?" he asked quietly.

"Yes, and lots more," she whispered, turning into his waiting arms.

Inside the cabin, Jebediah was helping Meg put everything back in order when he noticed she was crying. Taking out his handkerchief, he wiped her eyes and hugged her tenderly.

"Come on you two, let's go home," he called gruffly through the open door, destroying the moment of magic.

Over the ensuing days and weeks that led into summer, they all took turns walking the streets of Victoria with Dan, also taking several trips to Seattle. Still Dan's memory remained dormant. News from Europe told of a German retreat giving everyone hope that finally the war could be coming to a close. However, the next week the Colonist stated that enemy pleas for peace had included far too many concessions on their own terms, which were abruptly turned down by the allies.

Jebediah tried talking of the war to Dan but soon realized it was not going to help the lad, although heart warming stories of Americans feeding the starving British and flooding onto the battlefields of France and Belgium, rallied everyone's spirits.

Nancy took him to watch the troopships a few times, still regularly arriving with wounded soldiers and leaving full of excited new recruits—from what seemed like an endless supply of British Columbia's young men. Conscription was now a strong topic of conversation on the streets of the capital city. Opinions, often expressed by men already enraged by Premier Brewster's threat of prohibition, sometimes met with violence erupting on street corners and at political meetings.

A visit to Emerson Turpel at the Point Hope Shipyard, now working again on government contracts, told them he was desperately in need of skilled men. Wandering through the busy shipyard with Kenneth Macpherson, the man tried hard, but unsuccessfully, to jolt Dan's memory.

"Sorry love," the superintendent murmured to Nancy, as he held back to talk with her. "I really have no idea what to try next."

Undaunted, Nancy stubbornly kept to her plan, and slowly Dan became familiar once again with the city where he was born. They rode the streetcar all the way from Beacon Hill to the Uplands, visited Eliza Marshall at the Gorge Hotel, and alone he spent many afternoons with Harry and Waldo.

On the 21st of May, together with Meg and Jebediah, they watched the Victoria Day Parade. Led by the 5th Regiment's military band and two cars of wounded soldiers from the Esquimalt Convalescent Hospital, it brought joy to the onlookers mixed with stark reminders of the savage war still taking place so far away.

Proceeds from the day were to be donated to the local Red Cross. The surprising star of the parade was a goat, caged, and riding in an open-topped car driven by Maria Sweeney and accompanied by her mother. It was displayed with a giant notice that read, WE'VE GOT THE KAISER'S GOAT. It was followed by Chief Davis of the Victoria Fire Department riding in his shiny new white car. Behind him came a long line of firefighting equipment and, bringing up the rear, were three snorting horses pulling the aerial ladder.

Afterwards, many gaily decorated cars and tradesmen's floats made their way back to the showgrounds of the Royal Athletic Park on Cook Street. It was a warm day and many hundreds of residents also made their way to Athletic Park to partake of the afternoon activities. After tramping around the showground all afternoon, visiting the unusual booths and watching people playing games, Meg announced she was tired and wanted to sit down. Everyone agreed they had been on their feet long enough and, with Meg leaning on Jeb and Dan's supporting arms, they slowly made their way back to the streetcar stop on Cook Street.

As it rumbled toward town, the old Scot began to recover and by the time they reached Douglas Street she was pointing out shops she thought Dan might remember—the Dominion Bank on the corner as the streetcar turned into Yates, Dentist Lewis Hall's office, and the Brunswick Hotel with its usual complement of rowdies gathered around the door.

"I must make an appointment at the opticians," Meg chuckled, seeing Frank Clugson's shop across the street, its window full of eye glasses.

Rattling on down to Government Street, its wheels ground on the bend as it turned southward, passing the cigar and newspaper store on the corner. They noticed that the town was almost empty of people as stores had been closed for the holiday. When they got off on Wharf, Jebediah helped Meg down the steps to the street.

301

"I'll go make you some tea," Nancy called over her shoulder, hurrying ahead.

"No, no, Nancy!" Meg called to her, waiting as she came back to see what was wrong. "Let's call in at the restaurant and see Katherine. We don't get to see her very often anymore and we can have something to eat there."

Nancy smiled, knowing how much Meg liked Kate. Dan caught up with her and they crossed the street together. She started Jeb's car and Dan opened the doors. As the others approached, Nancy noticed the swelling around Meg's ankles.

"You've done too much walking today, young lady," she chided, receiving a sheepish grin in reply. "It's concert time in Seattle tomorrow, so you'd better sit with your feet up tonight, or you won't be going!"

The almost deserted city made for easy travelling and with only the streetcars for company, they followed the rail track up Fort Street to the Jubilee Hospital. They were surprised to see hundreds of soldiers and their relatives sitting about on the lawns listening to a military band, while Katherine and her new waitress, Dottie, who Nancy had stolen away from the Balmoral, dashed back and forth delivering trays of drinks and sandwiches.

Glancing up, Katherine saw Dan carrying chairs out for Meg and Jebediah. A young soldier with a twisted smile creasing his badly burned and mostly bandaged face, reached out for his beer. His eyes, heavily bandaged with small slits that he could barely see through, were stark evidence of the surprise gas attacks. She moved the beer into his hand and he looked up at her gratefully, asking, "Is Nancy here?"

"Yes, she is!" she whispered, looking across the street again. Tousling his hair gently, she was always overwhelmed by this lad's indomitable spirit.

"SING FOR US, NANCY!" he called loudly, not sure which direction to look.

Shuffling through his music, Captain Nixon looked up as several of his bandsmen began to chuckle as the lad's plea was taken up by others. Tapping the baton fiercely on his music stand, he couldn't help smiling to himself, as he listened to the eager voices shouting for Nancy to sing.

One of the bandsmen, dispatched by the conductor, made his way carefully through the audience, saluting smartly as he confronted the redhead. "Will you sing for us, Miss Nancy?" he asked.

"I would be happy to, I'll be with you in a minute," she replied, helping Meg get settled. Then, grabbing a drink of water off Dottie's tray as she went by, she took a sip and handed it to Meg. Following the bandsman, they made their way through the crowd toward the waiting band. As she moved confidently across the lawn, she had to pull her skirts about her legs often stepping over and around prone soldiers lying on the grass. She stopped to shake hands and tousled the hair of several others.

"Captain Nixon would like to know which songs you would like to sing, miss," her guide asked, coming up alongside her.

"Let's see, tell him *April Showers*, *It's Spring Time in the Rockies* and *Our Island Home.*"

Returning to the band ahead of her, the soldier delivered her message adding a thought of his own. "She said to keep it low, sir."

They were all professional musicians and knew the songs well. Tapping his baton, the conductor quickly led them into the introduction for *April Showers*. As she moved amongst the crowd, her voice and her smile reached out to the men and she often stooped to touch the arms or shoulders of the badly injured causing a smile or an embarrassed blush.

The streetcar, already late on its return run, stood silent and still as the driver and conductor stood on the track listening, enthralled by the unusual concert. Meg was enjoying herself immensely, beaming over at Jeb as the last notes floated through the still afternoon air. A moment's stillness settled over the crowd before erupting into deafening applause. She sang the two remaining numbers then began to make her way back toward the restaurant, looking for Dan.

A lady, plainly dressed in black, suddenly rose from the crowd and with skirts rustling walked directly over to Nancy. "Young lady," she said quietly. "That blind soldier you touched just now is my son. He thinks you're an angel, and so do I. You've given him a beautiful memory. May I shake your hand?"

Nancy took the hand she offered, feeling its strength and the creases of a work-hardened palm. "You're not from Victoria, are you ma'am?"

"No, we're from the Okanagan Valley and I'm taking him home tomorrow." She began to turn away, then murmured, "Poor lad, he has a hard cross to bear."

Nancy watched her help the lad to his feet, shocked and saddened to see how young he was. Her mind tried to imagine a world in total darkness for evermore. Then her attention was taken by the sound of familiar voices and she found Jack and Nellie Duggan behind her. She waved one last time to the crowd before turning to greet her old friends.

"What are you two doing here?" she asked.

"We were in the hospital visiting a sick neighbour, when we heard you singing," Nellie told her. "So we came out to see. We wanted to talk to you about your birthday party."

At that moment, Dan came up beside them.

"Hello Dan," said Nellie, "welcome home."

"Danny, this is Jack and Nellie Duggan, I've told you a lot about them. Jack's the person responsible for your orchard."

"Oh, yes, you have told me a lot about these people. It's so nice to meet you. I can't thank you enough for your work on the orchard, Jack. One day when I remember I'm sure I'll be even more pleased," he said with a grin. "You mentioned Nancy's birthday, is it soon?"

"No, love," Nancy replied. "It's still three weeks away."

"We're going to put on the party this year," Jack announced, "but we want to have it on the lawn at Cunningham Manor!"

"Who's we, Mr. Duggan?" Nancy asked with a giggle.

"Don't be so nosy, Nancy. Meg's given her permission, that's all we need," Jack teased. Taking Nellie's hand, they waved before disappearing into the crowd.

Nancy's group made their way back to the restaurant saying goodbye to Katherine and leaving by the back door.

"Mr. Duggan is a long-time friend isn't he?" Dan asked, trying to remember all Nancy had told him as they climbed into the car.

"Yes, Danny," replied Meg. "You introduced Nancy to the Duggans when you met in the restaurant many years ago. Jack built Cunningham Manor."

Dan stared through the car window, his mind puzzled by so many things. There seemed to be a never-ending list of people and places he couldn't remember.

Chapter 31

Eva called on Friday morning. She was carrying her large wicker basket which she lifted carefully onto the table. "I have a present for you, Meg; I know they're getting scarce in Victoria," she laughed, taking the towel off to reveal a bowlful of eggs.

"Thank you, Eva, this will be a real treat. I'll make a nice omelette for dinner. Perhaps I can persuade the others that we should get some chickens now that we have our orchard," she giggled, as Nancy came into the room to see what was happening.

Eva stayed all morning, talking with them about the widows and orphans and some of the local gossip. She sowed a seed in the redhead's mind that perhaps they should be thinking about opening their own children's home.

"Eva, what a wonderful idea. Now that comes close to my heart, but right now I can't see where I will possibly have the time," she sighed, obviously disappointed.

"Why don't you let me put some ideas together, Nan. I know you are already doing so much and what with Dan's problem to contend with …."

Eyes twinkling again, Nancy agreed they would talk about it soon and she would offer as much assistance as she was able.

Meg insisted that Eva stay for lunch and during the meal the young woman asked a favour.

"Are you going into Victoria today, Nancy?"

"We're all going, straight after lunch in the boat," replied Jebediah. "It's our concert day in Seattle so we can't bring you back home but you can certainly go with us into Victoria."

"Oh that's wonderful! Algy will ride me home," Eva explained gratefully. "I've never been to Victoria by boat but I have gone home with Algy several times."

After lunch they all went down to the dock and Eva was surprised when Nancy got onto the captain's seat. As they made their way toward Victoria, Jebediah and Meg pointed out several landmarks to Eva. She was especially impressed with the size of the explosives factory, never having seen it from the water.

305

Jebediah noted the scaffolding at Ogden Point had been removed and the massive stone blocks around the harbour entrance looked starkly new as they formed the docking for visiting ships. Men were still working on the road surface now high above the waves. When the *Stockholm* slipped into the harbour, Eva smiled at the hint of lavender touching the breeze as they passed the soap works.

Dumpy and Fred came to help with the loading, eager to talk to Dan.

"I must go, you're busy," Eva exclaimed, as she stepped onto the jetty. "Thanks for the lift."

"Don't go yet, Eva, I want you to meet these fellows," Nancy insisted, grabbing hold of her arm and taking her over to meet Dumpy and Fred.

"It's nice to meet you both," she said, waving as she hurried away.

"Are you any better, lad?" Fred asked with concern, lifting the hatch cover to the hidden storage.

"Leave it, Fred, he's fine!" Nancy snapped, scowling at their friend.

A smile crept over Dan's face, and when he glanced up she was watching him. "You're really looking after me, aren't you?" he murmured, handing Jeb a box.

"Yes, I am," she stated fiercely, her hands balanced on her hips defiantly, "just like you took care of me all those years ago."

"All right, that's the last of it. Let's get out of here," called Jebediah, helping Meg back to her seat.

"Life's strange. It's funny how roles can change," Fred murmured to Dumpy as they watched the *Stockholm* move away.

"What do you mean?" Dumpy asked.

"Them two," came the slow answer. "Danny used to watch over her. He never thought of anything else, always talking of what he was going to do for Nancy." He paused to light his pipe. "Now look what's happened—just one stroke of fate and their roles have been reversed."

Dumpy looked puzzled, not quite following Fred's line of thinking.

"You're not saying Dan won't get his memory back are you?"

"No, I'm not," Fred snapped. "I'm just saying you never know what's around the next corner."

"Which corner?" Dumpy muttered, watching Fred throw his arms into the air before storming off the dock.

Nancy turned the controls of the *Stockholm* over to Dan as they moved swiftly into the choppy waters of the strait. Far ahead they could see several small boats over toward the lighthouse at Port Townsend but otherwise it was a quiet day for shipping. A stiff breeze was blowing through the narrows and they carefully avoided the other yachtsmen watching for any trouble. Useless Bay was now devoid of any German freighters and appeared peaceful again with only the seagulls for company.

"We better call at Ezekiel's," said Jeb. "Meg has some jam for him."

"Swing over close to the coast and head for Kingston," Nancy murmured, her finger pointing to the right of the waterway.

"Have you got your whistles?" asked Dan.

"Yes, just take us in slowly." She moved outside, her eyes fastened on the entrance to the cove as it came closer. As they started through the trees, she blew the whistle then the duck caller, leaping back as the new spring growth of overhanging branches brushed the side of the *Stockholm's* cabin.

Just getting ready to do some fishing, Zeke was standing ankle-deep in the water beside his boat. He watched as they came through the trees, moving closer to catch the rope Nancy threw to him.

"Did you see them out there?" he growled.

"See who?" Jebediah asked, holding out a case of Hamsterley Farm Strawberry Jam for the old man.

Ignoring the question, Ezekiel grinned when he saw the box. Thanking them, he took the jam and moved back to the shore putting it down on a log. He spit a long stream of tobacco juice into the sand, then came back toward them.

"Why doesn't he answer?" Dan whispered to Nancy.

"Shh," she giggled. "They like to annoy each other. Watch what happens when I ask him," Nancy murmured. "Tell me, Ezekiel."

"It were them Egger boys again," the old hermit explained, his eyes shining as he excitedly gave her the details. "Two night ago, lots of shooting, then nothing. I found a boat smashed on the rocks out there and these glasses were in it." He held them up. "I'm going to keep 'em, too!"

Leaving the cove, after getting his assurances he wouldn't do anything silly, they moved down the coast toward Kingston. They found the wreckage just as Ezekiel had told them, still jammed between the rocks.

"Pull in as close as you can," Jebediah instructed Dan. "I want to take a closer look."

A cautious leap from the rail of the *Stockholm* landed the old detective on the rocks near the craft. He lost his balance and found

307

himself precariously clinging to the rocks, scrambling to keep out of the water. Dan leapt out to help him and Nancy found a safe place to tuck the boat in almost out of sight. Jebediah finished his inspection of the broken hull and the men made their way back to the *Stockholm*.

"Let's go, we're running late now," Jeb grunted.

Backing away from the rocks, the redhead turned south toward Magnolia, pouring on the power to make up for lost time. Dan stood behind her with his hands on her shoulders and she felt safe and secure.

Pacing the dock worriedly, Terry heard the speedboat coming and breathed a sigh of relief. "THEY'RE WAITING FOR YOU," he yelled to Nancy, as she backed into the boathouse.

Servants ran down to get their overnight bags as the Jorgensens watched from the window.

"You had us worried, love," Beth sighed, affectionately wrapping her arms around the girl when she entered the house. "Why don't you go get changed, there's an officer from Camp Lewis coming in a while and he wants to meet you."

"Oh, really, I guess I had better hurry then," replied Nancy, going toward the stairs.

Outside, Gus walked down to the dock to meet the others. "What's keeping Jeb?" he asked Dan as the young man came toward him.

"He's talking to Terry."

"Trouble?" the shipowner asked, shading his eyes to look below where Terry's men were unloading the cargo. "You go on in, son," he suggested to Dan. "I want a word with Jebediah."

"What's going on?" Gus asked when he reached the men.

"There's been an incident up near Apple Cove. Ezekiel thinks the Eggers are hijacking boats again," Jeb replied.

"It wouldn't surprise me," Gus murmured, "but, more to the point, what do you think?"

"He told us about a wreck and I had a look-see," said Jeb, "had the name of Webber branded on its planking. Terry said they were well-known for running liquor from the top end of Whidbey Island but he's going to make some discreet inquiries."

Their serious expressions told Jeb the others were concerned too, but it was time to get ready for the concert so they left the problem in Terry's hands. The shipowner was worried, inwardly churning over in his mind the possibilities of the danger to Nancy.

"You think she should stop bringing us liquor for a while?" Gus asked, as he and Jeb went into the house."

308

"Hell, no," the detective chuckled wickedly. "She's got me, Dan, and the cannons! She'll be all right." He paused to remove his pipe, glancing at the shipowner with flashing eyes. "That redhead has a fighting spirit you've never seen the like of. I'd hate to get her mad!"

"Don't you let her take any chances, Jeb," Gus said solemnly, as they entered the house.

Upstairs, Nancy enjoyed a quick shower, then began to get dressed nibbling on some sandwiches one of the servants had delivered. As she slipped into the luxurious silken underwear she left at the Jorgensen's just for these occasions, she felt the wonderful cool smoothness of the luxurious fabric as it caressed her youthful figure. When she stepped into the blue gown and looked at herself in the mirror she smiled at her reflection. As she began to fasten the row of tiny matching buttons there was a light tap at the door.

"Come in."

"You're dressed. Good! Oh, and you got your sandwiches," said Beth as she came into the room. "Come sit down and let me brush your hair, dear. It's a shame you have such a rush tonight but the concert is earlier and with that man coming …. the boys will be meeting us at the theatre, by the way," she added.

Nancy sat on the bench and Beth picked up the silver-backed brush she had purchased especially for her. As they talked Nancy ate. Beth pulled the brush gently through the long soft tresses watching as with each stroke little red stars seemed to dance about the surface. There was another knock at the door and Meg and Nellie appeared.

"What does that military man want with my Nancy?" asked Meg, stepping into the room and looking in the mirror at their reflection.

A quick smile lit up Beth's face as her hands gently smoothed the girl's hair into place. "He's the officer in charge of the concert at Camp Lewis. He just wants to meet Nancy and confirm she'll be singing on the 16th of June. He evidentially wants to give us a peek at the program of stars they have lined up for the show."

"Who's coming?" Nellie asked, with obvious interest.

"You wait and see," Beth chuckled. "If we're all ready now, let's go find out."

The men were talking in the living room, as the ladies entered.

"My, what a bevy of beauties!" the officer quipped, as the men all sprang to their feet. "You must be Nancy Wilson," he declared pleasantly, moving toward her and extending his hand.

"Yes, I am," she replied flashing him one of her dazzling smiles. As she took his hand, she noticed the array of badges and stars on his uniform. "This is my aunt, Meg McDonald, and my accompanist, Nellie Cornish." She went and sat down.

"You won't require an accompanist for our concert," he said brashly. "At this point, I simply need your confirmation that you will be arriving at Camp Lewis at 3 o'clock in the afternoon on June 16th."

There was a moment of uneasy silence in the room as Gus leapt to his feet scowling at the officer, but Beth moved quickly to his side. He whispered something to her and left the room.

Nellie stared silently down at the floor but feeling an arm go around her, she looked up and found Nancy beside her.

"Then the answer is No!" Nancy retorted, her eyes flashing. "You either want us both or none at all, sir!"

"B-but I have my orders, miss," the officer stammered, shuffling his feet nervously.

"Hold it right there, soldier!" Gus' voice rang from the doorway. "General Greene is on the phone. He wants a word with you."

Marching quickly across the room, the officer disappeared into the foyer, passing the shipowner with hardly a glance. He knew the fierceness of his commanding officer and wasn't at all pleased that he had to talk with him due to a civilian's interference.

"Come on, it's time we left for the theatre," Gus grinned. "Buck up girls. He had incorrect information; you'll see when the general's finished burning his ear!"

They were all in the Chrysler when the army officer came hurrying outside, shouting for Peter to wait.

"I'm sorry, sir," he said, addressing Gus through the open car window. He was clearly embarrassed by the turn of events. "The general says I'm to invite all of you, especially Miss Cornish, his favourite pianist. May I talk with you at intermission?"

Jebediah sputtered in the back seat.

"After the show, lad, I believe you've done enough damage for one evening," said Gus, trying to hide his smirk. "It's time we were off ... Peter!"

As the car moved away, Nellie leaned back against the leather seat and sighed deeply. Meg, sitting beside her, patted her hand.

"We didn't find out who will be performing with us," said Nancy, smiling at her friend. "Will you tell us, Beth?"

"Yes, I saw the list. It will certainly be a show of Hollywood royalty!" she chuckled as the limousine sped on its way. "Mary Pickford will be there and perhaps Charlie Chaplin." She giggled. "Gus and I saw him in New York. He's a funny little man who looks like somebody put his legs on sideways. They call Mary Pickford a film goddess. She's a petite little thing."

"Dan and I met Mary Pickford when we first started our delivery business just before the war. She and her director wanted to go whale watching and we took them out in the blue boat. What an interesting day that was!" said Nancy, looking over at Dan who shrugged his shoulders.

"Who else?" asked Meg.

"Fanny Brice, Bill Baker, Billy Robinson, he's the coloured wizard of tap dancing and, somebody just for you, Meg. Harry Lauder is a popular Scottish singer."

"I've read about him," Meg purred. "I'll enjoy that."

"So, who are they billing as the star of this show?" asked Nellie.

"Who else?" Beth asked cheerily, "but our own, Nancy, of course … and you! I think they're calling it *Nancy and Friends*."

"How delightful!" gasped Meg before the others all speaking at once, congratulated Nancy.

Peter pulled up to the curb and eager hands helped them alight. The two girls said their goodbyes and, gathering up their skirts, hurried down the hallway that led to the backstage area. The Jorgensen boys were waiting and Bill's wheelchair bounced forward when he saw the redhead, pulling her quickly onto his knee. He laughed when she hugged him, planting a kiss on his cheek.

"My turn now!" called Christopher, a little too loudly, causing a few people to turn around and stare. Grabbing her hand, he pulled her away from his brother and held her tightly with his one good arm. "You look beautiful, little sister!" he said, kissing her on the other cheek.

"Fifteen minutes to curtain," the harsh voice of the stage director rang through the backstage corridors. "All visitors must leave, if you please," he said sternly, seeing the group near the door.

James Moore appeared, also reminding the boys they needed to get to their seats before the lights went down. They said goodbye and allowed James to help them back up the ramp to his box. The girls hurried to their dressing room and rid themselves of their coats, checking their lipstick.

Nellie grabbed her music and put her arm around Nancy. "Take a deep breath," she said, sporting a radiant smile. Then giggling, they left the room, shutting the door behind them.

Intermission brought round after round of applause from the appreciative audience, which continued even after Nancy had left the stage. She raced up the stairs to the private box, brushed through the curtain and, hesitated when she saw the splendidly uniformed officer. He was a kindly-looking, middle aged man, round-faced with a bristling moustache and hair turning grey at the temples.

"Hello Miss Wilson. Well done as usual, my dear. Forgive me, I'm Major General Greene from Camp Lewis," his pleasantly deep voice rumbled. When he rose, he stood tall and straight, and he had a twinkle in his eye. "I'm an old friend of Gus and Beth's," he explained and instead of shaking her hand, he reached out and grasped her shoulders. "Young lady, we'd be proud if you'd be the star of our camp show."

"Nellie comes, too," she murmured.

"Whoever you need, my dear," he replied, smiling broadly. "Jorgensen will arrange it all, just say 'yes' to make me happy."

Standing behind the curtain, Nellie heard the whole conversation and tiptoed quietly away. She said a little prayer of thanks knowing her life had been blessed by an angel named Nancy Wilson. How many more times she wondered, would she have cause to be grateful to this girl. Memories flooded back of the first time Nancy sang in concert, when she quietly negotiated with James Moore for part of his bar profits to be donated to her music school. Paying the rent had become a much easier task since then. And now, it was happening again.

"It will be a pleasure to sing for you, general," she replied, smiling graciously. She noticed the orchestra returning to their seats and she quickly excused herself.

She found Nellie pacing at the edge of the stage holding a glass of water in her hand. Handing it to her, Nancy took a sip and gave it to a stagehand. Clasping hands, they walked across the darkened stage.

"You're a special friend, Nancy Wilson," she whispered. "I'm so blessed to have met you." Nancy could hear her sharp intake of breath before she squeezed her hand and went to sit down at the instrument.

Now what's that all about? Nancy wondered, as her attention suddenly jerked toward the curtain as it began to open. Nellie looked up at her and smiled coyly and her fingers came down on the keyboard for the introduction of *Pack up Your Troubles in Your Old Kit Bag and Smile, Smile, Smile*. At the end of the concert, the last notes of *It's a*

312

Long Way to Tipperary were still ringing through the theatre when the audience erupted with wild applause.

Later, at the Jorgensen's the two stars circulated together amongst the houseful of guests. Wine and spirits flowed like water despite Washington State prohibition laws. Hiram Gill, fresh from his day in the courts battling accusations from the notorious bootlegger, Logan Billingsley, loudly proclaimed his innocence to the amusement of the listeners. The Everett Massacre and the war were the main topics of conversation and when word circulated about the star-studded show at Camp Lewis, Gus and Beth were pestered ruthlessly for invitations having to explain it was only for the soldiers.

Enthusiasm for the war was now evident and Nancy shook her head in dismay as she overheard ladies talking about their husbands or sons in uniform sporting a chestful of heroes' medals. She'd seen it all before when Canada entered the fray and the depressed economy of British Columbia sent thousands upon thousands of laughing young men to Europe … but Canadians weren't laughing anymore.

Bright morning sunlight was streaming through the window when Meg quietly opened Nancy's door and found her weeping. Sitting down beside her on the bed, her aunt put her arm around her.

"Don't worry, my darling," she whispered, "everything will come out right in the end."

"But I try so hard, Aunt Meg," she gasped, "and Danny's no better."

Meg held her until the girl's body relaxed. "Come on, love, why don't you have a shower. That will help you feel better."

Meg was right. When she arrived at the door of the breakfast room, Nancy looked refreshed and radiant. The boys cheered.

"Leave the poor girl alone," Beth frowned. "I thought there were gentlemen at this table."

"You tell 'em, Ma," Bill chuckled.

"Billy Jorgensen if you don't behave …," his mother threatened.

Chris and Bill's eyes met and they burst out laughing.

"Now, what's amusing you?" their father demanded with sparkling eyes, as the servants began serving breakfast.

"He'll tell you, dad," Bill chortled, pointing at his brother.

Controlling his laughter, Christopher tried to explain. "Mother always threatened us as kids saying she'd smack our legs." Laughter overtook him once again. "But that won't work with Billy any more!"

313

Beth let out a big sigh, shaking her head sadly. As a mother, she couldn't bear to join in the jest, although she was very proud of the way her sons were dealing with their life-changing battlescars.

"Please, boys," Gus tapped the table irritably. "You're upsetting your mother."

"Dear Dad and Mother, Uncle Jeb and Aunt Meg, and not forgetting you, Nancy," Christopher addressed them solemnly. "We three young men have lost much … all in the name of freedom. Please don't take away our right to laugh, even if it's at ourselves."

His mother's fork slipped from her hand, clattering noisily onto her plate. Lips quivering, she levelled her eyes on her son. "I love and admire all three of you boys," she whispered emotionally, "but please don't joke about your injuries in my presence. I changed you and your brother's diapers and nursed you until you could walk, seeing that ability taken away from you is certainly no laughing matter for me."

She looked like she wanted to leave the table but she hung her head and clasped her napkin tightly to her chest and took a deep breath. Gus looked at her sadly and went to stand behind her placing his hands consolingly on her shoulders. He knew all too well the pain she was feeling and was proud of her for speaking out. One day when the boys had children of their own they would understand better.

Christopher was about to speak again, when Nancy surprised them by striking her fist sharply onto the table making her silverware jump. The oriental servant hovering nearby, leapt back in alarm and a silly grin crept across Jebediah's face as all eyes focused on the girl.

"That's enough, brother!" she snapped, looking right at Chris. "That's enough of your fooling around or I'm going to come over there and thump you personally!"

The tension broken, Gus kissed his wife on the cheek and went back to his seat. They all settled down to finish eating and only Dan noticed the sly wink Christopher threw at Nancy. "You're more woman than I can handle, little sister," he mumbled. Nancy made a face at him and everyone laughed.

With breakfast over, they made their way down to the boathouse. Dan, Bill and Chris charged ahead on the new concrete walkway with Dan pushing the wheelchair.

"They're brothers in spirit, that is for sure," Nancy commented, linking arms with Gus and Beth. "They've all shared the same traumatic experience and someday my Danny will remember it, for good or not."

314

Chapter 32

"They're coming," Eva murmured. "I can recognize the sound of Nancy's boat now."

"He's still watching us," Dorothy whispered, casting a furtive glance toward the darkness of the tree line.

"It's only Sam," Eva laughed. "He's harmless."

Walking to the clifftop, the women watched the *Stockholm* dock and the occupants begin their slow climb up the stairs. Nancy saw them and waved. Later, while sitting in their kitchen having a cup of tea, Meg told Eva of the Camp Lewis show and listed off the stars who would be present.

"I heard at school yesterday," Dorothy interrupted, "that Mary Pickford once visited Victoria."

"She did and not too long ago," Nancy replied, smiling at the memory. "Dan and I met her."

Their conversation was suddenly interrupted by the sound of a vehicle coming up the drive.

"Now who could that be?" Jebediah remarked, easing himself slowly out of his comfortable chair.

The truck stopped, a door banged, and quick footsteps sounded on the gravel. When Jeb went to the door he found an army corporal getting ready to knock. He had an envelope in his hand.

"Is this the home of Nancy Wilson?" he inquired.

"Yes. I'm Nancy Wilson," she replied, coming up behind her uncle. "What have you there?"

"It's regarding a medical check-up for Sergeant Brown, ma'am. I'm to emphasize, you must have him at Esquimalt Naval Hospital at four o'clock on the day of your appointment." He handed Nancy the letter, saluted smartly and left.

Ripping it open, she groaned. "June 1st, that's a Friday. Fiddlesticks! Now we'll be travelling to Seattle on the edge of dark."

Rising to leave, Eva whispered to Meg. "I hate to ask, Meg, but have we any money left in the kitty? The price of food is rising like crazy and we have two families that are really hard up."

Scuttling away into the next room, the Scot quickly returned with a crisp, new American twenty-dollar bill. She handed it to Eva.

"Thanks Meg. Good luck with your medical, Dan," Eva called before she turned and went down the steps.

"Thanks, Eva," Dan said quietly.

"Do you want to go downtown shopping today, Aunt Meg?" Nancy inquired.

"No love, I've had enough excitement for this weekend."

"Oh good, then I think Dan and I will have a quiet afternoon, too."

After having a cup of tea and some lunch they decided to go for a walk first going over to the orchard to see Kent.

"Did you know about the boats that are using the bay at night?" he asked.

What boats? You mean recently?" asked Nancy. "We've been away since yesterday morning."

"Sam told me about them. He's seen them several times and seemed to be concerned so I came back last night. We watched together from the trees atop the cliff as it was getting dark." He pointed beyond the orchard.

"And what happened?"

"SAM!" Kent shouted toward the tangle of undergrowth beyond the clearing. "COME OUT HERE."

Appearing like magic, the old hermit stepped out from behind a tree.

"Tell them what we saw last night," he urged, taking his pipe out and lighting it.

"No, no," the redhead laughed. "You tell us, Kent."

"Right," the gardener chuckled. "It was that lad who used to work on the Empress dock before the war … Johnny something or other." He paused to puff on his pipe for a moment, before continuing excitedly. "A truck came and flashed its lights. Then he came in with a boat and several men loaded what looked like bulky gunnysacks. We could hear clinking like bottles. I think it was booze."

"Who have you told?" asked Nancy, watching the lad shake his head. "Then don't. Here's what I want you to do. Fill two oil lanterns from the shed and get Sam to light them after dark, then ask him to keep moving them up and down the beach all night."

"Why, what good will that do?" he asked.

"If they're trying to keep it secret," she explained, "and they think somebody's there watching for them, they'll stop using that beach. We

316

don't want that sort of thing going on next to us at Cunningham Manor now do we, Kent?"

Jerking to attention, the gardener saluted the redhead briskly. "No ma'am, we don't. We'll do it just as you say. Leave it to me," he replied with a serious expression.

Smiling at the former soldier's reaction, they wandered slowly back through the small trees and Nancy stopped to sniff the sweet scent of the first blooms. She slipped her arm affectionately around Dan's waist; his went comfortably around her shoulders.

"Some day this will be your orchard," she said.

"Have you always been this way?" he asked.

"In charge you mean?" She stopped, turning to face him. "No, Dan, you were always in charge. You bought this land, you had the house built, and you taught me about boats. I was just the little sister you took care of." Her voice broke and she buried her head in his chest.

"Don't cry, love," he whispered, gently stroking her hair and thinking how soft it was. "One day I'll remember."

Dark clouds filled the Sunday morning sky and raindrops fell intermittently over Victoria as Nancy and Dan drove along Richmond to the Wounded Soldier. She'd made a decision to try something new, which involved Dan working at the restaurant. Perhaps talking to people would help his memory.

He seemed to enjoy his new role as he chatted to the soldiers and picked up snippets of news from local folks. It gave him something to talk about at dinner. One evening, he emotionally told them of the three convalescing soldiers who had drowned in the sea off Resthaven Hospital the week before. It hadn't been in the newspapers but the boys knew all about it. He also told of overhearing conversations on the subject of conscription and read that the shipbuilding industry was now booming locally as government contracts finally poured into the shipyards.

On Friday, the 1st of June, the sun brought its joy streaming through the windows at Cunningham Manor. This was the beginning of a day Nancy would remember for the rest of her life. It was a happy day with Jeb making them laugh as they loaded the *Stockholm*, using the chute for the first time in weeks.

At half-past two, Nancy and Dan set out for Esquimalt to keep the appointment for his medical examination. Slowing as she drove past the little church in Henry Street, she mentioned Dumpy and Katherine's wedding. They crossed the tramlines at Admirals and continued along the bumpy, dusty road to the dockyard.

They waited impatiently until an orderly showed them into a small office with an eye chart on the wall. A nurse entered a few minutes later. She performed some tests on Dan's hearing and checked his vision. She left and soon a short, bespectacled young man in a white smock arrived. He seemed in a hurry and didn't even introduce himself. He asked Dan some questions then tapped on Dan's head.

Nancy couldn't help but giggle. "If anyone's home," she chuckled, making a face at Dan, "tell them I'm out here waiting!"

Unamused, the doctor looked disapprovingly at the redhead. Keeping his temper, he scribbled something on Dan's file. "No change," he snapped. "I want you back here in three months." It was all over and he strode from the room.

It was nearly seven o'clock when they arrived back at Gordon Head and the sun was slowly falling toward the mountains. Dan noticed a dark cloud drifting ominously over from Port Townsend way.

"I'll call the Jorgensens," Jebediah muttered. "You two better hurry up and eat. We'll be leaving in half an hour."

She nodded, unable to speak, as she tucked into a bowl of stew. Meg told them she had wrapped up some of her freshly baked apple pie so they could eat it on the way. Hugging her quickly, they gathered their coats and hurried down to the boat. The *Stockholm*'s engines burst into life and Dan cast off the lines.

Meg stood on the clifftop and waved until they went out of sight. Raising her eyes she said a silent prayer, as had become her custom.

Darkness began to descend on the water as they passed Discovery Island. They sped confidently down the sound and it didn't seem like very long before they passed the Port Townsend Lighthouse. She slowed as they neared Edmonds, turning toward Apple Cove. She found the light at Kingston and, frowning in the darkness, strained to see Ezekiel's light but there was only black hillside.

"Can you see his light, Jeb?" she asked, concern in her voice.

"Not yet," he growled. "Move in a little closer."

They moved toward the pitch blackness of the coastline and suddenly, a rifle barked out of the darkness. A bullet slammed off the wheelhouse as Nancy screamed in surprise.

"Pirates!" Jebediah called in alarm. "Put the lights out! It's probably the Eggers." Leaping through the cabin door, his hands urgently searched the outside seat locker for the two Winchester rifles.

More bullets pinged off the surface of the *Stockholm* coming from other positions. Several bullets thudded ominously into the body of the boat. Nancy shot the speedboat forward, then stopped with a bone-crushing jar. Her hands flew over the controls as the craft jumped into reverse then she cut the engines and peered into the now-silent darkness. Only the angry slapping of the waves could be heard.

"There," Dan whispered, "look across the bay."

Silhouetted against the Edmond's lighthouse, for only a moment, they saw the dark shape of a sailboat moving slowly in behind them.

"Hold on tight, you two," Nancy snarled. "I'm going to run them down!"

"Oh my Lord!" groaned Jebediah. "She means it. Hang on, Danny and keep low!"

With engines roaring, the red-and-gold craft seemed to leap out of the water as Nancy poured on the power, shooting it forward like a tiger on the attack. She slowed when a spotlight's beam conveniently burst over the waves from their target and four guns aboard the shadowy craft spit fire. Bullets bounced off the *Stockholm*'s cabin as the hijackers tried in vain to stop them.

Jebediah and Dan went outside and, with both aiming at the spotlight, the scene was once more plunged into darkness. Jebediah managed to get inside before Nancy turned on the power again charging head on into the withering hail of gunfire. Her fingers caressed the triggers of the two starboard cannons, waiting for just the right moment. Swinging broadside suddenly, she pressed the triggers, lighting the water with her own thundering flash.

Screams, and the crashing of timber, could be heard in the darkness. Then silence took over.

"Danny, where are you?" Jeb whispered.

"Danny," Nancy's panic-stricken voice repeated.

"He's still outside, I'll get him," said Jeb, moving to open the door.

Suddenly two shots cracked out and as Jeb opened the door, Dan was flung against the cabin wall by the bullet's impact, moaning in pain as he dropped to his knees.

"Dan's been hit!" Jebediah hissed, "get the hell out of here!"

Looking fearfully over her shoulder, she saw Jeb's dark shape move to the rear of the cargo area but she was unable to see Dan in the dark. Jeb bent over him and called his name several times, but there was no response. Nancy's teeth bit deep into her lip as she turned the boat straight at the last spot she'd seen the gunfire, spraying the area with cannon fire as they tore by. Then she fiercely wiped the tears from her eyes with the back of her hand and opened the throttle. As they skipped across the waves, for a fleeting second she desperately hoped anything in front of her would be well-lit. The *Stockholm* responded just as she knew it would.

Jeb felt for Dan's pulse and found it too slow for his liking. His skilled hands moved quickly over Dan's body searching for tell-tale signs of an injury. He heard the cannon fire again and wondered what she was doing. Finally his fingers found what he was looking for.

Oh Lord, not again, he thought, cradling the still form in his arms as he tried to find the source of the bleeding. Although not a religious man, Jeb's prayer for speed and Dan's life was the only thing he could think of doing at the moment.

"HOW BAD IS HE, JEB?" yelled Nancy.

"HE'S ALIVE, JUST GO!" he called back, looking out to see where they were. *Hold on, Danny. Please hold on, son*, his brain screamed.

Fifteen minutes later they were past West Point. She was sure she could see the lights of the Jorgensen boathouse. Barely slowing as she swept up between two well-lit freighters, she looked back and saw Dan in Jeb's arms, his face covered with blood. Her heart almost stopped beating. She shook her head and took a deep breath.

"Something's wrong," the figure on the jetty warned his men.

Nancy brought the powerful craft to a shuddering halt, hitting the wooden jetty as it stopped. Leaping out of the cabin, she grabbed one of the ropes. "DAN'S BEEN SHOT!" she cried, summoning all her strength to throw the rope to waiting hands.

One of Terry's men was already aboard and as others followed she dropped to her knees on the deck beside Dan and Jeb. Gasping with shock, she realized with terror that Dan had suffered another head wound. His face was a mask of drying blood and she could hardly make out his features. She was finding it difficult to breath and grasped Terry's arm.

"He's alive, Nancy. We'll get him to the hospital right away," he said kindly, helping her up. "It always looks worse than it is." As she stood up her head began to spin and she realized her legs weren't going to hold her. Terry caught her as she fainted.

They were halfway to the city when Nancy's eyes flickered open. "Providence Hospital, Doctor Tyler," she muttered, shaking her head and trying to get her bearings.

"He's on his way," Terry replied, as the car swung wildly to avoid a pedestrian. "Jebediah told me about him and I phoned the hospital from the house."

Screaming up to the entrance of the hospital, attendants swarmed around the vehicle, alerted by Dr. Tyler. Loaded onto a gurney, the white-coated medics swung into action. One of the nurses went over to Nancy.

"He's not going to die, is he?" Nancy asked as she got out of the car, wobbling slightly but Jeb was right there and grabbed her.

"No, my dear, he's not," the nurse said, hoping she was right as she helped to support the girl. "Here, this will work better." She went over to an empty wheelchair standing near the elevator and helped Nancy sit down. "5th floor, please," she told the Negro attendant and he pulled the accordion-type door closed behind them.

Up in the 5th floor waiting room, the nurse ordered coffee and cookies from a porter. Then, making sure they were all right, she explained she would have to leave them. "Don't move from here," she warned as she turned to go. "I'll come and get you when they've finished the operation. It may be awhile, so make yourselves comfortable."

Curling up on a large settee beside Jebediah, she dropped her head onto his shoulder and tried to sleep, her body twitching as a nightmare tormented her. It was just after three in the morning when the nurse reappeared.

Terry gently shook Nancy. "I think the operation's over," he said, standing up.

"No, sir, I'm afraid you'll have to stay here," the nurse instructed. "Miss Wilson, would you like to come with me?"

Chapter 33

Hurrying along the silent corridors, she led Nancy to a small waiting room. Dr. Tyler was already there. He could tell she was very apprehensive, looking at him with red, puffy eyes.

"Is Danny going to be all right?" she asked in a small, fearful voice, totally unlike the girl he had met on the earlier occasion at the marina.

"He's doing just fine, Nancy," he reassured her quickly, trying to dispel the girl's fear. Taking her arm, he led her over to a chair. "We are fortunate that Danny's injury is not as serious as we first thought. However, he will have to stay with us for awhile." He watched as the girl breathed a noticeable sigh of relief. "I assure you, Nancy, he's going to be fine. Come on, I'll take you in to see him now. He's still pretty groggy but I must warn you it's going to be a shock."

Confused and unsure what he meant, she felt him take her arm and he led her into a small room where Danny lay. His head was swathed in bandages and there was a tube in his arm and nose. His eyes opened when they walked in.

"Don't move your head, son," Dr. Tyler warned. "We'll come where you can see us."

As they moved around the bed Nancy watched him closely noticing the bandages and how pale he looked. She wanted to cry with relief but she didn't want to upset him so she took a deep breath and went to his side.

"Hi Danny," she said softly, kissing his cheek. "You gave us quite a fright you know."

"N-Nancy!" Dan cried weakly, reaching out to her.

Nancy took his hand and squeezed it gently as tears welled in her eyes.

"What are ... you doing in Europe?" he asked breathlessly. "You must ... go home. It's ... not ... safe here ...." His words trailed off and he moaned softly.

Gasping, Nancy looked up at Dr. Tyler who was smiling and nodding. She looked back at Dan and realized that his hand had gone limp in her grasp and his eyes were closed. The doctor took her arm and they tiptoed out of the room.

"He thinks he's in Europe," she whispered when they were out in the corridor.

"Don't you see what's happened, Nancy?" asked Dr. Tyler, sitting her down on a nearby chair and joining her. "Dan's memory has come back, except he thinks he's been wounded on the battlefield and is there in hospital. He's still under the influence of the anaesthetic but when he wakes up, I think you'll have the old Dan back, and his memory, too. It seems you can thank that bullet he received last night. We'll be watching him closely. You may have noticed the window in his room through which the nurses can observe him."

In a daze she thanked him and the same nurse appeared who had brought her to the ward only a few minutes before.

"You should go now and have a rest yourself," she advised with a kindly smile.

When they reached the room where she had left Terry and Jeb, they were both pacing in front of a window.

"I'll show you to the elevator," said the nurse, "you can come back any time after ten o'clock this morning. Just come up to the 5th floor and follow the signs to King's Wing. Mr. Brown is in Room 534."

"We have to stay in Seattle, Uncle Jeb," Nancy said numbly, as they climbed into the car a few minutes later, too tired and afraid to tell them everything that had happened, in case it wasn't true.

"I know, love," Jebediah grunted. "I've already called Meg. How's Dan?"

"Dr. Tyler says he's going to be all right. He even said a few words to me but fell asleep again from the anaesthetic."

"That's great news, honey. You'll find he's even better after some sleep," Jeb reassured her, very relieved, and now eager to get to bed.

Rain fell steadily as Terry took them through the city and back to the Jorgensen's. Beth and Gus were out of town but the servants had long ago been instructed to make them welcome.

"You'll be fine there," Terry announced confidently. "I'll leave you a car and a driver. He'll take you anywhere you want to go." He yawned, rubbing his eyes.

It was nearly 4:30 a.m. when they passed through the big iron gates; several dim lights were shining inside as they pulled in under the porté cochére. One of Terry's men stepped out of the shadows and rapped loudly with the brass knocker.

"Everything okay, boss?" he growled, moving toward them as Terry told him it was. "You should see that boat, boss," he added excitedly, "it's full of bullet holes. They must have had a hell of a scrap out there!"

"Later Benny, later," Terry replied irritably, glancing at Nancy as the door opened and one of the female servants appeared. "We'll get them Swedish engineers over to fix it up tomorrow."

Nancy had no recollection later of how she made it to bed or the gentle hands that tucked her in although sleep came fitfully as scene after scene flashed through her head. When she relived the horrible sight of Dan lying unconscious in the bottom of the boat with his face covered in blood, she moaned loudly, but there was no one to hear her.

At half past 9, when her eyes focused on the dressing table clock, she leapt out of bed. Panic sent her racing for the shower, quickly dressing and hurrying downstairs. At the table, Jebediah sat calmly reading the morning newspaper. His eyes were smiling as she burst into the room.

"We'll be late, Uncle Jeb. He'll be waiting for us!"

"No, he won't, little one," he chuckled. "He's no doubt sleeping. You've time enough for coffee and toast. He probably won't even remember you were there last night, you know."

When their driver pulled up to the hospital doors, he told them he would wait for them in the parking lot, no matter what time they needed him. Thanking him, Nancy eagerly stepped out of the car and hurried Jebediah inside. There weren't many people around except some white-coated hospital workers who seemed to be hurrying in all directions. The elevator took them up to the 5th floor and Nancy quickly found Room 534. She hesitated before opening the door and Jeb noticed her hand was shaking as she reached for the handle.

"Calm down," he said, slipping his arm around her shoulder and squeezing her. "Get a grip of yourself, girl," he whispered, opening the door himself.

Dan's bandaged head was the first thing Nancy saw, his face now swollen and blue under the bandages but the tubes were gone. Hesitating briefly as icy fingers clawed at her spine, she smiled and moved slowly toward him. He was propped up on pillows and, except for the bruising, she thought he looked better than he had a few hours before and this encouraged her.

There was a nurse in the room and she immediately caught Jeb's signal, following him out into the passageway.

Dan held out his arms and tried to smile. "I know who you are now," he murmured, and she thought she could see a twinkle in his swollen eyes. Unable to contain her happiness and relief, she went over to him and sitting on the bed, he enfolded her in his arms and she burst into tears.

"D-do you really re-remember everything n-now?" she stammered, realizing she was wetting his shoulder as she cautiously hugged him.

"Not everything, love," he sighed. "But it's coming back, the Joyce brothers, Aunt Meg, Waldo Skillings, Jack Dumpford, Jebediah and, most of all, you." Wincing slightly, he allowed his lips to brush her cheek. "I've loved you for so long it would have broken my heart to forget you. I remember the orphanage and the day you arrived, so fragile and tiny, and I remember meeting you again in the restaurant so many years later."

Nancy sat up and took his hand, taking a deep breath. She felt his other arm go around her waist. The door opened behind her, as she kissed him.

"Easy, you two, we don't want you to move that head too much yet," the nurse said gently. "Dr. Tyler says he'll be out of here by Thursday or Friday, if everything goes well ...."

"Can I stay?" Nancy interrupted, standing up and facing her as Jeb entered the room.

"Yes, you can, but he needs a lot of rest," the nurse replied. "It would be better if you came later."

Her eyes flashed to the man in the bed whose own eyes fluttered tiredly as he shook hands with Jeb. Jebediah, who had learned of Dan's memory return from the nurse, laid a comforting hand on her shoulder.

"Come on, sweetheart, let's leave him to get better."

Kissing Dan tenderly on the cheek and promising to come back the next morning, she slowly backed out of the room. At street level, they found themselves in sunshine and, Nancy, alert once more, said she wanted to see the *Stockholm*. She instructed the driver to take them back to the house. As they ate lunch in the quiet of the Jorgensen's private apartment, the maid rapped lightly on the door and entered.

"Begging your pardon, Miss Nancy," the girl said softly, respectfully lowering her eyes. "Mr. O'Reilly said to tell you he is waiting at the boathouse when you are ready."

On the dock, Terry had been watching Gus' friend, Sven, the Swedish engineer and his partner, Hans, as they meticulously went over the *Stockholm*. They chattered away together in their native language pointing wide-eyed at the bullet holes in the woodwork. When Nancy and Jebediah appeared, Terry called them over to the cabin, running his hands over the unbroken, but badly scratched, glass in the windows.

"How?" Terry asked, but the redhead shrugged her shoulders.

"That must be special glass," Jebediah grunted, also running his hands over it curiously.

Chuckling with cold amusement, Hans nodded. "You're absolutely right, Jebediah. Gus ordered us to install Swedish armoured glass. You would call it bullet proof!"

Nancy's eyebrows shot up, amazed that Gus had such forethought and had apparently gone to such lengths to protect them.

A cold shudder shot up the old detective's back when he realized the danger they would have been in, if the *Stockholm* had been a normal boat. "Hell's bells!" he whispered under his breath, running his hands over the multiple holes in the hull and cabin. "We sure took a hammering out there."

"We gave as good as we got!" Nancy snapped, before turning to the Swedes. "Will the boat be ready by Thursday we'll need to be off by lunchtime?" she asked. The note in her voice warned against argument, as she rounded on Terry. "Have you contacted Gus and Beth, yet?" she asked, adding bluntly, "and you owe me some money!"

Jebediah smiled at the look on the gangster's face, taken aback by the girl's approach. Nodding, he stuck his hand into his inside pocket and pulled out an envelope.

"I talked to Bill at the farm," he growled irritably. "He said they would all be home on Friday."

Handing Jebediah the envelope, Nancy took Terry by the arm and led him out of the boathouse. "I'm not cross with you, love," she purred, holding onto his arm as they walked a bit farther up the jetty. "I'm just so eager to get things moving. I want to be out of here on Thursday evening so we can get back with the shipment on Friday. Then if the doctor says Dan is able to travel, we'll be taking him home with us." She glanced up at him, affectionately squeezing his arm as she smiled coyly. "But I sure need them Eggers kept out of my way."

"You don't have to worry about them for a while, honey," Terry laughed. "Roy Olmstead has them in jail and two of them are full of your buckshot, whining like babies, he said!"

"Right!" she giggled, as they walked back to the boathouse where Jeb was waiting. "You take care of the repairs to the boat. Now, it's a shower for me, a bite to eat, and I'm going back to the hospital."

Jebediah winked at Terry knowing they had the old Nancy back again. He knew the young man would follow her instructions to the letter, such was her magic.

They had a different driver that afternoon. He was a talkative man, born in the city and eager to relate its history as he manoeuvred the vehicle through the confusion of streetcars and Saturday traffic toward the hospital.

"That's Pike's Market," he pointed ahead through the crowds of noisy shoppers jostling around sidewalk stalls of produce and wares as they finished up their day. "We can stop if you like." Receiving no reply, he carried on with his impromptu monologue. "Over there, toward Puget Sound," he said, pointing, "are so many restaurants it would take a week to try them all and, some you wouldn't want to, I wager!"

"Are we close to the hospital?" she asked, obviously not listening to his chatter.

"Not far," he replied. "It's at 17th and Cherry."

Somewhere in the background a clock chimed the half hour as Jeb held the hospital door open for Nancy. Wasting no time, she ran to the elevator calling to Jebediah to hurry.

"5th floor, please," she told the attendant.

Entering the dimly lit room, she looked up at the observation window and noticed the nurse look up and put her finger to her lips. She and Jeb entered the room but Nancy quickly forgot that Jeb was with her, so intent was she on watching Dan. She quietly moved the chair closer to the bed but before sitting down she just stood and stared at him for a moment.

When she sat down, she gently laid her hand on top of his, feeling his warmth. She studied his face with its bandages and bruises and noticed that the swelling had gone down some more. She sighed deeply with relief and settled back into her chair. Wild thoughts began to run through her head unaware that Jebediah had left the room. She sat for almost an hour watching him breathe and then dozing off herself.

Suddenly, Dan groaned and she opened her eyes with a start, almost forgetting where she was. He seemed to be having a bad dream. He winced in his sleep and his breathing became rapid and shallow. Trying to comfort him, she stroked his arm but he moaned several more times turning his head and moving his body. His obvious torment alarmed her and especially concerned with his head movements, she tried to think of what she could do to calm him.

327

Of course! she thought, and instantly began to sing. A remarkable change came over his body and a smile momentarily crossed his battered face.

"Listen, she's singing to him, doctor," the nurse whispered to Dr. Tyler, who had arrived on late rounds. "What a lovely voice she has."

"Do you know who that girl is, nurse?" Morgan Tyler muttered, looking through the window at the two figures who had become very special to him.

"No, doctor."

"That's Nancy Wilson," he replied, solemnly. "Many would claim she is Seattle's favourite singer, even though she is a Canadian. I personally owe that girl a debt of gratitude for my own life."

The nurse looked up at him with a curious expression, understanding at last his extraordinary concern for the Canadian soldier. They listened to the singing as they worked and then the doctor said goodnight and left her to continue her quiet vigil.

Out in the waiting room, Jebediah was awoken by a gentle shaking. He sat up and stretched. "What time is it, nurse?"

"It's 10 o'clock, sir. It's time you took Nancy home, Mr. Judd, or you might find yourself staying the night!"

Jeb got up and went to find the girl who was also dozing in her chair, still holding Dan's hand. He shook her gently and indicated they should go, showing her the time. She shook herself and stood up. Giving Dan a light kiss on the cheek, she looked up at the nurse's window but no one was there.

Arm in arm they walked slowly through the hospital doors and out into the darkness of another pleasant June evening. Hardly a word of conversation passed between them. They stood for a moment and Nancy saw their driver wave from the parking lot. She could feel the energy in the air around her. In the distance, the city seemed to be lit by thousands of tiny lights pushing back the darkness with a feeling of friendliness. She felt remarkably calm despite her tiredness.

"This is a beautiful city," she murmured, looking up at the stars as the car pulled up. "But I'm quite exhausted. I suppose you've been sleeping in the waiting room. I'm sorry I kept you so late, Uncle Jeb. You're going to have difficulty sleeping tonight."

"No, love, I never have trouble sleeping. A long time ago, I got used to sleeping on stagecoaches. I can sleep anywhere!" He patted her hand affectionately as they pulled up to the Jorgensen's. He opened the car door thanking their driver.

On Sunday she stayed all day at the hospital, leaving Jebediah at the mansion to amuse himself. Nancy felt quite sorry for him wishing she could send him home. However, on Monday, he was invited to the shipyard to view the repairs being done on the *Stockholm* and it was quite obvious he was looking forward to it.

Dan was making steady progress and on Monday Dr. Tyler allowed her to wheel their patient along the passageways of the 5th floor. Nurse Baker provided her with instructions so they wouldn't get lost.

Tuesday brought a great feeling of relief when Dan began relating memories from their childhood, with such clarity that tears welled up in Nurse Baker's eyes as she listened and watched from the window. Amazed and enthralled by the hardships these two orphans had suffered, she had to tear herself away to tend to her other patients.

That afternoon they took away Dan's wheelchair, allowing him his first attempts at walking again. Jebediah was present and howled with laughter when Dan said his legs had turned to jelly. Nellie visited in the evening, looking grief stricken after talking with Terry who had told her of the accident. However, she quickly joined in the Canadians' laughter when she was made aware of the happiness of the situation.

On Thursday morning, she asked the driver to stop at a clothing store so she could buy Dan some new clothes. Then hurrying to the hospital, she was delighted to find him sitting in his wheelchair waiting for her by the 5th floor elevator. She made a striking figure with the sunlight sparkling on her red hair as she stepped out of the elevator, sending a thrill coursing through the young soldier's body. He had become quite aware of his feelings for Nancy over the past few days and greatly looked forward to her visits. He had also spent a great deal of time thinking about her.

The elevator attendant called her by name for the second time that morning. "Is Sgt. Brown going for a ride, Miss Wilson?"

"Oh yes, thank you," she replied, quickly pulling the wheelchair into the conveyance. "Main Floor, please," she requested and when they reached the bottom they both waved to the man as he took several more people aboard. "Busy morning," she commented as she pushed Dan over to the window. She bent down to hug him and passing hospital staff called out to her by name. She stood up and watched them go looking at Dan with a puzzled expression.

"It's no good looking at me like that," he said, chuckling. "Everyone knows who you are. Your picture is in all the newspapers as the star of the Camp Lewis Show. You seem to be a celebrity, love!"

329

Nancy rolled her eyes and grinned, patting his shoulder. They went for a walk in the sunshine and when they returned the elevator was waiting. Dr. Tyler joined them at the 2nd floor. With his stethoscope swinging from his neck she realized what a handsome man he was.

"Looks like we're going to the same place," he declared, grinning broadly. Stepping out ahead of them at the 5th floor, he turned to wait for them. "I'll sign Dan's release for four o'clock tomorrow, Nancy. I might not see you again for awhile so you two look after each other."

"We will, doctor, thank you," she replied, as the surgeon began to walk away.

"Wait a moment!" she insisted, her voice full of devilment. "Are you claiming salvage, sir?"

Morgan Tyler stopped in mid-stride. Turning slowly, he looked from one to the other and broke into laughter. "No, young lady, I'm not. I've squared my account and I thank you for the pleasure of being able to get to know you better. Let's make it under more pleasant circumstances next time, all right?"

Lips trembling as she tried to smile, Nancy went toward him. "I can't thank you enough, doctor," she whispered, giving him a hug.

"You do, my dear, every time I hear you sing," he replied. Winking at her, he spun on his heel and disappeared around the next corner.

They ate lunch in Dan's room giving Nurse Baker the thrill of her life by inviting her to join them. An hour later, Nancy told Dan she had to go and, stooping to hug him, he surprised her by grasping her tightly and kissing her full on the lips. Taken aback, she pulled herself away and stood up looking up at the empty nurse's window. She could feel the redness creep onto her cheeks as she broke into a grin.

"You be back here by five tomorrow, my love, and there'll be more of those waiting," he said slyly, winking at her.

Shaking her head in disbelief, she waved goodbye and hurried from the room. *This is certainly a new Dan I'm seeing, but isn't it grand?* she giggled, beaming broadly she hurried toward the elevator.

"My goodness, she is a nice girl," said Nurse Baker as she came to check on Dan. "She's the first big star I've ever met."

Dan nodded although he hadn't heard what she was saying. His thoughts were on his redhead, her hair flying in the wind aboard the *Stockholm* as she skimmed over the waves of Puget Sound toward home. *She'll be all right, Jebediah's with her and it's daylight,* he told himself, but the whispering voice of worry refused to leave his head.

330

Terry O'Reilly and Roy Olmstead were sharing stories as they waited on the dock for Nancy and Jeb to come down from the house. They were discussing last night's crazy antics of Hiram Gill's dry squad. Terry's contacts had informed him this morning that the squad had wantonly wrecked several of the backstreet saloons of Seattle's dockyard area causing more destructive riots.

The engineers had finished their repairs on the *Stockholm*, delivering it a short while before. To the naked eye, the boat looked to be in brand new condition, with no visible signs of the battle.

"Dan's got his memory back," Terry told Roy.

"You rat," Roy chuckled. "You've got somebody at the hospital feeding you information. You haven't been near them since Saturday."

The young gangster merely grinned.

A female voice caught their attention as Nancy and Jeb came down the path, interrupting further conversation. Dashing past them and into the boathouse her eyes flashed over the boat then her fingers searched the woodwork for bullet holes. Frowning, she climbed aboard, her gaze resting on the place where Dan had lain. Everything had been repaired and the blood cleaned up so well she thought for a brief moment maybe it was all a bad dream. She smiled wryly.

"Looks good as new, Uncle Jeb," she called. "I suppose we should be off."

Jebediah climbed aboard saluting Terry and Roy who hadn't moved but were watching them with interest. *Now there's a strange friendship,* he thought to himself, *a smart young policeman and a gangster, both in the rum running business*!

Terry's voice broke into his thoughts. "Your fuel tanks are full, Nancy. Cannons are clean and fully armed, ready for another battle."

"Cut that out, you twit," Roy snapped, punching him on the shoulder. "The Eggers are in jail, love, and I intend keeping them there. But they're not the only ones with hijacking in mind. So you be careful, run in daylight if you can, it's safer that way."

Thanking them both, Nancy started the *Stockholm*'s engines and slid the powerful speedboat out of the boathouse. Waving to the men, she swung the craft north and opened the throttle. Watching through the field glasses, Jebediah pointed to a German freighter as they neared Keystone. It appeared to be escorted by a U.S. gunboat and two coastguard vessels.

Smiling with satisfaction, the old detective watched them go by as the redhead's eyes focused far ahead into choppy Canadian waters.

331

Nancy was so happy to be back behind the wheel and Jeb noticed. He was glad to be heading home, too. He had missed Meg a lot although he had talked to her each day by phone. *A wonderful invention!* he thought as he trained the glasses on the water ahead.

The ride across the Straits that afternoon was tame compared to some of their trips and it seemed like no time before they were turning into the cove at Gordon Head.

Sam banged on the kitchen door, alerting Meg to the arrival of the *Stockholm*. Excitement gripped the old lady as she hurried outside and over to the stairs. She watched as they climbed out of the boat and started toward her.

"Golly, I'm glad to have you two home," she sighed, giving them each a big hug. "Sam's been keeping watch over things for me."

"Thanks, Sam!" Jebediah shouted to the disappearing native.

As they sat over a cup of tea on the porch, they related their adventure in as much detail as they dared, not wanting to worry her any more than they already had. They told of the help they had received from Doctor Tyler, of Dan's memory return, and the friendly staff at the Seattle hospital.

"We're bringing him home tomorrow, Aunt Meg," Nancy concluded, watching the sparkle return to her aunt's eyes. The sound of a truck in the drive brought her quickly to her feet. "It's Dumpy, what's he doing out here?"

"He's brought the shipment out from Victoria," Meg clucked disapprovingly as Dumpy waved, pulling his truck over to the workshop. In a couple minutes he was striding toward them.

"Howdy! Nan, you're back. How's Dan?" he asked eagerly.

"He's just fine and I'll be bringing him home tomorrow. He remembers everything. It's so wonderful. Why have you come out?"

"Big blow expected tomorrow. We'll get you loaded now."

"Good idea. I'll send them down the chute and you can catch them at the bottom," Jebediah chuckled, planning to get the ride he'd been missing in recent months.

Chapter 34

Morning brought the wind Dumpy had forecast, bending the trees that clung precariously to the rocky cliff and whipping the seas outside the cove into a boiling mass of thundering waves.

"It's going to be a rough one, Jeb," Nancy murmured over breakfast.

"Then wait a while," Meg suggested.

"We won't leave until noon but can't wait any longer than that," the girl replied. "Dan's waiting for us."

"He doesn't want you getting killed by being foolhardy. There's been enough accidents in this family for one year!"

"I know, Aunt Meg. I won't be foolhardy."

Fortunately the wind on the cliff eased a little and they got away as planned. Out in the Strait, however, the scene was different and they were buffeted by strong gusts and angry waves as they fought their way past Discovery Island and headed out into the open water. Suddenly, the wind dropped, and the boiling sea began to settle as sunlight peeked through the clouds. The redhead smiled, poured on more power and hurtled across the water for Port Townsend. The weather improved all the way and by the time they reached Edmonds, the smoke from the factory chimneys were rising lazily into the sky.

At the Jorgensen dock, Nancy leapt easily to the deck unaided and raced toward the house. Knocking on the great oak door, the butler gave her a startled look when he saw her.

"Are you staying again, Miss Nancy?" he asked.

"Only briefly, Joseph, I'll need a car in half an hour, please," she called over her shoulder, as she dashed up the stairway to her room.

"Would you like the kitchen to pack a meal to take with you?"

Stopping at the top of the stairs, she looked down at him and smiled. "That would be wonderful, Joseph, thank you. It's a lovely day for a picnic," she giggled.

Down at the boathouse Jebediah had just finished securing the lines when Terry hurried through the door.

"Well, where is she?"

Laughing, the old detective pointed to the house. "She's in a hurry and she'll need a car."

"Car's there, you go with her," Terry snapped, "I'll take care of things here."

Jebediah nodded, lit his pipe and walked slowly up the path to the porté cochére where a car stood waiting. He struck up a conversation with the driver until Nancy appeared. Her long hair was brushed to a sparkling shine and held back from her face by a blue ribbon; she wore a snow-white cotton dress embroidered with tiny blue flowers across the front. White shoes and a perky little hat completed the picture. The old man whistled as he sprang to open the car door.

"Good grief, what are you trying to do to Dan on his first day of freedom?" he teased.

"Are you going with me?"

"I think I had better!"

Heads turned as they entered the hospital lobby and walked to the elevator. Many recognized her instantly while others thought they did but weren't sure.

"Are you taking Sgt. Brown back to Canada today, Miss Wilson?" the elevator attendant asked, as he let them off at the 5th floor.

"Yes I am," she replied happily, striding out confidently. Tapping lightly, they entered and found Dan talking to Doctor Tyler and Nurse Baker. Wearing his new clothes and with his head only lightly bandaged, he looked happy and more like his old self. Even his bruising was disappearing. He stood up and came to meet them as they entered, kissing her on the cheek and winking, then shaking Jeb's hand.

Getting some brief last minute instructions, they said their goodbyes and took one last look around the room.

"Use a wheelchair down to the car," the nurse advised. "We don't want him tired out before he's left the premises!"

Saying goodbyes all along the way they finally arrived at the front entrance and the car was waiting. Before Dan got out of his wheelchair, he gazed up at the spire over the central area and knew he would long remember this place.

Terry's driver sped them swiftly back to the mansion, leaving them with a friendly nod of his head and a wave. Jebediah banged the brass knocker. Letting them in, Joseph informed them the family had arrived home and were expecting them.

No sooner were the words said then the Jorgensens converged from all directions shouting noisy, excited greetings. Bill almost overturned his wheelchair in his eagerness to get to them. Beth cried with relief when she saw Dan giving them each a lingering hug. Everyone listened intently when Dan proved his memory was back, by relating the story of their first meeting with the Jorgensens on a tram leaving Gorge Park.

"Tell me, son," Gus inquired. "Now that your memory's back, have you forgotten all the things that happened from being wounded to last weekend?"

"No, unfortunately I can remember it all," he replied slowly, "even the blackest moments of desperation and hell when the only thing that kept me going was the sound of an angel singing in my head."

"That's enough of that, Danny," Bill growled good-naturedly. "We know all about that hell and don't need to relive it, but for angel's sake we're sure glad you remember everything now."

Pulling out his pocket watch, Jebediah frowned. "It's almost six o'clock," he reminded Nancy. "Meg will get worried if we're too late."

"You're right, Uncle Jeb, and we don't want Dan to get too tired. He has a long stairway to climb when we get home," she laughed.

"Shucks, I thought maybe one of you would carry me!" Dan chuckled, grinning at them.

Suddenly, jumping out of her chair, she ran to the stairs. "I'll just be a minute." Going to her room, she quickly changed her clothes and packed her bag, hurrying downstairs and meeting them at the door.

Gus looked at her and smiled then noticed what Dan and his sons were doing—their hands locked together in a silent promise of unity and friendship. "*What a blessing to have such wonderful young people around us.*"

At the dock, the bow of the *Stockholm* sparkled in the evening sunshine and the redhead lovingly stroked the rail. The Jorgensens' eyes flashed over the craft, checking for telltale signs of damage.

"Terry told me Sven and his boys did a good job," said Gus solemnly. "I think I would agree with him."

They were saying goodbyes as Nancy started the engines. Suddenly Christopher remembered something and pulled out a package from the seat of his brother's wheelchair, tossing it up to Dan.

"FOR YOU ... OPEN IT!"

Dan's fingers quickly tore open the package to reveal a captain's hat, piped with gold braid. Embroidered on it were the words, *Captain Brown.* Setting it on his head carefully, to avoid the bandages, he saluted the Jorgensens.

"CAST OFF, CREW!" he yelled with a wide grin, throwing the rope to Gus. He put his arms around Nancy who stood at the wheel laughing, and kissed the top of her head.

Tree tops swayed gently in the evening breeze and daylight was fading quickly as Meg stood on the cliff straining to catch the familiar sound. A smile crossed her face when she heard the first whisper of the speedboat's engines in the distance. Clutching the woollen shawl around her shoulders she slowly made her way back to the kitchen to put the kettle on to boil. Twenty minutes later, she was gripped by an unusual feeling of expectation when she heard their voices.

"Oh my, look at you, you poor dear," she sighed, seeing Dan's bandaged head.

"Stop that Aunt Meg! I'm fine now," he laughed, hugging her and planting a big kiss on her cheek. "I'm back to normal, that bullet did me a huge favour. Then he whispered into her ear. "It's happy times again at Cunningham Manor!"

They sat around the kitchen table for a long time after dinner was over chatting of things that had happened in the years before Dan went away. Meg's eyes misted up when the youngsters talked of incidents that only the three of them would know. Yawning, Nancy reached for Dan's arm and tugged him toward the door.

"Come sit on the cliff steps with me, Danny," she whispered. "Let's see if you really remember!" she teased. "Maybe I'll sing to you, just like I used to do."

As they disappeared out the door, Jebediah also rose from his chair. He picked up Meg's shawl and slipped it around her shoulders giving her a squeeze. "Let's go sit on the porch and listen, love, just like we used to do!" he winked at her and she giggled like a schoolgirl.

Moonlight, shining through wispy clouds, sent brilliant rays of amber over Gordon Head as Nancy sang her welcome home to Dan— the soft sweet notes fading quickly as the breeze took them out to sea.

Sleep came easily that night, the pain and worry having been lifted from everyone's minds. Laughter and good-natured banter again filled the kitchen at breakfast as they all prepared for an outing into town to reintroduce Dan to his friends and familiar places.

Arranging to meet at The Wounded Soldier and have lunch with Katherine, they left in two separate vehicles. Jebediah took Shelbourne Street, now connected to Hillside, while Dan and Nancy drove the old way along Cedar Hill Road. Today it was Dan that chattered about the farms they passed, even remembering many of their neighbours' names.

"I think I'd like to go for a walk along Government Street today," he suggested, when they arrived on the outskirts of town. "I'm eager to see what's changed since I've been away … now that I remember what used to be there."

Pulling into the traffic at the fountain intersection, she stopped to allow streetcar passengers the right of way, as they wandered across the road near the iron foundry. She watched Dan closely for signs of panic or fear as the foul-smelling air touched their noses. Other than commenting about it, he seemed to have no ill effects.

They heard the thundering rush of smoke from the nearby E&N trains, the crashing of steel on steel as rail trucks were shunted to the rice mill on Store Street. The din of car and cart, mixed with the sounds of horses and the voices of Saturday shoppers. The rumble of streetcars and the horns of motor vehicles turned it into a typical summer's day in wartime Victoria.

"Oh, for the quiet of Gordon Head," Nancy sighed.

"It's wonderful!" he said as his eyes moved across familiar buildings and up and down once familiar streets.

She could see his excitement as they pushed through the Wharf Street congestion to turn onto the dock. He looked up and read the sign.

"Brown and Wilson is it?" he said in a teasing voice. "Let's go find Dumpy! It looks very quiet."

"The boat's missing. He's probably had to go on a run somewhere. He knows you were coming home today, so he'll be eager to see you."

They walked down the dock to where the *Belfast* was once moored and stood together silently gazing out at the water. Dan put his arm around her and finally broke the silence.

"They were good men, Nan."

"The best!"

"I wonder where they are now?"

"I sure hope they got back to Newfoundland all right. It was a long trip for them."

"They were tough fisherman. They'll have found a way to make it. Us fishermen don't give up easily," he said, taking her arm. "Let's go for that walk."

He noticed it right away as they walked along Wharf Street—Moore and Pleasant's motor vehicle showrooms were empty. The post office and the Belmont Building still stood guard at the edge of the harbour.

Standing for a moment to admire the stately Empress Hotel, they turned up Government Street. She could see his puzzled expression as he looked up and down the west side of the street.

"They've gone," he muttered in disbelief. "The Rogers' grocery store is gone!"

"No it hasn't, silly," she laughed, pointing across the street to an elegant-looking little shop with fancy copper-trimmed windows and leaded lights over the doorway. The sign read, Rogers' Chocolate Shop.

"My word, looks like it's a popular place, too," he declared, noticing a continual stream of customers coming and going. "I guess chocolates were doing better than groceries for them!"

He mentioned the Windsor Hotel on the next corner and the old cigar shop next door, still in the same location. His eyes glanced up the street checking for the West End Grocery store that now sported a sign for Victoria Book and Stationery and, he remembered a bakery that used to be here, but the name failed him. Two tipsy men with bowler hats, rolled out from the Brown Jug Saloon.

"Well that hasn't changed," he mumbled, noticing for the first time that people were watching him. He surmised that it was his bandages that made him a curiosity.

The Royal Bank, Woolworth's and E.A. Morris all brought memories flooding back as he walked on to the corner of Bastion Street. He stood looking down its rough wooden-blocked surface to Langley Street, and his gaze fell on the large, stone-fronted Bank of Montreal building on the corner. Grinning, he turned toward W & J Wilson's on the east side of the street at Trounce Alley. His mind went back to the night several years before when he had put a line onto a foundering freighter and the Joyces had claimed it for salvage. That act had marked the beginning of their business relationship with Gus Jorgensen, and the clothier had bought the British cloth they had salvaged from the wreck.

"That's enough for now, Nan," he announced, taking her hand when they reached the corner of Yates Street. "Let's head back to the dock and see if Dumpy has returned."

Nancy was now totally convinced that his memory was intact but she had forgotten that this was his first day out and realized he would be getting tired.

She took his arm. "Come on, I'll make you a nice cup of tea and then we have to get over to the restaurant to meet Meg and Jebediah."

As they crossed over Yates to the end of Langley Street, he stopped and looked around. "Is the Provincial Police office still along here?"

"Yes," she replied, "but look over there."

He followed her hand and noticed a crowd gathering in front of a building whose sign said, The Majestic Theatre.

"Music Hall?" he asked.

"No, silent moving pictures, they call them. I've never seen one but I've heard a lot about them. Waldo and his wife went and quite enjoyed it. We'll have to try it one day soon."

Screams of indignation from the corner of Wharf Street drew their attention as a bicycle rider and a pedestrian became entangled in front of Hugh Bains' tyre repair shop. Dan laughed as the two people yelled scorching abuse at each other while an amused crowd gathered.

Across the street, blacksmith, Jim Morrison, shouted a greeting to them, waving them to come over. "I heard you were back home, lad," he called. "Folks said you were wounded but I thought that was a while ago."

"Yes, I was wounded by a shell in Belgium but that's all better now." Dan chuckled. "This bandage is just covering a lump where Nancy belted me!"

Amused, the blacksmith spat a stream of tobacco juice onto the sidewalk and pulled out his tobacco pouch to refill his pipe, displaying heat-blackened fingers. Jim had known both of them since they were youngsters in their first jobs. The bond between these two young people was well-known by the traders of Wharf Street.

Cocking an eyebrow as he put a flame to the fresh tobacco, Jim Morrison's eyes twinkled with devilment.

"That's easily fixed, Danny lad, marry her!" Chuckling to himself, the blacksmith turned and disappeared into his workshop, his leather apron slapping against his thighs as he walked.

Blushing, their fingers entwined, but not looking at each other they continued on their way toward Bastion Street. Dan jerked to a halt in front of Harvey's wholesale liquor store.

"The old Ship Inn has gone," he exclaimed, looking around the square, "and no German Consulate!"

"The Germans left the consul at the start of the war. There was a big riot in this area after the sinking of the *Lusitania*. The saloon's been gone for at least a year."

The *Lusitania* was sunk?" Dan asked incredulously, remembering reading something about the ship while he was in England.

"Yes, unbelievable as it sounds. It's quite a story and Meg kept a copy of the newspaper for you. I'll tell you all about it later."

Heading over to Wharf they looked down toward the Brown and Wilson dock and saw Dumpy, Fred and Waldo talking together outside the office. She took his hand again and they walked slowly down the boardwalk. The men saw them coming and walked up to meet them.

"How does it feel to know who you are, Dan?" Waldo asked, grinning as he held out his hand.

"He must feel pretty good, he's just had a week lazing about in Seattle," Fred interrupted, with a grin.

"He weren't lazing!" Dumpy replied indignantly. "He was hurt. Leave him alone, Fred."

"Gee, he just told Jim Morrison it was because I thumped him!" Nancy exclaimed, trying to lighten the mood.

A clock began to strike noon in the background.

Dan, who had been very quietly ignoring this conversation, leaned over to Nancy and whispered into her ear. "Have you any money with you, Nan? I need to go to the bank before we go home."

"How much do you need?" she asked, taking her little purse out of her handbag and opening it. "I think there should be enough for your needs in there. Where are you going?"

"I don't know yet," he said, taking the purse out of her hand and striding up the boards toward Wharf Street.

"WHERE ARE YOU GOING ... Danny?" she cried, realizing it was futile, but not concerned in the least.

"Who knows," Waldo mumbled with a frown, "but he wanted to be on his own that's obvious. Does it really matter now he's got his memory back? It isn't often a man asks to borrow a woman's purse!"

Nancy looked at him and smiled. Waldo understood these things. She and Dan had shared everything since they had been together, this didn't surprise him in the least.

Grinning to himself, Dan started to run but found his head hurt so he slowed down and turned up Broughton knowing exactly what he was looking for. He crossed Government, dodged around a streetcar and found Henry Greenfelder's jewellery shop. Breathing hard, he entered the store and dropped Nancy's purse on the counter in front of the startled jeweller.

"I need a diamond ring, Henry, and quickly!" he gasped, his fingers pulling a small wad of bills from her purse.

"For a lady, sir ... or yourself?" Henry inquired, staring at the money but quickly regaining his composure.

"For Nancy, don't you remember me, Henry?" came the snappy answer. "Please hurry!"

The jeweller kept looking over at him as he went to a drawer and brought a selection to the counter. "Yes ... you're Dan Brown, aren't you, lad? Of course, I remember you and Nancy. I thought she was your sister?"

"If she was, I wouldn't be buying her an engagement ring now would I?" Dan said in frustration. "I need some help here, Henry. I don't have any idea what sort of ring a lady would like."

Picking a ring out of the display, Henry handed it to Dan. It seemed to Dan a rather large but beautiful stone. He knew right away that Nancy would love it. He frowned and the jeweller assured him it was a reasonable price. Asking what that price was, Dan checked his money and found he was $3 short.

"That's all right, son. Call it a wedding present for a nice couple."

Within ten minutes, Henry had it boxed and wrapped then handed it to Dan with his receipt. Heaving a sigh of relief, he slipped Nancy's purse into one of his coat pockets and the ring into another, hoping she wouldn't need any of her money until they could get to the bank. He thanked Henry and set out back to the dock, arriving flushed and breathless.

"Are you all right? Where have you been?" Nancy asked, taking her purse from Dan and looking at him quizzically.

"Buying a hope for the future," he replied evasively, kissing her cheek.

"And you think he's recovered, lass?" asked Fred, shaking his head. "Why he's just as daft as he used to be, but it's good to have him back!"

Waldo checked his watch, grunting it was way past his lunch time, as he marched off the dock.

"Oh, my word!" Nancy squealed. "We promised to meet Meg and Jebediah at Katherine's for lunch. I completely forgot!"

"Better hang on tight, Dan," Dumpy laughed. "When that girl is in a hurry, it usually means you're in for a wild ride."

Dan followed Nancy to the car and she had it started even before his door was shut. She forced her way into the heavy traffic at Wharf Street and amidst blaring horns and angry gestures they turned into Fort

341

Street, causing two sailors a moment of terror as they leapt for the safety of a crowded sidewalk.

"Do you always drive like this?" Dan asked sarcastically, cringing as the little truck veered around a streetcar disgorging its passengers as they passed Fort and Quadra Street.

"Police Chief John Langley lives over there," she laughed, pointing up Cook Street as they passed by. "He was a regular at the Balmoral."

"Are you trying to tell me that you bribe the local police so you can drive like this!" he laughed, not expecting an answer as they continued up Fort.

There was no let up in the traffic as they went over the crest of the little hill and onto Cadboro Bay Road following the well-signed route to the Jubilee Hospital. Pulling in at the back of The Wounded Soldier, Nancy recognized Jebediah's car, along with Jack Duggan's shiny new Ford, and Harry Maynard's big Chrysler.

Great, they're all here! she thought to herself.

Inside, they found Meg and Jebediah presiding over a long table of friends. Katherine, having removed her apron, was sitting between the Duggans and the Maynards and as they entered she ran to meet them. Greetings were exchanged welcoming Dan and everyone watched curiously as he comfortably joined in the banter.

As the meal progressed and the noise level calmed down, conversation turned to the war and the effect it was having on Victoria. This prompted several questions to be aimed at Dan, who suddenly looked quite uncomfortable.

"If you want to know about the war, go over there to the hospital and walk through the wards," he said slowly, picking up his spoon and turning it over and over in his hand. "I really don't want to talk about it if you don't mind."

"Me neither, lad!" The voice came from a table near the door. The young man rose from his chair, swinging a white cane in front of him and tapping it on the floor. He cautiously made his way over to their table and looking right at Dan, held out his hand.

"I'm proud to meet you, mate. Dan is your name? I'm John."

A silence fell over the restaurant, as Dan stood up and took the stranger's hand. "Yes, I'm Dan Brown. I suffered from amnesia until recently and now I'm mighty glad to be home. My Nancy is one of the owners' of this restaurant, John. So I'm sure we'll meet again," he said, gripping the man's shoulder.

John saluted casually to the group and left the restaurant.

There was no further talk of the war after that and the topic changed to prohibition and Brewster's hard-line attack on saloons and taverns. Now they had Dan's interest.

"I'm sure you'll all want to bring me up to date on the local news," he commented, grinning at Nancy. "I think Meg has kept a pile of newspapers from me. She must want me to catch up on my schooling ... reading and history!"

Meg made a face at him and they all laughed.

"Between rising food prices, the coalminer's strike in Nanaimo, and Victoria City close to bankruptcy, maybe we should all emigrate to Sooke and become farmers!" Harry joked.

Eva arrived unexpectedly just as the lively group erupted in laughter. Nancy waved her over.

"I never expected to find you folks here," she exclaimed.

"I think they were just leaving!" murmured Jack, winking at her.

"Come on, Danny," Nancy chuckled. "Jack's right, we have things to do."

"Where are we going?" he asked, when she turned onto Richmond.

"Esquimalt Hospital."

Turning onto Bay Street with its wide open spaces of farmland, they chugged along the narrow road and she squinted in the bright sunshine. He shaded his eyes with his hand as Nancy pointed out the older, established area of Fernwood on both sides of the street.

"Jack and Nellie live just up there," she announced, pointing southward.

Nodding, Dan's eyes roamed along the valley, taking note of the little houses at each side of the road. "It was at the Duggan's where we became a family," he reminded her.

They met a dray pulled by four steaming horses plodding up the hill toward Quadra Street and from here they could see the haze caused by the city's industrial factories. The Model T picked up speed going down the hill and past the Armouries, stopping at Douglas for some traffic. By the time they reached the Point Ellice Bridge the roads were very rough and unsurfaced and clouds of dust spewed into the air behind them. Nancy kept well back from the car in front as they made their way along Esquimalt Road, hearing a train in the distance. Finally they reached the rail lines at Admirals Road and turned into the dockyard.

"Commander Jackson!" Nancy called out the open window when she saw the Naval Base medical commander crossing between buildings. She hurriedly stopped the car, explaining to Dan who it was.

The commander watched as she ran toward him. "Don't yell at me, girl," he snapped, his lips in a tight thin line under his bristling moustache. "What is it you want?"

"Dan Brown, sir. He got his memory back! I'm his sister, Nancy. We met a few weeks ago at Resthaven Hospital."

"Oh yes, you're the singer." Still scowling, Commander Jackson watched Dan walk toward them. "You've had an accident soldier?" the commander's voice softened slightly.

"Yes sir, just a little bump on the head."

"And who says your memory is back?"

"I do," Dan said, squaring his shoulders. "So does Dr. Tyler."

"Morgan Tyler? You've seen Tyler in Seattle?" Commander Jackson's words came excitedly. Seeing Dan nod, the naval officer suddenly became more interested. "Come with me. Let me look at that wound."

He walked quickly away from them, heading toward the hospital block. Turning, he beckoned them on impatiently. "Come along, come along, both of you," he growled. "I haven't got all day!"

Ushering them into a small cubicle, Nancy stood curiously watching as the doctor removed Dan's bandage. He put the soiled gauze in a trash can and studied the ragged red wound on Dan's forehead.

"Bullet!" he muttered, under his breath. "Nice job of stitching. NURSE!" he called, immediately bringing a middle-aged woman in a nurse's uniform. "Redress this man's wound, but bring me Sgt. Dan Brown's file first."

Fifteen minutes later they were sitting in the commander's office, waiting as he finished flipping through the pages of Dan's file. Finally, he reached for the ink pad and, taking a small stamp out of a drawer, carefully stamped it with an imprint.

"There," he sighed, turning the page around to allow them to read the words … CLOSED. Commander Jackson chuckled dryly. "Now let me tell you the odds of that ever happening!" He paused looking over at Dan. "The odds are over a thousand to one. You're a lucky man, Sgt. Brown!"

When they were back outside, Dan put his arm around Nancy. "He's right you know. I am a lucky man! Let's go home, honey, we've got work to do."

Back at the restaurant, the group were making final plans for Nancy's birthday party on Sunday. Katherine was making a large cake, and the beer was being provided by Harry's brewery. Extra chairs, garden tables and the supply of beer would arrive while Nancy and the others were in Seattle. Jebediah, being cautious to avoid any confrontation, had already told Sam to allow them access to the workshop.

Chapter 35

As the first light of dawn appeared on Sunday morning and the sun slowly filtered its way through the mist on the water, Dan stood at the cliff and stared out to sea. His fingers played with the ring box in his pocket. He took a walk into the orchard strolling amongst the young trees and his mind flashed back to when he first went away—when this land still had many trees standing straight and tall. Suddenly, senses alerted, Dan looked around and saw Sam watching.

"Morning, Sam."

Lips quivering, as if he was about to say something, the hermit suddenly changed his mind and shuffled back into the forest. Smiling, Dan walked back over to the porch and hearing the sounds of Meg and Nancy's laughter in the kitchen, he decided to go inside. As he came around the corner he realized Jebediah was sitting there quietly by himself puffing on his pipe.

"You know something, lad," said the old detective, as Dan came up the steps. "You have your own little piece of heaven right here."

"It's yours too, Jebediah," Dan contradicted him as he opened the door. "HAPPY BIRTHDAY, LITTLE SISTER!" he called, going inside.

Dropping the frying pan onto the stove with a clatter, Nancy flew across the room and into his arms. "I'm twenty-one, Dan. I'm really twenty-one!"

Hugging her tightly, he carried her back toward the stove with her legs dangling in the air, set her down, and leaned over to give Meg a kiss on the cheek.

"So you're twenty-one, are you girl?" he laughed. "Getting awfully old is all I can say."

Nancy slapped him playfully on the arm.

"When is breakfast ready, girls? Me and Uncle Jeb are mighty hungry, we've been up for hours!"

"You may have been, but I happen to know Jeb has only been up long enough to light his pipe," exclaimed Meg, with a twinkle in her eye. "He was making a nuisance of himself, so I sent him outside."

After breakfast was over and the table cleared, they sat talking over a fresh cup of coffee. Dan suddenly pushed his chair back with a scraping sound and looked across the table at Nancy. Conversation stopped as they all watched him curiously. He reached into his pocket and slowly brought out a small box, placing it on the table. They all noticed that his hand was shaking although he tried to hide it by putting it quickly in his lap.

All eyes were riveted on the little box, but when nothing happened the others looked at each other and then at Dan. Finally, he took a quick breath and reached for the box. *Damn it,* he admonished himself, *quit shaking!*

"Nancy?" he began. His tone and expression was so serious Meg wanted to giggle. She didn't dare look at anyone. He clumsily pried the ring from the little box and held it up. Then he looked over at Nancy across the table and their eyes locked. "W-will you marry me, Nan?" he asked slowly, as if each word was hard to get out.

Jebediah almost chocked on his smoke and Meg's chuckle was loud enough for everyone to hear.

"Yes … I will, Danny," Nancy whispered instantly, holding out the fingers of her left hand as she bit into her lip. Tears filled her eyes as Dan slipped the sparkling diamond ring on her finger. She had known this day would happen but she certainly hadn't expected it so soon. She took a deep breath and as one lone tear rolled down her cheek she exhaled slowly. Dan leaned over the table and gently wiped the tear away with his finger, grinning at her. She looked at the ring and thought how lovely it was.

Standing up, he walked around the table and pulled her to her feet and into his arms. Their bodies melded together and he began to waltz her around the kitchen floor. Meg began to clap and Jebediah got his guitar and soon the redhead's, and Meg's, tears changed to laughter as they danced from room to room.

"What a birthday present!" Meg exclaimed, dabbing at her eyes with her apron as Nancy came to hug her and then Jeb, showing off her lovely ring. *And this day has only begun,* the Scot thought, looking over at Jeb and winking.

At 11 o'clock laughter again filled the air as the guests began to arrive, surprising Nancy all over again. Jack Duggan and Nellie were the first, followed quickly by the Maynards. Ten minutes later, Kate's merry laughter indicated the Dumpfords had also arrived. Katherine had organized her husband, who was very slowly and carefully carrying a huge, beautifully decorated birthday cake.

"Kate said if I so much as smudged one flower, she would kill me!" he groaned as he set it down thankfully on the kitchen table.

Tables and chairs were magically produced by the men who, under instructions from Kate, set them out in small circles around each table on the lawn.

Suddenly, the sound of blaring horns indicated the Jorgensen entourage had arrived and as the two cars stopped near the house Nancy was there to greet them. Terry was the first out, helping Bill into his wheelchair.

As the rest piled out Nancy was surprised to see Nellie. After hugging her pianist she called out, "Where's Christopher?"

"I'm here!" came the familiar voice from behind her as an arm wrapped itself around her and his parents were there to hug her, too.

Over the next hour, some of their neighbours dropped in to offer birthday greetings ... even some neighbours they didn't know very well. And everyone brought food. They had so much food Meg was trying to find places to put it, so they decided they might as well start eating. By 1 o'clock the Peases, Whites, Williamsons, Woods, and Dunnetts had been by and many of them stayed spreading out their blankets on the lawn. Everyone seemed to be enjoying themselves. The children played under the watchful eyes of their parents, worried about the cliff, and some of them even went swimming in the cove. For many, a local picnic was the only opportunity they had to socialize with their friends who might only live a mile or two away.

Billy and his sister, Rose, arrived with Tom Irvine surprising Nancy speechless at seeing the girl for the first time in two years. Waldo brought Fred Barrett, although they didn't stay long. They gulped down a couple of beers with a few sandwiches and went to say goodbye to Nancy and Dan who couldn't resist telling them about their engagement.

"Jack's going to announce it in a while but we wanted you to know before you left," whispered Nancy, showing off her ring.

Several others noticed what was happening and word went quickly around the party.

"I guess Jack won't have to announce it now! It's about time Danny came to his senses," Waldo grunted, as he and Fred walked back to the truck.

Eva and Dorothy arrived soon after and were both thrilled to meet the Jorgensen family having heard so much about them. Dorothy found herself the center of Bill and Christopher's attention doing their best to make the young girl feel important as they carried their war wounds with pride.

At precisely 2 o'clock, Jack Duggan stood up and tapped loudly on his bottle of beer with a spoon to draw everyone's attention.

FRIENDS," he shouted, going to stand beside Nancy. He put his arm over her shoulder. "A TOAST IN CELEBRATION OF OUR NANCY'S COMING OF AGE. I wonder how long it will take her to stop counting!"

Nancy looked at him puzzled at first then broke into a grin as glasses clinked and everyone repeated, "TO NANCY'S COMING OF AGE!

Someone began to sing *Happy Birthday* and everyone joined in.

"SPEECH!" someone else called out, but Jack held up his hand for silence.

"I HAVE ONE MORE PIECE OF INFORMATION I'VE BEEN ASKED TO CONVEY," he said. "No doubt many of the ladies will have noticed that Nancy is wearing a new diamond ring on her left hand! It seems she has also agreed to become Mrs. Daniel Brown! WHERE IS THE LUCKY MAN?" Hearing the news, everyone began to cheer and clap looking around for him.

Christopher was talking to Dan and gave his friend a little push toward Nancy. "Go on Danny. Don't keep the lady waiting!"

Nancy could feel her cheeks getting hot even before Dan ran toward her, taking her into his arms and kissing her. The younger members of the group erupted into cheering while some of the older ones tittered disapprovingly.

"Stop it, Danny, you're embarrassing me," she whispered into his ear as some of the audience yelled for more.

"Okay honey, but these are our friends. They'll have to get used to this. We're not brother and sister any longer."

Some of the ladies, who had not been aware of what was happening, hurried over to congratulate them and to see Nancy's ring. The men noisily congratulated Dan with handshakes and slaps on the back.

"Did you ever see a happier girl?" Beth whispered to Meg.

"They deserve each other, Beth," Meg replied. "It's been a mighty eventful week, and year, but Nancy's dreams are coming true at last.

We certainly never expected Danny to act so quickly. I think he's really come to appreciate all that Nancy has done for him of late."

"Well, I think that after all he has been through he has come to realize how important family can be," added Beth.

Meg clasped Beth's arm and looked over at her with brimming eyes, unable to speak. Later, as the buzz of voices settled down and people prepared to leave, Katherine, with her usual vigour, organized the clearing of tables and sorting out of dishes before leaving to wind up the day's operations at the restaurant. Eva and Dorothy said their goodbyes, surprising the Jorgensen boys as the young girl expertly manoeuvred the big Cadillac out of the parking area and up the drive.

Nellie Cornish watched with a fascinated interest when Dan and Nancy walked Tom, Rose and Billy to their truck, the young people all hugging each other with an obvious fondness.

"I get the strange feeling, there's a special bond of friendship between those three," Nellie said to Millie.

"There is," replied the older woman. "They were all young children when they met at the orphanage. They've been friends ever since."

"We have to go, too," announced Gus. "There's a boat waiting for us in the harbour."

"We'll see you on Friday," his wife interrupted. "Don't forget it's the Camp Lewis concert next Saturday."

Terry shook Dan's hand before climbing into the car, beaming a smile as he glanced at the redhead and muttered quietly, "You're a lucky man, Dan Brown. That Nancy is one hell of a woman! Think you'll be able to tame her?"

"I don't want her to change one little bit, Terry."

The Maynards and Duggans left one after the other, loading most of the borrowed tables and chairs into their trucks. When the dishes were finished the house slowly settled back into its normal, peaceful quietness. Meg sat on the porch rocking in her chair as she sipped on a cup of tea from her treasured china. Close by, Jeb stretched out in his chair, blowing black smoke into the fast cooling air. Dan and Nancy sat snuggled together on the top of the cliff stairs, watching Sam fish from the little rowboat.

The scene of tranquillity seemed complete as the sound of a cow bellowing mournfully in a nearby pasture joined with a faraway church bell beginning its slow call to evening worshippers. Half an hour later, a cool breeze drove them inside where they had a light meal of leftover sandwiches and cakes.

"Have you two decided when you're going to get married?" asked Meg.

"Not yet. I guess we'll have to decide what we're going to do, won't we, Dan?" asked Nancy. "Several people asked us today."

"I don't see why we should wait very long," he commented. "Now that we're engaged, you better not give me time to change my mind!"

"Oh Danny, you wouldn't do that, would you?" Meg's face had a shocked expression.

"I'm only teasing her, Aunt Meg. I think we should get married as soon as harvesting season is finished. What do you all think?" he asked. "Will it give you ladies time enough to plan your clothes and such?"

"Autumn, you mean?" asked Jebediah.

"Yes," Nancy giggled, "and right here on the clifftop if the weather will cooperate."

"If it doesn't we'll move it indoors. And who will you get for a minister?" asked Meg.

"Do you know who I would really like to have marry us?" asked Nan, "the old vicar who was so kind, finding Dan for me in England. We met him at the Esquimalt Naval Hospital. Remember, Aunt Meg? His son is an army doctor."

"Oh you mean that man who said he was the retired minister from the prairies," Meg replied. "Now what was his name?"

"Thomas William Burton," said Dan. "I remember him coming to see me in the convalescent hospital at Whitby, but I think he died soon after that."

Meg's mouth dropped open in surprise while three pairs of eyes suddenly focused on Dan.

"You mean you can remember the time you spent abroad?" Nancy whispered.

"Clearly," he nodded. "Everything except the last time I was wounded and even that's strange," his voice trailed off. "It's like I was stood outside my body watching. I can see myself laying there in the mud."

"Oh stop!" Nancy interrupted with a trembling voice. She went over to him, wrapping her arms around his neck. "You don't need to go through that again, love."

The conversation dwindled out and soon tiredness sent them all to their beds. Cold cotton sheets made Nancy shiver as she pulled the covers up under her chin. Just before drifting off to sleep, she sighed as happy thoughts of a wedding stole through her mind.

By Monday morning, news of Dan's return and recovery had travelled through Victoria's waterfront where he had spent all of his working life. Hudson Bay and Rithet's warehouse workers waved wildly as the Model T passed by on its way to the B&W dock.

Mid-morning the couple decided to go for a walk uptown. Going straight up Broughton, they were surprised by the sight of a funeral procession led by Mr. Hayward's new motorized hearse which his BC Funeral Company had recently purchased. Behind it came a long line of cars full of mourners. They were traveling very slowly and all had their lights on as they proceeded up Douglas Street on its journey of tears to one of the local burial grounds.

Walking up Burdett, they looked up at the grand wooden structure of the second Christ Church Cathedral, then they turned north on Blanshard. At Yates Street they stood to look across the corner at the imposing structure of the Carnegie Building which housed the public library. Nearby, black smoke curled over the rooftop of the V&S station as the engine got ready for its morning run. Staying on the south side of Yates, Dan stopped to watch as a dusty-booted businessman allowed Perri, the boot black, to put a shine on his footwear, before entering the close-by Dominion Hotel.

"The candy shop's gone!" he exclaimed, staring across the street. "Now it's the Sausage Kitchen. There seems to be an awful lot of restaurants in Victoria now."

"Wait until you see all the fancy feathers," she giggled, pulling him to the front of the South African Plume Shop with its wondrous array of fashionable feathers in every colour of the rainbow.

"Well, I'll be damned! What they won't think of next."

Nancy took him into Gordon's and stood back as his eyes flashed around the store.

"Was this here before?" he asked, pulling her back out to the street. "I was never in here, if it was. I think you're trying to trick me, Nan."

"You're right, I was!" she giggled. "Look over here, something else has gone. Can you work it out?"

A streetcar rattled noisily around the bend from Douglas and came to a screeching stop disgorging eager shoppers. He looked in the direction she was pointing and rubbed his chin.

"So many changes," he murmured.

"Remember this shop?" Nancy's eyes twinkled with playful devilment as they stood in front of Lange the Tailor.

"This was …," he began, fingers rubbing his bandaged temple, "Charlie McKeen's shoe shop!"

"That's right, love," she complimented him. "Oh, that reminds me, you'll need a new suit for the wedding, but we'll go to Wilson's for that."

"We've got lots of time, Nan."

"Not so much, Dan. The time will go very quickly to September. Maybe we'll be lucky and have a lovely Indian Summer this year. But you could also use a new suit for the concert next week."

Suddenly, as they waited for an opportunity to cross through the maze of traffic at the corner of Douglas, a clock boomed one o'clock. A gap appeared and Dan grabbed Nancy's hand. Laughing, they raced across Douglas jumping over the tracks and landing in the shadow of the Dominion Bank.

"Where's the time gone?" asked Dan, pointing across Yates at the White Lunch Cafe. "It's time we ate, I'm starving."

A tiny bell tinkled its warning as they entered the restaurant, bringing a young waitress scurrying toward them.

"Hello Nancy," the waitress greeted her shyly, showing them to a gaily decorated table with a red-chequered tablecloth by the window. "It's nice to see you. Are you having lunch?"

"Yes, two roast beef dinners, please Alice, and two teas."

"Who is she?" Dan whispered, when she had gone.

"That's Alice Turner, she was one of my dishwashers at the Balmoral. You don't know her. Her dad was killed right at the beginning of the war. It's been very hard for them."

Returning, the waitress brought a small tray with china teacups and saucers, placing them carefully on the table along with a teapot covered by a pretty tea cozy. The girl stepped back to admire her work.

"Condiments, Alice?" Nancy whispered.

The girl's cheeks went instantly red and she spun round and dashed away. She was back immediately with the necessary items. "Sorry, ma'am," she mumbled, her hand shaking as she set them on the table.

Dan watched enthralled, as Nan gently took the girl's hand and smiled warmly up at her.

"Stop worrying, Alice, you're doing fine. Just remember the little things Katherine and I taught you." Still holding the girl's hand, Nancy asked, "Are you and your mother still living on Cook Street?"

Shoulders sagging, Alice nodded. "It's hard to make ends meet Nancy, but it's much better since I got this part-time job." Then as if a door had opened, Alice's thoughts came flooding out. "If it weren't for that lady from Gordon Head we'd never survive. Mrs. Todd calls her Victoria's guardian angel. She pays our rent every month, she does, and never asks for nothing in return."

"Don't you worry, love," said Nancy, patting the girl's hand before she released it. She pressed on Dan's toe under the table. "Just be glad somebody's watching out for you."

A bell rang in the kitchen, abruptly stopping further conversation as Alice hurried away for her order. When she returned, she slipped the steaming hot plates onto the table in front of them. "Enjoy your lunch!"

"That's you she's talking about," Dan whispered across the table when she was out of earshot. "Aunt Meg and Uncle Jeb told me all about it. Eva distributes money from the concerts you give in Seattle."

Nancy could feel the colour in her face rising. "Hush, love, there are a lot of other people helping out, too. Let's eat before this gets cold."

When they were finished, they wandered down the street, gazing in shop windows. Whitney's Jewellery Shop had a fabulous display of gold and diamonds.

"Oh, look at how it shines, Dan. Just imagine, those gold nuggets that English Jack sent me would look just like this if they were made into jewellery. Poor Jack, what a sad end he came to."

"He was doing what he loved to do, Nan, and lucky for us you were the daughter he never had. He's at peace now and we have a wonderful home thanks partly to his legacy, and still some gold in the bank!"

They entered the darkly decorated men's clothiers, W & J Wilson, and stopped just inside the door. They saw old Mr. Wilson come out of a back room and he beamed with recognition when he saw the young couple. Snatching off his spectacles, he put them down on the desk and came over to welcome them, shaking Dan's hand.

"They say that you're better, son … you've recovered your memory. Is it true?" the old clothier's words rushed out.

"Yes, it is true, Mr. Wilson," replied Nancy, "and now he needs a new suit rather urgently. Do you have anything readymade?"

"I believe I have just his size," he chuckled, "a suit that some gentleman hasn't collected. If it fits, you can have it for a fair price."

Scuttling away into the stockroom he returned with a handsome-looking grey suit on a hanger.

"Try this on, lad."

Slipping on the jacket, Dan flexed his shoulders, fastened the buttons and looked in the full-length mirror.

"Fits you like a glove, Danny," Wilson observed. "Looks like it was made for you, now go try on the trousers."

While Dan was busy, Nancy quietly told Mr. Wilson she also needed a black evening suit for him, with all the accessories including socks and shoes, if possible.

"Is he not to know?" he whispered, frowning as Nancy nodded. "Then give me a moment."

Going over to the wall rack of evening suits, Mr. Wilson began talking to himself, fiercely at times. He selected a garment and rushed off into the back room. Muffled voices could be heard as two assistants came out from the rear, one was carrying Dan's boots as he hurried out of the store.

"Where's he going?" she asked the other clerk.

"To Robert Watson's shoe shop just over on Yates," came the whispered reply. "We don't stock shoes but this is the only way we can be assured we have the right size."

Stepping out from the changing room in the grey suit, Dan looked around for his boots.

"Who pinched my feet?" he asked, with a chuckle.

"Oh my," Mr. Wilson sighed, his face as blank as a coffin bearer. "I sent them to be polished; we do that for all our customers."

"Never mind your boots, does the suit fit?" asked Nancy.

"Mainly, yes, it's just a bit long in the leg, but that should be easily solved."

They managed to kill some time by looking at other clothes and the assistant returned, peering inside the store cautiously until he was able to catch Mr. Wilson's eye. The owner winked uncharacteristically at the girl then swung into action. He distracted Dan by telling him to stand on a chair and face the wall while he marked the trouser legs for shortening. The trick worked and he beckoned to the assistant who returned unnoticed with a large parcel in one hand and Dan's boots in the other. Dan was surprised to see his shiny boots back in their place when he went to change.

"Perhaps I had better try these with my shoes on," he suggested, sitting down and slipping his shoes on. "How do they look, Nan?"

"Perfect! Mr. Wilson must know how to make allowances for missing shoes," she giggled, leaving Dan and going back to the counter where Mr. Wilson was getting her bill ready.

"Shall I have all your purchases sent to the dock, Nancy? They'll be ready by noon tomorrow."

"Thank you, that will be fine," she nodded, very pleased to have that job taken care of so quickly.

Watching Dan lace up his boots, her thoughts turned back to Mr. Wilson and how for so many years he had been a man without humour, stern-faced and rigid. That image was now destroyed for the redhead, having witnessed his warm and friendly side.

Back out on the street, they continued toward Broughton, crossing over behind a clanging streetcar. They stopped to talk to Tom Ben who was raising the awning at E.A. Morris Tobacconist. They passed Woolworth's Five and Dime, and then the Royal Bank building with its imposing columned facade.

Clocks all over the city were chiming half-past four as they crossed Fort knocking on the window of Hagenbuch, the sign writer, and waving a greeting to the old man who was still busy at work.

They arrived at the dock and saw Dumpy coming up the harbour, towing the oil barge from Sooke. The *Ping Pong* waited just out in the channel, ready to push the barge into its mooring.

"Where's Dumpy been?" Dan asked.

"To Sooke, we've been running a regular service for the Village since 1914. I believe we were talking about it just before you signed up.

"DON'T GO YET," Dumpy yelled, as he shut down the engine and waved to them.

Going into the office, Nancy noticed Dan looking around at the four walls. She knew what he was thinking. It was just an office now, but it held many treasured memories locked in its rustic frame.

"Are you thinking what I'm thinking?" Dan murmured, feeling her eyes on his back and turning around.

She nodded, hearing the laughter of the Joyce boys and the ghostly creaking of the *Belfast* tied at the dock. The sound of Dumpy's boots on the boards outside snapped their thoughts back to reality.

"There's a hospital ship out there waiting to enter the harbour," he said excitedly.

"What's so special about that?" she asked.

"It's the *Marguerite*," he laughed. "She's come home!"

The S.S. Marguerite had been called into war service and this was the first time she had been back to Victoria.

It was almost six o'clock when they left the city, quiet now after the bustle of the day. Streetcars rumbled along the tracks with only a few passengers for company. The sun was still high in the sky, lazily drifting toward the mountains, as they travelled along Shelbourne in the quiet stillness.

"They'll be hungry," Meg muttered to Jeb when she heard the truck come down the drive.

Relating the activities of their day over a late supper, she conveniently left out most of the happenings at Wilson's, though Dan caused a ripple of laughter when he told them of his disappearing boots. Later, as the men stood on the cliff smoking their pipes, well out of earshot, she told Meg of the dress suit she'd bought for Dan, swearing her to secrecy.

"But why the secret?" the Scot asked. "When is he going to wear it?"

"It's a surprise for the concert at Camp Lewis," she whispered. "I want him to look like a million dollars."

During the next week Dan and Nancy visited Eliza Marshal and Eli Gainer at the Gorge Hotel, enjoying the streetcar ride through the rolling countryside of Esquimalt. It was on this same route they had first met the Jorgensens and they discussed how the mighty hand of providence seemed to have intervened in their lives. The brother and sister were so pleased to see them again and welcomed them royally inviting them in for a cup of tea.

They took the V&S to Sidney for the very first time, travelling along the side of the wetlands in the Blenkinsop Valley, skirting Mount Douglas and chugging on through the sparsely populated area of Cordova Bay to the terminus at the bottom of Sidney's Beacon Avenue.

They decided to take advantage of the short layover hurrying around to see some of the landmarks—the sawmill, the Rubber Company, the hotel, and the Government Wharf, before it turned around and went back to the city.

On Thursday, after returning from Victoria with the *Stockholm* loaded and ready for their big trip to Seattle the next day, Nancy sat Dan down in the kitchen and began to gently unwind the bandages from his head. As the last piece of gauze came off, the ugly red groove across his brow was exposed but Nancy thought it actually looked much better than it had a week earlier. A neat row of black stitches ran along its edge and she stood back and studied it.

Meg gasped.

"Boy, you were lucky, lad," Jebediah growled. "Half an inch lower and you'd be either blind in one eye or dead!"

"Hush, Uncle Jeb," Nancy snapped, stepping closer and studying the stitches. "Dr. Tyler said to take every other one out. Can we use your little scissors, Aunt Meg?"

Meg scurried off to get them, relieved for the excuse to escape. Meanwhile, Nancy got the tweezers from the medicine chest and when Meg returned she carefully picked up the first stitch, snipping it off just behind the knot and gently easing it out through the skin.

"Fourteen more to go," she whispered, dropping the tiny piece of black twine onto the saucer Meg had handed to Dan. "Did I hurt you Danny?"

"Not yet!"

Jebediah watched the concentration on Nancy's face as she removed stitch after stitch from Dan's forehead. It was warm in the house and beads of perspiration formed on Dan's brow. Nan gently wiped them away with a towel and finished the job.

"There you are, all done!" She handed him a mirror and was cleaning up her supplies when she saw him gently probing the wound with his fingers. "Leave it alone, get your dirty fingers off it!" she admonished him. "I'll put a new bandage on before you go to bed. We'd better take some extras with us." Reaching for his hand, she led him out of the door and across the lawn, to the clifftop. She was so happy. *I want this to last forever*, she thought.

Meg's noisy banging in the kitchen awoke Nancy the next morning and, seeing the bright sunshine, she hurried out of bed. She went over to the window and pulled back the curtains. Jebediah and Dan were talking below on the porch.

By mid morning they were packed and ready to go. Nancy was at the helm of the heavily-loaded boat as it left the cove. Meg and Jebediah had decided to sit outside it was so nice out. Dan stood behind her. They were passing Port Townsend with only a freighter for company, when a Coast Guard boat pulled out from the coast and seemed to be trying to catch up to them.

"Now what do we do," Dan grinned, "outrun them?"

"No silly, they're friends," she chuckled, pointing to the sticker on the windscreen as she eased back on the throttle.

Dan read the sticker in reverse. "Where on earth did you get that?"

Not aware of their conversation, Jebediah, alarmed at the sudden change of pace and the noise of the Coast Guard vessel coming up behind, leapt from his seat, reaching for his Winchester.

"NO JEB!" Nancy yelled back at him, stopping the old detective before his hands fastened on the gun.

Jostling in the swift-running tide, the two boats slowly came together. At the rail, a smiling young officer saluted them.

"HOLD STEADY, MISS WILSON, CAPTAIN GRAY IS COMING ABOARD," he shouted.

Helped by Dan, the handsome young captain jumped across the narrow opening. Tipping his hat to the ladies, he addressed the redhead.

"We're your escort, Miss Wilson. I'm John Gray, Captain of the Coast Guard in this area, and one of your fans, incidentally! General Greene from Camp Lewis has issued the Coast Guard orders to make sure you get safely to the Jorgensen dock." He saluted. "Would you do me the honour of autographing our log book?"

"Her autograph?" Dan retorted.

"Yes sir, she's a very famous person in these parts," retorted Captain Gray smiling at Dan. "It won't take a moment if she'll just step aboard my vessel."

"Not on your life," snapped the old detective, his Winchester leaping into his hands as the hair on his neck bristled. "Do you have some identification, Captain?"

John Gray cautiously reached for his wallet and flipping it open revealed his U.S. Naval identity card. A voice from the Coast Guard vessel's rail chuckled mockingly.

"Made a mistake, Mr. Judd?"

"Caution don't hurt in these waters, lad," the old man growled as he came to take the wheel. "You go with her, Dan."

"Capt. Gray, I'd like you to meet my fiancé, Sgt. Dan Brown, retired. Recently home from the war," she added quietly.

The effect her words had on the other Coast Guardsmen was dramatic as they sprang to attention, each one saluting.

Tension gone, laughter quickly solved their differences as Dan and Nancy scrambled aboard the cutter, helped by the grinning sailors. Glancing back at the detective, Dan realized how fiercely protective Jeb was toward them. *Jeb acts like we're his children,* he thought. *What a wonderful addition to this family he has been.*

Nancy signed the log book with a signature that, in years to come, would be her trademark. Neatly written across the log book it read, *Nancy Wilson, the Redhead.*

"Thank you, Miss Wilson … Sgt. Brown! Do you realize, we're in awe of you Canadians?" he asked, his eyes flicking up to Dan's bandaged head. "I shall welcome the chance to get into that scrap with you."

"Don't be too eager," Dan growled, as he helped Nan back to the *Stockholm*, "it's hell over there!"

The two vessels slipped apart and they continued down Puget Sound, the Coast Guard cutter taking up the rear. Nancy turned around to watch them and Meg noticed the wicked glint in her eyes.

"There's devilment in that girl's mind," she said into Jeb's ear, watching the girl carefully.

"Take the helm, Dan, and open her right up. Let's see if they could catch us! HANG ON BACK THERE!"

Dan opened the throttle and began the thundering acceleration. As the mighty *Stockholm* leapt through the water, the Coast Guard cutter responded, making a valiant effort to keep pace though slipping farther and farther back into their wake.

"Push her, Danny," Nancy called above the noise.

"NANCY!" Jebediah shouted, pointing eastward. "LOOK AT THE HILL!"

"Never mind, Danny, slow down. There's something wrong at Ezekiel's place." Focusing the field glasses, she watched carefully as tiny flashes appeared, barely discernible in the sunlight.

"That's an S.O.S!" exclaimed Dan, seeing them, too.

Making very little noise Dan headed for Zeke's entrance, all eyes on the hillside as the Coast Guard cutter came up behind them. Three boats lay at anchor outside the entrance, each flying the small red flag, but not a soul was in sight. Jebediah grabbed his rifle and waved the cutter alongside. They also cut their engines.

"What's wrong?" called Captain Gray.

"Come aboard," Jebediah replied in sign language.

The captain leapt aboard and swung round to face them. "What's going on?"

"It's the Egger gang, they're in there after Ezekiel Plunket," Jeb growled. "Look up there," he pointed. "He's flashing an SOS from that chimney on the hill."

"We might have trouble with three boats, I'd better call for some backup," Captain Gray snapped, preparing to return to the cutter.

"Wait!" called Nancy. "I've a better idea. If Aunt Meg can stand the excitement, I'll sink two of them for you. That'll bring the men out and you'll only have one boat to deal with."

"You'll do what?" the captain gasped.

360

Gunshots sounded from the thickly wooded area behind Zeke's house helping the captain make a speedy decision.

"DO IT!" he yelled, as he swung back aboard the cutter and gave the order to stand back.

"Will there be shooting?" Meg asked apprehensively, as they all squeezed into the cabin.

"You'll be all right in here, Aunt Meg," Nancy replied. "It's armour plated!"

Settling into the helmsman's seat, the redhead sent the *Stockholm* surging forward, watched intently by the crew of the Coast Guard vessel, now behind them. With speed building, she raced in close to the coastline, turned broadside to the boats and pressed the firing mechanism. Two sudden but separate explosions tore through the two Egger boats. The *Stockholm* screamed away with the two boats foundering behind them, their sides torn to shreds.

"My God!" Captain Gray gasped. "What the hell is she carrying for armament?"

"TOO LATE TO WORRY ABOUT THAT NOW, CAPTAIN," a crewman yelled. "HERE THEY COME!"

The intimidating sight of the U.S. Coast Guard vessel, her deck lined with rifle-carrying seamen, and two of their boats foundering on the rocks, took the fight right out of the Egger gang who quickly surrendered their weapons. The prisoners were handcuffed to the rail and with the surviving boat in tow, the cutter slowly moved away from the cove.

"HOLD IT, WE MISSED ONE," one of the sailors yelled. "There's an old guy standing on a rock over there. He appears to be waving a rifle."

"He's all right!" John Gray laughed. "That's Ezekiel Plunket, he's a harmless old codger … those mad Canadians were protecting him."

As Nancy sent the *Stockholm*'s cannons into action, Dan's hands tightened on her shoulders. They heard the shuddering impact and watched in silence as the Egger's boats smashed onto the rocks.

Glancing over at Meg, Dan saw her expression and realized she had a tight grip on Jebediah's arm. *She doesn't know whether to be excited or fearful,* he thought. *She's not going to forget this day any too quickly!* Dan chuckled.

Nancy swung them away and out into the channel where they watched as the Coast Guard moved in. Jeb picked up the glasses and searched desperately for his friend. As the Coast Guard rounded them up, he saw a lone figure climb onto a rock and wave his rifle into the air. He handed the glasses over to Nancy and pointed.

Nancy's laughter broke the spell and they all came out of the cabin to wave madly at the lonely figure standing on the rock.

"SIT DOWN, EVERYONE AND HOLD ON, WE HAVE A DATE TO KEEP!" Dan shouted as he saluted the Coast Guard vessel, then pulled down on the throttle. "Well done, love," he congratulated her as she came up behind him and wrapped her arms about his neck. Pulling her closer, he kissed her tenderly while she nestled up against him. "I think I'm going to have to watch my p's and q's. It looks like I have some competition as the marksman in the family!"

Chapter 36

Terry O'Reilly was toying with his drink when Al O'Malley, the owner of Finnegan's, called to him that the *Stockholm* was coming in. Gulping it down, Terry made two phone calls before running to his car. He pulled up to the Jorgensen dock as the speedboat was arriving. He watched the carefully oiled machinery of the Jorgensen plan as it was set into motion. Several servants hurried from the house and down to the dock. Gathering up the visitor's luggage they carried it back through the garden and disappeared into the house. Beth and Gus appeared.

"You're early," Gus greeted them. "Did you have a quiet trip?"

"As if you didn't know!" Jebediah declared. "You've got your spies everywhere."

The shipowner laughed heartily protesting his innocence as they went through the ritual of their greetings then set out for the house.

"Nellie's here," Beth announced. "She's staying overnight and travelling to Camp Lewis with us tomorrow. The boys are going to visit with friends in Spokane tonight and will meet us at the Camp."

"I'm so glad Nellie is here. It will be nice to visit with her without the rush for a change," said a delighted Nancy.

During dinner, Beth brought up the subject of Nancy and Dan's forthcoming marriage. "Have you made any plans yet?" she asked. "Why don't you let us do the wedding here for you?"

"Thank you, Beth, that's awfully nice of you but we have so many friends in Victoria … but I'm sure Aunt Meg would appreciate any help you might offer," Dan replied graciously.

"I suppose this means, I have absolutely no chance of winning your hand now," teased Bill, looking quite forlorn.

"I'll let you borrow her for a dance once in a while," returned Dan.

"We've always said you were a lucky man, Danny," Christopher added.

"I'm lucky too," laughed Nan. "I always knew Danny was mine. Thank goodness he got his memory back or I would have had to work even harder to turn him into a husband!"

As they got up, the boys said their goodbyes and the others moved toward the living room. Nellie stopped at the music room door. "Come on, Nan, let's hear you sing when you're happy!" She opened the French doors and went over to the piano.

The others loudly expressed their agreement following them into the room and pulling chairs up near the piano. Nellie sat down and began to play an unfamiliar but haunting melody.

"All right, let's do something light for a change. I know two or three fanciful songs from the music halls now," Nancy admitted, feeling quite giddy. "You probably know them, Nellie."

The Spaniard Who Blighted My Life surprised them all with her comic actions and they were soon clapping and laughing as she went through the verses. She followed with, *My Old Man Said 'Follow the Van'* doing her best to copy the English cockney accent that Susan White had taught her.

The butler interrupted, going over to speak quietly to Gus.

"Show him in, Joseph," Gus chuckled. "Seems we have company!"

Joseph returned and announced Major General Greene from Camp Lewis. Cap under his arm and moustache bristling, he stepped into the room and looked around at the faces, stopping to rest on Nancy.

"I heard there was trouble in the straits this afternoon," he announced rather seriously. "I thought I should check to see that your guests were all right."

"Your singer is fine, general," Gus chuckled. "Join us, please. What do you drink?"

"Scotch on the rocks, thank you."

"I'll get it, Gus," offered Dan, catching Gus' nod as the general went to sit in a chair near the piano. He was still watching Nancy and many in the room already suspected the reason for his visit.

"Where does your family come from originally, sir," Nancy asked casually, knowing exactly what he was thinking.

"Ireland, but it was a long time ago," he said brusquely.

She went over to stand behind Nellie and whispered, "*It's a Long Way to Tipperary* and *My Island Home*."

Accepting the drink, General Greene sat back in his chair appearing to finally relax as Nancy sang the lively tune. Taking a sip of his scotch, his eyes were on the girl but his mind was virtually spinning unable to fathom the truth he had discovered only an hour before. *Nancy Brown ... a rum runner? Why else would she have armaments on board her vessel? The pieces of the puzzle are coming together ...*

the boat ... the Jorgensens ... so many trips to Seattle. How fascinating!

A strange tingle ran up his spine as he suddenly realized she was singing about Ireland. He never thought much about having Irish roots but hearing her beautiful voice singing this particular song bit deeply into his thoughts and rum running was nearly forgotten.

He had also forgotten the drink in his hand which was now dripping onto the floor. As the last notes of the piano echoed about the room, General Greene jerked back to reality. Noticing his wet hand, he quickly realized, to his embarrassment, that there was a pool of liquor on the floor. He hastily wiped it up with his handkerchief.

"Wonderful, truly wonderful, ladies," he complimented them, handing his drink to the servant and clapping his hands. Soon afterwards, he made his excuses and stood up to leave. Thanking them for their hospitality, he made a point of talking to Dan as he left.

"I understand you are a sergeant in the Canadian Army, young man. I compliment you and all Canadian soldiers for their gallant efforts in the European conflict." He reached out to shake Dan's hand.

"Thank you, sir. We can only hope it will be over soon," Dan replied stoically, walking him to the door.

Nancy sang one more song and suggested to Nellie that she play something nice and quiet to end the evening then she went and sat next to Dan. Beth watched the two young people as Dan's arm went comfortably around her shoulders. They were so happy and she was thrilled for them. As the song ended, Beth noticed Nancy yawn.

"Well everyone, I think we had better let these young stars get some rest so they are in top form tomorrow. Thank you, Nellie and Nancy, for your impromptu concert. We are so looking forward to tomorrow."

As Nancy entered the breakfast room the next morning, a lively discussion was underway about the high cost of living at home.

"The miners are still on strike," Jeb muttered, "and now they're shipping in cheap Chinese labour who will take pitiful low wages that our men aren't satisfied with. It was bad enough when they decided to draft the men from the prisoner-of-war camp in Nanaimo. There's going to be trouble."

"I don't understand it," replied Gus. "Seattle is booming."

"It must have something to do with the war," suggested Beth.

The argument ended when Beth suggested she give them an outside tour as it was such a beautiful day. Everyone agreed and they moved outside. As they walked around the mansion's magnificent and expertly manicured gardens Beth explained that the property was utilized by various groups for garden parties in the spring and summer.

"We've even had a wedding or two here!"

Meg was so impressed by a delightful display of rhododendrons she decided instantly that she must have some for Cunningham Manor.

After lunch the cars were packed and they all piled into the two vehicles. At 3 o'clock, they pulled up to the closely guarded gates of Camp Lewis. Gus, driving the first car, identified the occupants to the two soldiers on duty and Terry followed him through.

A phone call brought two motorcycle riders who escorted them down a road to a huge marquee. Carpenters were still busy putting the final touches to a stage set into its open entrance. Half in and half outside of the tent, a stage of about 50 foot square was being put into place. Another group of workers were in the rear of the tent setting up the massive black curtain which was to serve as the backdrop for the performers.

"That's big!" Nancy gasped, climbing out of the car and looking around in wonder as a soldier came toward them.

"Miss Wilson … Miss Cornish, if you would follow me, please," he requested in a crisp manner.

The girls looked at each other and grinned, raising their eyebrows.

"Just do as he says," Dan whispered. "They'll take care of your bags. We'll follow you."

The young soldier led them to a group of small buildings off to the side of the marquee. It was grand confusion with people coming and going and all seemed to be in a hurry. It was noisy, too, as several musicians were warming up their instruments.

"This is your dressing room. We hope you don't mind sharing!" their escort informed them, opening the door into a small room sparsely furnished with two wooden chairs, a small table and a mirror.

Suddenly a voice screamed above the noise.

"NAN-CEE!"

Turning, Nancy scanned the room. Suddenly, the movement of a curly, blonde head pushing through a group of people and frantically waving caught her attention.

"Who's that?" asked Meg.

"It's Mary Pickford!" Nan replied, breaking into a grin as she went to meet the girl.

The Jorgensens had already recognized the actress having seen several of her movies. Now, they all watched in surprised fascination as the two girls hugged like old friends.

"Is this your family?" Mary asked.

Her cheeks pink from excitement, Nancy began to make the introductions. "Mary, you've already met Dan, he's my fiancé now."

"How wonderful for you both," the actress gushed.

"This is my Aunt Meg and Uncle Jeb. Nellie Cornish is my pianist, and these two people are my American mum and dad, Gus and Beth Jorgensen from Seattle. I have two adopted brothers too, but they're already out in the audience.

"Clear as mud, Nancy!" Mary laughed. "But it's nice to meet you all. Come on, let me introduce you to the others," she said, tugging on Nancy's hand. "Uh oh, no need. The general is bringing them over!"

The crowd parted and General Greene came striding toward them. Behind him, looking like a curious entourage came all the stars of his show: African-American, Billy Robinson, the world famous tap dancer; Fanny Brice, the singer-actress; cowboy, Will Rogers; and ragtime singer, Bill Baker. And, bringing up the rear were perhaps two of the most colourful gentlemen Nancy had ever seen, one of them a kilted Scotsman named Harry Lauder, was a short man decked out from head to toe in Scottish regalia and carrying a comical, twisted walking stick. He was drawing good-natured whistles from the carpenters. Beside him walked a dapper little man with a funny gait and an equally funny hat, who turned out to be the comic, Charlie Chaplin.

"We'll use the Officers' Mess, ladies, join us please. FOLLOW ME!" ordered General Greene as he strode by, appearing to be enjoying himself immensely. The group followed obediently behind and the three girls joined them. They were led out of the building and into another one a short distance away.

"Tea or coffee," an orderly asked as they all settled comfortably into the seats provided in a small room beautifully decorated with plush carpets and highly polished dark furniture.

"Tea or coffee, laddie!" quipped Harry Lauder. "That stuff's poison, it'll be whisky for me."

"Not in this camp it won't, sir," replied the general, glowering at the Scotsman. "It's illegal, and has been for some time in this area."

Mary introduced Nancy and Nellie to those near them and then the general went to the front of the room.

"ATTENTION EVERYONE," he bellowed, then waited for silence. "Our show will be starting in just over an hour and I want someone to volunteer to be the spokesman for the group."

Mary's hand shot up. "I don't have much to do," she said, giggling.

"Mary is volunteering. Any objections?" asked the general. For a moment there was a murmur of good-natured sarcasm and banter. "It looks like you have the job, young lady."

Bill Robinson stood up. "I have been given the list for our order of appearance if anyone is interested in knowing when it's their turn to wow the audience!" he announced jovially, his friendly black face and deep mellow voice no doubt capable of soothing the nerves of any nervous performer. "If anyone is unhappy about the order, this is the time to speak up." Receiving only sarcastic comments, he proceeded to read the list. Afterwards, there were some questions and re-arranging, as expected, and then they lined up for a quick rehearsal of the finalé.

"Bill, will it be all right if my pianist plays for the finale?" asked Nancy.

"Of course, we'd be delighted if Nellie would join us," he replied, giving them both a pearly white smile.

As they finished, the orderly appeared again, going to speak to the general. "One hour to show time, sir."

"ALL RIGHT, FOLKS, YOU HEARD THE MAN. YOU'RE DISMISSED! BE BACKSTAGE IN 45 MINUTES READY TO GO," shouted the general.

The performers began to disperse.

"I've never heard of Nancy Wilson," Fanny Brice whispered loudly linking arms with Will Rogers as they walked away. "Who is she?"

Bill Robinson, walking behind them, chuckled. "I was lucky enough to catch her concert at the James Moore Theatre in Seattle about six months ago. She's a new Canadian singer and a show stopper, too. She'll bring the house down, Fanny, even though she's only an amateur. Just you wait and see."

"Not nearly as good as you though, Fannie darling," Will teased.

When the girls returned to their dressing room, they found Meg and Beth trying desperately to get the small room organized with the three men underfoot.

"It's time for you boys to go find your seats, except you, Dan … you need to change," announced Meg.

"We know when we're not wanted," Gus retorted, quickly wishing the girls luck and ushering Jeb out of the room as the door began to close. "We'll wait outside for you, Dan!"

"Your clothes are in that box marked W & J Wilson," said Nancy.

"No, they're not, I saw Aunt Meg pack my new suit in here," Dan retorted, holding up his bag. He saw Nancy grinning at him in the mirror, winking mischievously when their eyes met. "You little devil, so that's what you were up to in Wilson's!" He looked over at Meg who was holding the other suit and new boots in the air. "Another new suit, and boots, too! Is that why my boots disappeared?"

"All right ladies, let's let Dan get changed!" Meg interrupted, ushering the women outside. "Don't take too long, Dan," she advised, closing the door.

"It won't take me long to get ready," Nellie murmured, releasing her bun and running her fingers through her hair. "I'm already dressed."

"No, you aren't! I have a surprise for you both," Beth said secretively. "But you'll have to wait until we get back into the room."

In a few minutes the door opened and Dan let them in while he put on his shoes. Fumbling with his tie, Meg went over to help.

"I'll finish up, Dan, you go on ahead with the others," she offered.

He wished the girls luck, gave Nancy a quick kiss and a hug and was gone. Meanwhile, Beth opened the bag holding the girl's dresses.

"Look, Hattie sent you girls matching dresses!" She took the dresses out of the clothes bag and held them up.

Both girls stood with their mouths open. The dresses were lilac and pink shot-taffeta. Nancy's had a slim skirt and a scooped neck, and Nellie's had a fuller skirt. Hattie had also got shoes to match.

"Oooh, they're beautiful! Let's see how they look, Nellie!" exclaimed Nancy, already beginning to undress.

Nellie followed her lead but it was obvious to everyone that she was overwhelmed by the surprise. Thirty-five minutes later, amid much laughter and many compliments, the girls left the dressing room to join the other performers backstage. A stagehand came by shouting an urgent last call to Mary Pickford, who ran by them laughing as usual.

At precisely 3 o'clock, they heard the audience go suddenly quiet and a booming voice introduced America's Sweetheart—Mary Pickford. Mary made a little speech first introducing the orchestra and its conductor then explaining why the concert was named *Nancy and Friends* telling them who Nancy was. Next, they heard the words 'the magical tapping feet of Billy Robinson, the wonder of the music hall boards and the tap-dance king was on. After Billy came Bill Baker, singing two of his most popular ragtime numbers, including the servicemen's favourite *Rag Time Cowboy Joe*.

Fanny Brice brought the house down with her comedy routine *Becky Is Back in the Ballet*, sending the soldiers into howls of laughter. Will Rogers was next with his slow, drawling humour and country boy jokes performed while expertly twirling his lariat.

Whistles again taunted the tiny Scot, Harry Lauder, some making loud comments about his long socks, hairy knees and kilt, but his talent quickly reduced them to silence. His haunting Scottish melodies and a rousing battle song soon had them eager for more but Harry turned the stage over to his good friend, Charlie Chaplin. Totally transformed into a walking stick twirling, foot shuffling idiot, Chaplin again had the audience alternatively cheering and howling with laughter as he portrayed his famous comic character of Music Hall fame.

"We're on!" Nellie whispered, squeezing Nancy's hand.

"Break a leg," she retorted, grinning.

They waited until the stagehands had the piano back into position and Nellie pushed Nancy in front of her. Grabbing her hand, they stepped through the curtain. Approaching the footlights, 10,000 soldiers held their breath. The spotlights picked them out as they walked to center stage and took their bow. Their matching dresses and long hair made them look almost like sisters from a distance and the soldiers loved it. The audience burst into applause and whistles. There had been so much publicity about this Canadian singer, everyone felt they knew her already.

With the sun behind the hills, and the stage in almost total darkness behind them, they became the center of attention. A hush fell over the audience as Nellie took her place at the piano and set up her music. She looked up at Nancy and saw her take a deep breath and nod. Nellie winked at her then looked over at the conductor.

At the same moment her fingers came down on the keyboard, the orchestra began the introduction to *Pack Up Your Troubles* and the audience screamed with delight. Nancy knew instantly that Nellie was also enjoying herself. She looked out at the audience and sent a mental kiss to Dan, wherever he was. She took another deep breath and began to sing.

The soft breeze picked up each clear, thrilling note floating it through the air to the spellbound crowd. Before the first verse was ended this virtually unknown Canadian's talent had tugged at their hearts and there was absolute silence beyond the footlights. Red hair flashing in the spotlights, she moved to the edge of the stage and slowly began to descend the steps. Her dress snagged on a splinter of wood, but one of the soldiers quickly released it, receiving the reward of a blown kiss for his efforts. The audience hooted their approval and many reached out to touch her hand as she sang, moving along the first row then returning to the stage.

"By God, you were right!" Fanny whispered to Billy Robinson as they stood in the darkness of the wings. She gripped Will's hand so tightly, he had to pry it loose.

Nellie felt a dampness in her eyes as she watched Nancy return to the stage, finishing the last verse of her song and taking a bow. But the audience weren't finished yet and thousands of solders leapt to their feet, stomping wildly in a tumultuous standing ovation.

Stunned, but quickly trying to gather her wits, she ran back down the steps sweeping up a hat from an officer's lap. He grinned at her and, balancing it jauntily on her head, she returned to the stage and began her last number. The audience reluctantly resumed their seats but when she again finished there was another deafening roar.

Nancy was relieved when the rest of the cast appeared from the wings to join her. With arms linked they moved forward en masse into the spotlights. The orchestra played a few bars of the final number and, recognizing it, another cheer arose. The noise was overpowering as the standing crowd became an amazing chorus of thousands of male voices joining the stars in the popular soldiers' anthem, *Over There.*

As the concert concluded and everyone took their last bow and began to leave the stage, an almost imperceptible yet spontaneous chant began in a back corner. As it spread through the audience it built in momentum, finally erupting as one thunderous roar.

"NANCY! NANCY! NANCY!"

Nellie watched emotionally from the piano as Nancy stood in the middle of the stage looking alone and overwhelmed. The pianist went to stand beside her and hand-in-hand they took another bow.

"What do I do, Nellie?" she asked helplessly.

"Enjoy it, love ... this is only the beginning!" Nellie replied, her voice cracking, as she gave her friend's hand one last squeeze. Then she waved to the audience and walked off the stage leaving Nancy alone.

Nancy stood for a moment listening to the applause and chanting that seem to be growing even louder. Fleetingly she wondered where Dan was sitting. Nellie was right, this was only the beginning ... the beginning of her new life.

She felt Dan's ring on her finger and peered out into the darkness, but it was hopeless to see anyone. Taking a deep breath, she stepped closer to the footlights.

Suddenly new energy coursed through her body and, smiling broadly, she raised both hands to her lips. Blowing a kiss to the wind, she waved jubilantly ... and walked off into history.

The End